Entertaining Ambrose

Deirdre Purcell

Entertaining Ambrose

MACMILLAN

First published 2001 by Macmillan
an imprint of Macmillan Publishers Ltd
25 Eccleston Place, London SW1W 9NF
Basingstoke and Oxford
Associated companies throughout the world
www.macmillan.com

ISBN 0 333 71823 2 (Hardback)
ISBN 0 333 90517 2 (Trade Paperback)

A CIP catalogue record for this book is available from
the British Library.

Typeset by SetSystems Ltd, Saffron Walden, Essex
Printed and bound in Great Britain by
Mackays of Chatham plc, Chatham, Kent

This novel is dedicated

to the memory of Charles Pick

✦ Acknowledgements ✦

When in future I look back on the writing of this novel, I will remember many encouraging and cheer-leading friends with love and gratitude, primae inter pares: Pat Brennan, Patricia Scanlan, Jacqueline O'Neill, Carol Cronin, Patricia and Frank Byrne, Jacqueline Duffy, Laly Calderon Cortes, Jonathan Curling and all those whose patience I stretched. From Townhouse, I should like to thank Treasa Coady, Joe Hoban, Felicity Dickson and Amanda Kiely; from Pan Macmillan: Suzanne Baboneau, Kirsty McKie, Imogen Taylor and Hazel Orme; from CPC, Martin Pick, Sandra Sljivic – and Charles, much missed and to whom this book is dedicated.

Most of all, I should like to thank, as always, Kevin, Adrian and Simon. When I think of them, it is all worthwhile.

⇥ One ⇤

My name is May Lanigan. Today is my forty-fourth birthday, 20 April 2000, and I'm going quietly out of my mind.

The disintegration started nine calendar months ago exactly. To the day. Saturday, 20 September 1999. Half past six in the morning. Thunderous knocking, on and on with no let-up.

Half dead from lack of sleep, I stumbled out of bed. 'For God's sake, shut up – you'll wake Johnny!'

Although I knew full well this had to be bad news, the desire not to wake Johnny remained foremost as, my own sleep still misting in front of me, I ran down the corridor towards the front door before it caved in under the onslaught. I'd had a bad night with him. He always reacts to cola drinks and someone, probably Esmé, had given him one. He had been like a dervish after it – you try controlling a nineteen-year-old six-footer – and it was after three o'clock in the morning by the time I had him settled and was in bed myself. So you can imagine how I felt when I woke to that noise less than three and a half hours later.

They were polite enough, I suppose, in retrospect.

Two of them, and another sitting in the unmarked car out in front of the house. The engine was running, that's a detail that always sticks in my mind. It sounded so loud in the quietness of the street where the only movement was of a Corporation worker picking papers out of the gutters and flinging them into his dustcart.

'Good morning,' says the first character, an uptight sort with a moustache, who must have just scraped the height requirements for entry to Templemore training college. I recognize him, as it happens, from being about the place. He's a local, I've seen him going in and out of the Bridewell down the street. 'Is your husband in?' he asks, civilly enough.

'Is there a problem?' I try to stay calm – or at least not to give them the satisfaction of knowing I'm panicked.

'We just want to ask your husband a few questions,' says the second one. 'May we come in?' He is a little bigger than the first. Mutt and Jeff? Little and Large? Laurel and Hardy? It's surprising what goes through your mind at times like this.

I plump for Zig and Zag as I take off the chain and open the door wider. Our lobby is narrow and they have to push close together to fit side by side, which seems to increase their bulk. I am still semi-stupid from sleep, or shock, or both. Before I close the door, I notice another detail: the dog from next door is peeing at one of the tyres on the unmarked car at the kerb. Will that rot the rubber?

'What now?' I ask.

They exchange a glance. 'Could you wake your husband, please?' the familiar man, Zig, says, looking at me with what is probably pity. I jump as though I'm guilty. Oh, yes, sorry, say I.

Clem is sleeping like a new puppy in our big four-poster. I shake him hard. 'Wake up, Clem, wake up . . . Wake *up*!'

All his life, Clem has boasted that he had never lost a second's sleep from worry about anything. Well, he has something to worry about now. I shake him harder. '*Wake up!*'

'Wha—' He finally opens his eyes.

As I had feared, the commotion has woken Johnny, I can hear him shouting. We have him at home for the weekend from St Anthony's; sometimes we take him from the Friday. He is always disoriented when he wakes.

'Hold on, Johnny, love,' I shout back. 'It's Mammy – you're at home. I'll be down with you in one minute.'

By this time Clem is sitting up, none too pleased. 'What's going on?'

I tell him the news – which sure wakes him properly. He dives out of the bed, so smartly that I know there is no mistake here. Those men downstairs have something to be calling about. The realization is quite a shock, and all of a sudden I can feel icy rivers running through the veins of my arms and into my cheeks. 'What have you done?'

'Nothing,' he mutters. 'It's just that those gougers have nothing better to do than harass people in their beds.'

I look at him. I know he is lying. I have lived with this man for twenty-seven years, have borne six sons for him, have kept his house and cooked his meals, and continue to make love with him on a regular basis. There is no way that Clem Lanigan could fool me. Or so I had thought up to that morning. (And even for a while afterwards, God help me.) But right now the presence of the two men inside our front door is all that engages my brain. 'What have you done?' I ask him again.

But he is looking over my shoulder. I look too. The two police officers are no longer at the front door: they are crowding into the doorway of the bedroom.

Clem puts up no resistance. They allow him to get dressed but watch every move as he does so. I simply stare. I could not have spoken. I have no voice.

As he is being led out of the bedroom, Clem twists his head over his shoulder towards me and gazes at me with a peculiar intense look in his eyes. 'You'll hear things, May,' he said, 'but just remember me and you the way we were. Ring Tony. He'll know what to do.' Tony Malone is Clem's best friend and business partner and I suppose you could call Joan, his wife, my best friend too.

'We'll let you know where he is, Mrs Lanigan,' says the policeman I had recognized, the one with the 'tache. Ten seconds later, I hear the front door slam behind the three of them.

For some reason, I check the alarm clock, which is ticking loudly and erratically as usual. It is now exactly half past six. The entire episode has lasted less than five minutes. The sun is slicing through the gap where the curtains do not meet. Johnny's shouts are becoming wilder.

I sit on the bed.

Not quite, actually. If the truth be told, my knees give way and, afraid I will fall, I find myself back amongst the bedclothes. They are still warm from Clem. They carry his smell.

From that moment, my world began to unwind. It's only now, nine months later, that I see how carefully I had cocooned and constructed my existence to shield myself from the truth of our station in life. From where Clem got his money – our money. I suppose I should now call it ill-gotten gains.

I'm still more than somewhat confused in that area. Whether you believe it or not, and a lot of people clearly don't, I'm not at all sure how much money we have or where it is. It never concerned me. And Clem always believed you should never show wealth, that throwing cash around in full view serves only to make people jealous and suspicious. You lose friends by showing money.

All I knew was that we always managed well and certainly, in latter years, we were more than comfortable.

For instance, take this house, suitable to our needs and, if I'm honest, a bit more besides. Clem took his own advice about vulgar displays, and about eight years ago, he made the neighbours on both sides an offer they couldn't refuse, and knocked our cottage into both of theirs. On the inside only, so you'd never know. Kept the outsides exactly the same, three front doors although we use only the middle one, which opens directly into a new, artificial little lobby between the kitchen and sitting room, three separate gardens, three sets of railings and gates. We got an architect to do the drawings and then a few of Clem's builder mates turned up trumps. It worked really well. It's now what the estate agents call "full of character" and we have oodles of space. The end cottage, number 22, has four bedrooms and a bathroom in it, the kitchen, lobby and sitting room take up all of number 21, and number 20 contains the two other bedrooms, both *en suite*, one for Clem and me and the other little one for Johnny.

It's a waste now, to have all this space, because as well as Esmé, I've only Martin with me now – and Johnny, of course, at the weekends. One moment you have a full house, three adults, six lads. The next, there are all those empty bedrooms – maybe they'll come in handy if I ever have any grandchildren.

That's a big if: they all seem to be slow off the mark these days.

Hindsight, hindsight – if I had not been so protective of the family maybe I could have circumvented what happened. Could I have intervened with Clem? Should I have been less blinkered, complacent, even? Asked more questions? Insisted on answers?

Maybe.

In my own defence, however, I was one hundred per cent engaged in other matters. All through my married life, there have always been other people who needed my full attention and support, whose lives have been more important than mine and whose crises have always been far more urgent. Added to which, I was brought up to be unselfish. But maybe—

Maybe. Such a wasteful word. The facts are the facts, May, might as well face them.

The article that really cut my heart wasn't even specifically about us but the person who wrote it used our situation as a jumping off point to give an airing to what is obviously a bee in his own bonnet about families like ours. He appeared to believe that because we are related to a criminal we're as guilty as the person who is officially judged and sentenced. 'Get the wives and kids' was the gist of what he wrote.

What gives any other human being the right to judge me without ever having met me? Judgement is Mine, saith the Lord. I've been up before no court, have been charged with nothing.

For instance, what if I genuinely didn't know what Clem had been up to?

I can see the guy's face. Pshaw! How could she not know?

Well, I have a question back for him. Would he know if his wife was having an affair? Yet doesn't he live in the same house, talk to her every day, sleep in the same bed? How could he not know? But aren't most spouses the last to know?

I rest my case.

So whether I am believed or not, I'd like to state, for the record in the strongest possible terms, that I did not know my husband was a crook. Up to the time he ran and left me holding the baby, as it were, I had nothing whatsoever to do with the finances in this house. I had no cheque book and never saw the need for one because Clem gave me a Pass card and taught me how to use the hole-in-the-wall machine for whenever he wasn't around and I needed cash. He took care of business, I took care of the family. That was the deal.

Did I never ask Clem what he did for a living? Of course I did – near the beginning of the relationship when everything about the other seems fascinating. He sat me down and explained how he and Tony Malone, who have been pals all their lives, made money from being middle-men. They bought surplus goods on the open market, Clem said, in England or Holland or the North of Ireland or wherever they could get them, and sold them at a profit to the street vendors or the cut-price retailers here or anywhere else they could find buyers. Tony runs his own taxi and long-distance trucking business and his trucks and vans carried the goods.

I was grateful for the family benefits when, for instance, Clem arrived home from time to time with a boxful of runners or sports strips for the boys, or a microwave oven or a toaster or the very latest TV or video.

It all sounded perfectly legitimate to me so why should I have suspected otherwise? We never had a visit from the law until that first morning I've described.

None of them was ever in trouble except our eldest, CJ. And up to that awful morning I had thought CJ was the only problematic apple in our barrel.

In many ways, I can see now, I switched directly from my Da to Clem in being minded and cosseted from the more mundane details of the world's works.

When I was young, if I needed anything for school I just asked. Similarly, after Clem and I were married, if we needed anything for the house or the kids, I asked and it was provided.

I never wanted much anyway. Yes, I do like things to be nice, but not for their own sakes. I'm not greedy or covetous and I don't care whether the pictures on my wall are velveteen prints from the pound shops or original van Goghs. If I like it, or if it has sentimental value, that's all I care about.

As it happens, most of the pictures on the walls of our house are family photographs because always central to me was the health and welfare of my little gang. Having grown up motherless and as an only child, I wanted a crowd in my house and was certainly contented, happy even, that I was the spool around which so many young lives were wound. I think I am – or was – a born wife and mother.

Maybe if you can accept that the arrival of the police that morning was completely shocking to me you have some idea as to how I have felt since. And writing this memoir will, I hope, put the record straight for the boys. Despite what they've read in the newspapers I want them to know, should anything happen to me, that even if their father was a criminal, he took care of them – and me – up to now at least, and that they should never doubt his love for them even if it was from a distance. If there is an earthquake to happen between Clem and me in Spain, it will not negate the past twenty-seven years.

I say that now. Who knows what I'll feel like in two weeks' time?

Through these eight months Clem's been away, I've honoured my side of the bargain. As ordered, I waited for him to contact me, made no efforts to get in touch with him in case some nosy-parkers were listening in. Therefore, communication between us has been infrequent at best, and — now that I am confronting the issue — I'm forced to recognize how it has become even more infrequent lately. As a matter of fact, the last time I heard from my husband was more than four weeks ago. The kind of communication that is no communication at all. Just a quick 'Hello, howya, how're the lads, everything's fine here, how're things there . . .'

But now, given what Esmé has told me, I have no option but to challenge him. I'm leaving tomorrow. I'd be gone already if today wasn't my birthday. We've always made a big fuss about birthdays in this family and I don't want to deprive others of a party. At present my preoccupation, source of stress, obsession, is not what crime or crimes Clem has or has not committed, but his whereabouts, what he is doing wherever he is, and with whom. I've been alight with fury ever since that conversation with Esmé, and if what she hinted at is true, I'll kill him. Or maybe I should kill myself and be done with it.

I don't mean that. I take mortal sin very seriously and the sin of despair is very serious indeed. What has been keeping me going through the normal routines of each day is a fierce sensation of hard, cold fire — if that's not a contradiction in terms.

Don't think about it, May. Concentrate on the present. Get to the next moment.

I can't, most of the time. It's no use pretending I can be rational about this. I pound wildly around a circle of rage, disbelief, horror, and back towards rage again. How dare Esmé allege what she did? Clem unfaithful to me, after all these years? Clem? No way. Not Clem.

But then horror approaches and I see his hands on some other woman's body. I see him kissing her, licking her throat, the two of them sharing a bottle of wine, giggling in a bed. I go berserk.

I have to be fair, however. Esmé, who is barking, might be wrong. But I couldn't just ignore what she said, could I? Esmé's the last of Clem's aunties. Into each life some rain must fall.

I used to think it odd that someone like her, who has had a most unusual life by my standards, has ended up here with us although there isn't much about people or their behaviour that can surprise me any more. She is tall, thin and willowy as a whip – and on first acquaintance you would probably take her for a con-firmed spinster in the old-fashioned, self-contained, almost careerist sense of that word. But Esmé was married and widowed three times. She had no children, however, and this is probably why you would never associate her with the rough-and-tumble of ordinary married life. All her husbands were Frenchmen – the first, a young navy lieutenant, bore her off from Dublin to his home port of Marseilles – and that is as much as we know personally about any of them. I've tried to get her to talk about herself, about her husbands' deaths or even about France and Frenchmen: this was curiosity on my part, as much as an effort to figure out why she can behave so outlandishly, but she's as tight-lipped as a clam.

What we do know, however, is that after the third husband died it was discovered that, despite the aristocratic way they lived, he hadn't left a bean. The house, a château that had apparently seen better days, had to be sold to pay all debts and taxes. Esmé was over seventy at that stage and had nowhere to go so Clem took her in. She arrived here with only a single trunk fourteen long, long years ago.

Anyway, she's sitting here one day – it's only ten days ago although it feels to me like ten years – in the big Dralon recliner we bought for her, reading some book in French, feet up on the extended footstool. The Queen of Alder Cottages. I'm doing the sitting-room floor around her and, of course, she makes no move to help me or even to move her feet.

I finish the Hoovering, switch off the machine and start in on the mantelpiece with the Pledge and the dusters. I get the feeling that she's looking at me and when I look around at her, sure enough she is. She's staring at me over the tops of her glasses. Come here, May, she says to me. I have something I wish to say to you. Esmé's long sojourn in France has coloured the way she speaks, to the extent that her English is very correct.

I probably should have ignored her that afternoon: there's a contrary, spiteful streak in Esmé, as there is in a lot of old women, and I could see that whatever it was she wanted to say, she was going to enjoy it and I wasn't. I had had a go at her that morning about treating this place like a hotel, and now I had a feeling she might have cooked up some sort of revenge. But I'm a sucker for punishment so I put down the duster. All right, I say to her, what is it?

Then she tells me. Clem Lanigan has a fancy woman. She says it just like that. I thought you should know, she adds, picking up her book again.

I'm staring at her. I'm like a fish gaping at the fisherman that's just hauled him out of the water. If this is revenge for my outburst earlier in the morning, she has certainly achieved it.

Of course, as soon as I get my breath back I dispute with her. What's her evidence?

I just know, that is all. Her gaze is milky.

I start to cajole: Esmé, please . . .

She holds up one hand, the long fingers as graceful as a ballerina's: Do not urge me, May. I do not tell you this for my own benefit. What you do with the information is up to you.

I continue to stare at her and then the dam breaks. I start yelling. She's no relative of mine – I don't have to keep her here, she's nothing but an ungrateful old bat. I can throw her out – and I would in a minute. What's she going to do then? How is she going to survive living in the Morning Star hostel with the plebs? Or maybe she'll have to sleep in a doorway.

All to no avail. She has gone back to her book. Esmé knows me. She knows full well I'd never throw her out because she has nowhere to go. And that even if I did some day reach breaking point and do it, she knows I'd be out combing the city for her within the hour, that I couldn't rest easy picturing her in some indigents' hostel with tatty sheets on the bed.

I'm stuck with her – we're stuck with one another.

In one of those strange coincidences that can't be called coincidences because they happen in Dublin families all the time, she actually knew my father, my mother too, but only slightly. Before she left for France, she worked as a secretary in the union in which Da had an interest and they used to be cordial to each other. We didn't make the connection until after I was married.

Esmé cordial. Now that's a sight I'd like to see – but that's definitely the phrase my father used about her.

I keep banging away at her, trying to get her to tell me what she's talking about and eventually, with a small sigh – Esmé is never less than ladylike – she snaps shut the bloody book.

I sit down opposite her: Well?

I am warning you, it is not pleasant—

Esmé, stop with the drama. Just tell me, for God's sake.

The gist of the thing turns out to be that about a week before the police burst into the house on their dawn manoeuvres, Esmé claims that at some ungodly hour of the morning she saw my husband with another woman in the passenger seat of the Humber. Clem has always driven classic cars because of the cheaper insurance premiums. According to Esmé, she was looking through her bedroom window and spotted the car idling outside the new Spar shop across the street.

Clem came out of the shop, she says in her cultured voice. He returned to his car. He got in beside the woman and they drove away up Church Street.

She could be telling me about some art exhibition. I realize my hands have curled into fists. Carefully, I uncurl them and spread them on my knees, placing each one so the palms are exactly centred on my knee caps. How could you have seen them at that hour, Esmé? Were you walking the streets at three o'clock in the morning?

Esmé looks into the fireplace: I am an old woman. I do not sleep much or very well, and when I do, my dreams disturb me. So rather than stay there for no purpose, I get out of bed. I spend time at my window, watching the night-time pass by.

It was dark, you might have mistaken Clem for someone else.

I saw them clearly, May, she says quietly. It was his car and there is no mistake.

All right – I start clutching at straws – supposing you're right and it was him. He was there, I'll accept that. But he could have been merely giving this woman a lift.

Her eyes, like old marbles, look beyond me now as though she is tired of the conversation or is already moving ahead of me towards the next item of interest. This is a habit of hers.

Esmé, for Christ's sake – My voice has risen so that I sound like a screaming magpie. I bring it back down and speak as slowly and calmly as I can manage. Listen, Esmé, are you sure? Could it have been something you saw on the box?

Like me, Esmé has been watching too much television lately.

She shakes her head.

Or even something you dreamed? Esmé, please, were they kissing or what?

She sighs again, closing her blue-veined eyelids in genteel tolerance: No. They were not kissing. But they were obviously together. One can tell . . .

Well, if they weren't doing anything to each other, how could you know, from a bedroom window on the other side of the road, that he and this woman—

Girl, Esmé interrupts me. Girl.

Girl? How did you know what age she was? What did she look like? And why are you telling me this only now? Why tell me at all?

She looks steadily at me, her expression pained but remote, as though she is a kindergarten teacher and I am one of her charges who is way past nap-time. Please, May, I know nothing more. I wish now to read again. She picks up her book and from then on, no matter how I nag, she won't say another word.

I look down at the Hoover, at its squat, ugly body and snake neck. It has turned into something evil. Everything in the room is now soiled, evil. I need to be by myself. But as I walk to the door some instinct makes me turn back to look at Esmé. I catch her looking after me and our eyes meet. To my astonishment, I don't recognize the expression in hers. She breaks the contact immediately, buries her nose in the book again.

Had it been my imagination or had I surprised a blaze of sympathy in those old eyes? Had Esmé for a moment resembled a human being?

The image she has conjured up has continued to

scrabble like a live crab inside my brain and I can't shake it out. Fancy woman. The words grow to monstrous, overwhelming proportions, smothering all others. For those first few minutes after Esmé's revelation, I believe I will never be able to think about anything else. I hadn't thought of myself as a jealous or an insecure person but, then, I had not had cause before, had I? Or had I? Had I been a complete blind eejit?

One situation at a time, May, I say to myself, one situation at a time.

Right. If she had been making it up just to upset me she'd have made it more dramatic, surely. Wouldn't they have been in each other's arms? Crawling all over one another? And why would she lie anyway? She has no history of lying. On the contrary, she is straight to the point of blunt tactlessness.

Yet still my mind argues with itself. Clem and a fancy woman. Preposterous.

No. It happens all the time. You read about it all the time. Yes, I have been blind. Blind and smug.

And subsequently I discover it's not knowing the extent of it that's the worst. Maybe he had a one-night stand. All right, that's bad. But it's not the end of the world. Even two or three escapades of that nature. That would make him a complete shit, but he wouldn't be the only one in this imperfect world and so long as he didn't shake it in my face, what I didn't know at the time couldn't hurt me. What I'm afraid of, I suppose, is something more sinister. Like a one-night stand that took. Like a real girlfriend.

Girl. She did say girl. What a cliché. The younger model. All of a sudden I feel hard and used-up, like a dishrag too long on the line.

It won't be long now, anyway, before I'll find out for once and for all. These things have to be sorted out face to face. I have to catch him red-handed.

→ Two ←

The whole family comes here to the house every Sunday for a traditional Sunday dinner. I wait until they are all seated in the sitting room after the meal to tell them I'm going to Spain to visit Clem. I'm tense, expecting consternation, even objections, but after all the screwing up of my courage, my announcement is somewhat of a damp squib.

Good on you, seems to be the general drift as they all go back to *The X-files* on the telly and I'm left standing there with my big speech deflating in my mouth. None of them even asks me why I'm going. On reflection, this is hardly surprising – they'd think it only natural that I would want to see my husband after all these months. I had been prepared with all sorts of rationalizations. I was going to be firm but fair. Look, I was going to say, I've done everything I can for all of you, I've cleaned the house from top to bottom, the freezer is packed with food, and St Anthony's is going to keep Johnny for the weekend so you won't have to worry about him. I don't get to say a single word of it. It is a lesson. Maybe I have an exaggerated idea of my own importance within this family.

Like a gom, I look around at them all, fully re-
absorbed into the world of Mulder and Scully, except
for poor old Johnny, of course, who is banging away
at his pots and pans with the wooden spoons and who
would not have understood my announcement in the
first place. Johnny, as you may already have gathered,
is a *duine le Dia* – he was brain-damaged at birth and has
a plethora of other problems besides. And although I'd
be happy to look after him full-time, it's better for him
that he's in residential care because he loves lots of
company. We were lucky to get a place for him.

Nonetheless, I know that I continue to be an incorr-
igible mother hen. At least we have a state-of-the-art
microwave oven that everyone can use – even Esmé,
although her aristocratic nose turns up at any mention
of it. Unless it involves lots of slow bubbling, chopping
and fine herbs, Esmé doesn't want to know.

As I record this, she's out on one of her trolley raids
again. I'm forcing myself to ignore her because, at the
moment, she and her exploits are the least of my
worries. I should paint the picture for you although it
is hardly edifying. Think of Esmé, stylish, tall and
straight as a telegraph pole, standing at the kerb with
an empty shopping trolley from Tesco. Nice as pie,
this is an old lady minding her own business. Now
think of this old lady running her trolley at motor
cars – as if she was one of those advance men in a
bullfight who, before the matador comes on, runs at
the bull with little darts to madden him. I told you
she's bats. She'll be all right, she never comes to any
harm.

I used the word record just there because I'm

dictating into a little tape-recorder that Eddie, the second eldest, gave me. Since half of Ireland seems to be writing its memoirs, why not me? I'd been toying with the notion of writing something substantial in any case and, in my present circumstances, it may even keep me sane.

Unfortunately, pen and ink, or even typing, would be too slow for the state I'm in now. I read somewhere that the writer Edna O'Brien loves the slow, sensuous way ink flows blackly from her pen on to her paper. But I bet that while she's writing, her world isn't raining in pieces around her and her fingers don't dance jigs.

I always knew I'd write something some day, if only to recycle some of the trillions of words I've ingested over the last forty years or so. Reading was one of the better legacies left to me by my father. Our house was stuffed with books and periodicals of all kinds: they jostled each other for attention and shouted, Read me! Read me! from every corner of the house. Since, unlike my lot here, I had no one to play board games or cards with and we had no television, I read myself nearly blind.

At school everyone, even the teachers, said I was very good at English. Anything to do with English – even acting in the plays. I played an abridged Hamlet one year and loved it, I also played an abridged Malvolio, a Macbeth and a St Patrick, but apart from learning lines and practising the roles, writing essays was my favourite homework although I was whammed by the teachers for my style. This varied wildly from week to week so that a year's output resembled a

patchwork quilt of manuscripts authored by P.G.
Wodehouse, F. Scott Fitzgerald, Annie P. Smithson,
Catherine Cookson, Thomas Hardy, Arthur Conan
Doyle, Agatha Christie, plus whomever I'd last read.
Looking back, I suppose I was a bit like a sponge.

Similarly nowadays I would say I'm very influenced
by the hours of TV I watch. Emily, the facilitator in
my creative-writing workshop (it's only once a week,
but I love it), thinks so and criticizes me for writing
sometimes like Colombo, sometimes like Hyacinth
Bucket. On the other hand, she is always telling us not
to dickey around with trying to achieve a perfect piece
of literature first go. Dive in, she tells us, and don't be
pre-editing yourselves as you're going along. She's
good on tips. Work hard on the first and last para-
graphs, she says, and you'd be surprised how the rest
fills in.

So here I go. Diving in.

I was born in Kimmage, Larkfield Park, in one of
the Guinness houses, but except for the death of my
mother, which I don't really remember because I was
only three at the time, my early childhood was standard
fare: cycling to school, homework at the kitchen table,
playing with my pals, boring Sunday walks with my
father in Poddle Park, bus trips to the zoo or to the
Museum of Natural History to see the elk and the
whale skeleton and a lot of dusty old animals.

May is my real, birth-cert. name, not short for Mary
or anything else. I'm named after the month. My
father, a Guinness clerk all his working life, even
though he wasn't a Protestant, harboured secret Communist sympathies and, although out of loyalty to the

firm that paid his wages he didn't want it known, he spent a lot of his own time doing voluntary work for the Workers' Union of Ireland – for instance, helping in the writing of their pamphlets. When I was born, he seized on the chance to immortalize his commitment – May Day and so forth. He was so dogmatic about his beliefs, my poor mother probably had little say in the matter.

From my Da's perspective, we were as good as any and better than most in Dublin or even in the whole of Ireland, despite being working class. I suppose that that attitude has rubbed off on me to the extent that if the Pope himself came waltzing down Church Street, I wouldn't be slow in waltzing up alongside him to have a chat, equal to equal. According to Da, brains, application and the best education possible are what counts, not background or privilege. This works both ways: in Da's scheme of things, you shouldn't judge the privileged by their wealth, accents or sports cars any more than they should judge you by your flat vowels or broken-down shoes. The rich have a right to be heard and are as honourable and straight as anyone else until they prove otherwise.

I don't know all that much about my mother and now it's too late to find out since none of the older generation of my relatives is still alive. Not that there were all that many relatives to start with. My father was an only child and was never close to any of his cousins, all of whom continued to live in Co. Cork. He was the only one who had made the break for Dublin.

I asked him about my mother, naturally, but he was

uncharacteristically vague in his answers. I always had the impression that to talk about her hurt him a great deal so I didn't persist. Anyhow, when you're young you seem to accept the cards dealt to you and I was not a brooder. I did find it strange, however, that the only photo Da had of her was their wartime wedding photo, which is one of my most precious treasures. He brushed off my queries about this. They didn't have money to waste on fripperies like Box Brownies.

As I get older, though, I find I'm hungry for details about her. Even the sort of detail Esmé might be able to supply woman to woman — like her taste in clothes, the way she wore her hair: in the wedding photo it's concealed by a hat and her slim body is encased in a serious tweedy costume. Studying her face in that photograph, I endow her with a musical laugh — Esmé, the infuriating old biddy, says she doesn't remember what her laugh was like. I do not recall her laughing, was the way she put it.

I wouldn't wish harm on a hair of Esmé's head, of course I wouldn't. I can even recognize, objectively, how elegantly unusual, even fascinating she is — to others. And if she were someone else's responsibility and house guest, I would greatly admire her, I'm sure. I might even regard her eccentricities as amusing.

But as a living presence in the house, her other-worldly detachment is not only annoying, it feels haughty, even sometimes quite spooky. I feel her looking right through me, as though there is something far more interesting on the other side, and I find my flesh tingling. It's hard to live with.

Speaking of living with, there is something I have to reveal to you before we go much further. Take it at face value or discard it, it's up to you.

Deep breath, May. Introduce Ambrose.

Ambrose?

Ambrose.

I have deliberately waited until now to tell you about Ambrose. This is for fear you might think I am as bonkers as Esmé.

Ambrose arrived here in the late afternoon of the day Clem was arrested. As you can imagine, given the drama of the morning, I was in bits by tea-time, barely managing to function. Hour after hour had vanished down some sort of sensory swallow-hole, and if you were to torture me to reveal the actions and events of that day in proper sequence after Clem's arrest, I would have to die on the rack.

I remember making telephone calls to Eddie, Con, Frank and Martin, although probably not in that order. Despite what Clem had advised, I know I rang them before contacting Tony Malone. I needed to talk to them before hearing Tony Malone's version of why Clem had been arrested. I needed them with me before I set foot again in this appalling world – as I've said, up to that morning I had thought that the eldest, CJ, had been the only Lanigan in that particular arena.

I remember that Tony, when we eventually reached him, indeed knew what to do.

I remember that Clem was bailed and out of custody by lunch-time.

But if you were to ask me now how much the

bail was, who delivered it or who else we talked to, I would have to say that I haven't a clue. All I know is that Tony didn't seem to have much difficulty in coming up with the money and whatever else was necessary. And that when I wasn't tending to Johnny, I seemed to spend most of that day sitting by the phone. And that Esmé seemed, mercifully, to stay out of my way.

I also remember that Clem didn't come home after he was released, he went to Tony's. He was still there when Ambrose appeared to me.

When a crisis occurs, my first impulse is not to weep but to clean so, sometime around five o'clock, I'm polishing our few bits of silver while trying to take my mind off the merry-go-round of worry by half watching Ricki Lake. Today's topic is Women Who Want To Remarry Their First Husbands (whether or not said husbands were happily ensconced elsewhere).

One of the Women – so enormous that she over-flows the armrests of her chair on each side by at least a foot – is in full flight when I hear the church bell across the road ringing slowly. I know that bell. Some poor soul's coffin is being brought to the church. So I stop with the silver and turn down the television to concentrate on saying a little prayer for the repose of his or her soul.

Then I get that prickling feeling at the back of my neck, the sort I get when Esmé is giving me one of her spooky looks. I'm being watched from behind.

I whirl around to confront her: Esmé, will you for God's sake stop creeping around like—

The sentence dies. I am being watched all right. By

a very, very large person, whose head is only inches from the ceiling. He is wearing a long smock, very full, made of a fabric that looks like coarse linen, shot through with different colours, like children's bubbles. (He tells me subsequently it's his seamless garment — that's Ambrose's idea of a joke.)

Right now, though, the silence stretches and stretches as we gaze at one another, as I take in his bare feet, his dark, collar-length hair, curly with a purply sheen, his pale blue eyes, the blue you see on the cloak of Virgin Mary statues.

Does my heart start to thump? No.

Am I afraid? No — surprisingly.

Do I know right away that this is an angel?

I do. If this is not an angel, I'm in serious need of brain surgery or at least several long sessions of therapy.

The questions start to form in my throat — why, how, when, am I imagining things now?

I am real, says the apparition. I am not a figment of your imagination.

And this is without my having asked any of the questions.

May I sit? he — it — asks politely. His voice chimes, harmonizing with the bell that is still tolling from the church across the street.

Of — of course.

Next thing I know, he's in Clem's armchair. I haven't seen him move. One second he's standing, the next he's sitting six feet away, and somehow I've missed the bit in between.

Seriously flustered now, I put the half-polished

candlestick back on the mantelpiece and start to pull off my rubber gloves. I'm – I'm sorry you've caught me like this. I wave haphazardly, taking in the general disorder of the room, my frayed apron, the wadded polishing cloths.

Please, do not apologize, he gestures with one hand, this is your home. You were not expecting me, of course. He smiles, showing two rows of perfect pearly teeth. Naturally.

Even in the state I'm in I realize there is no point in offering a cup of tea or coffee to an angel so I don't know what to do next. I start to pick up some of the cleaning stuff scattered on the floor. The sun has come out, lighting a corner of the sitting room through the lace curtains on the window, but for the first time, I notice that it is cooler in here than it has been all week. Cold, even. I could seriously do with a drink.

Have a drink, if you wish.

Mouth open, hands full of dusters and tins, now my heart is starting to thump.

He smiles again: Please do not be alarmed. Think of it merely as a parlour trick.

I'm – I'm not alarmed, I say faintly. But I will have a drink if you don't mind.

The tolling across the road stops as I do a fast cosmetic tidy-up, piling all the cleaning stuff on to the hearth, into a corner of the fender where it will be hopefully out of sight. Outside I hear two women shout greetings at one another. Then an articulated truck roars by, drowning their voices. Quickly, I pour myself a generous measure of brandy from the bottle we always keep in the sideboard. I take a large slug and then, holding the brandy balloon tightly as though it was a lifebelt, I sit carefully on the edge of the sofa opposite my extraordinary visitor. Now what? Although Johnny is taking his nap and is not due to wake up for at least half an hour, I can't guarantee he won't start roaring soon, or even come tumbling in here. Or what if Esmé comes back from her trolley excursion?

We shall not be disturbed, says the angel. How is Esmé?

I almost fall off the edge of the sofa. This is terrible. How am I going to control my thoughts so that I don't think something awful and make a fool of myself? Could I mask them somehow? But then I do worse than that. Is that why you're here? I ask him. Is it time for Esmé to go?

I was merely enquiring, he says gently, so gently that I nearly die from embarrassment.

Or course. He knows that I'd have liked it to be Esmé's time to go. Then – the brandy must be starting to work – mortification veers towards annoyance. After all, this is my sitting room and this person, being, whatever it is, has arrived uninvited. Look, I say firmly, if you can know everything I'm thinking, what's the point of having a conversation about anything?

Exactly, he says.

So will we just sit here? I sound belligerent – I don't mean to but this is all too sudden.

If you wish, he says. Then: You have had a trying day, May, but please be assured that you are never alone.

We stare at one another, he mildly, me taking this

in. A thought strikes me, so terrifying and at once so wonderful it takes my breath away. Could this be my mother come back to me? I hold my breath, keeping my gaze steadily on the angel, trying to formulate the question in a way that won't sound too stupid.

I needn't have bothered. The creature's eyes widen briefly. We continue to look at one another as I wait, more than half hoping. Then he shakes his head a little, his expression compassionate.

The disappointment is huge: All right, you're not my mother – you're my guardian angel, is that it?

If that is what you believe. Yes.

I take another slug of the brandy: If that's what I believe? Are you my guardian angel or aren't you?

I've learned many times since that you don't ask Ambrose direct questions because he deflects them with the utmost charm and that smile that would start a stopped clock. He does it now and I can see there is little point in questioning him further.

So, more to fill the silence than anything else, I find myself telling him a bit about myself and about the family, but after only a minute or two, I can see that although he seems to be listening, it is out of courtesy and I'm not telling him anything he doesn't know already. That conversation, too, peters out.

I finish the last of the brandy, place the glass on the coffee table in front of the sofa, face him squarely: I suppose there is no point in asking you why you are here?

I am here because I am here. Do I disturb you?

I shake my head: Not in the least, actually.

Whether it's the alcohol or what, I find I've spoken

the truth. I'm far from disturbed. Actually, I'm calm. Much calmer than before he came. And I seem already to have accepted this bizarre occurrence. Even the sounds I now hear from down the corridor are not bothering me. Johnny is awake and calling, and ordinarily I would be up like a shot and running to him. Instead, I stand up slowly, almost casually, taking my time. I'm sorry, I have to go, I say to the angel.

Of course. He inclines his head. We shall speak again. And before I know it, he is instantly standing too. It's like looking at two separate snapshots: Angel Sitting; Angel Standing.

Calm and all as I am, it's still very new to me and I find I am still trying to control my thoughts, to let them trickle in slowly so I can immediately banish any that I wouldn't want him to see. I swallow a couple of times. So you're coming again? When?

He doesn't answer that, just smiles. I can hear Johnny banging on the cot sides of the bed. We hate using them but they're for his own safety. Distracted, but not wanting to be rude, I glance towards the door: I really will have to go now.

When I look back towards where he is standing, there is only chair and carpet. The angel has vanished.

The room seems warmer again.

Three

No wings. He let me feel once and I couldn't detect even bumps that might indicate where wings might sprout. He says he doesn't need wings to get about. We were given wings, he tells me, by artists who don't trust people to have imagination or intuition. Little about his physical appearance is constant. For instance, his height is variable, and when sitting in a chair, as he did that first day, he is a person of normal stature. His voice changes too: sometimes it's like bells, sometimes like birds, or gurgling water, or wind or rain, or a harmonica or the faint music of a church organ. Not that he uses it all that much and we do seem to spend a lot of his visits in silence.

He is deficient in one crucial area. He cannot laugh. Can you believe that? He was sitting in the kitchen one afternoon as I was preparing the tea. I was giggling at a satirical sketch running on the radio but when I glanced at him to see if he was joining in — you know how infectious laughter can be — I saw he was wearing an expression of what I can only describe as rueful regret.

What's the matter, Ambrose? I ask him. Don't you find it funny?

He smiles. I find it very funny, May, but laughter is a gift specific to humans. We can smile but we cannot laugh. I can remember everything in creation but I cannot remember laughter.

Well, how can you reply to that? I turn off the radio. It's hard to laugh alone.

Yet Ambrose can certainly be amused. He adores jokes, both listening and telling. It's an angelic characteristic I had certainly never heard about before I met him. Unfortunately, though, our sense of humour does not concur. For instance, while I continue to cringe, he continues to remind me how hilarious it is that on our first meeting I automatically assumed he had arrived to collect Esmé.

I'm not even sure that Ambrose is this angel's real name, you know. It's probably something far more complicated like Lochinvar or Iker or Xerxes. But one afternoon not long after he arrived – it was raining, I remember – we were in the kitchen where I was cooking a mince stew. He was ensconced in one of the fireside chairs flanking the old fireplace, Ronan Collins was nattering happily on the radio and the atmosphere between us was peaceful.

I look over at him suddenly: What's your name, by the way?

He smiles gently: Guess, May.

Ambrose? It pops willy-nilly out of my mouth. To this day I don't know if he prompted it or not. The only other Ambrose I ever knew was from the old days in Kimmage and he was the pernickety, rheumaticky coalman.

He nods, smiling: Well done.

Given the way I talk about him here, I don't want you to get the impression that I'm ho-hum or blasé about him — far from it — but after the initial shock of his arrival wore off I suppose I got used to him. You can get used to any phenomenon, particularly when you have other things on your mind. You can't stay surprised for ever, can you? In fact, you could say I think of him almost as part of the family now.

Mind you, he is the hidden-in-the-attic member and will remain so, because I know perfectly well what the rest of the family would say about him and about me if I mentioned him. Therefore I have never told them. Strangely, I don't find it all that difficult to keep his existence to myself, especially as he appears only when I am alone in some room of the house.

I do find it unsettling that I never know when I am going to see him. Ambrose comes and goes as he pleases — and very much as he pleases. There is little doubt as to who is top dog in this relationship.

He can be moody, but also amazingly kind. The day after Esmé made her chilling revelation, I was going through a turbulent few minutes of serious upset, trying to visualize the appearance of the bimbo — as I had to think of her in order to salve some of my own hurt. I was slumped in Clem's big chair in the bedroom, staring at the bedspread, and had been sitting like that for what seemed like hours. Ambrose appeared right in front of me. Stand up, May, he said softly.

I stood.

He shepherded me across to one of the mirrored

wardrobes and stood so close behind me I could feel his cold breath on my neck. What do you see?

I was alone in the mirror, of course, there was no image of an angel although, by a half-turn of my head, I knew I would see him. I was used to this phenomenon and didn't give it more than a passing thought as I stared at myself. What I saw was hardly encouraging: a middle-aged woman wearing mismatched clothes and down-at-heel sandals, one torn toe-strap carelessly mended with Super-glue. How could this sad sack compete with a glamorous bimbo?

Then Ambrose breathed right into my ear: I know what you see, May, but your eye misleads you. What the world sees is a lovely woman with dark brown eyes, curly fair hair and a small waist on which childbirth has made little impression. When it looks at you, the world sees heedless beauty.

I stared and stared, and a strange thing happened. Maybe I didn't look quite so bad after all, I thought. Maybe if I stood up a little straighter, raised my chin a little, tucked a few of the curls behind my ears so I would look less like a sheepdog – and I resolved there and then to throw out those bloody wrecked sandals.

Thank you, Ambrose, I whispered. He had succeeded in dispelling at least some of the gloom.

But he was nowhere to be seen on the day our solicitor, the one who was handling Clem's case, arrived here unexpectedly a month ago. This was the day I first heard about the CAB.

Sit down, Mrs Lanigan, says this solicitor gravely, after I've shown him in. There's something I have to tell you.

I sat. I knew by his face and tombstone voice that I'd need to. It was lashing rain, I remember, and that damned bell across the street was ringing again – this time for no obvious reason. It wasn't angelus time and because it was still early afternoon, it was hardly a removal or a funeral.

It might as well have been mine because by the time that solicitor had finished with me I was as numb as a corpse. The dry words were all the more shocking because they were spoken so quietly in his reedy little sing-song voice. We're sitting opposite one another across the coffee table in front of the fireplace – I've lit a fire for comfort and company – and there's mist floating gently from the wet cuffs of his trousers.

Apparently there's a very powerful division within the Irish police called the Criminal Assets Bureau. It seems all they have to do is tell a judge they have reason to believe people like us are living on the proceeds of crime and that's enough to have everything frozen while an investigation starts. Root and branch, that's what the solicitor has said. Until this investigation is finished, we can't touch anything, not Clem's bank accounts, not even the pathetic little post office account I set up years ago, which I added to as each of the kids was born and which I was keeping as a little nest egg for any grandchildren. We can't sell this house or anything in it.

The good news or bad news, depending on your point of view, of course, is that they have seven years to prove their case. If they do prove it, everything can be seized and confiscated permanently.

And even that isn't all. Eddie and the two married ones, Con and Frank, all have their own places but the solicitor informs me these have also been frozen because the CAB maintains they were bought and set up with Clem's financial help. Which they were. Of course they were. Of course Clem would help – like any parent who wants to support his kids who are try-ing to put a foot on the hideously expensive property ladder in this country. Eddie's apartment, apparently, is still a grey area. They're working on that one.

Get the wives and kids.

The solicitor, solemnity and sympathy personified, is watching me. Do you understand, Mrs Lanigan? Of course I have made representations about your disabled son and provision has been made for his expenses.

Well, that's something, I say, just to say it. What would have been funny in any other context is that I can see, reflected from the telly in his spectacles, two beetles going at it hammer and tongs – I'd been watching the National Geographic Channel before he arrived, and although I've turned down the volume, the picture is still on.

When I don't respond further – because I can't – he puts a hand over mine: You've had a shock. Would you like me to fix you a drink, Mrs Lanigan?

No, thank you. The feel of his dry warm skin is repellent and brings me to some sort of sense. I shake off his hand and stand up. I can't wait now to get rid of him so that I can take this in privately. I try to keep my voice level: Just as a matter of interest, how are we going to live if all the money is locked up?

He stands up to face me. Arrangements will be made, he says, and he explains to me that where this house and my living expenses are concerned, the court will dole out money as I need it.

I straighten my shoulders so he won't see how devastated I am. I make myself sound scornful: So now I'm a charity case.

Don't look at it like that, Mrs Lanigan, he says earnestly. I'm sure everything can be sorted out before too long.

A picture of Clem, sunning himself on the Spanish Riviera, flashes in front of my eyes. I can smell Brylcreem from the top of the solicitor's head — he's a tiny man, only about five feet two. The smell is almost sickening and I try to rise above it, stretching my spine as straight as a telegraph pole: Does Clem know about this?

He looks cautious now. As you are aware, Mr Lanigan is — ah — not within the jurisdiction. We would hope that the next time you are talking to him you might ask him to contact us. Something he sees in my expression upsets him. He looks at the ground: In strictest confidentiality, of course. Solicitor-client privilege. He hesitates. You see, Mrs Lanigan, it's your husband I represent and there are certain matters I cannot discuss even with you, but what I can say to you is that if he would be willing to come home and — ah — help the police with their investigations, it might benefit all of you in the long run. He looks at me, his glasses glinting in the firelight. Your husband is not the main target of the investigation, Mrs Lanigan. If you could manage to persuade him . . .

He stops, his implication as clear as clean glass. Clem is small fry, but if he leads the police to the sharks, a deal can be done.

I stare at him. Already I'm thinking of what lies ahead. Own brand sliced pans, baked beans, shin beef and the cheapest mince, worrying about the cost of making a daytime telephone call, home perms, Johnny's treats curtailed. I can't promise anything, I tell him, but I'll try.

After he goes, I take his advice and pour myself a brandy. I am burning to confide in someone, anyone – but the only other person in the house is Esmé and I certainly won't tell her. I think about telephoning Joan but I decide against this: she would be dripping with sympathy and, for the moment anyway, I would find that deeply cloying, even insincere.

What I need is someone to tell me what to do. I'm entirely competent when it comes to domestic matters but this is like waking up and finding myself alone on a desert island in the middle of an unfriendly black sea and there is no one coming to take charge. So, as the fire crackles, I just sit there, gazing at the grainy, silenced pictures from the Negev, or wherever those beetles are doing their thing, while I sip my drink quietly and contemplate the ruins of my life.

There and then I decide I'm not going to feel sorry for myself or lie down meekly. Think of it as a challenge, May, I say to myself. Nine-tenths of the people in this world don't live like you do, going up to Tesco and filling your trolley with whatever you need or even what you don't need, without looking at the price tags. You leave lights on all night, use the

central heating as though you're an oil baron. This all
has to change. Make it a mission, an adventure. Beat
the system—

I stop abruptly. I can't stick this situation, which is
not of my making. I don't care what the consequences
might be or who's going to listen in – I go to the
telephone and dial Clem's mobile number, even though
I know he never has the phone switched on. I leave a
message. I say that it is a matter of the most extreme
urgency that he calls me back.

When he does call back, about fifteen minutes later,
he has assumed I've rung because of something to do
with Johnny: What's happened? Is Johnny all right?

When I tell him Johnny's fine but explain what's
actually occurred, he flips. He yells down the line that
he thought he had made it clear I'm to call him only
on life-or-death matters, that this is just a blip, that it
could have waited, that we're not going to starve, are
we? And now, thanks to me and my knee-jerk reactions, I've ruined everything for him and he'll have to
move again.

This is so unfair it makes me almost dizzy. I finally
lose it. That's tough, poor Clem, poor baby, all that
freedom, all that sunshine. We, of course, will not
be free to move anywhere or to buy a pair of socks
without permission, but he's not to worry about
that, he has all that swimming, all that sunbathing
to do—

He tries to interrupt but there's no interrupting me
now, I have full steam. I've been loyal and faithful and
have stood by him through thick and thin and what

have I got for it? Running up and down to Beaumont hospital with Johnny, having to put up with his crack-pot auntie – your auntie, Clem, not mine – and from now on, of course, I will be re-using my tea-bags. But not to worry, isn't recycling all the rage these days? And maybe when the blankets wear out we'll be able to cadge a few out-of-date newspapers from the news-agent's to put on the beds to keep us warm.

Through the harsh sound of my own voice I hear him saying something. His tone has dropped, become conciliatory. I cut short the diatribe: What?

Listen, Maisie, he says quietly, it'll be sorted out, I'll deal with it, I promise.

I take as much air as possible into my lungs to calm myself down. Will you come back, Clem? Things have changed now. You need to deal with this. I explain to him quickly what the solicitor has implied. When I have finished, there's silence from the other end.

I'll see what can be done, he says then, but I'll need a few weeks, a couple of months at most. He rushes on before I can say anything in response: Nothing drastic is going to happen before then, I'm sure you'll have enough – and I do appreciate all you've done, I do. Trust me. But I have to go now, right? I'll talk to you soon, I promise. I've been on too long, they've probably traced this by now. I'll get another mobile – I'll make sure you get the number.

He hangs up and I'm left with the receiver buzzing in my hand. Not before I have heard the scream of a seagull.

Slowly I replace the receiver. A fucking seagull.

I turn round, and Esmé, standing at the end of the corridor, is looking at me without expression. I remember that remark I made – yelled – about her to Clem. If she'd been there she'd heard it. I take a few steps towards her but she turns back into her bedroom.

As it happens, I am just back from collecting the old so-and-so. The trolley. Again.

Esmé's stomping ground is the junction where the road widens into Broadstone just beyond Church Street. It's busy at the best of times, and what with all the construction work going on, the traffic is almost always snarled around there. Today, as I get nearer to the junction, I see the northbound cars, which have jackrabbited away from the lights at North Richmond Street, swerving, almost crashing into one another. She's obviously on form.

I arrive at her station just above the junction and shout at her, trying to make myself heard above the roar and general chaos. As usual, she ignores me and I have to wait until the lights go red. Then I dart out to her, grab the handle of the trolley, to the great amusement of the crowd, not least the pedestrians who happen to be passing by and who have stopped to watch the spectacle. I'm not a weakling but she has a grip like a mechanical grab and within seconds we're wrestling for possession, like the two fishwives fighting for the looted pram in *The Plough and the Stars*, which, true to form, was my father's favourite play. He never forgave the Abbey Theatre for rejecting Sean O'Casey.

For God's sake, Esmé! Maddened, I eventually shriek at her at the top of my voice and she lets go suddenly, causing me to stumble. Then she threads her way to the kerb, leaving me, red-faced and puffing, to follow in her wake.

God knows what goes through her head when she does this. I've asked her, of course, we all have. But all she'll say is that she'll mind her own business and we're to mind ours. She never actually hits any of the cars, her timing is impeccable, she seems merely to enjoy frightening the drivers.

In the house, she behaves as though she's still living in France and we're all the underlings. She looks down her nose at our cutlery and ware, and wouldn't wash a cup to save her life. She gets up at the same time every morning, a quarter to eight on the dot, washes herself from head to toe in her *en suite*, then dresses herself perfectly. All in black. Down to stockings, Cuban heels and her string of black pearls, which is worth a fortune and is all she has left out of what, by all accounts, must have been a fabulous collection of jewellery.

I've tried and tried with her where that trolley is concerned, threatening, arguing, cajoling, but all to no avail. Although, as I've said already, she never comes to harm, I suppose there's always the possibility she could mistime her runs and get killed or injured. The last time we went through the charade of me hauling her home, she made a show of me in front of the entire rush-hour population of Church Street.

Dublin's grinding to a halt, you know, and it's only a matter of time before we have total and permanent gridlock. Bring it on, I say. Bring on the gridlock. Then they'll have to do something about it. At least gridlock will be *something* they can't blame on the Lanigans.

Sorry. Overreacting again. The public exposure we got at the time of Clem's arrest and – more prominently – after his escape – still stings. It's almost as humiliating as the discovery that I had been the last to know I had been married all along to a lawbreaker. But, in truth, we were a nine days' wonder, and except for the occasional mention of our name now when they write generically about criminal families, we don't feature all that much any more.

Yet I feel so upset and humiliated that I still can't go outside the house without looking around to see who's pointing at me. As a matter of fact, as usual, I saw a couple of unsavoury characters hanging around out there in doorways, people I wouldn't like to meet coming down an alley on a dark night. This area used to be respectable – and it still is around our part of it, the settled part. Our cottages are set in one of a few cul-de-sacs of tranquillity and we have very decent neighbours but you'd never know who'd be buying or renting the piled-up dog boxes that are being thrown up all around us. Little corner shops suddenly sprouting seven storeys and becoming huge apartment blocks, glitz on the outside but rows of tiny, identical kennels on the inside, apparently. I heard that in one complex, just up the road, one unfortunate couple had to saw the end off their bed to get it in the door of the bedroom. Honest to God, it's true. I met Melanie Malone, Tony and Joan's daughter, in the new Spar a few months ago and she told me. Nice girl, Melanie, blonde, gorgeous little figure. She lives in one of the new complexes – or she did before she went out foreign. Brazil, or Guatemala, or someplace, Joan told me, I can't remember. Melanie is a whiz with computers and her company was sending her out there for a year.

Esmé goes straight to her room when we get back into the house after her little excursion and, in a thoroughly bad mood now, I go into the kitchen to make myself a cup of coffee and maybe to lace it with something stronger. What do I find? Ambrose. King Angel is deigning to grant his humble serf a visit. Fat lot of good you are to me, I grumble at him, without thinking, then, of course, have to apologize.

Feel free, May, he says quietly, and there is something in his tone that causes me to put down the Nescafé jar and look sharply at him. His expression is bland, his hands are folded like a bank manager's across his garment, but his eyes spark: I am never far away, he says. I am the drunk who accosts you for a few pence but who forces compassion upon you by looking directly into your eyes. I am the irritating dog that barks at night to keep you awake and focus your mind on something I wish to bring to your attention. I am the fat unwashed bag lady who prompts you to count your blessings. I am the butterfly that lands gently on the arm of your garden chair and brings you a moment of pure joy.

I gape at him as he pauses for effect, then, his lips twitching: I am also the drugs dealer loitering in the doorway of a half-completed apartment block on the street outside.

I sit down. His smile this time I can describe only as complacent.

So he is all around me. Fine. But on his terms. Recently, for instance, when I was particularly exasperated with Esmé, I asked him to intervene and talk to her but he said he couldn't. That as of now – that's the way he put it, as of now – the only person with whom he wished to communicate was myself. It was news to me that angels have discretion over their own actions. We were always taught that they were messengers of God. Like, God being the Head Honcho and nothing moving without His say-so. Not so – at least not in the case of our Ambrose.

I'm not sure if he could be said actually to be living here. Does he sleep here – however occasionally? Do angels sleep? And even if he does, it's only forty winks. I share him with others, but I have to say I'm in good company – he mentioned Stephen Hawking, for instance, plus a Mexican poet, whose name escapes me, and some Aids nurse in a South African clinic.

Disbelieving – wouldn't you be? – I asked him at the time if he had any other just-a-housewife like me but he smiled patiently. No such thing as a just-a-housewife on Ambrose's books, apparently. We're all stars.

I do feel for sure that when the time is right Ambrose will reveal his mission and why he chose to put me, of all people, on his roll.

By the way, Clem was right about one thing he said in that phone call – we didn't or won't starve, and of course I've calmed down. The whole apparatus is chugging along: the subsistence cheques from the court, measly as they are, are enough for our needs, if I'm careful, and where our financial future is concerned, I'm at present acting like Hear No Evil, See No Evil. If I don't think about it, it mightn't happen, right?

→ Four ←

I'm in bed now, all packed. I'm not taking much with me. My wheelie-bag is on the floor, yawning open to take last-minute items. It has started to rain again but I'm snug in bed, the heavy curtains are drawn and my bedside lamp is making velvet shadows.

I was afraid the birthday party this evening would turn out to be terribly morose, not only because of our straitened circumstances but because of the long shadow cast by those missing from the table this year. Actually, though, it turned out very well.

To be honest, it wasn't that much of a hardship to have the party here in the house. Plain food, well cooked, has always been my motto and I've brought the boys up to believe the same. So where the food was concerned, although I say so myself, I did very well on little money, basing my meal around two frozen turkeys from Aldi, the cheap German supermarket down in Parnell Street. With good vegetables from the markets across the road, soup to start, ice cream to follow, it was a real feast. We wouldn't have got better in the Gresham.

By six o'clock everything was ready. The aroma of

roasting filled the candlelit house and mixed with the sweet, pungent scent of six dozen white roses. A chap I know in the markets wouldn't take any money for them because a few of the blooms had frost damage and because I had told him straight out it was my birthday. People can be really nice sometimes, can't they?

I'd set the big kitchen table with the damask cloth that had belonged to Clem's mother, all the bits and pieces of silver cutlery and Waterford glasses we had acquired over the years and, as a centrepiece, the big twelve-branched brass candelabra Eddie had found years ago in some junk shop and which had cleaned up brilliantly. My presents and cards were heaped on top of the microwave.

My determination to put on a good show, this year of all years, must have been catching because everyone had made an effort. Esmé was wearing one of her best dresses, lavender and black, its little cascades of jet beads soughing with her every movement. Amanda, married to Con, and Sharon, who is Frank's wife, had also dressed up; Sharon is a hairdresser and Amanda works in a boutique. Their skirts were a little too short and their necklines a little too low for my liking but that's how young people dress nowadays. They're nice girls and they love their husbands, which is the main thing.

As I said grace and glanced around at everyone, at the flowers, the steaming birds, at the young healthy skin glowing in the soft lozenges of candlelight, I thanked God for all His blessings and actually meant it. I even grinned at Esmé and surprised her into a return smile, faint but recognizable.

Even Johnny, whom we had taken home for the occasion and who loves candles and lights of all kinds, was entranced into quietness. I've accepted now that he will need minding for the rest of his life, although when he was very young I trailed him in and out of hospitals and doctors' offices until I was heartily sick of the sight of white coats. One of my main worries in life – that there will be no one to step into my shoes to look after him should I die before he does – has been taken care of, thank God. St Anthony's is wonderful and he thinks of it as home now. It broke my heart to put him in, but he didn't seem to mind one bit. My fervent prayer is that there will be enough money, somehow, to keep him there. It's a private home and the state only pays so much.

The others tell me not to worry, that should anything happen to me they'll take care of him, make sure St Anthony's stays up to scratch – but you know how it is. They care about him but not the way I do, motherhood being a life sentence.

Every year with Johnny is a bonus. At the beginning we were told his life wouldn't extend much beyond his teens because even if he hadn't been brain-damaged he would have been delicate. When he was only three months old, we discovered that he had an inoperable heart defect – nothing to do with the brain damage, just one of those random afflictions with no seeming cause. As he gets older, his other organs are being affected and every virus and infection can be life-threatening.

So far so good, however, and despite having to dash to the hospital now and then I have a feeling that he's going to confound everyone. Although I was very upset at the beginning, I suppose I have now stepped back a bit and can see the overall picture. The way to look at it is that I was lucky the first five were born perfect. Family is everything to me. Family is probably everything to everyone, when you come right down to it. That's why I pity the homeless so much and why I sometimes go down to give the nuns a hand with the Penny Dinners.

Half-way through the birthday meal, as I try to guess what's in my cards and presents – no word from Clem, of course – I am visited with an awful thought. Which one of us will be missing from this table next year? Instantly I dismiss it. That's in the hands of God, May. Enjoy this slice of happiness while you can.

Clem is not in our apartment in Nerja; as an asset, it has been locked up by the courts, but even if it hadn't been seized, it's the first place the police would have looked. I have fond memories of the place from when the boys were very young, but Johnny's birth and subsequent difficulties put an end to my going there. Clem has used it a few times over the years, usually with friends like Tony and Joan and others, including their kids, and because we had always talked about retiring there, we never sold it or even rented it out.

It was Martin, whose job as a bouncer affords him the most amazing contacts, who found out where Clem had moved to, and I keep picturing his face when he sees me walking into his new hideout, a resort called Sitges, somewhere near Barcelona. Won't he get some shock?

I feel anger rising but then the back of my neck prickles and I look sideways. Like a benign spectre at the feast, Ambrose is in a corner of the kitchen. He makes a curious gesture: he holds out both hands to me, palms upward, as though gifting something. I flash him a smile, turn back to the table and feel good again.

Near the end of the meal Eddie, who with Clem and CJ both away is the senior male present, taps on his glass with his spoon and stands up. It's time to give Ma her presents, he says, but before we do, I'd like to propose a toast. Then, looking directly at me: Ma, you're going away from us tomorrow. We want to wish you good luck and *bon voyage*. We also want to say that we know how difficult it's been for you lately, in more ways than one, and in our opinion there is not a mother in Dublin who can hold a candle to you. You deserve the best, Ma, and I, for one, am always going to see that you get it.

Hear hear! Frank shouts.

Then they all cheer and clap and with huge smiles on their faces, sing 'Happy Birthday To You' followed by 'For She's A Jolly Good Fellow'.

Johnny, surprised, joins in, shouting his head off and banging one of his tins off his helmet. Even outside the epileptic fits, his movements are unpredictable and can be a bit wild so, God love him, he has to wear a crash helmet at all times so he won't injure his head if he falls. Esmé doesn't sing, but she wears an expression that, in strong light, could even be taken for good cheer.

I'm stunned and can barely hold back the tears as I look around at my smiling boys and their wives, at my family. Although we do celebrate birthdays properly, as I've said, we don't go in for speeches or shows of emotion, and this is the first time in my life that this has happened to me. Now I can say with my hand on my heart that, despite all our troubles, I know firsthand what happiness feels like.

One by one, ceremoniously, they extract their presents from the pile and give them to me. A T-shirt, an embroidery kit, chocolates, slippers. They are terrific presents, of course they are, and I am very grateful to get them, but I recognize a lot of the stuff from going around the pound shops, and can't help thinking of the cornucopia of other years. I dismiss this as being unworthy and ungrateful. Everyone is very sweet even to make the effort. Sharon, God love her, gives me a big art book about Christianity. I open it at random, and what's the first thing I see? You've guessed it. A huge colour reproduction of a painting depicting a flock of angels. All sizes. All with wings. Reflexively, I look around for Ambrose to share the joke, but he's not there.

The book is beside me here on the bedside table but I have already flicked through it, and, where the angels are concerned, it seems to be more of the stuff I've read before. Does no one know anything for sure about angels? Yet I, of all people, should best understand why definite information on them is so thin on the ground and why there is so much speculation in all the books I've read. Look at me, for heaven's sake. I'm in a good position, you might think, to get real information and I've been able to find out damn all. He has just left – as a matter of fact he materialized just after I snuggled into bed.

Whereas in the kitchen during the party he was normal-sized and quite relaxed, tonight he was regal, almost off-putting. His back was very straight, his head held high on his neck, and he wasn't in one of his happy-clappy moods. He also seemed distracted, as though his mind was on one of his other clients.

I wish you a good birthday, May, he says in formal tones.

Thank you. I hesitate, then come out with what is really on my mind. Can I rely on you during the trip, Ambrose? Will you be coming with me tomorrow?

I'll be there if you need me, May.

I can see that he continues to be only half present mentally but I know better than to press him. It went well this evening, I say to him. I was glad you were there.

Did you like your gifts?

I look sharply at him but his expression is remote. I loved them, I say firmly. Then, quickly: What did that gesture mean – the one you made with your hands?

He raises an eyebrow: You understood perfectly.

I think hard. I'm to enjoy it while I can? Live in the present – count my blessings, all that stuff?

You understood perfectly.

His back becomes even straighter and he grows a bit. He always grows when he's in a bad mood.

Relax, Ambrose, I say to him, you look like you have a poker up your—

He shoots me a fierce glance and I subside. I suppose the wine I had drunk during the dinner had made me less than cautious. Ambrose hates bad language.

I study him, the way he holds himself, his haughty

demeanour. I've done more than a bit of reading in the angelology section of the local library. My bet, I think, is that what we have here is a Principality—

You are mistaken, May, he says coldly, and once again I remind myself that he can read what I'm thinking. It continues to be very unsettling.

He's not going to put me off tonight, however. I push myself up on one elbow: Then what are you, Ambrose? I'd really like to know. He flashes me what you could only categorize as a glare but it doesn't faze me and I keep my gaze steady. If you must know, he says at last, the human passion for pigeon-holing and classification is just that. Human. These appellations have no relevance. I am no more a Principality than I am a Seraphim, a Cherubim, a Throne, Dominion, Power, Chariot, Virtue or an Archangel. I am myself.

Come on, Ambrose. I'm taken aback at the dismissiveness of the response. I only asked—

The conclusion is inescapable: he cuts across me with icy disregard. The concept of a universe swarming with formless, ageless spirits is too frightening to accept even for those of most open mind. This, no doubt, is why our presence, when acknowledged at all, is not only defined by type, but clothed in myth and metaphor. We are ancestors, fairies, elves, trolls, spirits of the trees. We are Santa Claus, the Good Fairy, the Witch of the West. And before you ask – he grows larger – you have wondered also, no doubt, how, like Santa Claus, we can be expected to attend many charges all at once and in widely separated areas of this world and others. His eyes widen, his brows come together: Perhaps you will remember, he says with chilly intensity, when I tell you once again that we do not exist in the dimension generally referred to as time. Eternity is not an infinite extension of time, it is its absolute absence.

And with that he vanishes. Definitely in a huff for some reason. I flop back on to my pillows.

That was about an hour ago. I do hope he's going to show up tomorrow.

I'll miss our bedroom – I haven't been away from home for donkey's years. The wine is still working its magic and, sentimentally, I cast around the room, as big and plumply luxurious as the drawing room of a plush hotel with its red carpet and pale pink walls reflecting in the mirrored doors. All Da's books and my own are neatly ranged along the shelves of his old mahogany breakfront bookcase – my most precious material possession. We had a devil of a job getting it in here, we had to remove all the door-frames.

I'm gabbling, I know – but it's something to do. I'm trying not to be nervous because, as you can imagine, the coming confrontation with Clem is chuffing round and round in my brain like a clockwork train.

Because the CAB confiscated my passport, I had to get a false one. It's in the name of Crowley – an omen, maybe, because my maiden name was Crowe. I'm leery about using it, to tell you the truth, because I'm the type who feels guilty even doing something as simple as going through those tag detectors installed at the doorways of shops in Henry Street. Eddie has been trying to convince me I won't be committing any crime. That, as a citizen of the EU, I'm entitled to travel freely inside the EU boundaries without any passport at all and I am entitled simply to wave the cover of my EU passport at the border officials. This is called the Bangemann wave because the law was brought in by some European official called Bange-mann.

I've become close to Eddie in the last few months and have leaned on him a fair bit. There was a time when I thought he would never do anything with his life – but he's been grand for the past couple of years, has a good steady job managing a record shop in town. He's certainly not into anything crooked. At least I don't think so.

You see? You see what a state I'm in? I can't even trust my own instincts any more. And I wouldn't dream of asking Martin – he's the fourth – how he got the damned passport for me. I hardly know what to believe about anyone or anything any more.

It's not only as a result of what happened to Clem. Coming to terms with what happened to CJ was bad enough. In retrospect, maybe CJ getting into trouble should have warned me about Clem: like son like father? But the plain fact is that it didn't.

CJ's trouble? All right, I suppose I have to be up front about him too. Clem Junior, the eldest, is in gaol. I hate thinking about him in there, I hate thinking about what he did to get there, I hate the whole sorry mess of what has begun to happen around my life.

Where CJ was concerned there were no dawn raids or anything like that, but the shock was every bit as bad – worse, really, in many respects, because it was my first intimation that things were going off the rails in this family.

We got a phone call from a solicitor asking us to come down to the Bridewell. Clem was away on business in the North, Martin was asleep – because of his job, he sleeps during the day. I didn't like disturbing Con, Frank or Eddie at their work so I had to go down there by myself. I had no idea what faced me: the solicitor wouldn't be specific over the phone, merely said that my son was at the station and my presence was required. It was a beautiful day, I remember, birds, sunshine, summer dresses and white shirtsleeves on the street, the whole shooting gallery.

By the time I got there the solicitor had already left and, by contrast to all that brightness and gaiety outside, the room where I waited to see CJ was dingy, to put it mildly. The walls were scored with initials and curse words, while the air ponged of cigarette smoke with an undercurrent of alcohol. Although I was nervous, I felt fairly confident that this would turn out to be a misunderstanding, or at worst some street fight that had run out of control. None of the lads had ever been in trouble before, thank God. Yet as I waited, my unease grew. Maybe it would be something more serious after all. I had been somewhat out of touch with CJ lately. Since leaving home, he had shared a flat in Rialto with a builder pal who gave him steady work on the sites around the city and, except for weekend visits when he came home to see us – to see Johnny, really – we rarely met up.

The first thing I notice about him when he comes in

is that his clothes are in tatters, muddy and torn. The second is that as he sits down and drapes one arm across the back of his chair, he doesn't seem all that upset: Hello, Ma.

You're filthy — what happened to you?

I had a bit of an argument with a bush, he says.

CJ, this isn't funny. I want to reach across the table and slap him, hard, but of course do nothing of the sort.

OK. He sits up properly. There's no point in not telling you, Ma, you're going to find out anyway. We're going to plead guilty, and because it's a first offence, we'll probably get probation.

Guilty of what? And who's we?

Calmly he tells me what happened. Just as what happened with Clem's arrest later, just as with Esmé's recent revelation about the fancy woman, it is all too much to take in at one go.

So here's a summary, as CJ told it to me. Early that morning, he and the flatmate had been in the flatmate's Ford Transit van, which was loaded with stolen cigarettes, when ahead of them they saw a Gárda checkpoint on the Ashbourne Road just south of Slane. CJ was driving. As he slowed the van in response to the guard's signals, the flatmate panicked and jumped out while they were still moving, spraining his ankle. His panic was contagious because CJ slammed on the brakes and jumped out too. He ran across the fields, but the police gave chase and called in a helicopter to assist. It took them less than fifteen minutes to corner him.

I'm serious, Ma, you're not to worry. CJ shrugs

when he's finished relating this tale of mayhem. It sounds worse than it is, it's nothing, really, I keep telling you, it's only a first offence.

Stolen cigarettes? My voice sounds like that of a ninety-year-old.

He shrugs again. It's no big deal. It's a game we all play with the cops. He looks aggrieved now. Do you know how much this government rakes in with taxes on cigarettes, Ma? We're doing the public a service.

I can't believe what I'm hearing. You mean this isn't the first time? I feel now as though I might choke. You've done this before? How many times? How long have you—

That's enough! CJ pushes back his chair and stands up. His expression has tightened. I told you we're pleading guilty, we'll get probation. Thanks for coming, they shouldn't have bothered you. I told them to ring Da.

I look up at him, at this firstborn son who is now a stranger. At what point exactly did I lose him?

Da wasn't home, I say. I can now barely hear myself.

The rest of that day, and the entire week following it, are blurred in my memory, because Johnny chose that day of all days to take one of his periodic fits, quite a serious episode this time. He was rushed into Beaumont Hospital from St Anthony's and poor Eddie, whom I rang from the ward, had to bear the burden of spreading all the bad news, not only about this but about CJ. For several days after that I was so fully occupied with Johnny's crisis that I didn't even make it to the court for CJ's trial.

Johnny pulled through but CJ's predictions of getting

probation proved wrong. He got four years. His builder pal, who apparently had a record of convictions, received six.

I must go to sleep now. The next twenty-four hours are going to be quite something. One way or another.

→ Five ←

If Clem had said to me a year ago that I would brazen my way through French immigration on a false passport waving like Bangemann, or that shortly afterwards I'd be sitting beside an angel at the back of a coach travelling from Beauvais to Paris, accompanied by hordes of youngsters munching Tayto crisps and fizzing up bottles of Fanta, I'd have said he was nuts. But lives change in the course of a few seconds, don't they? I'm the living proof of that.

Preceded by his scent, Ambrose materialized on the seat beside me just as the bus was pulling out of the French airport yesterday afternoon. Have I mentioned this scent? It's very delicate. I can't put my finger on what it reminds me of. The nearest I can come to it is that it resembles that sharp, bittersweet waft you get from roses after a heavy shower of rain. As distinctive as the ringing of a bell, it's permeating the air up and down the coach – as we gathered speed, I could see some of the kids breaking off from their mobile-phone conversations, sniffing the air and looking around to see who was using this exclusive new perfume.

Today, my angel is in chirpy good form: Good

afternoon, May. I must say that Beauvais airport was charming. He looks through the window at the receding terminal: Yet airports have become a peculiarly ingenious instrument of torture – have you noticed? He raises his eyes skywards, shrugging like a Frenchman: Bangkok – ouf! Addis Ababa! And as for Heathrow – the tenth circle of hell! But, then, I have always liked the French, you know, civilized, self-sufficient people . . .

He settles deeper into his seat, for all the world like an ordinary tourist bent on enjoying the passing scenery.

He has obviously recovered from whatever had been bugging him the previous night. I should have left well enough alone, of course, but being me, I blow it: Feeling a bit more cheerful today, Ambrose? What was that all about last night when you were so sniffy?

He freezes. His neck elongates: You are not my only charge in this universe.

That's me put back in my box. I don't want him vanishing on me in a huff – I need him with me for what's coming – so I rush to repair the damage: Sorry, Ambrose. Humbly.

Oh, never mind, apology accepted – he waves a hand, good humour instantly restored – think nothing of it.

It was a close one.

I have to agree with him about Beauvais: it was quite a contrast to the airport in Dublin where the departure area was bedlam, even though it's still only April. I have rarely seen so many young people in one place, and at my age I was probably as conspicuous as a hen on horseback. But, then, I had never flown Ryanair before and you can't beat a ten-pound round trip to Paris, plus another tenner for the taxes and so forth, can you? It's a pity, I like Aer Lingus, always have; we had always been Aer Lingus passengers, Clem and I.

Feck Clem. I won't think about Clem until I have to.

I concentrate on first impressions of France.

It is true that they look after their own: our coach is surrounded by Renaults, Citroëns and Peugeots as we approach the outskirts of Paris. Over there is one of those huge hypermarkets I'd read about. And what an amusing name for petrol: Elf.

And, would you believe?, far away in the murky distance, there's the top of the Eiffel Tower. If my mother could only see me now – Paris must have been an unattainable dream for someone like her. These days, I find myself thinking more and more about her, wishing, for instance, that she could have known the boys, or see what we've done with our house.

Would Mammy have liked it? I'm sad not even to know what her taste was. The few memories I have of her are just impressions, mostly sensory. She smoked a lot and I remember the musky, sour smell of her breath and from her skin. She always wore a wide brown slide to keep her hair to one side – I remember the smooth, warm feel of that when I grabbed it. I remember also that she used to wear a lace collar, or perhaps it was a lace dress. White, anyway, or cream. I remember the tight sharp pain of my fingers getting caught in it as I reached for something around her neck.

That's it, unfortunately. Not much, is it? A few smells, a few memories of touch. Although I've studied her face in photographs, there is no pull of recognition. The woman smiling up at my father in their wedding photograph is a complete stranger.

I've asked Ambrose about my mother. Has he met her? Could he describe where she is? Is she happy? Is she with friends? Does she remember me? Although at present he tells me he can't answer questions of that nature, something tells me he will eventually. He will, if I have to drag it out of him.

It was dark when our train pulled out of the Paris station for Barcelona. I went straight to my sleeping compartment, to find that I had been given one of the top berths. The accommodation was adequate, I suppose, although my three immediate companions, who had also decided to retire early, were surly and unresponsive to my tentative smiles of greeting. One of them, very tall and overweight, even turned her back, which was just as well because, guiltily, I have to admit I found it difficult to look directly at her. The poor woman suffered from an awful disfigurement: on one side of her face, a purplish birthmark, livid as a fresh bruise, extended from below the jawbone, over her cheek and nose, and into the middle of her forehead, crinkling and shrivelling the skin of her eyelid so that her eye, twice as large as its companion, stared whitely from its socket. She was probably fed up with being stared at and mistook my overture of friendship for voyeurism. It's no wonder she turned away.

Miserably, I climbed the ladder into my bunk, struggled out of my slacks and blouse and stretched out as comfortably as I could. The bed linen was clean and crisp enough at first, but it was very hot and within minutes my legs were entangled in a slithery mess. In addition, whereas I'm accustomed to sleeping against a high, downy pyramid, this miserable excuse for a pillow was only about an inch thick. I tried to raise it by putting my travel bag under it, further decreasing the space between my face and the ceiling, but the pillow's sliver of foam was inadequate to the task of smoothing out the lumpy contents of the bag. It was like trying to sleep on rocks in a small, suffocating cave and within minutes I had removed the bag and had resigned myself to a night of wakefulness.

Yielding myself to the motion of the train, I managed to drift off, but shot awake when the luminous dial of my watch told me we were only about an hour or so out of Paris. I was puddled in sweat and my heart was thumping. Hard. Most scarily of all, I seemed to be having difficulty inflating my lungs to their fullest extent. Every puff of air around me seemed to have been sucked away.

I forced myself to lie still while I worked out what was wrong.

We had stopped. All around I could hear sporadic clanging and a tumult of engines.

Up on one elbow, I peered through my window – bumping my head in the process – but it was too dark outside to see what was going on so I lay back again: Relax, May, relax, relax, this too will pass. Close your eyes.

The more I tried to rest, however, the more breathless I became, until I was actually panting, struggling for each puff. I tried to sit up – bumping my head for the second time – but, given the space restrictions, could manage only a sort of sideways foetal curl. My heart pounded faster but I was so caught up in catching gobbets of oxygen to feed my tortured lungs that I was only peripherally aware of its speed.

Across the way, behind the privacy curtain of her bunk, the disfigured woman was snoring explosively and out of rhythm like a choir of bursting volcanoes. Fleetingly, I envisaged a person of her height and bulk confined to such a small space and knew she must be seriously uncomfortable but all that really concerned me was the burning in my chest and the sensation that my ribcage was going to disintegrate entirely with the pain and effort of breathing. Was I having a heart-attack? Was I dying here of all places? Did I have a call bell? Where was Ambrose? Gasping, I scrabbled wildly around. I had seen a light switch somewhere – where? Please, God, where's the light switch?

I was faintly aware of something changing in the compartment but, mainly intent on staying alive, it took me a few seconds to realize that the snoring across the way had stopped. Then the drape alongside my bunk was gently pulled aside and, in the darkness, I could just make out the disproportionate eye of the birthmarked woman.

Then she did an extraordinary thing. She reached upwards and placed one fat hand on my sweating forehead. I shuddered at the touch – her palm was as cool as a river. She maintained the contact as the

coolness extended downwards across my nose and
mouth, along my throat and over my breasts until it
reached my stomach then my thighs and feet. My heart
slowed, my lungs seemed to inflate again of their own
accord. Even the commotion outside seemed to recede
until it was just a murmur.

I fell asleep. At least I think I did. Well, I hope I
did.

Because the next thing I know, I become aware that
the carriage roof is lifting to give me breathing space.
Lazily, like the petals of a flower filmed in time-lapse,
it opens so that now above my head there is nothing
but blue sky and white, puffy cartoon clouds, the kind
drawn by a child on an Easter card. The most wonderful feeling of airiness radiates from my heart through
my veins, and I find myself, young and light, floating
along through a scented sky with the train far below
and shrunk to the size of a toy.

I know that scent, I think. That's Ambrose.

There is no sound at all. The silence in this sky is
like balm.

I start to enjoy myself. Looking down from my
eyrie, I can see no train now, although the tracks glitter
from horizon to horizon across an immensity of open
fields. Ahead of me is a green mountain, studded with
wild-flowers. I come to it and float into a meadow,
finding myself waist deep in big white daisies. I lie back
to look at the sky through the undersides. The daisies,
soft as feathers, pat my face. I turn my head sideways
and Ambrose is sitting beside me. His face is luminous,
plated with silver and gold. Aquamarine light streams

from the palms of his hands as he holds out his arms to me. I turn in to him and he enfolds me. His garment is soft and billowing and feels like a warm breeze all over. I'm not at all conscious of my own body as his silky hair grows into mine. I look at his shining face. His eyes grow larger and larger until I'm looking into one great eye, as deep and blue as the Pacific Ocean and in it I float exquisitely and infinitely free. I hear his voice, like riffling leaves: How do you feel, May?

This is bliss, I say back to him.

This is happiness, May, he says. This is how you should feel all the time.

And then I wake up – or come to. The carriage ceiling has closed over again, inches from my nose. I am still in my cramped bunk. The snoring from the disfigured woman across the narrow passageway is like an insult.

I discover that my face is soft with tears, but I am serene and untroubled. I feel I will never worry again.

How much I slept for the rest of the night, I don't know. I must have napped some, however, because sometime after dawn when I descended from my perch to go to the bathroom, the drape across the disfigured woman's berth had been pulled aside and her berth was empty, the linen already gone. I had not heard her leave.

Meaning to thank her, I searched for her when we got into Barcelona – scanning the train windows along its entire length. Then I moved up and down the platform but could not find her either amongst the disembarking passengers, or in the throng of silent, beautifully groomed young men and women with gleaming hair and buffed luggage, who were waiting to board.

I gave up the search and followed directions for the Sitges train. I sat on a curved bench and tried to order my thoughts. Strangely, despite what was facing me during the coming day, I continued to feel calm, but my brain struggled with the surrealism of the dream, the tendrils of which still clung. Could I have dreamed the entire episode, the incipient heart-attack, the woman's action? Could I have dreamed her existence?

No. Definitely not. Those snores were very real. And so was that blemish, the wheezing bulk, that awful eye—

What's wrong, May? The temperature goes down a few degrees. Ambrose is beside me: Is something the matter?

Railway stations in Spain have a quality that makes you feel like a traveller, rather than just someone who has to be shovelled into a carriage. It might be the tiles, or the cleanliness, or the different, vibrant colours. I keep my eyes firmly on the red, green and white under my feet: Nothing, Ambrose, thank you for asking, there's nothing wrong. I hesitate: Although I did think I was going to have a heart-attack last night.

That was a panic attack, May.

I risk a look at him. His face is arranged in the angel equivalent of a smirk.

It's too complicated. I decide to let the hare sit. I'll

bring it up some other time, when I've properly mulled it over.

He vanishes when the local train pulls into the station at Sitges but his parting smile makes promises: I'll be around, it says.

I certainly hope so, I think, as the train pulls out and I am left alone with my wheelie bag.

Where to go now? Somehow, in what passed for the planning of this trip, I had not accounted for the bit between arrival here and actually finding Clem. Should I check in somewhere first?

Pulling the bag behind me, I set off through the shady, narrow streets, instinctively making my way downhill towards the gleam of the sea, eventually coming out on to a wide, steel-smooth promenade which, lined with elegant old palm trees, stretches for miles. The trees undulate gently over fountains, innumerable flowers and – I see gratefully – lots of seats. I sit.

I'm facing out to sea, which is as flat as a glass table. The bright sand on the beach is patterned with circular ridges – I reckon they must use some kind of a raking machine to clean it. Along the prom, skateboarders, rollerbladers, cyclists and joggers weave calmly through the more leisurely paced strollers. Behind me, bathed in the clean yellow sunlight, are the souvenir shops, cafés and some of the bigger hotels, immaculately kept.

So now what? Enough of this slinging and swinging the lead. Stir yourself, May Lanigan. You're procrastinating again: you should already be half-way through your search.

I'm so tired, though, and so unexpectedly relaxed that I can't summon up the energy just yet to jump back into the storm. The task of locating him is daunting: this resort is not as small as I thought it would be and although it's still out of season and a lot of places seem not to have opened as yet, I don't quite know where to start. It's so agreeable here, with a little breeze from the sea stroking my cheeks and sunshine like slow, warm honey pouring over my shoulders.

He's probably as brown as a chestnut now.

Look, once and for all, I want to put on the record that I know Clem committed crime and deserves punishment. But in mitigation, what did he do that was so desperate? Nobody died. Nobody got hurt. He never owned, used, or even handled a gun – I asked him that at the first opportunity and he told me his conscience was clean on that score. This I believe, God help me.

The sheets of charges against him as read out in court – samples, the prosecutor called them – can be boiled down to a few, mostly to do with stolen goods and conspiring with others to defraud the state of its excise taxes by smuggling dutiable merchandise. Cigarettes, tobacco, electrical goods, alcohol, sports socks, Manchester United strips, that kind of thing. So what he did comes down only to evading taxes, and when you contrast this against what many another in high office did and got away with in this country – illegal offshore accounts, payola, bribery – Clem Lanigan's crimes have to be small potatoes.

And on a smaller scale still, who doesn't think twice

about milking or even defrauding the social welfare system? Maybe a few extra pounds here and there claimed illegally on the dole or disability might not seem to amount to much for each individual person, but if you add it all up together it must come to millions, billions even. And where the principle is concerned, I can't see all that much difference between Clem's crimes and what these people are doing *en masse*. Yet very few of these so-called watchdogs seem to bang on about that.

Am I being too defensive? But it is two in one flesh, as God has ordained, isn't it? Until death do us part? On my wedding day, I promised I'd stick by my husband until the very end, didn't I? It was my duty. You either trust someone or you don't. You can't trust them just a little bit. Trust is like love that way. That's what makes those articles about Get the Wives and Kids so unfair.

And I'm still loyal.

Until I find out for sure that he has given up the right to my loyalty and that I have the right to knock his block off.

Which vitamin is it you get from sunshine? Whichever one it is, my insides have shrivelled for lack of it and I didn't realize it until now. I might even doze off if I'm not careful—

Jesus!

That's him – Clem! I'm sure of it – across the road on the other side, at that souvenir shop there. I don't know if he's seen me. Jesus, help me. I'm not ready.

Hey, hold on! Why am I feeling guilty, like I'm the

one on the run? He's strolling in the sun looking as though he hasn't a care in the world.

That's my husband over there. I've every right to talk to him.

→ Six ←

I turn instantly into a pillar of salt, or ice or something completely dead. And then in one of those
strange, out-of-body moments a person can sometimes
experience, I withdraw from myself and, for a few
moments, can see myself as others would see me, as if
I'm looking at myself in the freeze-frame of a video or
in the harsh, X-ray lens of an all-seeing camera.

Despite what Ambrose said to me that time about
my reflection in my bedroom mirror, what I see right
now isn't attractive. I see a middle-aged woman, sitting
in the soft sunshine, but bound and harnessed into a
type of psychic armour, very thick, heavily plated like
a tortoise or an armadillo. Nothing soft – such as love,
humour, enjoyment, affection or fun – can get in or
out through that barrier. The only impetus from within
is duty, the only emotion that can penetrate it is fear:
I see anxiety and panic crouched inside that skin in
which I now exist and know for sure that these are the
only emotions I have experienced for a long, long time
– and this is what made the freewheeling blissful
feelings of the dream on the train so unusual.

The revelation is so sudden I feel I've been hit. I

wasn't like this as a girl. I don't know when that armour began to wrap itself around me or when the fun leached out of my life. I realize I can't remember any more what fun feels like.

When Clem was arrested, something started happening to me, some form of self-analysis started to impose itself and I'm not sure I like it. Maybe I'm going mad.

The impact of the vision, if that's what it is, is so real it may have lasted half an hour. But then I see that Clem has sauntered on only a few yards and it cannot be more than a second or two after I spotted him. He has stopped to look into the window of another souvenir shop so I have enough time to scrutinize him.

He hasn't seen me yet.

Are you chicken? I castigate myself. What are you playing at? What are you afraid of? If the truth is bad, it can't be any worse than what you've been imagining. And at least you'll have been put out of your misery.

I stand up and, leaving my little suitcase safely under the bench – this isn't Dublin after all – I walk across the road to intercept my husband. Knees bent slightly, hand cupped against the shop window to cut out the sun's glare, he is examining a big model of a sailing ship. He is wearing clothes I've never seen before, smart Spanish jeans and loafers under a navy cotton sweater with a boat neck. His ankles are bare and, as I get closer, I see he does indeed have a tan, that his hair has been cropped so short it's virtually stubble and that what's left of it has been dyed a reddish blond. Quite natural-looking too – although that's not surprising because hairdressers in Spain are masters of colour. What's more, he now has a little moustache, dyed to match.

I hesitate, taken aback. This man looks quite unlike the Clem I last saw in court. He could be any sophisticated, relaxed Euro-man and looks ten years younger than when I last saw him. Quite dishy as a matter of fact.

He is so engrossed in his model ship that I can get to within two yards of him without him noticing my approach: Hello, Clem.

To say that he is surprised to see me is the understatement of this new millennium. When he hears my voice, he straightens up so quickly he nearly loses his balance and I swear to God he goes grey under the tan: May— He croaks it. What – what are you doing here?

It's a strange experience to have caught him on the hop like this. Clem likes to act as though suave is his middle name.

What are you doing here? He repeats himself like an echo. Where did you come from?

I do my best to sound jaunty: From Ireland. I've been travelling for the best part of twenty-four hours.

It's great for once to inhabit the high ground, although inside my chest the old panic button has already been pressed and I can hear the first alarms. The gratifying thing – I think – is that I can see panic behind his eyes too. This man is definitely not happy with me appearing like this. He looks around quickly and grabs my arm: We can't be drawing attention to ourselves – come on over here.

But as he starts to draw me towards a café he sees the little tape recorder in my hand: What's that? He tightens his grip on my arm: What the hell is that? Are you recording me?

Luckily I can show him that the machine is not on. Let go of my arm, Clem, I say quietly. I'll go and get my suitcase and then we can talk.

All right, he mutters, but he looks hard at me, frowning: Who sent you?

Nobody sent me — look, Clem, this is stupid. I laugh, but the sound doesn't ring humorously in my own ears. I just wanted to see you, that's all, I say, as calmly as I can. Anyone would think you weren't pleased—

Of course I'm pleased to see you, he says quickly. You're right, this is stupid. I'll order the coffee — you go get your bag.

He hurries ahead of me into the café. But not, I notice, before he flicks an eye all around again to see if anyone is watching us. It stands to reason, I suppose, but he needn't have worried. There were still very few people around and none was looking in our direction.

Or maybe he was in fear of his fancy woman coming along and catching him with his wife.

As I go back across the road to pick up the suitcase, I'm kicking myself for my carelessness with the recorder. I glance over at the café. The front is all glass and I can see the pale dish of his face looking out at me. I'll have to brazen it out. As I drag the suitcase from under the bench, I realize something odd has happened. For a brief moment there, I thought I was actually afraid of my husband. I shrug off the notion as being absurd.

When I get into the café two cappuccinos steam on the bistro table at which he sits. As I settle myself into the small, uncomfortable metal chair opposite him, making sure its little red light is not on, I put the tape-recorder on the table between us, to show him I'm not trying to hide anything. Before you ask again, I say, I'm writing my autobiography and as a first step I'm talking into this. It's for my own use. And it's private, like a diary. I wouldn't read anyone else's diary. Would you?

His eyes shrink to cinders. An autobiography? You? Since when are you writing your autobiography?

Since a little while ago, I tell him.

He picks up the little recorder, holds it so it is out of my reach and juts his head across the table so his nose is only inches from mine: This is about me, isn't it?

Of course it's not — it's about me.

I'm in it, though, amn't I?

Yes, you're in it, Clem, I say calmly, you're my husband. Everyone is in it, Da and my mother and you and your ma and Johnny and Esmé and all the kids. This is my life and you are the people in my life. It wouldn't be an autobiography otherwise. It's for the boys, really. And it was something to do when you weren't around. I challenge him with my eyes, although inside I'm begging: Please, Lord, please, don't let him turn it on.

Thank God we're the only people in the café, if you don't count the waiter who, lounging against his counter with his back to us, has brought boredom to a fine art.

Clem's face relaxes and he chortles: Autobiography? Here. He slides the machine back towards me across the table. Keep me out of it, do you hear? I reserve

the right to vet this before it's published. He laughs
again. That'll be the day! Have fun! He continues to
smile as he takes cigarettes and a lighter from the
breast pocket of his sweater, taps out a cigarette then
concentrates on lighting it.

He draws deeply then blows smoke through his
nostrils, staring out of the window through the haze,
and while I'm putting the recorder safely away in my
handbag, I'm covertly studying him, trying to find
chinks and cracks and indications of what's been going
on. Something is tugging at the back of my consciousness but won't come to the surface. Does an unfaithful
husband carry some sort of identification mark? Do his
eyes shift more? Does his belly shrink?

If that is one of the telltale signs, Clem is certainly
guilty. To tell you the truth, and being as objective as
I can in this situation, I can't get over how well he
looks. He had never got fat, or even chubby, but the
years had softened up his muscles so that what I had
last seen in the bed beside me before he did his runner
was a somewhat blurred outline of the firm, compacted
body I had married.

Have you been exercising? I ask abruptly, trying to
goad him into God knows what kind of admission.

He laughs and I have to smile with him. Clem always
had a chuckly, infectious laugh. A bit, he says. Every
side street in this place seems to have a gym. For the
poofters. Place is crawling with them.

I glance around to make sure the waiter has not
reacted to this and when I look back, Clem is no
longer smiling. So what's going on? You're hardly here
for the good of your health. His voice is soft but, alert

as I am, I can detect deep wariness and I can see his brain is ticking like a metronome. He leans forward on both elbows, eyeballing me, pupils like awls: You could expose me, Maisie, don't you know that? You might have been followed.

But I wasn't followed, was I? I do my best to appear matter-of-fact: I wanted to see you, Clem. It's been eight months—

Then I have to stop abruptly because of the bile that has surged up my throat demanding expression. I want to scream at him at the top of my lung power. Who is she? Who the fuck is she?

I force myself to take a pause so I won't blow it. The object of this exercise is to get at the truth. I have to surprise him – there is no point in accusing him when his wits are this sharp; he will simply deny everything, vanish to some other small town and this trip will have been a frustrating waste of time. So I laugh lightly, or try to: Come on, Clem, I'm your wife. Why shouldn't I want to see you?

He stares hard. Yeah, right. His chair scrapes on the tiled floor as he pushes it back from the table: Have you finished your coffee?

I look down at the full, frothing cup in front of me. Between leaving home and arriving here, I've had enough coffee to do me for the rest of my life, I say truthfully. And I'm very tired.

He throws a couple of peseta bills on the tabletop: Let's get you into a hotel. I don't like hanging around any one place in public for long. Too dangerous.

As he stands up, I notice he has a swish metallic mobile slung on the waistband of his jeans. I suppose

you get used to seeing these things attached to everyone's anatomy and don't really notice them. I push
back my own chair: Is that a new phone?

He grabs it as if he hadn't wanted me to see it but
at the last minute mutates the gesture into one of
examining the keypad: Yeah, it is – gazing minutely at
the little numbers as though fascinated with them: I
only got it this morning – it's the latest model. I was
going to buzz you tonight to give you the number.

As I follow Clem out into the sunshine, I don't
know what to think. He's definitely agitated but, then,
he has plenty of ordinary reasons to be nervous. Like
the police, for instance.

Ambrose is lounging like a tourist against the sea
wall across the road, his hair glowing like stained glass
in the sunlight. I'm about to wave but, just in time,
remember who I'm with. I can imagine how Clem
might interpret a signal to what seems like empty air.
Where are we going? I ask, as he hurries ahead of me.

He turns and grabs the handle of my bag: We can
talk in the hotel.

Coming from a man who has so recently loitered at
a shop window for so long, I think that's a bit rich but
I decide not to challenge it: What about your place?
Where are you staying? I'm having difficulty keeping
up with him as he goes towards a small street.

I'm about a mile down that way – he gestures
vaguely towards the distant end of the promenade as
he turns the corner. It'd be too far to walk dragging
this thing – what have you got in here anyway? Bricks?

Again I let this pass.

A few streets later – he obviously knows Sitges

inside out – we stop in front of the doorway of a small hotel, decorated with tiles and stained glass as ornately as a church, and he goes inside to enquire about a room. I'm glad to have a breather. The pace has been killing and I am suffering from a stitch.

Within seconds, he is back beside me: This place is always full of Germans and French, he says, grabbing the bag again and bouncing it up the marble steps. You won't run into any Irish.

He books a double room.

What happens next is completely unexpected. I am feeling knackered and filthy from all the travelling, and as soon as Clem lets us into the room, I undress and go straight into the shower. I have been standing under the water for only thirty seconds or so when the glass door is slid roughly aside and, naked also, Clem comes in, grabs me and starts to kiss me like he hasn't done in years.

After a second or so of shock, I respond gladly and fully, and I leave the rest to your imagination.

In fact, I had a great time, we both did. It was wonderful just to close down everything, all the nerves, the questioning, the half-formed accusations. My husband and I made energetic love like we hadn't done for years. Half-way through, we left the shower enclosure and, dripping wet, continued on the bed. And for a few blessed moments afterwards, all questioning, all doubts were submerged in a warm, fuzzy daze.

A little while later, panting and perspiring beside him, I turned my head to look at him. The pillow on his side had fallen to the floor and he was lying on his back, throat exposed. A small pool of sweat had dribbled into the hollow below his Adam's apple and in the sunlight from the window, I could see the line of demarcation in his hair, grey roots, dye job above. It was endearing, in a way.

I must have smiled at the thought because he sensed it and, turning towards me, smiled back. What is it?

I raised myself on one elbow and stroked his forehead. I've missed this, I've missed you, although I didn't realize how much until now. Come back with me, Clem. Whatever we've to face, we'll face it together. You can't spend the rest of your life hiding. Your solicitor says that it would really be the best thing in the long run.

There was silence for a few seconds and then he rolled over, got out of the bed, muttering something that I couldn't catch. He started to dress.

Confused, I sat up fully, pulling the sheet around my breasts: What's wrong – what was that you said?

He turned to face me and I couldn't read his expression. It was flat. Like a piece of unused typing paper. So you'd want me to spend the rest of my days rotting in Mountjoy? That'd suit you, wouldn't it?

Immediately I pulled the sheet further up around my chin to cover the rest of my nakedness. All intimacy and emotion – I had taken it for love – that had so recently passed between us had been so crudely bludgeoned I couldn't think of any reply. Numb as a kipper, I merely sat against the headboard, while, with his back to me, he finished dressing.

He was slotting the mobile phone back on to the waistband of his jeans when he turned again to face me: I didn't mean it to come out like that, Maisie.

We'll talk about it over dinner, all right? I'll go and get my things and we'll talk again.

Yet I could see by his expression that he had mentally left the room. I couldn't answer him anyway. Suspicion is a strong poison and I was already wondering if his jumping me like that was a cover-up.

He came over and touched me briefly on the shoulder: All right?

I nodded.

He smiled at me warmly: Keep the faith – I shouldn't be more than an hour. I'll find us somewhere to eat on the way back. Eight o'clock all right?

I nodded.

Right then. He patted his pockets to ensure he had everything. Have a little nap. I'll see you soon.

On his way out, he closed the door very carefully behind him, as though he were not my husband and he was leaving this hotel bedroom illicitly. The doubts flooded back in earnest.

It has been an hour and half now since he left. Through the french windows, I can see my big balcony where the sun is dancing along the old, crazed but shining tiles, patterned with red and blue stars, diamonds and triangles.

Am I a total idiot? Have I made a lot of fuss about nothing, based solely on the word of a cracked old woman?

He could genuinely be delayed by scouting for a restaurant. I'll wait another while before I go out again looking for him. I'm sure it'll be OK.

The physical sensations of our lovemaking continue

to tingle. Talk about being shocked when he jumped into that shower with me – but maybe I should have expected it. Clem has always been very highly sexed and brilliant in bed, I have to hand him that.

Our wedding night was everything I had hoped for, and more. Clem was all I expected, even gentler – as much as that sort of thing can be gentle, given that we were in such a frenzy to do the real thing because we had waited so long for it. It was probably because of all the rehearsing that, for me, the actual event wasn't all that much of a revelation, and not half as painful as I had expected it to be.

Thunk! To this day, the solid thud of the hotel bedroom door closing behind us, leaving us alone and maritally licensed, remains the sexiest sound I have ever heard as instantly, my bouquet and bag are on the floor somewhere and his hands are on the shoulders of my dress, peeling them slowly down my arms. Or as slowly as he can manage. With my arms held out, like I'm being crucified, I stand as passively as I can, waiting, shaking with excitement. I close my eyes to make the moment last and to experience every second of this. I want to remember. Because everything is going to be different in my life from this moment on.

But I can't hold out. The brush of his fingers against my back charges the skin everywhere else; my mouth goes dry, my knees and ankles feel weak.

I realize his hands are shaking too – I can hear his breath.

The bra fastening finally gives and my breasts fall free.

That's it. After years of this, of torturing ourselves by taking one another to the brink but never falling over, neither of us can wait a second longer. I open my eyes, see his are shining and I leap towards him so violently he falls backwards, and with everything flying, arms, legs, my shoes, we tumble on to the chintz-covered bed, me fumbling at his zip, him at my tights—

We do it with him still in socks and shoes, fully dressed from the waist up and with both sets of feet and ankles tangled in the voluminous skirt of my wedding dress. It's wild.

When you see sex portrayed in a film or on the television it's all moody and spread with shadows and like a choreographed dance, but the reality, sweat, noise and effort, is so far from that that when you think about it it's funny. After that first crazy sex, we collapse into the ruins of my dress and his suit jacket and we laugh our hearts out, Clem and I.

In all, we do it four times between the moment we first hit that bed and breakfast time and each episode is different as we begin to get used to the sensations and techniques and even to experiment a little. I can't get enough of Clem's shoulders and the little hollow on his back just above the waist, of the soft bit behind his ears; I tear and probe and pinch and clutch at his lips and eyes and fingers and thighs. He can't get enough of me, of my breasts and my bottom and my stomach; he flips me up and over and about, like I'm on a barbecue and he's the chef.

Next morning, physically shattered but ready to start all over again, if you can believe that, I wake a few minutes before him and gaze around the room, which, in the unforgiving daylight, looks as though it's been blitzed. The sheets are badly stained and one of them is even a little torn, where Clem put his knee through it.

I shake his shoulder: Clem, Clem, wake up! We have to do something about these sheets!

Wha——? Sleep like cataracts filming his pupils, he sits bolt upright: What are you on about?

These sheets – this bedspread, we'll have to wash them – we'll get into trouble. Will we have to pay?

He flops back: For God's sake, woman, what do you think we're paying for? C'mere – he grabs me around the waist, fastens his mouth to my breast and we're off again.

Afterwards, when hunger forces us to get up and face the real world, I continue to worry but he pooh-poohs me. Do I think we were the only couple doing it that night in that hotel? What do I think hotels are for? He takes the little notepad and pencil from beside the bedside telephone and draws a quick, crooked cartoon of the hotel bouncing down the street by itself. I still have it.

He was very good at drawing cartoons.

The longer he is gone, the more convinced I am that all my suspicions are well founded. I should have asked him for the name of his hotel.

All right, that's it, time's up. I'm going out to find that bastard. I'll be systematic about it. I'll start on the promenade and go up and down the streets running off it. If it takes me all night, I'll find him.

But hang on — the way that man made love to you in that shower . . . could he do that and say the things he did while he was involved with another woman?

I don't know, that's the problem—

—and I don't care. This just isn't good enough.

→ Seven ←

It's the next morning now and, like an insult, the sunshine is again glittering on the tiles of my balcony. I don't know what time it is, and I'm too miserable to move out of this position to check. It no longer matters much – the longer the absence, the more certain the infidelity.

I must have called to every hotel and guest house in this entire resort, all that were open anyway. Because of all the trips we had made to Nerja over the years I have a smattering of Spanish and I was able to make myself understood where they had little or no English. My ruse was to ask if they had any Irish guests in each of them: I had made up a story about someone I had met in a bar whose name I didn't know but who had maybe gone off with one of my credit cards by mistake. A few tried to help me, others just shrugged.

One detail I forgot until I was standing at the reception desk in the first place I tried – a shiny big place, full of trees and marble – he had almost certainly not registered in his own name. But I can now tell you one thing for sure – there are very few Irish people resident in Sitges in the month of April.

I had a row with Ambrose last night, if you could call it a row. How do you fight with an angel who won't answer back, who just keeps agreeing with you like a nodding dog? I'm sorry about it now; I can see I was just taking all my own frustrations out on him. After all, Clem's perfidy, that's the only word for it, perfidy, is not Ambrose's fault.

He materializes beside me a few minutes after I get back here following the fruitless search. I'm pacing up and down the room, trying to decide what my next move should be, when I notice the scent and then he's here, twice as large as life.

He gets some welcome from me, I can tell you. I explode when I see him, shrieking at him like a fishwife: Thanks a lot, Ambrose, thanks a whole bloody lot! Fat lot of good you are to me.

He remains very still: Please do not upset yourself.

Upset myself? Upset myself? I am now actually spitting with rage: Upset myself, Ambrose? What the hell can you know about things like this?

I understand perfectly how you feel, May, he says, nodding, which infuriates me all the more.

No, you don't – you can't. Like hell you can. Don't patronize me, Ambrose. I collapse on the bed, too furious even to weep. No one, least of all an angel, could have a clue how red this anger is and how shocking this sense of betrayal. It feels like the entire universe has shrunk down to a single small wheel spinning round and round inside my head, going by so fast that as quickly as I can grab a handhold, it's torn away. Go away! I yell at Ambrose, not looking at him. Go away and don't come back!

You will find him, he says quietly. If you are sure that is what you want.

I calm down abruptly, at least enough to look at him without wanting to hit him: Of course it's what I bloody want. Why am I here in this poxy hotel instead of in my own bedroom in Alder Cottages? Why are my feet like turnips from all the walking?

If you're sure – He repeats it solemnly, like a priest would. Or a shrink.

And, of course, with that he fills me with dread. Will it be that horrible?

Why wasn't I more assertive when I met Clem on the prom? Why didn't I confront him immediately? Born a fool, live a fool.

In all the years of our marriage, I kicked up seriously only once. That was when I was very pregnant with CJ and Clem was absent night after night for more than a week, trying to arrange a warehousing deal, he said. On the ninth night, I snapped. Full force, I threw a plate of congealed dinner at him when he came in just after two in the morning. I caught him square in the chest.

He didn't move a muscle, even to look down at the damage to his shirt and jacket. Instead, he listened carefully to me while I yelled at him and cried and whinged and then, still as immobile as a lump of iron, he explained that his job was to supply the cash to keep me and the house going. My job was to be a wife and soon, hopefully, a mother. And he didn't want to hear any more about it.

Calmly, he took off the destroyed jacket and shirt,

let them drop to the floor and went to bed, leaving me to clean up the mess I'd made with the plate. He hadn't raised his voice, but something about the way he spoke warned me that from then on I should keep my complaints about his absences to myself. That was the basis on which we conducted the years of our relationship.

And so here I am. Stranded. Why didn't I smell a rat when he didn't bring me to his own hotel? Why didn't I cop on when he froze on me after I suggested that he come home?

A lifetime's conditioning, that's what it was, just going along with whatever he suggested. Damn him to hell. He has no right to put me through this. The bloody traitor, the Judas, the coward, the bastard, the shite, the fucker – I can't think of a word bad enough for him. And the awful thing is I can still feel him the way we were in that shower a few hours ago – I'm absolutely disgusted with myself for my naïveté. When I think of the things I said to him in the heat of lovemaking. Love? If that was love then my name is Princess Diana.

I have a good mind to call the Spanish police. That would put a stop to their gallop. Whoever little Miss X is, she'd be in for a right land then, wouldn't she? I suppose he represented himself to her as a rich businessman or something.

That's another thing. There we at home, scrimping and saving and going around pound shops and making do with bloody mince four days a week and eating day-old sliced pans. And to save a bit of money me taking the bloody train from Paris to here instead of flying. And here's him, living the high life in hotels. Jesus wept.

They've been knocking on the door here at regular intervals, trying to get in to clean the room. They can knock until kingdom come – my horizons are seesawing. I want to be wrong.

Deep down, though, I know I'm not.

How dare he? It's his bloody cockeyed auntie that I'm left to look after. And Johnny is his son too.

To think that I stormed heaven from the moment that shite was arrested. To think I thanked God for his escape. To think I was convinced that the poor judge's death was an answer to my prayers and that it was the doing of an all-merciful God that Clem should appear before that particular judge, whose time, He knew, was up.

I was sitting at the back of the packed courtroom when the poor man keeled over. They were on the fourth day of the trial, and I think the seventh or eighth Gárda witness, a weaselly fella from somewhere down the west with a sharp nose and eyes too close together. To be fair, I suppose I wouldn't like the look of any of the witnesses they put up against Clem.

Because CJ had pleaded guilty at his first hearing, the big deal of a trial was new to me. The place was crawling with policemen, if I looked right or left I caught their eyes – and if it wasn't them, it was the reporters. So, with Eddie and Martin on either side of me, I tried to keep my eyes front, on the back of Clem's head. His hair had never been so neatly combed.

I don't know if you've ever been in a courtroom during a high-profile case, but it gets very warm from body heat. And on this particular afternoon the central heating is clanking away, even though the sun is beaming through the windows. All in all, it's very uncomfortable. My feet have swollen in my new shoes.

Anyhow, this Gárda guy is being put through his paces when, all of a sudden, the judge gives sort of a quiet gasp and his head cracks on to the blotter on the bench in front of him. I happen to be looking towards him at the time so I see the entire episode from beginning to end.

It's the first time in my life I ever saw anyone die. It's quite undramatic, as a matter of fact.

Of course none of us know right then that the poor man is dead. The Gárda fellow falters in the middle of what he's saying and, for a few seconds, everyone in the room just looks at each other. All you can hear is a particularly loud clank from one of the radiators under the windows. No one knows what to do next.

Clem glances around at me and shrugs, then resumes looking towards the front.

My lord? says the barrister who's been asking questions of the Gárda in the witness box.

No answer.

My Lord? he says again.

I think at that point – we all do – that the judge has just fallen asleep. Too much lunch.

But then, when there's still no reply after the barrister addresses the judge for the third time, in quite a stentorian voice, a sort of quiet pandemonium breaks out. The court clerk, the barrister who's on his feet, and a few other people all move towards the bench. Everyone else in the courtroom is on tenterhooks. The barrister touches the judge on the shoulder.

No response.

A wave of loud babble rises and spreads. Silence, the clerk shouts, on automatic pilot, I suppose, but no one pays him a blind bit of attention. People are running, the door is open and other people are coming in, to see what all the commotion is about.

Meanwhile, I can't see the judge himself any more, there are so many people – guards, barristers, solicitors, prison officers, all crowding around the bench . . .

Next thing, I see that for a really brief spell, Clem is unattended and no one is looking at him except me.

We're in one of those modern courtrooms where the defendant is put into a low enclosure behind a little gate. With no one minding this gate, it's a matter of half a second for Clem, quick as a squirrel, to step out of the dock and to slip out behind the two prison officers, both of whom are at the bench and who are goggle-eyed staring at the corpse.

A few people as well as me see Clem go but they're members of the public and they say nothing. In retrospect I find that odd – but anyway, you can take it from me that's what happens. No one cries Stop That Man, or anything like it.

Clem escapes. And by the time – it couldn't have been more than thirty seconds or so – someone in authority notices he's gone, it's too late.

One of the two prison officers glances around, sees

the little gate open, sees the dock empty and lets out a roar. His colleague looks round – and then the two of them sprint for the door, nearly knocking down Martin, who is also running, closely followed by the detective I now know as Zig. For some reason, this character throws me a look as he barrels past me, looking at me personally, why, I don't know. He's gone past too quickly for me to analyse the expression in his eyes. It was probably contempt, but in any event, I've more on my mind than worrying about policemen. I'm in a blind funk. I don't know whether mentally to cheer Clem on or to scream at him to come back here immediately, that he's only making things worse for himself.

I still don't know how he got out of the building, but he managed it. Our courtroom was quite near the staircase, and because even to me Clem looked quite ordinary now, middle-sized, middle-aged and, on that day, dressed in a suit and tie like an ordinary person, I suppose that most people in the corridor outside didn't give him a second look. In any event, people were pushing their way into the courtroom to get a glimpse of what all the hoo-ha was about

The rest you know. Clem got to Spain, via Belfast.

The authorities don't like defendants escaping from courtrooms, it leaves them with egg on their faces, so they raised a hue and cry, alerting the security people on the train stations, ports and so forth, but to little purpose. They took in Tony and some others of his friends and questioned them, but nobody said a word. And, of course, they started coming to our house but, thank God, we were all able to be truthful. None of us had heard a word from him.

It turned out to be a few weeks before Clem rang from a public box quote, somewhere in Spain, unquote. It was a very short call and he spoke like a machine-gun, because he figured that all our telephones, including the mobiles, were tapped. He asked about the kids but cut me short when I launched into detail about Johnny. Good, good, he said quickly, then told me we weren't to worry about him, he was safe and well, being looked after by friends of friends and that he'd be in touch again as soon as he could.

Wait, Clem, wait! I shouted. What kind of friends? Who?

No names, he cut me off again and, speaking so rapidly I had trouble following him, told me he had had no difficulty getting out of the country – through the Larne ferry in the north: I have friends, you know.

So how are you living now? I was frantic for information.

The answer to that one was that he was being looked after by a few Irish fellas in Spain who owed a few favours to a few other Irish fellas back home.

Good-bye now, Maisie, he said breathlessly. If you need anything, Tony'll take care of it. I'll call again soon.

Before I could ask him any further questions he had hung up.

Of course I feel sorry for the poor judge's family but the man had to go sometime and he didn't suffer because the post-mortem showed he died instantly from a cerebral haemorrhage. And he got a lot of lovely obituaries and a big, terrific funeral.

I owe St Jude for that one. Unfortunately I don't have the cash to pay my saintly debts right now but I'm keeping it all on record as an IOU. I owe St Anthony a fortune.

Mind you, both St Anthony and St Jude can whistle for their money if I find that shagger with another woman.

God, please God – where is he?

Sleep, when it eventually arrived, was no sleep at all. And this morning my eyes feel like sucked sweets. I've no idea what to do now. Should I crawl back home? How would I face the lads? What would I tell them?

All my imaginings and scenarios had led up to a conversation with Clem. I hadn't got as far as picturing what was going to happen after that – happy every after? Hardly. But something concrete, either an affirmation of Clem and me as a couple or a total split. Then I could pick up whatever pieces I needed to pick up to resume some version of my normal life. The problem is that now my brain is just a big, empty no man's land.

It is probably obvious to every fool in Christendom that Clem doesn't want me. But as soon as I think that, other thoughts pile in. Again, that lovemaking – why did he make love to me? If he doesn't want me, how could he physically be capable of it?

I start in with the excuses. He could be a victim of crime, he could be lying somewhere in some Sitges alley with his head stove in. He could have had a heart-attack and be prostrate in a Barcelona hospital with drips hanging out of him and no way to get in touch with me. These things happen, you know.

But at rock bottom, I need to know, have to know. I hate loose ends.

There's that knocking again at the door of the room. It's driving me insane. I should have hung out the Do Not Disturb sign. I suppose I'd better make an effort and climb out of this bed. The sun is blinding, this room must be south facing.

I do not know why, but my head is full of memories of Clem. Perhaps it is because I am so tired. There is no logic to it: one moment I am raging at him, the next I am awash with pictures from our past. It is almost as though he is dead and I am leafing through the photograph album of our lives together. Have I already accepted the inevitable? Already said goodbye?

All right. Enough. I'm getting up now. Why the hell didn't I ask him for his mobile phone number? No answer to that, is there, except the obvious? You're a thicko, May Lanigan.

✦ Eight ✦

22 April 2000

The hammering at my door was a continuous percussion accompaniment to a strident voice: '*Permeso? Permeso?*'

I pulled my dressing gown around me, crossed the cool tiles and pulled open the door to be faced with a small, thickset woman. Bucket in one hand, mop in the other, she glared at me with fierce black eyes: 'You staying tonight, yes?'

'Yes,' I answered meekly, although up to that moment I had not thought about this. I had been able to think of little except Clem, his whereabouts, what he was doing, and with whom. '*Permeso.*' The woman marched past me, pointing at the bed. In one fluid motion, she dropped her mop and bucket on the tiles, tore off the coverlet, the blanket and the sheet. I fled to the bathroom, locked the door, turned on both bath taps, then poured the mini-bottle of hotel bath foam into the flow.

When the bath was three quarters full, I turned off the water and listened. Clanking and huffing from outside: the housemaid was mopping the tiles on the balcony. I stepped into the foam, slid down until the bubbles rested just below my mouth, closed my eyes and begged for peace.

Predictably, my imagination started at once to run riot about Clem. I saw him doing to another body the same things he had done to mine in the shower less than twenty-four hours previously. More upsetting even than that was the vision of him sitting across from Little Miss Fancy Woman in a restaurant or a café, the two of them looking into one another's eyes with that gooey, knowing, simpering look all lovers adopt while love is still in Cellophane wrappers. I read somewhere that this mutual gaze has to do with bonding and with searching for 'the soul within' through the windows of the eyes. Balderdash. It is not the soul you seek when you are in that state.

I closed my eyes and sank completely under the strongly scented surface, attempting to block out Clem by concentrating on the sensations within this muted, underwater world. The sounds from outside were now remote, muffled by the regular swish! swish! of blood in my ears. Was this the last sound heard by someone who has given up the struggle against drowning?

I stayed under as long as my breath held and when, spluttering and gasping, I had to surface and open my eyes again, the brightness of the bathroom was like a physical jolt. From outside, the clanking halted, the patio door was slid shut, followed by clunky footsteps, spraying and the rattling of a plastic bag. A short pause, then a huge rapping on the bathroom door: 'I go now.'

'OK,' I shouted back.

More clunking footsteps, door opening, door closing. Blessed silence. Only the lapping of the bath
water.

Time passed somehow until the water got cold, and
until internal nagging about being such a disgusting,
slothful coward forced me out to face the rest of the
day. I said a little prayer to my mother and, stepping
out on to the tiles, noticed that through the frosted
leaf pattern on the bathroom window, the sun had
splayed prisms of colour all over my bare wet feet.
Snatching at omens, I felt that this was the way my
mother was telling me she had heard my prayer.
Foolishly, I was consoled.

Knowing full well I was killing time, I spent a long
time carefully hanging my few clothes in the wardrobe,
folding my underwear and putting it in the drawer of
the locker beside my bed, tidying away my toiletries as
though I was settling in for a long stay. I pulled on the
only summer dress I had brought with me, a yellow
polka-dotted shirtwaister Sharon had found for me in
the Phibsboro Oxfam shop and that still smelt as though
it was almost new.

I decided to telephone Joan.

After Tony and she married, the four of us used to
go to the pictures together, or out for a meal. And at
the beginning, too, Joan and I baby-sat for each other,
although after Melanie she had no more children and
we dropped it – understandably because it was certainly not fair on her. Little comparison can be drawn
between babysitting one well-behaved little girl and
going to war with my lot.

Before Clem's arrest, I had started wondering if he

had developed some kind of a grudge against Tony and Joan because he seemed never to want to go out any more as a foursome. Yet any time I tried to talk to him about this he denied that anything was wrong and changed the subject. In retrospect, Joan and I have not been all that easy with one another either. As soon as Melanie left for foreign parts, Joan went on a FÁS back-to-work scheme and retrained in her old profession of hairdressing so it is possible that not only might she be too busy – and too tired in the evenings – for socializing, she might have a dose of new friends who have more in common with her than I have now.

Or it might be that they are furious about Clem skipping bail – although the last time I was talking to her Joan assured me I was not to worry about that aspect of things one iota. That Tony and Clem would sort it out between them.

I do miss her.

The line was wonderful, clear as ice, when Tony answered but it seemed to take an age for him to fetch Joan. When she eventually came to the telephone, her voice was subdued. 'Hello, May. It's been a long time.'

'Yes,' I said, and hesitated. She sounded cautious, not as ebullient as the Joan I was used to. Joan Malone is always the life and soul of any party and there is nothing that cannot be cured by a good stiff pink gin. 'Is there anything the matter?' I asked her.

'Not at all,' she said, then: 'Well, that's not really true. I've been to the dentist. I'm still a bit stiff and sore, but I'm all right.' My sympathy for this was genuine and heartfelt because for years I lived in mortal fear of the mere word 'dentist' until I finally found one in Dorset Street who did not hurt me. We gabbed about this for a bit. She seemed to cheer up.

'What's up?' Joan asked then. 'Are you on the mobile? Where are you?'

Instantly, I lied: 'I'm in town, shopping.'

Why had I done that? Why could I not confide in Joan? Had that not been the purpose of the call?

'Really?' She sounded surprised. 'It's very quiet there, isn't it? What time is it?' I could hear her fumbling with something, obviously her watch.

I cut in quickly: 'You probably think it's quiet because I'm actually ringing from the ladies' in Arnotts. I just called for a bit of a chat. We haven't been in touch for ages, and since you crossed my mind, I thought I'd strike while the iron was . . .'

I trailed off. To me I had sounded unconvincing but she did not pick up on it. 'Oh, May,' she said, 'I'd love to come in and have a cup of coffee with you, but with my teeth . . .' It was her turn to trail off.

'Not to worry,' I said brightly. 'Sure we'll catch each other again.'

'We will,' she said, too eagerly. Was it my imagination or could she not wait to terminate this call? We said our goodbyes and I was left looking at my little blue Nokia. Something struck me. It is so easy to lie on a mobile. Mobile telephones must be God's gift to adulterers.

Outside, on my balcony, two birds chattered, their speckled feathers glistening in the sunlight. The air in the streets was thick with the growl of mopeds. Women called to one another, a man laughed loudly. I gave myself a mental shake. I was in Sitges. Sitges is a lovely place. I was in Sitges on a lovely day with time to call my own. Was I going to spend this opportunity skulking around waiting on Clem Lanigan's pleasure?

The girl on the desk at the foot of the stairs smiled at me when I passed her. As far as she was concerned I was an ordinary tourist, going about ordinary tourist business.

Reality slammed home: her smile was shocking. Did she not know that the world was falling apart? I glanced towards the little lounge bar to the right of the desk. Two businessmen were talking quietly over an open briefcase. A couple sipped coffee, smiling at one another. Did they not know either?

I went out into the street. A woman sluicing water from a saucepan over the front doorstep of the house opposite looked across at me. 'Buenos dias,' she said, her voice as merry as if everything to her, also, was normal.

I walked slowly down towards the sea-front. The street was narrow, cool and shaded by the tall buildings on both sides. Geraniums, pelargoniums, giant busy Lizzies and other flowers I could not name, all in full bloom, tumbled from window-boxes and balconies. Palm leaves thrust through cracks in the crumbling courtyard walls of old houses and from open windows I could smell garlic, olive oil and that fresh, soapy smell of the cologne beloved of Spanish men. I should have been having a wonderful time.

I gave myself a mental scolding: Don't think ahead. Don't let what might or might not happen ruin this. Feel it, smell it, see it. It's marvellous – experience it!

Three old men sat at a small metal table on the

footpath directly ahead of me. As gnarled as old woodcarvings, they leaned on their sticks, tiny glasses of honey-coloured liquid in front of them. One of them turned his head as I approached and appraised me. I had to step out into the street to pass them and as I did, one of the three murmured: '*Guapa!*' Pretty.

Pretty? Me? May, the middle-aged mammy? May, the cuckolded wife? May, the miserable, frightened, abandoned, discarded, second-choice woman, so stupid and grasping and possessive that she is pursuing a man who does not want her? I straightened my back and deliberately felt the warmth of the street through the thin soles of my sandals. Step, step, feel this, enjoy this . . .

Ahead of me I could see the shining sea. I fixed my eyes on its glitter so that I would not cry.

At the end of the street, I saw one small shop open. On impulse, I went inside and bought a blue and yellow beach ball. I blew it up as I came out into the sunshine of the promenade and attracted yet another smile, incredulous, no doubt, from a young boy free-wheeling by on a mountain bike. I know I looked absurd yet I continued to blow into the mouthpiece of my beach ball. At least it was some kind of action. If I could not be carefree, I could mimic being carefree.

Ambrose was sitting on the beach when I got there, the featherweight toy now sturdy and firm between my hands. I sat down beside him. 'Sorry,' I mumbled. 'I'm sorry about last night.'

'You look very pretty, May,' he said. 'Yellow suits you.'

'Pretty' was obviously the word of the day. 'Help me, Ambrose,' I said, 'please help me. Tell me what to do.'

He shook his head slowly. 'I cannot tell you what to do, May,' he said quietly. 'Nobody can. But be assured I will be with you when you yourself decide what is best. I know you are finding the situation difficult and that you feel confused, but please do not think you lack the resources to make the correct decision in your own interests.'

This was not what I wanted to hear. I wanted him to be on my side. I wanted him to tell me to go home and to try to forget the bastard. To tell me that I was hard done by. That just around the corner I was going to win the lotto and meet a wonderful new man who would sort out my life. I wanted him to say that Clem Lanigan was the biggest shithead in creation. I stared at his caring, compassionate expression and I wanted to shred those smooth cheeks. To hell with him, I thought. To hell with all angels and the whole holy works. You have managed by yourself up to now, May Lanigan, and you will manage again. I briefly considered getting up and stalking off, but my legs and arms were slack with fatigue.

We sat staring into the water for a while, Ambrose and I, without further conversation, he an exotic anachronism, I an awkward, straight-backed contrast to the relaxed, sprawling bodies of all of the other beach-users. I do not know what people would have thought had they been able to see him. At least his feet were appropriately bare. I kicked off my sandals then felt stupid and uncomfortable with the sand grains penetrating my tights so I surreptitiously eased my feet back into them.

Because it was a Saturday, I suppose, there was a lot more activity than there had been the day before. The lounge chair vendors were unchaining their stacks and sorting their umbrellas. Awnings were coming down over the beach restaurants. Although it was probably still too cold for swimming, children splashed in and out of the fringes of the calm water and waves of rapid-fire chatter ebbed and flowed as small family groups set up their pitches for the day. Mothers smeared lotion on babies, spread out towels, shook sand off water bottles. Several pairs of men wearing thongs and a lot of body oil strolled by. Having noticed them, I realized that there were more such pairs on the beach, rubbing one another's backs, pulling one another into the sea. I remembered Clem's disparaging remark about poofters.

Ambrose noticed me watching them. 'Are you shocked, May?' he asked.

'Shocked about what?'

As it happens, I was not shocked, merely surprised at the numbers. Anyway, fair's fair — Clem and I are not exactly lifestyle role models, are we?

The beach ball rolled off my lap into the sand and, out of the corner of my eye, I could see a little boy, maybe four or five years old, eyeing it. 'Go ahead.' I managed to raise a smile for him and fisted the ball a few inches towards him. He hesitated for a moment, looked over his shoulder at his mama, who was paying serious, beady-eyed attention to me. I couldn't blame her. If I had seen a lily-skinned woman sitting stiffly upright and alone on the sand wearing a wide-belted shirtwaister dress, Dunnes Stores' tights, sandals and with a big handbag firmly attached to her elbow, I'd have kept an eye on me too.

I nodded a bright, mother-to-mother smile at her and, leaning over, palmed the ball further towards the little boy. This time, he ran towards it, scooped it up and gave it a kick. The ball travelled only a short distance before bogging down in a sand moat dug by another child. The little boy bustled forward to retrieve it.

There is something about little boys that always gets to me, especially at that age – and even older, I suppose. Even lumpen adolescents, with their slouching and their pretend-angry expressions, exert a pull. But the little ones, all earnest independence and always about some serious secret errand of their own, are those who beat a path straight to the mushy side of my heart.

I continued to watch as a bigger boy of about eleven attached himself to the possessor of my beach ball, and the two of them raced with their prize to the edge of the water. They both turned and looked questioningly towards me for permission. I smiled and nodded, so the little boy threw the ball on to a small, lazy wave and started to surf on it. The bigger boy joined in. I discovered my eyes were filling with tears. 'I'm going back to the hotel,' I muttered to Ambrose. 'I look ridiculous sitting here in this outfit.' I scrambled to my feet and, not waiting to see if he was coming with me, bolted from all that simplicity and enjoyment.

When I arrived back at the hotel, the smiling girl at

the desk stopped me as I hurried past. 'Señora, your passport.'

I took it from her, thanked her, and then she nodded towards the lounge bar. 'You have friend to see you.'

When they say in books that hearts lurch, that is only the half of it. Hearts lurch certainly, but within a split second they have rocketed up to collarbone height to fill throats. Friend? It could only be Clem.

I looked towards the lounge. The couple I had seen earlier had left but the two businessmen were still conducting their meeting.

The only other person there was a blonde girl, back to me, staring out through the open double doors towards the hotel's garden restaurant. Puzzled, I looked back at the receptionist. 'Are you sure? Is he out in the garden, perhaps?'

She looked towards the lounge, frowned, then came out from behind the desk. For a moment I thought she was going into the garden, but she stopped at the blonde girl.

The blonde girl looked round and I was staring into Melanie Malone's young face.

→ Nine ←

Everything in the world became very, very quiet as Melanie and I looked at one another. As yet, stupidly, I did not quite grasp what was going on. Then Melanie, her little face set in serious lines, stood up and came towards me.

'Hello, Melanie,' I said uncertainly. 'I thought you were in South America?'

'Hello, May,' she said. Now that should have tipped me off because she had always called me Mrs Lanigan. But you have to understand that I was still off balance.

'This is amazing,' I said. 'How did you know I was here? I was talking to your mother this morning and she never said . . .'

It was only then that it dawned on me fully. Because I had lied to Melanie's mother, there was only one way Melanie could have found me; only one person on earth knew exactly where I was and in which hotel, and that was Clem Lanigan.

If I may again refer to books, at moments like this everything is supposed to go into slow motion, or the room is supposed to spin, or the woman faints, or at the very least her knees wobble. Nothing of the sort happened to me. I went blank. My body was a void, my brain like a virgin snowfield.

I am not sure how this conveyed itself to Melanie, but I registered that she looked concerned. 'Are you all right, May – Mrs Lanigan?' She put out a hand as though to steady me.

With all my might I hit it away from me. The ferocity of the action surprised me yet it gave me satisfaction to see Melanie stagger a bit from the unexpectedness – and, I like to think, the force – of the blow. The receptionist, who had begun to walk away from us, turned back; she must have caught the action in her peripheral vision.

'Is – is everything OK, Señora?' she asked, frowning again, looking from me to Melanie and back again.

'Everything is fine,' I said, and my voice did sound fine right then. I think I might have been playing catch-up. My brain had started to kick in and was now racing ahead of my physical reactions. 'Let's sit down, Melanie,' I said.

As we take up our positions on two stools at the little bar, I start to flip through the possibilities. Could there be any mistake? Could I be wrong? Surely this child, who is the same age as my Martin, this young girl whom I have always treated as one treats the child of a friend – with cheerful, somewhat proprietorial good humour – could not be out here rolling around *in flagrante* with my husband? Surely if she was my husband's mistress she would not be standing here in front of me as cool as spring water, calling me May – therefore having elevated herself to my equal? 'What would you like to drink, Melanie?' Yes, that was my voice and it sounded clear and steady.

'A margarita, please,' Melanie says, crossing her glossy legs. She is wearing a snowy sleeveless T-shirt and well-pressed khaki shorts, and I notice that, like Clem, she has a tan. Her upper arms are smooth and toned, her waist, cinched into a belt of soft green leather, measures perhaps twenty inches.

I keep cool, or try to. 'One margarita, please,' I say to the barman, 'and I'll have a gintonico. *Doble, por favor.*' With the way they pour, a small gin in Spain is usually big enough for me but this is one occasion on which it certainly is not.

Side by side, Hear No Evil, See No Evil, we sit in silence, Melanie and I, staring straight ahead, watching with deep concentration as the barman pours the drinks. There is nothing so balletic as the movements of a barman at the top of his profession. Poetry in motion.

Thuk! Thuk! The two glasses are placed in front of us on two coasters, slid under them with superb precision at the very last moment.

'I sign,' I say. '*Habitación número dos uno . . .*' That gives Melanie and me another few moments' grace while he punches out the receipt on the computerized, softly clicking register then hands it to me along with a little gold pen.

In elongating the signature process to give myself a few extra seconds to deal with this, I almost make a fatal mistake. I start to write 'M-a-y' – but remember just in time to ripple the line leading to the 'y' so it could be taken for an unconvincing 'r' as in 'Mary'. As

I scribble 'Crowley' I hear the clincher dropping like the last snooker ball into the pocket. She had to have asked at Reception for 'Mary Crowley'.

I turn to face her, to stare into those limpid pools of blue. She has achieved perfect separation of individual eyelashes with her mascara wand. She's worth it, is what she probably thinks.

She does not flinch: 'We have to talk – er – May,' she says.

'I'm all ears,' I say. 'Shoot.' I raise my glass and tilt it a bit so the liquid hits my lips but they're shut tight and I don't open them. It is something to do.

Melanie clears her throat, coughs while I sit, holding my cold hard glass, looking at her. Waiting.

'We're both adults, May,' she begins and glancing at her immaculate shorts – thighs as smooth as her arms – she flicks away an imaginary speck of dust. The cool is assumed, I think. She is nervous. If it had been any other situation, I would have felt sorry for her but I quash that thought immediately. I am not sorry for her. She is the enemy.

I let the silence run on. I am laying the siege. I am forcing her to bring it into the open. I find myself raising my glass to my closed lips once again and once again the icy liquid moistens them.

She takes a gulp of her margarita. Faces me squarely. 'Look,' she says at last, 'there's no way to say this gently. Clement and I are together now. I'm sorry, but that's the way it is.'

Clement? *Clement?*

That does it. I jump off the stool and stand with my face inches from her dotey little nose. Not even Clem's mother, with all her pride in her white-haired boy, ever called him Clement. 'Clement? How dare you call him Clement?'

She looks at me in surprise but she stands her ground. 'What?'

Written down in broad daylight, it does seem to be an asinine basis for the beginning of a row about such a serious matter. When you are faced directly with your husband's mistress for the first time, however, you are in no condition for the niceties of warfare and you cannot plan in advance which way the progression of hostilities is to go or where the first engagement will be. 'My husband's name is Clem,' I say. 'Clem. At least get that right.'

She stares at me. 'So it's all right, then? I'll call him Clem and it'll be all right?'

She has a dusting of pale freckles across her nose. I can feel myself starting to shake with rage and shock so I sit back on my stool. I have to use every ounce of willpower to prevent my nails raking tramlines along that porcelain skin. 'No, it's not all right,' I say. 'It is most definitely not all right. I can't understand what you are doing here, sitting in front of me. How you can have the cheek—'

'I'm here to explain,' she says, interrupting me.

I stare at her but she is not unnerved in the least. She clears her throat again and then launches into the speech she has clearly rehearsed.

What is most striking about it is that, even in the state I am now in, hours later, I recognize that Melanie's speech was constructed on a bedrock of conviction. I hear her saying these outlandish things about me and my husband of twenty-seven years and to her they apparently do not seem outlandish in the least. Let me paraphrase and compress because it would be too upsetting to repeat verbatim all she said to me (although, believe me, I could recite every last word of it).

Melanie started her argument with Clem's report to her that I wanted him to go back to Ireland to face the music, i.e. to go to prison. That proved beyond a shadow of a doubt that I did not have Clem's best interests at heart, whereas she did. She loved him for his own sake, wanted him to be happy. I just wanted him in my possession. As a possession.

Furthermore, she was able to quote from some article she had read, which argued that an extramarital affair never started outside the primary relationship unless the primary relationship was in serious trouble in the first place. Melanie has obviously read a lot of women's magazines.

To summarize the substance of what Melanie believes: Melanie believes that I no longer need Clem but that she does. Our family is reared, we are all comfortable (albeit going through a temporary glitch – one that 'Clement' assures her will be sorted out ere long as a result of mechanisms he is putting in place in Ireland). *Ergo*, since she needs him now and I no longer do, she can, and should, have him. QED.

How am I to fight that?

Is it worth fighting?

Her reasoning is so novel – so fantastically off-beam – that I cannot take it in. In my view there is something seriously amiss in Melanie's brain.

I am exhausted and although the drama did not end
with Melanie's cute little prepared speech, the index
and middle fingers of my right hand are grooved so
deeply from writing that my pen is stuck painfully to
them.

The light is dying, the pale pink sky outside my
french windows is filled with little black sickles —
swallows, swifts or martins — on their last hunt of the
day. I have had nothing to eat except the Mars bar I
always carry in my handbag for emergencies, and all
I have had to drink is some water out of the tap in
my bathroom. I do not care if I come down with
salmonella, hepatitis, beri-beri or whatever it is you
get these days from dodgy water. I shall go to bed.

To hell and back with Clem Lanigan and his doxy.

23 April 2000

Surprisingly, I slept. I am usually a good sleeper and a
creature of habit in that regard. Even more surprisingly, given my mental state, I woke with a huge
hunger.

I dressed quickly and went straight down to the
walled garden restaurant where they were setting up
the buffet under the trees. The sun had not fully risen
and it was quite chilly.

After some palaver, because breakfast was not due
officially to start until eight o'clock, one of the waiters
brought me a pot of coffee and an enormous jug of
hot, frothing milk. Uninvited, as they were still arrang-
ing the fruit and the juices, I helped myself to the

heftier side of the buffet – chorizo and salami, pale, anaemic cheese and a couple of hot bread rolls – then picked a table in a spot where the sunshine was trickling through the budding branches. Shoulders warming, I stared at the food and it was only then it occurred to me that this was the first time in nearly thirty years that I had sat down to a meal in a restaurant without Clem. This was the future. My hunger died, and although I ate, my tongue differentiated neither in taste nor texture between the spicy meats and the cheese, or even between them and the bread . . .

Having delivered her carefully thought-out and off-the-wall reasoning about herself and 'Clement', Melanie waited for my response with a serious, periwinkle stare. When there was no response forthcoming, she leaned forward slightly. 'I know this has come as a shock to you, May.'

'Do not, under any circumstances, call me May again.'

She was so startled by the suppressed venom that she jumped and a little of her margarita slopped on to the front of her very, very clean T-shirt.

What difference did it make? What's in a name? I don't know. But names sure seemed awfully important to me during this little interlude barside, as they would say in California. I studied her as one would study the most interestingly poisonous fish in the poison-fish aquarium.

'Let me ask you a question, Melanie,' I said to her quietly, trying to keep my tone as conversational as possible. 'Do the expressions 'adultery', 'cheating',

'fornicating', 'lying' or 'snake-in-the-grass' mean anything to you?'

She wrinkled her perfectly smooth forehead as
though she didn't understand what I was getting at. I
don't think Melanie is the brightest. 'What?' She shook
her head as though to clear it and her silky, naturally
blonde hair moved a little on her creamy neck. Melanie
was always blonde. As a baby, her hair was so white
that if she hadn't had such big blue eyes we would have
thought she was an albino.

'Was there some word you didn't understand?' I
asked her. 'Will I repeat the words for you? Maybe
I should explain.'

She came to life. 'I know what the words mean, I'm
not stupid, you know. Look Mrs Lanigan, I – we –
Clement and I didn't mean for this to happen. It just
happened, that's all. These things happen. They happen
every day, in every city and town and village in Ireland
and everywhere.'

I'd had enough. I stood off my stool once again and
summoned every last ounce of dignity and authority I
could find. 'Where's Clem now?' I asked it so harshly
and with such apparent strength that, without thinking,
she answered truthfully.

'He's in the apartment.'

A pile-driver into my throat. 'Apartment?' I asked
faintly. 'What apartment? How long? When? Where?'

Realizing she had spoken out of turn, she froze, and
as she hunted around for a plausible lie, I pressed
home. 'Right,' I said. 'I want to see him. Where's this
apartment?'

For a moment I thought she wouldn't tell me. I

snapped the clasp of my handbag, although it was already firmly closed. 'If you don't tell me where it is,' I said quietly, 'I'll go straight to the police.' To show I was not kidding, I turned away from her and asked the barman if he had a book for the *teléfono*. I meant it too. I was not thinking then, only feeling.

'Wait, wait,' she said, or bleated, in that oh-so-pleasant, homogeneous, call-centre-bred accent. 'I'll show you.'

So it was that I found myself walking behind Melanie Malone through the bright little streets of Sitges and on to the main drag that, lined with shops, curves down a long, slow hill towards a square within sight of the promenade and the sea. No calls of '*Guapa!*' this time, or if there were, I did not hear them. Instead, one foot doggedly after the other, step for step, I padded behind her, watching closely in case she should get it into her head to make a dash for it. (Now that I write this, even as the situation gives me pain, I can see the ridiculous side. Inspector Clouseau comes to mind.)

'Here it is.' She stopped in front of a camera shop. From behind the counter inside, a beautifully groomed girl waved a languid greeting at her and before she had thought about it, Melanie had waved back. My husband's apartment, the one he had shared with Melanie for at least as long as it takes to become on familiar terms with the neighbours, was on two floors above this shop.

Silently, Melanie inserted a key in a metal door-frame beside the shop's entrance, and when the door opened, stood back politely to let me go through. Now she might have been an estate agent and I her client embarked on viewing a property. We had not spoken a word since leaving the hotel. In retrospect, she was probably as fearful as I, although she betrayed none of it.

Ahead of me was a flight of stairs between rough concrete walls and at the top a wooden door behind a gate of wrought iron, painted white. 'Excuse me,' Melanie said politely, as we came to this gate. I stood aside and she selected a second key from her ring, inserted it in the gate's big lock and turned. Inside, she punched a few numbers on a keypad on the wall beside the door and turned the handle. The door swung inwards, directly into the living room-cum-kitchen.

Clem was in residence. Slippered feet comfy on an upholstered pouffe that was half buried in a black shag carpet, he was ensconced in a leather chair, watching grand-prix racing on an enormous TV. His face, turned towards me and Melanie, was frozen around the big round surprise of his open mouth.

On the instant he saw us, he dived for the remote control and shot to his feet. He forgot actually to punch anything on the remote, however, and as we all three stood there, the screaming of the cars seemed to grow louder and louder as, for what might have been five seconds or five minutes, I travelled to hell and back as I scanned the cosiness and domesticity.

Oh, look – their dinky little stereo with their CD rack tidily beside it; and over there, on the countertop, their black ceramic bowl filled with nice fresh lemons. See their stainless-steel fridge-freezer humming busily beside their stainless-steel sink, their set of colourful crockery neatly stacked on a shelf above it — and on top of the huge TV, what killed me altogether: a photograph in a silver frame of the two of them, arms around one another's waists, smiling happily into the camera against a background of snow-capped mountains; beside it, also framed, one of Clem's cartoons. The same scene, but showing the foothills as a pair of breasts and I leave the peak to your imagination. Tasteful. Not.

Clem saw me looking at this cartoon and, fussing with the remote control, moved to block my view of it. The racket on the TV died as he turned back to face me. 'It's a national park,' he said — or, rather, croaked — into the abrupt, knife-edged quiet. Then, as if this made it all right, 'Picos de Europa. Mel and me went up there for a little trip.'

Mel 'n' me, me 'n' Mel, Mel 'n' Clem, Clem 'n' Mel, the duo made for each other. All they needed was a guitar and a tambourine. Before I could stop myself I had walked across the floor and hit my husband across the face as hard as I could. Then I snatched the framed cartoon and threw it against the wall. Hard. Little bits of glass flew, then lodged, glinting, in the tufts of their shag carpet. They would have quite a Hoovering job to do.

That was twice in less than half an hour I had been instinctively violent. I hoped I was not developing a vicious streak.

→ Ten ←

Clem did not react to being hit. He did not even put his hand to his reddening cheek. He just looked at me for a second before dropping his eyes. This sheep-like creature was not the Clem I knew. What had she done to him?

'Excuse me,' said 'Mel', from behind me. 'Would you mind if I spoke to Clement alone for a few minutes?'

'I would mind very much,' I said calmly. 'Anything you have to say to Clem, you can say in front of me.' I turned back to Clem. 'I'd be interested to know why you made love with me in the shower yesterday.'

From behind me, I heard a small, high-pitched squeak. I turned to face it. Little Mel was puce in the face. 'Sorry,' I said pleasantly. 'Didn't he tell you, Mel? He couldn't wait – even for me to come back into the bedroom.' I turned back to Clem as though we were discussing a Sunday drive: 'We had a fun time, didn't we, Clem – even if it was a bit slithery?'

She flew past me and hit him. To my immense satisfaction she had cracked him on the same side as I had. Obviously we are both right-handed.

That made me the only one of the three who had not been hit. It would have been very funny in a TV sitcom. It was not funny in the least.

Clem and Melanie were facing one another, both furious. 'Is it true?' She was so upset, she sprayed him with spit.

'So what if it is?' he spat back. 'She's my wife—' And then he had to raise both arms to defend himself because she screamed and flew at him again, this time with both fists. He caught her by the wrists and his voice sank to a low, deadly pitch. 'Shut the fuck up,' he said quietly. 'If you hit me again, you'll regret it.'

She went white and I felt she might be about to fold, like a concertina, and who could blame her? From my experience, I don't believe he would have resorted to actual violence, but what did poor little Mel know? She probably had not seen this forceful, threatening side of Clem before – certainly not while they both still tingled with the first flush of Love's Young Dream. Once again, I almost felt sorry for her – but not quite.

To give her her due, she was the one who recovered first, and within seconds. 'Let's all sit down,' she said, while the two of them were still standing, locked fist to wrist.

'Certainly,' I said, and checking first to see there was no glass on it, immediately sank into their very soft, creamy coloured sofa. 'Is this your furniture, Clem?' I asked conversationally. 'Because I would be very interested in knowing where you got the money for it. Those of us still in Alder Cottages could do with a few bob. We're sick of sausages and yellow-pack baked beans and of buying our Brillo pads in Pound World.'

'The flat is rented furnished,' he said, and let Melanie go. She glared at him for a bit, rubbing her wrists, then trod carefully across the shag to sit on a wood-and-chrome stool set at the counter that divided the kitchen area from where we all were. He sat back in his leather chair. But I noticed he did not put his feet back on his pouffe. For the moment, at least, I felt I was still in charge.

'Right,' I said, 'who's going to go first?'

'I'm not going anywhere,' Melanie said instantly.

'That's not what I meant,' I said patiently, as though to a dim child. 'What I meant was, who is going to speak first?'

Silence. She tucked one of her legs under her, not an easy task on a hard stool. It must have been uncomfortable but the image was beguiling. Clem was staring at the floor and the thought again occurred to me: what had happened to this man? Clem had always been decisive. This was not even the Clem I had met the day before in the coffee shop. With all his faults, there had never been any doubt as to who was the head of our household, but with her around, he seemed to be at sea.

For my part, the adrenaline was still turning my white cells red. I gazed around the three of us and then directly at him: 'Have you nothing to say?'

He shrugged. 'What's there to say?'

'Well, for a start, how long has this been going on?'

They locked eyes in that lingering eye-to-eye, lovey-dovey look of fond recognition I had anticipated earlier. I flipped. Somehow my hands had now found their way into my hair and were pulling hard. It was a substitute for grabbing the Toledo sword mounted over their mock fireplace and wreaking havoc with it. 'Stop this!' I yelled. 'Stop this rubbish!' It worked. I had gained their undivided attention. Four wide round eyes, all blue, stared at me: *The woman is bonkers. What's she going to do next?*

Melanie shifted a little. The bone of the ankle under her must have been giving her hell. 'May,' she said, 'we really feel your pain—'

'Get her out of here,' I said to Clem. 'Just get her out of here before I'm hauled up before someone for infanticide.'

She jumped off her stool. The carpet crunched as her feet hit glass. 'I told you,' she squeaked, 'I'm not going anywhere. And may I point out that you are in our flat. My flat, actually. It's me who pays the rent and has to work damned hard to earn it. I work nights,' she added, with pointless clarification.

What did she do? Haunt the nearest cave?

Everything comes into sharp focus, tight as a pinhole. I concentrate on Clem but, out of the corner of my eye, see that Melanie has seated herself back on her perch. Leg Two has now been tucked under her pert little bottom, giving Leg One a rest. 'Is this it, then?' I say to Clem. 'Am I to take it, so, that you aren't coming home?'

He stares at me and then his eyes flick towards her.

For permission? For understanding? I feel the fury start to pile coal upon coal inside me. Is this prick worth fighting for?

'Look at me, Goddammit – at least give me that courtesy.' Despite my resolve, my voice is beginning to rise and betray me. He will not meet my stare. I swallow hard. 'Am I to take it that our marriage is over?' I ask, with a semblance of calm.

For some inexplicable reason this rattles him. 'Of course it's not over, May. You're my wife. You'll always be my wife.'

I ignore the explosive sound that comes from the direction of the countertop. 'Then what are you at?' I work hard to keep my voice level. 'What the hell are you doing with her?'

He spreads his hands, then looks at me with the little-boy-Clem look which has rarely failed with me in the past on any (rare) occasion he had admitted to being in the wrong. 'I was lonely, May,' he says softly. Again he glances towards her: 'And we had such fun together . . .' When he looks back to me again he is almost aggrieved: 'You have to admit there was very little fun in our lives, May.'

I nearly faint with anger but I hold up my hand like a traffic policeman to stop what he might say next. I have the running and I am not going to lose it: 'The game is up, Clem. It's time to choose. Her or me.'

It is dangerous – I think – although I am not sure now what I am playing for. All I know is I have had enough and he has to make some choice, any choice. If it is the wrong one from my perspective, so be it. I will live with it – even though at this precise moment I do not even know whether or not I would want him or have him under any circumstances. Which would be the 'right' or 'wrong' choice for me? If I 'win' this tussle, will I ever, for the rest of my life, be able to put this bizarre scene behind me?

As Clem and I stare at one another, every choice seems to have narrowed down to the thinness of a credit card. Yes or no, no in-between. No subtleties, no grey. 'Don't push me, Maisie,' he says softly.

'That's rich,' I say, just as softly. We're locked in together now, excluding your woman: 'Do the twenty-seven years we've been husband and wife mean nothing to you?'

'You know better than to ask that.'

'What right have you to come in here?' Outside the intense circle Clem and I have created, Melanie starts to bluster.

'The rights I've gained with twenty-seven years of faithful slogging and six sons,' I answer her, but keep my eyes on Clem. 'Not to speak of Esmé.' I realize that the pressure exerted by my nails on the palms of both my hands is excruciatingly painful and I attempt to relax a little by opening them wide.

'Esmé?' He was taken aback.

'Yes, Esmé,' I press on, 'your crackpot auntie, who is literally off her trolley. Your relative that I have to mind and feed and rescue and put up with, while you're out here with your – your—' I could not think of an epithet that would have been insulting enough to both of them. 'It was she told me.'

Melanie jumps in to rescue him again. 'It's just as well. You were going to find out anyway. I was going to tell you.'

I ignore her: 'Have you stopped loving me, Clem?' It kills me to ask such an intimate, limp question in front of her but I have no option, or so it seems to me at the time.

He hesitates. Then, appealing for understanding like a bold puppy: 'I love both of you. It is possible to love two people at the same time, Maisie. I never thought it was, but it is. I didn't ask for this. I didn't go looking for it.'

It is so utterly outrageous, so straight from a Richard Gere video that I cannot deal with it. So I say the first thing that comes into my head. 'What's to stop me,' I say to Clem, 'from going to the Spanish police and telling them where you are?' I pull my mobile from my handbag. 'In fact what's to stop me using this mobile and making a call right now to Mountjoy in Dublin?'

'If you do that,' he says quietly, 'I will never speak a word to you again.' I know he means it and he knows I know. He also knows with whom he is dealing: 'But you won't do that, will you, May?'

'Can I say something?'

Clem and I turn simultaneously towards Melanie. It is almost as though we have temporarily forgotten her and are surprised to hear her cheep. 'I think it's probably a good thing we're having this meeting,' she says. 'Things had to come to a head and out in the open.' She climbs daintily off her stool and, moving a piece of glass aside with one toe, comes to sit on the shag carpet by Clem's feet, facing me. Two against the world, two against the Big Bad Wife. She runs the fingers of both hands through her silky hair – and her firm young breasts lift against the snowy T-shirt. It is a cheap trick, but effective. Somehow I manage to hold my tongue as I see Clem's eyes, like a snake's, flicker downwards.

'I believe you are being very judgemental, May,' she says earnestly, 'but we'll let that pass. In my opinion,' she goes on, looking up at Clem now, 'May is right, this is make-your-mind-up time. You need to make up your mind between the two of us.' She looks back in my direction: 'I don't want to hurt you, May, but Clement has said certain things to me that indicate that there have been problems between you recently and that you weren't really all that happy together . . .'

'What problems?' This is news to me. I look incredulously at Clem. 'You've been discussing our marriage with her?'

It is a dreadful mistake, I have handed it to her on a plate. Somehow, she has managed to take the high ground and here am I conducting a marital counselling session in front of my husband's mistress. But Clem is looking at Melanie. Melanie's eyes are candid. Enormous. Somehow, one of her little hands has landed on his knee and the fingers are resting on the inside of his leg, ever so lightly: 'I don't want to go into it, May,' she says sympathetically, 'it would be too painful for you and, anyway, those are your private problems, yours and Clement's.'

He smiles down at her like an indulgent parent proud that his little girl has come top of the class.

How can they behave like this in front of me? I
cannot believe that my husband is sitting here like a
lamb, listening to this and allowing this touchy-feely
stuff to happen with me sitting right in front of him. I
am his wife, Goddammit. Has he no loyalty – even
residual loyalty – to me at all? I shoot to my feet.
'Stop this!' I yell. 'Stop this immediately.' I round on
Melanie: 'Where do you get off telling me I'm judgemental?' I turn to him: 'What problems, Clem?' I ask
again, repeating myself like a cuckoo clock. 'What
fucking problems?' I have to stop because I feel spittle
gathering in my mouth.

He makes a move as though to stand to face me but
she intervenes, locks an arm around his calf. 'We don't
need to go into that right now,' she says swiftly. 'Your
relationship with your husband has nothing at all to do
with me, any more than my relationship with Clement
has anything to do with you.'

'Wha—?' Her effrontery is breathtaking. I mean that
literally. The air seems to expel itself from my body in
one great whoosh over the half-completed word.
'What fucking problems, Clem?' I cannot seem to
leave it alone, although I know I'm doing my cause –
if I have any now, if I want any now – far more harm
than good.

'Clement,' she leans a little closer against him, 'I am
only talking the truth, isn't that right?'

Clem pushes her off and jumps to his feet. 'Stop it,
both of you, stop it. I can't stand this. I'm going for a
walk.'

'No, you don't!' Both Melanie and I say it simultaneously, so abruptly that he hesitates. She, too, stands

up and the three of us teeter, literally three sides of a triangle.

While he is temporarily wrong-footed like this, Melanie walks towards me. By doing so, she cuts him out of the loop and it is just her and me now in the arena. 'You talk about your rights,' she says (although as a matter of public record, this is something I have barely yet got around to), 'but what about my rights?'

It is so stark it bewilders me. 'What rights?'

'My rights to this relationship,' she says briskly. 'All I have invested in it. It hasn't been easy for me either, you know – I had to change jobs, leave my family—'

'Tell me, Melanie,' I cut across her, 'does the morality of this not impinge on you, even in the slightest?'

She takes offence. Her body stiffens. 'I am a deeply moral person,' she says, 'deeply moral. This is not a moral issue. No human being owns another human being and everyone has a right to happiness.'

'I can't stand this any longer.' From behind me, I hear Clem make a move towards the door. Before either Melanie or I can stop him, he has reached it and gone through. I can hear his feet, muffled by the slippers, descending rapidly towards the street. 'Clement, wait – wait!' Melanie runs after him and I am left there on my own.

All the piss and vinegar drains out of my veins. I want to cry, but not yet. Not while there is still a chance that one or both of them will come back and find me. What was the point of fighting, anyway? My marriage is over, that is plain. Clem, whatever he thinks, cannot have both of us. That is realistic only in exceptional cases and I am not an exceptional woman. If I did not want to know the truth, why did I come haring out here in the first place?

I have lost him to her and I might as well face it. If I am very honest with myself, I had half suspected something along these lines anyway even before Esmé's little revelation. All right, he could not use his mobile for fear of the calls being traced. But in the course of eight months? He couldn't have managed a few brief hellos from the Picos de wherever-it-was he went on his little trip? Or from some train station?

Clem had not wanted to talk to me – it is as simple as that. I have been played for a sucker and I fell for it because I wanted, needed, to continue with the fantasy that I was still a busy married woman, still the essential hub of the family, still propping up my spouse, errant or otherwise. Stand By Your Man. Tammy and Hillary and me.

It is almost time to leave for the airport. I have just read back over all of this so far and an insidious thought occurs to me. Why am I so catty about her and not about him? After all, she is single and, by the lights of today's Dublin, where it is a dog-eat-dog world and where the young and beautiful snare the most succulent prey, she was not betraying anyone, nor had she anything to lose. In fact, on the surface, she had everything to gain. Married, single, divorced or separated, if a man in Dublin has two arms, two legs and does not resemble the Creature From the Mummy's Crypt, he seems to be fair game for any number of predatory females. This is a piece of received wisdom about which I used to smile tolerantly, until it came to live under my own front doormat.

So why is it that I seem to come down harder on her than on him? He, after all, is the real villain of the piece. He is the one who made the vows all those years ago.

I realize I am still leaving a door open for him. Why, is the mystery. I suppose that if I was as clear-eyed about him as I seem to be bitchy about her I could not countenance ever living again with such a bastard.

Sad. I am sad in the Californian, TV meaning of the word. Although I try to convince myself that he is a pathetic cradle-snatcher – little Mel having just passed her twenty-first birthday – I'm sure that she and her ilk would think it is I who am truly pathetic.

And when I think back on it now, what takes my breath away is the unexpectedness of her reaction. If I had been in her shoes, I would have been covered in mortification. As the wife, I am the wronged party, or so I would have thought, but I am far from that in her eyes and she is far from mortified. To her, it seems, I am just an incidental irritant in her life with Clem, and she seems genuinely not to understand why on earth I would think I have a prior or more valid claim on his allegiance than she.

What have I missed in this new Ireland? Is this now what defines the generation gap?

In that context I cannot shake from my head what is, no doubt, her vision of the two of us lining up for battle: a settled, past-it mother of six, shackled in the stays of nineteenth-century morality, versus a toned, thoroughly modern CK babe. To the young and free go the spoils.

My suitcase is packed and I am now ready to leave here, and I have nothing left to do before I have to check out of this room at twelve noon. I do not have to be at Barcelona airport until four o'clock for a five o'clock flight to London, connecting with another to Dublin at Heathrow. Unfortunately this morning's direct flight on Iberia was full.

As you can see, I'm sure, with so little to do I've been trying to divert myself from rage and pain by puzzling things out. It is not difficult to see why my husband is attracted to Melanie Malone. It is her logic that's so hard to follow. Like a psychiatrist or even an anthropologist, I have been trying very hard to follow the way the Melanie-brain works.

The only logic I can remember to match it is that of Dinny Crowe, a schizophrenic cousin of my fathers. On one occasion, for instance, having crossed the Irish Sea on the boat to Holyhead, he set out to walk to London because he had used up his small store of money. It started to rain. Dinny was getting wet and he was always one who hated getting wet.

Approaching him, he saw an English gent, walking his springer spaniel, both sheltering under a large umbrella. Dinny walked up to the gent. 'Give me that umbrella,' he said – quite pleasantly, by all accounts, but naturally, the gent demurred. 'Give me that umbrella,' Dinny insisted, more heatedly this time, 'I need it.' The gent held on to his property as he attempted to pass but Dinny was having none of it.

'Give me that fucking umbrella,' he yelled, hit the gent a dunt on the nose, grabbed the umbrella and walked on, quite contentedly, without a backward glance.

Thus doth the Melanie-brain dictate: Melanie needeth Clem, Melanie taketh Clem. What's the fuss?

At least I had the satisfaction of leaving that grotty flat and pulling all the doors shut tight behind me, hoping like hell they had both run out without taking their keys.

❖ Eleven ❖

A week has passed since I arrived home from Spain and I'm trying very hard to pick up the pieces of normal life. Right now, I have a casserole and a round of brown bread in the oven and I've been peering around the kitchen, wondering what to do next. More cleaning, no doubt.

All week I've cooked for the freezer, cleaned like a dervish and the poor little yard outside doesn't know what hit it, having been mowed and clipped and manured and watered and generally tidied up to within an inch of its scrubby little life. I even whitewashed the walls – all it took was one large can of emulsion from a stall in Moore Street, £3.99.

I have learned one big lesson. If you force yourself to act as normal, some semblance of outward normality follows, even when you are at your most wretched. I know I have to make very large choices, but I'm in such turmoil at present that it's probably as well not to force decisions about anything major until I'm calmer.

I've humiliated myself enough about the débâcle of that afternoon in their flat, so I won't go into too much detail about what happened when I went back that night – solely because I needed money to change my airline ticket.

Suffice it to say that I got a chilly reception from little Mel and a hangdog one from Clement. It was he who opened the door, with her hovering like a harpy on his shoulder. The stare she gave me would have given hypothermia to a penguin but I have to say it gave me more than a tiny dart of satisfaction to see that the baby blues were puffy and red. Ignoring her, I told him straight out that I needed cash to get home as quickly as possible.

Wait here for a minute, says he, and he goes inside, half shoving her ahead of him and leaving me to cool my heels on the little landing outside the security gate. I could hear a kerfuffle going on between the two of them inside, although I couldn't make out what was being said. He came out then, took me to the nearest ATM machine and used her Mastercard to get me the money. I doubt if she was happy about that, but I did not hang around to watch the fallout.

I'll refrain from painting the scene of Clem and me together during that short march. I don't think I'd need to. We spoke maybe ten words.

And how do I feel about taking her money? Damn good. Let them work it out between them. She's welcome to him now. At least, that's how I feel for this split second as I speak these words.

So where was Ambrose while all this was going on?

Actually, he materialized beside me in the back of the taxi, just as we were going through the toll booth on the motorway to Barcelona airport. He didn't say anything but his strong, comforting presence at last brought on the waterworks.

You know, I have no memory at all of calling Ambrose into my life. Or of calling any angel. I'm not into angels, or wasn't. I'm more of a saint person, St Anthony, St Jude, the Little Flower. I give pennies to them all, over in the church, light their candles, say their novenas when I think of them.

Shortly after Ambrose arrived for the first time, I went to the library to check up on angels as a species – or why angels appear to some people and not to others – but I didn't get very far. I found a plethora of books all right, about angels appearing to people in times of need, on how to contact angels, on angels' roles as interpreted by scholars, but each seemed to regurgitate identical information or variations of it.

The most entertaining image I retain comes from a video Eddie brought home once, starring John Travolta, where he was this Archangel who moved in with an old lady in Iowa – I think it was Iowa – in the United States. But this Archangel had to have been a complete figment of the writer's imagination. For instance, he was filthy, loved fighting, poured pounds of sugar over all his food, smoked like a chimney and went with women. Far from our Ambrose, I think you'll agree.

Vaguely, without him saying so, and despite my sulks and complaints about the opaqueness of his function in my life, my understanding of how he operates is beginning to glimmer. Although he was never going to hold my hand, literally or metaphorically, he pads alongside me like a silent cheerleader.

The silence in this kitchen is unnerving but I don't feel like music today.

Half relieved to find something to occupy me, I see that the hob could do with a bit of a going-over.

For the umpteenth time this week, I open the door of the press under the sink to take out my trusty cleaning sprays, sponges and scrapers when I notice that the air temperature has dropped. I look over my shoulder and sure enough, Ambrose has plonked himself into one of the fireside chairs: Dear, oh dear, May – cheerleader? John Travolta? Come, come, now!

From the way he has pursed his lips, I can see he is in one of his more patronizing modes – he calls it elucidating – and although I find it thankless to debate with him, on this occasion I welcome the diversion from the endless carousel of dismal thought and rage.

Just a minute, Ambrose – I open the oven door to check on the contents, find everything in order and close it again, then settle opposite him – what's wrong with cheerleader? It's a positive image.

It well may be, but it is misleading. Might I explain something, please, since I have wished for an opening in our discourse in order to correct a universal misunderstanding about us?

Be my guest.

He stands up and begins to pace as though he were a professor in front of a packed lecture hall. Sadly, for lyricists, screenwriters, popular novelists and poets, he says with some pomposity, singular concern for individuals – the Guardian Angel concept – is not within our remit. He stops pacing and turns to face me: Yet in itself, the physical image of cheerleading is half correct,

May. My presence in your life is parallel, that is true. But unlike the motives and objectives of sports person and cheerleader, yours and mine are not entwined. The cheerleader encourages, even influences, the participant on the field towards a mutual goal. I have no goal. I may lay out possibilities, even argue them with you, but the decision to take any direction will be yours alone, choices you must make every waking instant.

I shake my head. The old free will routine again, Ambrose?

He frowns. Again? Always, May. You could choose to go to university, you could move into an apartment and take in a cat, you could paddle a kayak along the length of the Amazon or enter a convent. Instead, you have chosen – and continue to choose – to be the self-sacrificing linchpin of your family

I splutter indignantly: That's a bit much. I really resent that!

He holds up his hand: I am merely trying to illustrate a principle here. Humans are whimsical, paradoxical creatures. The more freedom is offered, the more diligently they seek fetters. Much as they protest, they like containment, because containment means certainty and the illusion of control.

He is very quiet now, his expression bland: What is difficult for you is that your husband is equally free, to love whom he wants and to walk the earth wherever and however he wants. If he chooses to scoff at the law, he is at liberty to do so. He may become a drunkard, a philanthropist, a philanderer or a recluse, the choice is his.

This, of course, is like a red rag to a bull and I shoot

to my feet. That's quite enough, Ambrose. What about vows, marriage, till death us do part?

My objections die away in his blue gaze. He waits until he knows he has regained my full attention, then: Freedom is equally available, May, to the private in the army platoon, to the adolescent in the first flush of romantic love, or to the pair of married nonagenarians habituated to one another's presence. Only when this is understood can progress be made towards contentment.

Of its own accord, it seems, my chin thrusts itself belligerently outwards: So everyone is an island, then? In your scenario, the poor homeless drunk with no friends or family must be the most blessed of all?

He, too, has choices, Ambrose says quietly. And I am sure you have wondered why I chose you rather than one of the needy souls you mention — is he not more deserving than you? He looks away as though hearing something, then answers his own question: I chose you because I chose you. No one is deserving, and the concept of fairness is an entirely human invention.

But now the usual frustration — I can see my time slot has been exhausted — he is already moving on. This frequently happens when he drops in with one of these heavy discussions on his mind and I know from experience there is no point in trying to contain him. One question, Ambrose, I say quickly. If, as you say, you specifically chose me, what's in it for you?

In good time. He is no longer physically with me. His voice has chimed in tune with the clock in the hall.

Very interesting, highly illuminating, I think, sulking, as I turn back to my life. And yet these assertions of his are impossible to ignore and I know they will niggle away at me now for hours.

Despite his frequent pontifications about free will, I do feel Ambrose is pushing me. I can't put my finger on it exactly, but as an example of what I mean, take the sudden impulse to join a creative-writing group. That seemed to come completely out of the blue. Or did it?

After CJ went to gaol, to distract myself I had started to fiddle around with a few bits and pieces of writing, usually late at night when I couldn't sleep. Then one day, quite soon after I started, one of those free-sheet newspapers was pushed through the letter-box. I never read these, usually put them straight into the bin, but for some reason, I felt impelled to pick this one up and open it. A recruitment advertisement for a writing group immediately caught my eye; the sessions were held every Friday night in the Father Mathew Hall, attached to the church just across the road from our house. (It has fallen into disrepair in recent times but parts of it are still sometimes used.)

Now it might have been coincidence that this was a Friday and that this was the first and last free-sheet I've ever read and it happened – just happened – to be the one that pointed me towards the Father Mathew Hall on this very day. But that newspaper plopped on to my doormat just ten days or so before Clem's arrest and before my angel materialized to me for the first time.

One of the reasons I was attracted to the workshop, apart from the writing aspect, was the notion – which arose abruptly – of having some sort of identity outside the walls of Alder Cottages. It might be nice, I thought, for the first time in my life, for someone to view me other than as Mammy.

As well as the moderator, there were seven of us there, that first night, five women, a nice man named Joe, who went out of his way to welcome me, and another, very silent, intense young fellow with long, tangled hair and three earrings in his left ear, who didn't open his mouth that night but who, I subsequently discovered, wrote obscure poetry.

None of the fragments I had left with the moderator for assessment was any good, I already knew that, but after she gave them back to me at the next session I heard myself telling her I was planning to write a personal story about myself and my family. Again, I heard this as though someone else was saying it. It was a complete surprise to me: I'd had no idea I was going to say it until I heard the words flowing from my mouth.

Now here's the point of this story.

When I began to feel comfortable with having Ambrose about the place, I mentioned the memoir project, and although he didn't react overtly, I'm convinced I caught a flash of triumph on his face.

See what I mean?

I should probably go for a walk, but I hate walking for no reason. It's an acceptable activity in order to get from point A to point B, but I could never see why anyone would walk around here for the sake of inhaling the fumes of the juggernauts thundering up and down Church Street and along the Quays.

I can't clean any more, I can't do anything. Because I can't ignore the bucketload of feelings and sensations ignited by that confrontation with Melanie and Clem.

I have to face it. I am middle-aged. I have certain fixed views and they have little to do with modernity and *ménages-à-trois*. Plus, I no doubt give the impression of a person who no longer cares about her appearance. On the other hand, I'm certainly not going to fall into the trap of putting myself through a makeover. Since I've been guilty of nothing but neglecting myself, I'll control what I can control, do what I can do and leave the rest for another day. Clem and that little cow will not defeat me.

Money continues to be a problem, of course, and although, as I've said, we manage, since I got back I have had to fight waves of bitterness about the difference between our lifestyle and theirs.

Esmé can't contribute to the general coffers because her only income is the non-contributory old age pension, a pittance because she is not living alone. And anyway, she spends every penny she gets on her personal food delicacies, patés, special coffee and so forth. I don't begrudge it to her, but thank God for my sons. Since this sequester or freezing order, or whatever it is, applies only to the existing assets and bank accounts, they have all rallied around. Martin, who gets paid in cash, has most to spare but even Frank, who is between jobs at the moment, slips me a pound or two out of his dole. Without this help, modest though it is, I would be struggling to buy even one cut-price can of paint.

Eddie must have spread the word that something serious had happened in Spain because I've had un-expected visits from Con and Frank. Even Martin, whom I normally don't see from one end of the week to the next, took a night off to sit with Esmé, Johnny and me in front of the television on the Saturday night. To what do I owe the honour? I yell at him, barely hearing myself above the yowling car chase in the film and Johnny's happy banging. No big deal, Ma, he yells back, I feel like a night in, relaxing, that's all.

Yet despite their tact, all during the last week the unasked questions hung around the house like clanging wind chimes. So much so that I couldn't stand it any more and a couple of nights ago, when I was making a cup of coffee for Con in the kitchen, I faced him about it: was he – was no one – interested in what happened?

We're interested all right, Ma, he says, but the fact that you came home so quickly is not a good sign. We've decided that you'll tell us when you're good and ready.

Then he couldn't resist it: How is Da, anyway? How does he look?

That, at least, I was able to talk about truthfully but although he seemed to listen, I could see he was worried and cut short my laudatory descriptions of Clem's new look: Something on your mind, Con?

His face reddened. It's none of my business, Ma, but is it going to be all right, you and him? Then, hurriedly: Don't answer, you're right, it's nobody's business but yours, yours and Da's. He grabbed the coffee mug from my hand and fled the kitchen.

Sadly, I looked at the empty doorway. Con, who is a clerk in a bookie's shop in Ranelagh, was always, with CJ, one of Clem's favourites and must miss him.

And speaking of missing, although he can't express it, of course, I can tell that Johnny badly misses CJ. Maybe it was because they were the oldest and the youngest, but CJ and Johnny always seemed to get on particularly well. CJ was always able to calm Johnny down, more than the rest of us, and when CJ was here, Johnny followed him around like a happy little Pekinese.

All of this teaches me another hard lesson: there is little I can do about their pain. I've finally recognized that, much as I would want to, I can't carry their burdens for them. It remains to be seen how successful I will be in detaching.

Her eyes knowing, Esmé has been watching all this activity of mine, all this coming and going of the boys, over the tops of her glasses. But she hasn't said anything, the old witch, and neither have I. And, thank God, she hasn't gone on one of her little trolley runs since I came home. I'd probably leave her out there to rot. Maybe this is her way of showing she cares. Yeah.

I haven't told any of them here what happened between me and Clem, but I threw caution to the winds and used the mobile to ring Eddie so he could meet me at the airport. Needless to remark, you could have knocked him down with a feather. I hadn't been expected home for at least a week.

He took one look at me in that arrivals area and knew something had happened but had the good sense not to push it, although I could tell by the way he was talking and acting that he might have a fair good idea of what had gone on. Had I been the only person in the world who had been living in Cloud Cuckoo Land?

He used the new motorway as far as Whitehall and neither of us spoke until we were coming down Broadstone. That would be unusual, because Eddie, unlike most males, is a chatter. Then, as we were passing King's Inns, he said to me that I didn't have to tell him anything if I didn't want to. I was very grateful for his tact. I'd tell him sometime, I said, but not now. All right, Ma, was all he said.

He continued to be a brick when we got home, wading in to save me from Esmé, who was ensconced in the sitting room watching TV Cinq, some documentary in French about Algeria. He told me to go straight to bed, said he would tell Esmé that I was too tired even to say hello.

There are some times when I want Clem back no matter what. Under any circumstances. Please, God, I hear myself praying in the darkest, deepest night, I don't care what he's done or who he's with, I'll forgive him anything, please let him come back and let everything be as before. I'd like to think that those times are getting rarer but so far they continue to occur with unpleasant frequency. Please don't press me as to why I might want him back – I don't know why I'd want him back. I just don't know. It makes no sense.

But in the throes of feeling these feelings, I'd even be prepared to forgive Little Mel.

I think.

So now what? When contrasted with the spiky silence in here, the rumble of traffic outside makes this kitchen feel like prison. The dishes are done, the floors are spotless, the rasher and sausage casserole for tonight's dinner is ready and cooling, the bread is on its wire rack and, on close inspection, the hob didn't need cleaning after all. Esmé has retired to her room, claiming to have a headache, and even Martin has pulled himself from the scratcher and gone out.

I can't concentrate on reading any more and, in my current state, daytime television drives me bonkers. There are hours to put in until it's time for my workshop tonight. Anyway, my short story is crap and unworthy of rescue, even if I could find either the energy or the focus. Which I can't.

I need to talk to someone.

There is nothing further I can do to avoid thinking about Tony and Joan. I haven't faced up to it all week. Did they know? Of course they did. How do I feel about this since Joan is my best friend? Now that I think of it, she is my only friend. I've been too busy and wrapped up in my family to cultivate others. The answer to how I feel about her deception is I feel like shite.

Am I obsessed? Yes. Beyond reason? Yes.

I find myself standing on Joan's doorstep without any clear memory of how I got there. I'm breathing hard, from tension, I suppose, but also because I've walked so fast across the cobbles of the new Millennium Plaza that some shin muscle I was barely aware I owned until this minute is hurting me from the unusual exertion.

I'm trying to calm myself down before I knock. They live in a conventional semi-d, part of an infill development on the other side of Smithfield. They're at home, at least Tony is, the tractor unit he owns is parked outside the house.

A stern voice inside my head is asking me what good this is going to do me. I already know the worst. How is attacking Joan and Tony going to change anything or make anything any better?

I've been pushed here by a demon called information. I want details. The details will kill me, to know them is in nobody's interest, certainly not in mine, but I want them. I need them. When did it start? How long has it been going on? Was she out there first? Did he run to her? Did he give her any presents? What were they? Where did they have their trysts in Dublin? Does Joan have any other details she'd care to share with me, other than the glaring one that she, too, has betrayed me? She was supposed to be my friend.

Horrible word, trysts, but it's the only one I can think of at the moment.

I feel like a perverse Dorothy following not a yellow brick road but a road running between walls of black, grinning question marks. I'll follow this road until the pain is so strong that I'll be consumed by it and I'll stop only when there are no more details to be had.

Poor May? Poor Ambrose. Having to watch this from the sidelines is no bed of roses, you know.

→ Twelve ←

The door opens after the second knock. Joan is standing there in her dressing gown and slippers? Please! It is twenty past two in the afternoon. That pale turquoise colour certainly does her no favours; and as for the blotchiness of her skin — what has she has been doing to it? She's never been Mona Lisa, but my God!

My own face almost cracks with the effort to smile. Sorry, I say, although I don't feel sorry, is this a bad time?

No, not at all, she says, come on in. Don't look at the state of me, for God's sake, I'm just out of the shower. Tony and I are going to an afters.

She turns and walks ahead of me down the hall. Every sense in me is singing as tautly as a musical saw. She hesitated before inviting me in. She's nervous. She definitely has something to hide.

I hate the idea of afters, you're either at the wedding or you're not. The afters, in my opinion, is just a way of maximizing the presents while minimizing the layout on the meal.

There she is again, that newly hatched bitch. I don't

mean what I said just there. Of course I don't hate
afters, young people nowadays are sensible enough to
rationalize the insane cost of weddings. Who's getting
married? I ask Joan, as she puts on the kettle. Their
kitchen is very unlike ours. Whereas we like pine and
homely baskets – the country-kitchen look as seen
through the eyes of a Dub – she and Tony went for
hi-tech. Black countertops, stainless steel kettle, a little
contraption that squeezes juice from oranges when you
pull down a lever. Plain white linoleum on the floor,
murder to keep clean, I'd imagine.

You wouldn't know them, she says back to me. The
girl is the daughter of a second cousin of Tony's –
that's why we're only invited to the afters, I suppose.
Too far out as relations to be invited to the real
wedding.

She sounds jumpy, or so my highly tuned hearing
informs me. She wasn't thinking of afters, or weddings.
Neither was I.

How's Melanie? I ask her.

Her back is to me as she busies herself with teabags
and two mugs. Funny you should ask, she says, I
haven't heard from her for several weeks.

Still in Brazil, is she? Or was that Guatemala? I watch
her very closely. I can see the sudden creasing of the
dressing-gown between the shoulder blades. Then she
sags. She turns round to face me; her expression is
desolate. I know you were out there, May, she says
quietly. She rang us and told us what happened.

From upstairs, I can hear Tony whistling, hollowly,
the thin notes enhanced by bathroom acoustics. He's
probably shaving. Joan is gazing at her white floor. She

looks thirty years older than she is. She buries her face in her hands. I'm sorry, May, I'm so sorry. I don't know what to say. I'm so ashamed.

So this is why you couldn't look me in the eye? Fury with Clem 'n' Mel is surging through every plane of my body. And while we're at it – I'm leaning forward on my stool, so far that it's in danger of toppling – that whole palaver about Guatemala was a lie?

She doesn't answer. Her shoulders shake and she presses her fingers to her eyes as big fat tears snake from underneath.

I sit back. I hadn't been expecting this reaction, I had been expecting a ding-dong battle: I would lay into her, she would fight back; she would be as mad at me as I was mad at her. Clem was my husband, after all: he was the instrument in destroying her lovely daughter; I was guilty by association. I see now that I had been looking forward to the fight as an outlet or catharsis for the way I was feeling. What do I do now?

As she continues to weep, every harsh word I'd planned to say, all the horrible thoughts, drain out of me in one big whoosh. This new bitchy me can't go so far as to take her in my arms, which would have been my reaction up to two weeks ago, but after a long, long pause, I hear myself telling her it's all right: Not to worry, Joan, I understand. I just wish you'd told me, that's all. You might have saved me an awful lot of heartache.

As soon as I say this, I know that, in such a dilemma, nothing she could have told me, however gently, would have saved me from one second's worth of heartache.

Stop crying, Joan, please, I say then. Sure how could you tell me? She's your daughter. I probably wouldn't have told you either if the situation was reversed.

Will we able to rise above this, the two of us? She looks up at me then, and if she had looked bad before, the wreck of the Hesperus has nothing on her now. It's hard to know where Melanie got her looks.

I'm sure we will, Joan, I say, but we have to be honest. It's not going to be easy.

We didn't do anything after all, she said then, with a quaver of hope in her voice, it wasn't us. We can't be responsible for two other human beings and they're both over twenty-one. She tries a conspiratorial, we're-both-in-it-together smile, a ghastly caricature of a smile. Joan never had great teeth and, without lipstick, they look as grey and miserable as I feel.

Before she can say any more, the kettle starts to whistle and she turns to flick it off. Isn't that right, May? she says over her shoulder. The two of us have done nothing wrong.

You're absolutely right, I say.

She pours the boiling water over the teabags as the air between us bristles with what she had left unsaid but undoubtedly feels. Like, Clem Lanigan has to take most of the blame and responsibility for this ruin. He is a lot older than twenty-one, old enough to know better. He is also the married one, the prime adulterer. Her Melanie, thinks Joan, is only the accommodating accessory.

And something more, as clear between us as an Easter bell. She had hoped for something better for her twenty-one-year-old and only daughter than an adulterous liaison with a criminal in his fifties who can't ever come back to his own country.

She has a point.

Watching her fiddling around with milk and sugar, trying to compose herself, the more I think about it, the more I doubt that my friendship with her can survive. It has got too complicated all of a sudden, with too many layers and too many trigger points. Too many areas we can't now discuss.

If she is willing to try, though, so am I. Maybe I'm a sucker. But I suppose a sucker with half a friend is luckier than a wiseass whose friendship quota has run out.

I decide not to test the theory at present and stand up quickly: Look, Joan, thanks for the tea, but I don't think it would be a good idea for me to stay now. It's too soon. I promise I'll get in touch.

If you're sure? This, gallantly, after a tiny pause.

I nod fiercely. I'm sure. I'll give you a ring in a week or two and we'll see where we are then – OK? In the meantime, you're right. They are independent of us and we're just part of the fallout.

As she sees me out, her relief is unmistakable. She doesn't go so far as to give me a hug because both of us know that something has broken.

The walk home took me by the Spar shop Where Love Stories Begin.

And now there are lists of places for ever more associated with Clem and Melanie and that will inflame the pain: that Spar, Sitges, Paris, Barcelona – the very word Spain. Ryanair. Dublin airport. Smithfield, where

Melanie was brought up, the apartment complex up the road where she lived, and presumably fornicated with Clem.

I don't know which is worse, the finding out, or the trying to adjust afterwards. Overnight, from knowing everything about a person – or thinking you know everything about a person – that knowledge is no longer relevant and now you have no idea even what he had for breakfast this morning. When an abrupt split like this happens, you lose two out of three entities. There has been you, him – and, third, your life together. You lose the latter two – him and the joint life. He loses two as well, you and coupledom, but replaces them instantly with Her and New Couple-dom – and, in addition, has all the fun of laying foundations under a new joint experience. He got away with murder in our house because by the time I was experienced enough to find out any different – that, for instance, other husbands were actually on nodding acquaintance with Hoovers and dish-towels, even nappies – I had a houseful of kids and was too busy to make a fuss. Clem has the privilege of reinventing himself. He can become New Man if he wants to now.

Yet if you can believe this – knowing what you do about him now – I always thought of him as a very good husband and a very good father: he never knocked me around or laid a finger on any of our sons, we ate the best of everything and every one of my kids always had shoes that fitted properly and warm jumpers.

So here I am, hiding from the world in my big, messy four-poster. Since Clem went, his side is now covered with books, my workshop scribblings, and recently, of course, tapes and tape boxes. I've been trying to put the episode with Joan into some sort of perspective, but the arguments on both sides are extreme. Of course she'd stick by her own daughter. So I could still be friends with her, couldn't I?

Absolutely not. If she was a true friend she would have come clean and you could have faced the situation together.

Do I hear you sigh with disbelief? All this *Angst* about a criminal?

That criminal was my husband. We had built a life together, no matter how the media scoff about it now, we shared a bed, we made wild love in the beginning, we whispered secrets to one another, we had six sons.

Or, to be more accurate, I had six sons for that lying, cheating bastard.

Ah, the hell with this. I'm going to take charge of my life. You won't know me. Mary Poppins.

No, she's too nice. I Am Woman, Hear Me Roar. That'll be me. I'll divorce Clem, laugh at Melanie, I'll wear plus-fours and I'll take up cigars. Ambrose won't know me.

I haven't been outside the door since my little excursion to Joan's — Eddie did the shopping for me this week. I'm due at my creative-writing workshop tonight and I'm damned if I'm going to let all this energy and effort go to waste, although the temptation is to stay here and pull the duvet over my head.

Everything has been infected, that's the only way to describe it. Last night, for instance, knowing that I have to have something to show the group, if I'm to continue with it, I tried to cobble together the beginnings of a short story. By page two, I found it was turning into a blood-curdling account of an adulterous affair, and I was unleashing such a gale of vindictiveness that I was even beginning to feel sorry for the wrongdoers.

I suppose it is still too soon to expect a diminishing of pain but I still wake up at four o'clock in the morning with Clem and Melanie there beside me in the bed, or I lie there all night without closing an eye, watching them romping, watching his arms around her teeny tiny waist, his head between her perky breasts. One of the most hurtful aspects is their brand new bank of shared memories. I cringe when I remember how I triggered that simpering, locked-together look when I asked how long it had been going on.

If I hadn't been so hell-bent on confronting the truth I could still be plodding along under the illusion that my marriage was fundamentally sound and that Clem's legal predicament was the cement that bound us even closer together; sooner or later, I would think, something would happen and it would all work out. Now, under this new, harsh light I'm forced to cast on myself, I see all too clearly that I was not only as thick as the wall on this one, but in a larger sense, I had cast myself as the voluntary martyr, smug in the halo of my indispensability.

The horror is compounded by memories of my own behaviour while out there. These days, while I cook, clean, dust, do the brasses, even watch TV, my own performance unreels again and again. I'd give anything to have that time back. I'd retain my dignity. I should have used that precious span of my one and only life to practise karaoke, to paint the window-frames, to do anything other than what I did.

And in front of her. Oh, God. Toe-squinching.

Up to now, hatred has been something foreign to me. You can be consumed by it, or so the wisdom goes, burned to a little crisp so you cannot function at all or be able to distinguish what is right and good. Well, I have a little bit of news for you. It is possible to hate and still to live an everyday life in this world, on the outside at least. Hate can be good. It is very real. It feels pure and unsullied and it can live cleanly alongside other sensations, even highlight them, so that coffee in your mouth tastes more coffee-like, hot water on your skin from a pumping shower feels more invigorating, or the smell of a good chicken curry in your nostrils makes your mouth water twice as fast. It has occurred to me more than once recently that active hatred can certainly get you up in the morning.

No sooner thought, of course, than Ambrose is in the bedroom, sitting in the big rocking chair Clem had bought me for our silver wedding anniversary. I sup-pose hatred had to be too juicy a subject with which to trust me alone.

Sure enough, he launches straight in. You have touched on an extraordinarily interesting debate, May. Take Adolf Hitler, for instance. Were his putative killers motivated by hatred of him personally or by service to the common good? My view, which might surprise you, given that by popular reputation I deal only in love, is that they certainly were.

I cover my face with a pillow: Please, Ambrose, not now.

Silence. Stretching. I look up to see if he has left. He hasn't. He is staring at me: How are you feeling, May?

Immediately I can feel the tears begin to well up: Don't do that, Ambrose — please don't do that. I've had enough of feeling sorry for myself. I stare at the ceiling rose: I'm fine. I manage fine until someone asks me how I am.

There is another long pause and I know he is continuing to look at me. Stubbornly I won't meet his eyes. At least I've controlled the waterworks.

He's the one to break it. I think you need cheering up, he says. Shall I tell you a joke?

That does bring me round. No, Ambrose, I'm in no mood for a joke.

If an angel can be crestfallen Ambrose is crestfallen, but at that moment, I certainly couldn't have coped with one of his performances. I've continued to spare you Ambrose's jokes. It's an aspect of him I find surreal — even more surreal than his being here in the first place. A stand-up angel comic? It isn't even necessarily the jokes themselves, it's how he tells them, the big build-up. All he's missing is a microphone and a pork-pie hat.

He loves *Fawlty Towers*, would you believe? We have watched the whole series on video. Frequently. At his request. Ambrose's favourite character is Manuel, his favourite episode the one with Manuel and the hamster.

Now he tries to persuade me as usual: Are you sure? I have practised.

I'm sure, Ambrose.

He's no longer paying full attention, his gaze has become opaque as if he hears something far away. Then, a second later – I swear to you this is true – he grows six inches as a powerful, monumental sound swells from somewhere behind his mouth without disturbing the lips. An enormous voice fills the room, it lays words over the pounding notes of a church organ: For your Father knoweth what things you have need of before ye ask Him. Each word burns a brand into my brain. Then, as though throwing a switch, as if the trickery had been a figment of my imagination, he reverts to normal size. Matthew, six, seven, eight, he says comfortably.

I'm sitting straight up in the bed without noticing the effort required to do so. I'm gaping: What was that all about?

So you will remember, he interrupts.

I'm about to argue, to tell him to stop being so mysterious, when I'm interrupted a second time – this time by a huge knocking at the front door.

The air against my cheeks turns frigid. My first thought, naturally, is that here come the police again.

The knocking again, louder, more impatient. I look at Ambrose and his expression is composed, as ever. Who is it? I whisper. He inclines his head a little, his expression impenetrable. Ambrose, please? I am completely panicked now – what's wrong?

Why don't you go and answer it? he says quietly.

Somehow I find myself in the sitting room looking through the little lobby at the security chains and bright blue paintwork covering the inside of our front door. I take a few steps forward, look through the peephole.

All I can see from the fisheye perspective are two black rubbish bags. I pull the door open a crack.

What took you so long, Ma? Standing behind the bags is CJ.

Thirteen

*P*erhaps the pyrotechnics were a little excessive in such a confined space as May's bedroom but I wanted her to remember those words of Matthew's. (I realize that John holds the high ground these days but personally, I enjoyed Matthew. He was one of mine.)

I do wish she had allowed me to tell her my joke. Human jokes intrigue me. It is difficult for me to ascertain precisely the degree of humour inherent in each but I have closely watched another of my charges, one who makes a handsome living in the entertainment profession. I flatter myself that such study has yielded a comic technique of my own.

Perhaps I might tell this one to you?

A farmer was married to the same woman for nearly sixty years. They were compatible except that the farmer's wife could not cook. One day this farmer was out and about the farmyard and looking forward to his tea. Or not looking forward to it, as the case may be. When he arrived in the kitchen, he found his wife in floods of tears. Boo-hoo. Boo-hoo. The farmer managed to interpret his *wife's words as she continued to weep: Boo-hoo, boo-hoo, I made a batch of buns for your tea, boo-hoo, but the cat ate them.*

The farmer thought hard. Do not worry, my dear, we shall get you a new cat tomorrow.

Yes? It is a good one?

CJ's skin is clear and his eyes are bright, but his head is shaved to baldness and I see he has put an earring into one of his ear-lobes. CJ has two more years of his sentence to run. I saw him last week at visiting-time.

On one level I'm delighted to see him, of course I am. But parallel to that is the thought: Oh, no! More trouble! This is the last thing I need. Over his shoulders, I search the street to see if the police are anywhere about: What the hell are you doing here?

Well, that's nice, he says, offended.

Immediately I'm ashamed. This is my firstborn son. I pull the door as wide as it will go: I'm sorry, honey, it's just that you took me completely by surprise. Come on in. Are you hungry?

He picks up the rubbish bags. I put my arms round him to hug him as he passes me in the door but he doesn't return the hug and walks on. The brief contact with him has told me his body feels more muscular than I remember.

Have you been exercising? It's a few minutes later and we're in the kitchen, he's sitting at the table, polishing off the last rashers and eggs I have in the house and I'm pouring coffee into two mugs.

His mouth full of food, he nods: Yeah.

It's on the tip of my tongue to ask him if he's out

legitimately but I manage to stifle it. It must be the effect of my encounter with Clem and Melanie. I seem to trust no one, these days.

He continues to wolf the food, talking all the time. The story is that he has been released early, on licence, for all kinds of reasons, including pressure on space and, I'm glad to say, good behaviour. I believe him, I think – well, those two rubbish bags did hold his personal effects.

While he was inside, I'd heard nothing but horror stories from him about Mountjoy, but now that he's out, he has to admit that, in all fairness, Mountjoy is trying to get its act together. It's still way too over-crowded and the building is atrociously run-down and dilapidated but it's swarming with social workers and people, including the governor, who genuinely care about prisoners. People who want to rehabilitate and improve themselves are given opportunities do so. Yet as I watch him and listen to him there's definitely something about him that makes me feel off kilter. Even more so than usual. I have the impression of being in the presence of danger barely contained.

I'm uneasy, ashamed of being uneasy, but I can't help it. Seeing tonight's workshop slip over the horizon, I find myself being selfish, wishing he had come home a little later when I was safely closeted with the group.

Confidentially, I've never been totally at ease with Clem Junior. Not since he hit puberty anyhow. Since then I've always felt a secretive and closed-in aura around him, some deeply abrasive attitude to the world. And he never seemed to grow out of it.

It's an awful thing to say about your own son, but I

think I got on better with him while visiting him in prison than ever I did when he was at home. It was certainly easier to talk to him in there: it was formalized, and unless he wanted to refuse visits altogether, he had to make an effort. There were also a few obvious topics of conversation that suggested themselves and which safely spun out the half-hour: the food, the regime, the screws, court appearances, his cellmates, other inmates, visitors, classes, the gym, what was on the TV.

Maybe it was because of this projection of latent aggression that the others here always accorded him the status of top dog and rarely, if ever, argued with him. Rooms in our house were never rowdy when CJ was present. He was never violent, nor ever showed me anything but the height of respect, but he frequently came home with black eyes and split lips from fights he had had outside – and would never talk about what had happened.

Although it seems as though he expects to move in, for the moment anyhow, I'm not inclined to provoke him by asking how long the arrangement will continue. I'd never admit this to anyone, but I think I'm even a little afraid of him. And yet CJ is always the one who will give me the most thoughtful present at Christmas and my birthday, always the one who will remember dates and anniversaries. Riddle me that.

I'm worrying about how I am going to answer any specific questions about his father. Does he know anything? Was he in on it? If Clem were to confide in anyone about Melanie, he'd choose CJ. And if he did know from the beginning, where does that leave me?

It's so easy when they're young.

So what's the plan now? I ask him. Having moved on to sounding off about various things that he's not happy about, mainly the Criminal Assets Bureau and the Gárdaí in general, he's now sitting back in the chair, looking around him as though assessing the kitchen.

No plan, he says. This was a bit sudden, you know? When he stares back at me, there's a belligerent look in his eyes, as though he is challenging me to blame him for not having a plan. I decide not to pursue the matter. Sure you've plenty of time anyway, I say, removing the empty plate from in front of him. Take your time.

Thanks, he says. I will. He drains his coffee and stands up. He has always moved very swiftly. I'm going out for a bit, he says, looking expectantly at me.

I know what he wants: I'm sorry, I say, I'm completely skint. I've only a fiver left in my purse.

He holds out a hand: That'll do. I'll pay you back.

Three pounds of that fiver had been earmarked, two as my subscription for tonight's workshop and a pound for the coffee afterwards. I feel I've no choice, though, and I'm getting up to go into the bedroom to fetch the money when the front door slams and Eddie comes in. Naturally he, too, double-takes when he sees CJ, and echoes me to a word: What the hell are you doing here?

CJ takes offence. Does no one around here think I've any rights to be here? Get me that money, Ma, I'm out of here.

Wait a second, Eddie says, what money? You can't swan in here and throw your weight around or go ordering her about like that. We managed fine without you.

CJ goes very quiet. Did you now? Well, I'm back. And, as it happens, I'll need those wheels tonight. He holds out his hand towards Eddie to receive the car keys.

Eddie laughs. You can piss in the wind for them, sunshine. I'm going out myself.

It's not like Eddie to behave like this. It worries me that trouble might already be starting. CJ has been away for a while and I'm still not sure about the effects gaol has had on him.

Eddie turns to walk back out the way he came in but, quick as an eel, CJ has blocked the doorway. I want those wheels, he says again. They're not yours, they're Da's.

As Eddie looks over his shoulder towards me for help, I make a lightning-fast decision. This has nothing to do with me, I say. I'm going across to my workshop. I'm late. I make for the door. This is so uncharacteristic of my behaviour over the years that even CJ is dumbstruck and stands aside to let me pass.

As you have already noticed, I'm sure, I hate confrontation, particularly within the family. That plate-throwing incident aside in the first year, my mission all along has been to placate and appease, to do or to say anything within my power to restore peace or to keep my mouth shut in order not to exacerbate war. I'm sorry for Eddie but he's an adult, and this time I put May's interests first. Heady stuff.

For your Father knoweth what things you have need of before ye ask Him.

The headiness didn't last long and as I walked across the road towards the church hall, I was asking myself again if this was what I needed. CJ around the place, adding complications to an already complicated situation? Am I an unnatural mother?

Hello, there, May. Emily, the workshop moderator, seemed genuinely pleased to see me: We missed you last week.

The group was already in session and a couple of the women moved up to make room for me as I apologized for being late. We meet off the side of the stage in the hall, in a large, decrepit dressing room, its mirrors peeling and spackled. And because we don't want to use up too much electricity, Emily lights us with a couple of Anglepoise lamps on long leads. She joins two big tables together with a lamp at either end to make one long bench. It's cosy: the twin lights pool around us and create an atmosphere of togetherness, but the venue is startling too, in that if you look up in an unguarded moment, you'll catch your unvarnished self in some mirror or other. It's only since joining this workshop that I realized how I have subconsciously adopted the habit of rearranging my face before looking at myself in a mirror. The real me looks like a stranger.

There were eight of us there that night, including me and Emily, four of the other women, Joe, and the second solitary male who's also been there since I joined and who never seems to miss any of our sessions.

Joe's my favourite of the lot. He specializes in bucolic vignettes about Co. Laois, where he was born and brought up. It's hard to believe, I know, but I have never once been to the country. Clem and I headed into the Dublin mountains once for a Sunday drive, but we had Johnny in the back, being obstreperous, and there were so many other cars crawling along the little twisty roads that Clem got impatient and turned back. Life was too short, he said, and anyway, who needs the bloody country?

Diversity, I suppose, has to be a beneficial feature of group workshops. Like Alice Taylor's, Joe's material, light years from the other man's poetry, concerns domestic animals, bastibles and village pumps, local carnivals, fêtes and patterns and is also very far removed from my own personal and *Angst*-ridden urban diatribes. A bus driver from the Broadstone depot up the road, he has the ability to become a good writer too — although I think he flattens out a lot of the originality in his pieces by overworking them. I suppose it's a bit presumptuous of me but I've had the temerity to tell him this, and for some reason he now seems to depend on my opinion. After each workshop, a few of us go around to Chief O'Neill's for a cup of coffee and he's usually among us.

Joe had been reading aloud when I came in. He smiled at me and I smiled back as I sat down and shoved my ring-binder under the table beside my feet in the hope that I wouldn't be called upon that night.

I was called on, as it happens, but I told Emily that I was still polishing my short story. A blatant lie.

Seriously, I made a mental note to do some genuine work on the bloody thing before next Friday's session but Johnny comes first this weekend. Eddie took him home as normal while I was in Spain, but routine is terribly important to Johnny and although he wouldn't have the emotional or mental wherewithal to say it, I know in my heart that he would have missed me terribly around the house. I have to make it up to him.

I might even risk an outing to McDonald's with him. Eddie has every weekend off and he'd come with us, I know. We've done it before and it has worked out reasonably well. The staff there are young and I suppose the young are more tolerant of difference. The customers are another story, but at this stage I'm fully armoured against people staring and the hostile looks we get when he makes noise. And with CJ home, which always has a beneficial effect, he might be quieter than usual.

CJ was still in bed when Eddie and I got into the house having collected Johnny from St Anthony's on the Saturday morning. We hadn't told him in advance what to expect because CJ can be an unpredictable time-keeper and Johnny reacts badly to disappointment. He gets very fixed ideas.

Esmé was in the kitchen, using the blender to concoct one of the breakfast health drinks she makes from goat's milk and vegetables. She ignored Johnny as usual, immediately leaving the kitchen to go her room. Johnny, of course, didn't notice: he rushed in search of his pots and pans and his candle. This is battery-operated, an artificial but realistic red candle with a yellow, flame-shaped bulb, which trembles a little as though it's flickering. Martin found it in one of the pound shops about two years ago and it's been a lifesaver. Johnny will spend literally hours staring at the shivering little bulb. He adores coloured light. Put him in front of a fully lit and decorated Christmas tree and he is struck dumb with happiness.

So we switched on his candle for him and put it in the middle of the kitchen table. I gave him his milk in his special lidded cup, and left him happily absorbed while I started fixing food for us all and Eddie went out about his own business.

I usually organize it so that there's food *ad hoc* throughout the morning and afternoon. The two married couples drop in at some stage on a Saturday to say hello to Johnny and, with him being a night worker, you never know what time Martin will get up; now, with CJ added to the mix, my kitchen table had to be as good as a hotel buffet. That is, if any hotel is reliant on yellow-pack cooked ham, cheese and yoghurt.

Ten minutes after his arrival, Johnny was still sitting gazing at his candle at the kitchen table when CJ walked in, rubbing the sleep from his eyes. The instant transformation in both of them was astounding.

John-see! CJ's face split into a wide, delighted grin as he saw his brother.

In response, Johnny shrieked and almost did himself an injury attempting to get out of his chair and throw himself at CJ in one movement. Luckily CJ darted forward and managed to catch him before he fell on the floor. He swept Johnny off his feet, John-see, John-see! and swung him round and round as easily as if he were a rag doll, while Johnny screamed like a train whistle.

CJ is not all that tall, about five feet nine, I'd say, whereas Johnny is the guts of six feet, yet they ended up sitting on a chair together, Johnny on CJ's lap and wound around his neck, as though he were a small child. Which I suppose he is, in a sense.

All right, John-see, said CJ, when Johnny had calmed down a little. I'm back now. Where's Bonzo? Where's my Mála? He unwound Johnny's arms from the death grip around his neck and thrust his face forward, pretending to scowl. No messing, now. Where's my Mála?

Má-a, Má-a – Johnny screamed with delight, throwing his arms in the air. Má-a. No Má-a. He jumped off CJ's lap and raced out of the kitchen and – with CJ in hot pursuit – raced down the corridor towards the sitting room, laughing hysterically.

It's a game they've always played. Every time Johnny comes home he is supposed to have a dog made from Mála as a present for CJ. Every time he comes home without this Plasticine task completed, CJ pretends he is going to spank him – but he has to catch Johnny first. He never does, of course, and by the time the chase is over, Johnny has always forgotten its purpose and has been distracted by something else, usually the television.

I had to swallow hard so as not to betray myself. Johnny certainly brings out whatever soft side is latent in CJ. It's extraordinary, really, it's like CJ is two different people and only Johnny can reach one of them.

The weekend continued successfully. The married couples came and went, Martin went to work and CJ went out, too, at about eight o'clock, leaving the house to Esmé, Johnny and me. Johnny and I watched his favourite videos — he loves *Fantasia* most of all — and we both went peacefully to bed.

On Sunday, Eddie, Martin and I brought him to McDonald's in Phibsboro. I really appreciated Martin struggling out of bed so early because his job means he sometimes doesn't get in until nearly five in the morning. CJ, who came in even later than Martin that morning, had been supposed to come but none of us was willing to risk going in and waking him up. It's not a pleasant task, never was. CJ enjoys very deep sleep and is not at his best if dragged out of it.

So we were just four as we set off at lunch-time. It was a lovely day and my spirits were high — anyhow, with Johnny hanging so heavily out of my arm, it was impossible to think about anything else. As happy as a pup with a marrowbone, he had a great time, reacting to each passing car and bus and making a deafening racket by clattering his stick all along the run of railings at the front of King's Inns.

In the restaurant, the only sticky moment occurred when he managed to get away from our table and ran over to talk to a baby in a high chair nearby. He is very attracted to babies but unfortunately he scares them rigid by thrusting his face right into theirs. He means only to be friendly, we know that, but on being loudly accosted by a large, crash-helmeted nineteen-year-old, the poor baby and its parents certainly don't, and naturally this child, who was about a year old, started to howl.

I retrieved Johnny before too much damage was done and apologized to the parents, who were, to put it mildly, stiff in their acceptance.

What do these people want us to do? Hide the Johnnys of this world for all of their lives? Lock them into attics, cellars and barns like they used to do in Ireland until recently?

Poor old Johnny. Whatever did he do to deserve such a fate?

Fourteen

When we got back after our outing, CJ was up and around. He had bought a pair of Beanie Babies and immediately lay down on the floor of the sitting room alongside Johnny so they could all play games together. Barney and Beanie went to the seaside and built sandcastles. CJ produced a tube of Smarties and Barney and Beanie had to have their Smartie dinner from little plates made of ashtrays.

Then Barney and Beanie made a tent with an old sheet over two chairs pushed together, which was a runner only until Johnny demolished the lot with a wild swipe of his wooden spoon. Looking at him, eyes shining, laughing like a drain, it was hard for me to believe what the doctors had said about his probable life span. To me he looked as healthy as a trout.

One thing I've always regretted and that is that I did not get his teeth straightened. While sound and healthy, they protrude a lot, so much so that he has difficulty closing his mouth and drools a fair bit. I'm convinced now that he might have spoken more clearly if I had insisted on getting some orthodontic work done on him when we could have afforded it. Ironically, one of his few decipherable words is Mel, a corruption of Clem. This is what he calls CJ.

The upshot of the weekend was that Johnny, clutching his Beanie Babies, travelled back to St Anthony's last night so tired and happy that, after babbling for a while to himself and to the Beanie Babies, tightly clutched one in each hand, he fell asleep in the back seat of the car.

But having deposited Johnny, as Eddie was driving us home along the Quays, the Clem 'n' Melanie saga smashed its way back into my stomach. I mean that literally. All the fury and hurt rose again, sour as bile, so quickly and harshly that I thought I might be physically sick.

I tried to reason with myself: I have to accept that, for the moment anyway, Melanie and Clem are a background hum in my life, no matter what I'm doing or whatever the current trauma or preoccupation. Yet this was more than background as the rage tumbled over itself inside my gut. Both Johnny and CJ were Clem's sons too. Where the hell was he? Where did he get off leaving me to manage everything? The fact that I had been managing perfectly fine until Esmé's bombshell sent me off to Spain seemed no longer relevant.

I didn't want Eddie to worry so, despite all of this, I tried to maintain a stream of casual chatter about the traffic, about how the weekend had gone, but as we pulled up at a red light just beyond the Four Courts, he looked across at me: Is everything all right, Ma?

Fine, fine. I plaster on a smile.

Are you sure you're OK? Eddie slows the car. You've gone very quiet.

I force a yawn: Sorry, Eddie, I'm a bit tired, that's all, lost in my own world. Are you going to come in for a cuppa or are you going out somewhere tonight?

He hesitates. No, Ma. As a matter of fact, actually I have a bit of news.

Oh? I say. Is your job OK?

These days, when anyone in this family says there's news, it's never good news.

He seems to brace himself against the large brown steering-wheel of the car. Everything is fine on that score, he says quietly. In fact really good, and I might even get a promotion in the near future. The place is expanding. But the news is personal.

He hesitates again while my mind races. It occurs to me that Eddie has been so much of a prop to my life that I haven't given him half the attention he deserved. Be a problem and be the hub of May's heart — that seems to have been my motto.

Don't keep me in suspense, love, I say. What is it?

He seems unhappy now. Look, he says, this is probably not the time or the place, especially with — with that little bollocks come back to haunt you.

It's so vehement — and the mid-sentence change so obvious — that I know Clem Senior and not Junior had been his first concern. I play along, however. Come on, Eddie, I say. CJ's your brother. You shouldn't talk about your brother like that.

The light goes green and he's silent for a few seconds, concentrating on driving through the heavy

Sunday-evening traffic. Ahead, the pollution haze over the city centre is streaked with pink, and at the mouth of the river, twin plumes of steam from the chimneys at Poolbeg rise straight as poplars into the air. It's a lovely evening. He looks across at me again. You know what I mean. There's always some excitement or other going on in that bloody house – I've been waiting for an opportunity to talk to you, Ma, but there never seems to be a good time.

Again there is silence between us, filled with Clem and with my sorrow that my twenty-four-year-old son has to have such an old head on his shoulders. I look at my feet. I'm just not ready yet to talk about it. My voice sounds hoarse.

Whatever, he says, sounding panicky, it's your call, it's none of my business. Then, desperately, Look, Ma, I have to tell you – I'm getting engaged.

Oh, God! It was so unexpected that it was shocking in a way and I find my hands jammed against my mouth: That's fantastic, Eddie, I had no idea. When? Who is she?

You're really pleased? You don't mind?

Mind? Of course I don't mind. Why should I mind?

He shrugs, glances sideways at me again through eyes that are too old and too worried, and I'm stricken. I want to hug him and kiss him and give him back his childhood. Instead, I reach over and pat him on the knee. Details, I say, I want details.

I rejoice at the way his voice lights up and races with happiness as he outlines his sweetheart's attributes and the plans they've made together. He got to know her in a coffee shop near where he works, she does part-time waitressing to help with the fees at one of the private colleges where she is studying law. She already has a business degree, she's a girl from the north of Ireland, from Bangor, she'll be graduating in June and then looking for a job. They don't plan to get married for at least two years so they can save up for a deposit on a house.

She sounds terrific, I smile at him, really and truly lovely. What's her name?

Tracey Ervine. And, yes, before you ask, she does kick with the other foot. I laugh, genuinely happy for him: I don't care if she kicks with her knees – all that stuff is old hat.

I've surprised myself, I hadn't known I'd become so liberal.

You're sure you don't mind? he asks again, anxiously. You're so religious, Ma.

I pat his knee again: Nonsense. That girl is welcome into our family and I hope we're welcome into hers.

Am I that religious? Well, maybe I am – or used to be anyhow. Maybe it's because we're surrounded by a flush of churches. Off the top of my head I can think of at least fifteen within a radius of less than a mile – and that's not to include all the little chapels and convents tucked into the back-streets, lanes and alleyways. We're as good as Italy – I suppose it's in case you're ever caught short for a prayer you're never far from a pew!

Being a late developer, as it were, maybe I get more out of religion than most. I certainly depend on it for comfort. I am probably attracted to religion because it was forbidden to me for so long, and one of the first things I did after my father, the Communist, died, was get baptized. In many ways, it's not the institutional Church itself that's so enticing, it's the trappings, the dark shadows, the smells, the whispers, the confidentiality, its deliciously mouth-filling vocabulary: chalice, ciborium, monstrance, alb, benediction, absolution.

To console me for not letting me make my first Holy Communion with my schoolmates, Da bought me a greyhound pup called Tarzan and took me on an outing to the dog track in Harold's Cross so I could get a smell of all the fun that was in store for me when the dog grew up. I didn't give a damn about either the dog or racing. All I wanted was to be like everyone else, to wear a spangly satin dress and white veil, lacy gloves and to carry a little white handbag filled with money — and to faint with hunger because I had been fasting.

Poor Tarzan lasted less than a week as it happened, he got out of the garden and was run over by a milk lorry.

It's only as we pull up on the street outside the house that the implications of Eddie's announcement begin to sink in. Goodbye, love, I give him a quick, strong hug to hide my tears. Bring Tracey to see us, won't you?

I will, Ma. He smiles at me, his eyes like lamps. You'll like her, I promise.

I'm sure I will.

I'm sure I will, I repeat to myself as I let myself into my silent house, the place that this son will no longer refer to as home. Don't get me wrong, I'm thrilled for him. But in the midst of the joy is the worm of loss. It's in the nature of the world that boys turn to their

wives' families. I'm lucky I've been left so long with a
son as good as Eddie, and although I gladly let him go,
there's no doubt it'll be a wrench. Letting this one go
will be different from letting go any of the others. I'd
never admit that to a soul.

So that brings us to today, Monday.

I had a lunch-time telephone call from Eircom. Good
afternoon – Mrs Lanigan, is it? The voice was pure
sugar, Blackrock College out of UCD. We're just
checking the lines in your area, have you been having
any difficulty lately?

I was surprised. I hardly use the phone at all now
but it seemed to be working fine: Do you mean making
calls or getting them?

Either, said Mr Sugar.

I assured him that, as far as I was aware, my
telephone was working perfectly. We have six extension phones, installed in the good old days when money
was plentiful. They were all working too, as far as I
knew. I told him this.

Perfect, said Mr Sugar.

Is that all? I asked him.

That's all, he said sweetly, then wished me a very
good afternoon and thanked me for my co-operation. I
put down the receiver and thought no more about it.

Until an hour later.

I answer the door to find two detectives on my
doorstep. Would you believe they're the same two
clodhoppers who arrived to arrest Clem at six o'clock
in the morning all those months ago? Mrs Lanigan? asks
Zig, the one with the moustache. I nod. He knows full

well who I am but I'm suddenly too weary even to feel upset. Zag, the taller one, asks if they can come in for a few moments. I step aside.

Esmé's in the sitting room but she gets up without a word and leaves when the three of us troop in. I close the door behind us and we all sit down. Tea? I ask.

No, thank you, says Zag. No thank you, says Zig, who's not looking at me but fumbling to open one of those diminutive elastic-bound notebooks beloved of police. His little biro has got caught in the black elastic.

I wait. We all wait while he untangles it.

I understand you made a call to this house from Spain, he says, having finally managed to open his notebook. He flips through the pages until he lights on one: From a mobile phone, he adds, on the twenty-fourth of April, one week ago. He glances at me, and then his gaze slides away towards my fireplace.

It was a Monday, says Zag, helpfully.

The reason for Eircom's solicitude has become apparent. That's right, I say, yes I did make that call.

Zag looks surprised and exchanges a glance with Zig. They had obviously expected a fight. I did make a call, I say again, emphasizing each phrase, to this house, from Spain, on Monday, the twenty-fourth of April. I made another one too, to my friend, Joan Malone. Did you not get that one?

It's a relief, in a way. I am through lying for Clem. All criticisms or questions from now on are to be addressed to Clem Lanigan, c/o Melanie Malone, Sitges, Spain.

So you don't deny that you called here—

From Spain. How many times do I have to tell you? I rang Ireland from Spain a week ago. Twice. The first call was to this house, to my son, Eddie, asking him to pick me up from the airport.

We already know that, says Zag, as though it was a matter of no consequence. He seems to be the one in charge. What we want to know is what you were doing in Spain and who did you meet there?

And how did you get there, Mrs Lanigan? Zig chimes in, but Zag interrupts him: It is our understanding that you have surrendered your passport.

I travelled on an old one, I say. Then, maliciously: You haven't heard of the Bangemann wave?

That seems to get both of them. The what wave? This is Zig.

I explain the Bangemann wave to them.

And no one checked this old passport you were waving? Zag asks.

I shake my head. I have them cold. They can't prosecute me. I'm back safely and they're hardly going to go interviewing every immigration officer in Barcelona and Dublin. I make a mental note to destroy the false passport, at present concealed snugly in a box at the back of my wardrobe.

Again they exchange glances. They've been taken down a road they didn't expect. Could we see this old passport? asks Zag.

I threw it away when I got back, I say. I've been overtaken by some sort of recklessness I never knew was in me. Lying? Fabricating? Must be the writer in me, I think as I meet their eyes.

Where did you throw it? This is Zig, who is watching me with the sort of inscrutable expression that would get Spock a bad name in the Andromeda Galaxy.

In the bin, of course, I tell them, and before you ask, our rubbish collection is on Fridays so if you're interested in finding it you'll have to go out to wherever it is they're dumping Dublin's rubbish now. County Kildare, is it?

Zag looks at Zig, whose head is low over his notebook. They don't know what to do with me. They had obviously expected the Little Flower, not Joan of Arc. Of course, before that trip to Spain the Little Flower is what they would have got.

Zig is the first to recover. The passport is not important anyhow, he says gravely. What we really want to know, Mrs Lanigan, is exactly where you met your husband?

Despite my blithe U-turn on the subject of lying for Clem, a twenty-seven-year-old habit does not wither in one week and I start automatically to build defences: I didn't say I met my husband, did I? Then I stop. Why should I? Let Melanie do that. But since I'm not all that fond of Zig and Zag, what have I to gain by co-operating with them? I have nothing at all to say about my husband, I tell them.

There's a pause. They glance at one another. Zag nods at Zig. Zig clears his throat: We know you made this call from the Barcelona region.

If you know that, why are you asking me?

It's Zag's turn. You are not in a good position here, Mrs Lanigan. Your husband is a fugitive criminal. You could be taken in for questioning on suspicion of aiding and abetting.

I shrug. This airy, daredevil me is momentarily lost in admiration for herself. Then the door of the sitting room opens. Their eyes swivel and come to rest on CJ who, on seeing them, stops dead in the doorway. The air tightens all over the room. Well, hello there, says Zag.

What Clem Junior says next is unrepeatable. This man with cold eyes and a filthy mouth bears no resemblance to the Beanie Baby kid who got down and played sandcastles with his brother.

There's little point in going any further with painting this scene. Clem is safe from them, for the moment anyway, and so is CJ. CJ and the policemen all know this so the three of them ignore me. Zag and CJ exchange insults and swear words and CJ leaves. Shortly afterwards, so do the detectives. All the fire has gone out of me and I spend the rest of the afternoon drearily going about the housework.

But I've saved today's best surprise till last. I can hardly credit what happened and I don't want anyone, least of all me, to read any more into it than is warranted but it has cheered me up no end. I actually feel like a human being as opposed to a pale grey shadow. No, even better than that. I feel like a woman with real blood in her veins.

Here's what happened. Around tea-time, Esmé and I are having a bowl of soup at the kitchen table when she gazes up at me with those cynical, all-seeing eyes: Aren't you going to answer it?

Answer what? I didn't hear anything.

There's someone at the door.

Sighing, humouring her, I get up and go to the front door.

Standing on our doorstep is Joe. The Joe from the workshop. He's smiling nervously. And he has a newsagent's bunch of flowers in his hands. Happy birthday, May, he says, I was just passing, it was an impulse. He holds out the flowers. The price is still on them: £3.99.

I'm stupefied: But it's not my birthday – then I could kick myself. Why couldn't I be deft enough just to say a simple thank-you and take the bloody flowers? It's just that no one has presented me with flowers for the longest time and I don't know how to behave. I always buy my own flowers – or used to before the financial difficulties.

Oh my God, the first of May, I thought. Oh – oh, my God, I'm sorry. His acute embarrassment is catching but we sort it out, somehow, both of us as red as beetroots and stammering. It turns out he has remembered a piece of writing I read out in the workshop about my father's reason for calling me May after May Day. He put two and two together and got five.

Fancy you remembering that, I say to him. Please come in, have a drink or a cup of something – I really appreciate this, the flowers are lovely.

Ah, no, no, I won't come in, he's still seriously off balance, sure I'll see you next time in the group? You can buy me a cup of coffee? He scuttles off.

As I'm closing the door with the bunch of flowers in my hand – wet from the newsagent's bucket – I realize I don't even know his last name.

But even now, nearly five hours later, the boost I got from that gesture is keeping me warm. I've arranged the flowers in a jug on my dressing table so I can see them from here in the bed. To be perfectly honest, they're not all that much to write home about — two stems of yellow chrysanths, three white daisies and a couple of raggedy unopened sprays of carnations — so he was ripped off at £3.99. To me, however, they mean that at least one person — one man — thinks I'm interesting enough to buy me an impulse gift. I wonder how he found out where I live. From Emily, probably.

Please don't go jumping to conclusions about romance or anything like that. At least on my side. I can't answer for him, of course — he's a bachelor, I know that from one of the pieces he read out.

Oh, my God — I can't believe I said that. Stop it, May . . . You're a married woman and you intend to remain married.

But still, that was a good May Day, and it was lovely to get them. Maybe I'm not so unattractively middle-aged after all. So stuff that in your little cotton socks, Melanie Malone.

I refuse to think of Melanie tonight. Go away, Melanie. Go away, Clem. Shag off.

He's quite good-looking too — Joe. I never really noticed before. A bit paunchy, but now that I think about it, nice eyes and mouth and, yes, good hands. I suppose they get a lot of exercise and stay supple from clutching that huge steering-wheel all day. I was never on his bus. I wonder what he looks like in his uniform?

This is pathetic, May. Uniforms, hands. Will you,

for heaven's sake, turn off this tape-recorder, turn out that light and go to sleep? Good night.

Good night, May. And if I may be permitted a small pun: Angels guard thee.

⇥ Fifteen ⇤

17 May 2000

They say happy people do not make good writers because they have no need of exorcism. I have made the disconcerting discovery that 'they' might be correct. It is so much easier to record misery than mirth. The details are sharper, the words come faster.

I used to be instinctively happy, I think, if anyone can be objective about personal feelings, but recent events have pushed happiness so far into the past now that I cannot remember what it felt like. Happiness did stir itself a little on the night of Monday, 1 May, when Joe, whom I now know to be Joe Rooney, gave me the bouquet of newsagent's flowers. They are still here in my bedroom, as it happens, brown and stinking, since I cannot bring myself to remove them and throw them out. As a matter of fact I have been unable to do much of anything since 3 May.

Three incidents, as the police would call them, occurred on the same day two weeks ago exactly. On Wednesday, 3 May. One of them was pleasant. That day Eddie brought Tracey round to meet me at lunch-

time. I gave them soup and ham sandwiches and she
was really taken with the house, which pleased me. It
was immediately clear to me that this girl adored my
son and it was uplifting to be in the presence of their
mutual childlike joy. When I had turned away for a
moment to the sink and they thought I wasn't watching, she pinched his bottom and he returned the pinch.
I had to wait until their stifled giggles had died away
before I turned back.

Tracey is very attractive, tall, red-haired and articu-
late. As an aside, my friend (former friend?) Joan
has always maintained that red-haired people are not
to be trusted, and although it is difficult to believe, I
have heard that in Ireland there is even a prejudice
against red-haired babies amongst prospective adoptive
parents. That is rubbish.

This red-haired lovely girl gave me a refresher course
in my own son. Fond as I am of Eddie, I had probably
begun to take his intelligence and practicality for granted
and it was therefore instructive to see him through her
eyes, not least in the way she deferred to him as in,
'Eddie thinks this', or 'Eddie says that', or 'Would you
agree with that, Eddie?' And she certainly has his best
interests at heart in that she seems to be encouraging
him to better his position in life. She has suggested he
take extramural evening courses at her college.

When she went to the bathroom, temporarily leaving
Eddie and me alone, I took the opportunity to tell him
how much I liked her: 'She's wonderful. I hope you
will be very happy. I really believe you will.' But then,
speaking slowly so he would remember it, I told him
that she was the one getting the bargain: 'You're a

marvellous son, Eddie, and thank you from the bottom of my heart for everything you've done for me. You've also grown to be a really good man. And I'm sorry I haven't said that to you before.'

I embarrassed him, of course, and she came back before he could respond, but I could see he was fundamentally delighted. I do not intend to write more about this at that stage. The memory of their joy will make me cry.

They had not long gone and it was about ten past three, I think, when the telephone rang. I was in the kitchen, Esmé was up in the sitting room, dozing in front of the gas fire. For once we had had none of the usual arguments about her wasteful use of this appliance. She keenly feels the cold yet refuses to wear what I would regard as adequate layers of clothing. On this occasion, however, I had not been interested in conflict of any kind because I was basking in the memory of Eddie and Tracey's young delight and had even succeeded in pushing Clem 'n' Melanie to the back of my brain. So I had contented myself with a small glare to let her know she need not think that this was to become a habit.

I have to admit that Joe Rooney's flowers were continuing to work their magic too. All day on the Tuesday I had felt a little taller, a little lighter, and that night I had even reworked my wretched short story towards resembling something I might dare to read aloud. So much so, I could even enjoy thinking forward to the workshop to come on the Friday.

Stupid, stupid, stupid. Stupid to think that May Lanigan could get away with any sort of lightness. Or plans.

Just before the telephone rang, I was humming a little tune down amongst the ratty sponges, bottles of drain cleaner, Weedol and Jif as I cleaned out the cupboard under the sink, a job I normally detest.

'Hello!' I hear Ambrose's voice and, turning my head, I see he has perched himself on the edge of the kitchen table.

I start to heave myself to my feet and crack my head on the rim of the sink. This hurts, but does not dent my spell of good-humour. 'You might consider some sort of early-warning system,' I say to him, rubbing the crown of my head.

Although he smiles in response, I can see he is in sombre mood underneath; not as tall as usual, always an ominous sign. 'Anything wrong?' I ask him.

His eyes do not flinch from mine. 'Give me your hand, May,' he says.

I chuckle uneasily as I hold it out. 'What are you going to do? Tell my fortune?' He does not reply and when he takes my hand in his, I am instantly afraid. 'What?'

'You have strength,' he says quietly, 'and I am with you. Do not forget the way you feel when you laugh. Laughter is a great gift to humans. You will laugh again.'

This is when the telephone shrills.

I turn towards it, hesitate. At the same time, I hear the front door close quietly. It is not followed by footsteps. Someone has gone out. Esmé, damn her, probably on one of her excursions. My reprieve is too enjoyable to last.

The telephone continues to ring. When I glance back

towards Ambrose to seek guidance as to whether I should answer it, he is no longer there.

I decide not to answer the telephone. Counting the rings, I stare at it, reaching ten before the instrument cuts itself off abruptly mid-ring and silence descends on the kitchen.

I pick up the rubber gloves from where I have discarded them, fold them tidily one into the other and place them precisely in the plastic bowl I use to hold my J-cloths. I take off my apron, hang it on the back of the door and leave the kitchen. It is my intention to go into the sitting room and to switch on the television.

I am passing the front door when the knock comes. It is too soon after the telephone call. The two occurrences could not be connected. It could simply be Mormons, or Witnesses, or even one of the desperate, slick-haired young boys they send out now as salespeople on commission to sell anything from double-glazing to tree-pruning. It could be kids playing Knick Knack.

I know full well it is none of these because of the way Ambrose has behaved. I ignore the front door and walk past it towards the television. I turn it on, turn up the volume. There is a brief pause, then the knocking begins again, strongly enough to be heard above the bellowing of the compère on the afternoon talk-show. Esmé has not returned; no doubt she has already wreaked havoc on the afternoon traffic.

A sort of fatalism takes me over. I know that this summoning will continue until I respond. I go to the front door. I am calm and blank as I pull it open.

Why does it not surprise me to find Zig?

But in place of Zag, he is accompanied by a uniformed Ban Ghárda. With strange detachment, I notice she has thick ankles and has not shaved the shins inside her tights. 'Good afternoon,' I say politely. In the street outside our cottages, two little girls are turning a rope and chanting, 'Jelly on the plate, jelly on the plate,' while a third is jumping. The skipping season must have started, I think.

'May we come in, Mrs Lanigan?'

This respectful demeanour from Zig is so different from what I had become used to that I am momentarily thrown. Then I see that, like biting bees, doom swarms around their shoulders and I know their presence has to mean bad news. 'Who's dead?' I have remained composed.

They look at one another. 'Mrs Lanigan,' says the Ban Ghárda, 'please may we come in for a moment?' She is so solicitous I know that (a) I am correct – someone is dead, and that (b) she has received training in this.

My mind has slowed. Like a ponderous grandfather clock it mentally ticks off the possibilities.

Johnny, he's the most likely.

Or Eddie's had an accident taking Tracey back to work. Tracey too?

Martin. You read a lot about bouncers and grudges.

Con or Frank? Anything could have happened to either of them.

One of the wives? No. The police would go to their families, not to me.

'Who's dead?' I insist.

'Please, Mrs Lanigan,' the Ban Ghárda touches my arm, 'please let us come in, won't you?'

I stand aside. She steps in first, with the uncharacteristically hesitant Zig close behind her. I shut the door and lead them into the sitting room. The television spiel now is from an expert on how to dry and preserve garden flowers. I turn it off and sit on the settee. 'Who's dead?' I ask, for the third time.

The telephone rings. 'Would you like me to answer it?' This is Zig. 'I'll take it for you, if you like.'

'Take it off the hook,' I say.

As he goes to remove the receiver from its cradle, the Ban Ghárda sits down beside me, on the edge of the settee and, looking me directly in the eye, begins to speak.

You have heard, I am sure, about death by a thousand cuts, none on its own lethal but cumulatively fatal. Each word this pleasant girl says, in her well-modulated, well-rehearsed voice, administers one of these cuts.

CJ.

It is CJ. In my mental enumeration, I had not considered CJ. I doubt now if the guilt arising from that omission will ever fully leave me. (It was only later, much later, that I realized I had also omitted Clem. This bothered me hardly at all.)

Although she did not want to tell me why or how CJ died, was dead, I was so strongly insistent and clearly in control of myself that she told me as much as they knew.

The story is as follows: CJ had apparently made

arrangements with another prisoner, with whom he had become friendly while in Mountjoy, to steal a container-load of cigarettes and tobacco with a street value of close to half a million pounds. The relevant container would be identified for them by an accomplice who worked as a temporary security guard at a storage warehouse. This man would also let them in.

The theft, on Monday night, went as planned at the warehouse but the Gárdai mounted a road block and stopped the truck on a back road in Co. Monaghan at four thirty on Tuesday morning. The warehouse accomplice, CJ and the truck's driver were arrested.

CJ was released at lunch-time on Tuesday while his colleagues were both held in custody.

This morning, CJ's body was found on a patch of scrubland near a building site in Blanchardstown, west of the city. 'It's early days,' says the Ban Ghárda, in her soft country accent. 'We don't have the full details as yet.'

With my right shoulder-blade, I can feel the line of braid that strengthens the seam between two pieces of the sofa's upholstery. Zig is leaning against the wall near the little telephone table – I can hear a protesting whine from the displaced receiver. The Ban Ghárda, leaning forward from the waist, is frozen in an attitude of concern.

'How did he die?'

She shifts a little. I notice she is married as she clasps her hands in front of her: 'There's to be a post-mortem, naturally—'

'Was he shot, stabbed, beaten, buried alive, what?' My voice remains strong but is rising.

'We don't know for sure,' she says, 'we have to wait—'

'How did he die? I want to know.'

I don't know why I need to know. I just do. The Ban Ghárda darts a glance at Zig for help. He frowns quickly, shakes his head, so quickly that I almost miss it. She looks back at me: 'I'm not being obstructive, Mrs Lanigan, but it really is too early to tell. I promise we'll keep you informed but we do have to wait for the results of the post-mortem.'

My brain has gathered speed again, clacking like an abacus, absurdly in time with the skipping rhyme outside: one possibility, two possibilities, three possibilities, four . . . 'Why did they release him? Why him and not the others? He was out on licence, surely he shouldn't have been released if he – that's obviously why he was killed, isn't it? It was assumed he was the one who – he was set up?'

Zig comes away from the wall, takes a step towards me: 'Don't jump to conclusions, please, Mrs Lanigan. The truth is we don't know any of this yet. The investigation is at a very early stage. Very early.'

I ask where I can see my son. They tell me he is in Beaumont Hospital but that I cannot see him just yet. 'Would you like a cup of tea, Mrs Lanigan?' The Ban Ghárda is so sympathetic she releases something very deep inside me and I think I'm going to blurt all over her polished shoes but I refuse to let them see the storm. I stand up. 'Thank you for coming.'

The Ban Ghárda rises too. 'Is there anyone we can telephone for you?'

I shake my head. The enormity of the situation has not begun to register. Whom should I telephone? I have no husband, no eldest son. My eldest son, whom I did not understand, whom I probably neglected because of all the others, whom I probably drove to crime in the footsteps of his father because my attention was on my other sons, is now dead. Clem Junior, whom I left to his corrupt father's care and attention, is now dead. Dead.

Dead.

And I did not even accord him the courtesy of worrying about him. His name was not on my roll-call.

Something must be showing through because both of them look concerned. Maybe Zig is not such a bad egg after all. From outside I hear the distant squeal of brakes. Yes, it has to be Esmé, up to her old tricks.

'Are you sure there's nobody——?' The Ban Ghárda hunkers down in front of me. 'You shouldn't be on your own, Mrs Lanigan. I'll stay with you, if you like.' I shake my head again. I refuse to cry.

'A priest maybe?' This is Zig.

'I would truly like to be by myself,' I say. 'And I will make my own telephone calls. But I would appreciate it if you would tell Beaumont Hospital, whoever is in charge of that – that department,' my voice wobbles but I fetch it back, 'that I will be going to see my son as soon as possible. Within the next hour.'

'We'll drive you, Mrs Lanigan.' The Ban Ghárda stands up. 'We'll call back for you in half an hour.'

'And we're very, very sorry for your trouble.' Zig comes forward and shakes my hand.

My mouth won't move, my eyes feel like dried plates. I am too tired to argue. I want to protest, to tell them I will take a taxi, thank you, but all strength has gone into keeping up appearances. 'Just one thing,' I say to them, dredging for the last ounce of composure, 'I would greatly appreciate it if you would go out to the junction of Broadstone and Church Street. You will find an old lady there in the middle of the traffic, wielding a trolley. I usually go to fetch her back – but now . . .'

'Of course – of course. We'll see you soon . . .' Zig hesitates, then thinks better of what he had been about to add and they leave, repeating condolences and sympathy but also telling me that some of their colleagues will be along to examine CJ's belongings – if that is all right with me, of course. I am abandoned to my jumble of woes in the hard-packed silence of our house.

I sit down and try to think clearly.

I had thought nothing of it when CJ did not come home on that Monday night, or indeed on the Tuesday night either. He was twenty-five years old, had a lot of catching up to do with friends, I had supposed. He was also long past the time when his mother dared to ask him about his activities. Not that I had ever been granted access to knowledge of what was going on in CJ's life.

I shoot to my feet again. Clem. Clem should be told about this. I glance towards the telephone receiver, still whining on the telephone table. I find myself with it in one hand, dialling Joan's number with the other.

She answers on the first ring: 'Mel?' Her voice is nasal as though she has a cold, or has been crying.

'It's me,' I say, holding the receiver as though it's a lifeline to sanity. 'Joan, would you do me a favour, please?'

'May?' Her voice sounds incredulous. 'Is that you?'

'Yes, please don't talk. I need you to telephone M-Melanie.' Despite Melanie and Clem's affair having slipped many places in the crisis ratings, the name still sticks in my throat. 'There's been a terrible accident and Clem needs to be told.'

There is silence at the other end of the line.

'Joan? Are you there?'

'Haven't you heard?' She is sniffling, obviously starting to cry again. 'Clem was taken this morning by the Spanish police. He's in gaol over there, in Barcelona. They want to extradite him. Melanie's in bits—' She starts to sob.

And that was the third occurrence of 3 May.

Slowly, gently, I replace the receiver, cutting off the sound of Joan's sobs. The phone rings immediately. I pick it up. 'Hello, is this Mrs Lanigan? This is the *Irish Independent* here—'

I put my finger on the hang-up button and dial Eddie's work number. I hold myself together while the girl who has answered goes to get him to the phone.

Eddie comes to the telephone. I break down completely then, and cannot tell him what has happened.

'Ma – Ma – what's happened? Is it Johnny?' Eventually, his frantic voice brings me to my senses. I tell him and ask him to come home.

I leave the phone off the hook again and try not to collapse while I wait. I give myself the task of walking a set number of steps forwards and backwards behind the mocking brightness of the blue hall door. I cannot seem to release myself from this lobby with its brass potfuls of mother-in-law's tongue and its solitary lonely ficus.

Eddie has said he will ring the others, and I assume they will come home too. Martin is the only one who might be doubtful. He did not come home last night either. It is possible that, like Eddie, he too now has a girlfriend. One I don't know about yet.

I see a bubble in the blue paint, right under the peephole. Together they are like two eyes on top of one another. A Picasso. The ficus has been overwatered: the edges of some of the leaves are turning brown.

The door opens at just about the time I would have expected Eddie but it turns out not to be Eddie. It is Esmé, whose existence and possible adventures I had wiped from my mind since the departure of the police. She closes the door carefully and turns to me, looking over her glasses. 'Here,' she says. 'You're going to need this.' She holds out a neatly rolled wad of money.

I look at it as though it is a foreign body. 'What—'

'You'll need it,' she repeats, 'so take it.'

I am so stunned I hold out my hand and accept the gift. 'Where did you get it?'

'Never mind that,' she says, but involuntarily her hand touches her throat and I see that she is not

wearing her black pearls. This breaches the dam and
sets me off in floods. 'Please,' says Esmé, an expression
of distaste on her face as she turns to go down to her
room.

The money, when I got round to counting it, came
to two hundred pounds. Not a lot for those pearls. She
had to have gone to the local pawn shop, which, given
Esmé's history and personality, had to have been the
greatest humiliation of her life, and the greatest sacri-
fice she could ever have made for me and for this
family.

They all arrive together. I am still crying, still
standing near the door, when I hear Eddie's key in the
lock. I snatch it open to find on the threshold not only
Eddie but the Ban Ghárda and Zig, plus Father Blaise,
one of the friars from the church across the street. I
also see Con and Frank approaching the house from a
taxi, which is just pulling away. With the door still
open, this friar puts his arms around me and allows me
to weep on the rough brown cloth of his habit. It
smells of old bread and tobacco.

We make an odd, sad procession heading towards
the hospital, the friar and I in the back of the squad
car, with Eddie, Con and Frank following behind in
the Humber. It is still the middle of the afternoon but,
this being Dublin, the traffic through Drumcondra and
Whitehall is very heavy. I notice as we turn into
Collins' Avenue that a circus is setting up on the site
beside Whitehall church. The Big Top is almost
complete.

Along the approach to the hospital, they are building
an extension. The workmen call out to one another,

scratch themselves; one looks at his watch, another drinks deeply from a can of Coca-Cola.

In the hospital itself, visiting time is over, yet in the packed foyer the shop, the coffee shop, the telephone booth and the ATM machine are all very busy and a long queue of people sits in the rows of blue chairs outside the admissions office. I overhear two queuers complaining one to another about the lengthy wait and I am stabbed with the Sitges feeling on that morning when no one except myself knew that the world had stopped turning.

And then I remember something weird. Esmé left for the pawn shop before the Gárdai arrived.

Sixteen

We waited for someone to appear to tell us where CJ was and to take us to him. Outside the hospital's entrance doors, groups of patients in wheelchairs or wearing plaster casts huddled together, pulling the guts out of cigarettes while clutching tightly at the collars of spruce, Paisley-patterned dressing-gowns in a vain attempt to shield themselves from the wind snapping at them from its lair in the Irish Sea.

CJ would smoke no more cigarettes.

I turned away from watching the door and found myself facing the gift shop where people, a mixture of visitors and patients, were buying tubes of Rolos and bottles of Lucozade or browsing through the vapid greetings cards adorned with cartoonish nurses and hangdog patients. On the floor of the shop, an assistant was unfastening bundles of the *Evening Herald*, ripping off the coverings and bindings. Underneath the torn plastic, the headline screamed:

HORRIFIC ACID ATTACK ON
DUBLIN GANG MEMBER

My eyes felt as though they were on pulleys and I followed the pull, taking a step closer. CJ was not named but in the secondary headline I saw the words 'wasteground' and 'Blanchardstown' so I knew. The main text of the article was set around a photograph of a horizontal, sheet-covered mound with a Gárda in attendance. The Gárda was looking away from the camera, out of the photograph. Judging by his body language, he was quite bored.

I stepped closer to read the text but Zig interposed himself between me and the shop, blocking my view. 'Don't pay any attention, Mrs Lanigan.' His tone was urgent but lacked conviction.

I looked at his face, at his moustache, at his eyes, wide with anxiety: 'Acid?' To me, my voice sounded perfectly normal but the next thing of which I was aware was the heavy pressure of someone's hand on the back of my neck and an overall sensation of great physical lassitude as my head hung a few inches above my lap. All around me I heard the low murmur of shocked, yet semi-thrilled voices. Word of my identity and the reason for my visit had spread.

Although my brain had returned to full function, I opened my eyes only a crack and saw the lobby's tiled floor and a segment of blue under my left knee. I had been seated on one of the admissions chairs. A woman's voice – the Ban Ghárda's? – was urgently requesting the presence of a doctor.

I could not bear just yet to face what was to come or to meet any stranger's pitying look so I closed my eyes again and remained limp. But then, behind the lids, I saw the steady, technicolour munch of acid into my son's flesh and it took me all my willpower not to scream. From somewhere I trawled the strength to zap that dreadful image. I forced my screen to replace it with Tracey's red hair, Ambrose's smile, with the little boy who took my beach ball in Sitges. I hammered at those colours. Yellow and blue, blue and yellow, ball tumbling up and over, over, blue sky, yellow sand, blue sea, yellow, blue, yellow . . .

I kept the blue and yellow in place while I allowed my knees to straighten under the urging of several pairs of hands propelling me to my feet. With head bowed, I allowed those feet to move one in front of the other until my ears told me I was in a quiet room away from crowds. It was only then that I yielded and fully opened my eyes.

I was sitting in a swivel chair at a small desk, the veneer of which had peeled away to expose the chip-board underneath. I surveyed: I had been moved to a small storage room, little more than a walk-in cupboard lined with shelves holding reams of paper, file covers, boxes of rubber bands, staples, Bic biros, computer disks, cartons of toilet paper. Eddie, the Ban Ghárda, and a woman wearing a stethoscope over a white coat were crammed together in front of me. The Ban Ghárda was holding my shoulder.

'Are you all right, Ma?' Eddie's anxious eyes were on a level with mine as, squashed in beside the Ban Ghárda, he bent towards me. I nodded.

The door behind the group opened and a small tray was handed in by a disembodied hand. On it was a cup of steaming tea and two Goldgrain biscuits. The doctor took the tray and laid it on the desk in front of me while the door closed again.

No one seemed to know what to do next. I took a small sip of the tea, which in this country is seen as the panacea for all ills, or at least as a limbo inn on the journey to hell. Irrelevantly, I remember *The Kennedys of Castlerosse*, a radio series from my childhood, in which at every new revelation of disaster Mrs Kennedy always said, 'Will you have a cup of tea?'

'Are you sure you're OK?' This was the Ban Ghárda, as much at sea as everyone else. I nodded again and took another sip of the scalding liquid while they watched me as though afraid I was a new and fragile species that might disintegrate if left unattended for a second. 'I left a note for Martin on the kitchen table,' Eddie said, after this pause. 'I also rang the club. He might call in there.'

Silence came down again on the stuffy little room. I could smell Lenor from the Ban Ghárda's shirt while I continued to sip my tea.

'If you're sure you're all right, Mrs Lanigan,' said the doctor then, 'I'd better be getting back. I'll make sure someone calls you when——' She did not, or could not, finish the sentence.

I looked at her properly for the first time. She was very young, bad casting for this job as I probably represented her first encounter with a dead gangster's mother. I tried to smile but the smile would not come.

Ten minutes later, or maybe fifteen, Father Blaise, Zig and the Ban Ghárda were waiting tactfully outside in a corridor while the rest of us sat in a small room off one of the wards. Being no stranger to this hospital because of Johnny's frequent admissions here, I knew it to be one of those used by consultants.

The hospital chaplain came in, whispery as a breeze. He shook our hands, each of us in turn, then turned respectfully to me. 'No hurry in the world on ye, Mrs Lanigan. Stay here as long as ye like,' as though this was a gift from God. His accent was soft, from some mild part of the country. Then, aiming his words largely at Eddie, Con and Frank, he talked in a low, soothing voice. God and His Blessed Mother would see us through this tragedy. We had to have faith. We must not let hope die. He sat behind the consultants' desk, careful not to scrape the legs of the chair: 'Was your son a religious person, Mrs Lanigan?'

I thought of what CJ must look like after a 'horrific acid attack'. I thought of the sneaking fear of him I had harboured in the latter years. But most of all I thought of my own guilt. I looked steadily at the chaplain, the expression on whose round, guileless face showed no trace of fudge or even of the irony inherent in his question. 'Religious? I don't think so,' I said. It came out as a low mumble. 'I have no idea,' I said, in a clearer voice. Out of the blue, I felt strong, in control of my role in this play. I knew my cues and I knew I was playing the lead. The previous weakness, all that crying earlier in the house, was owned by someone other than me.

'We can say a decade of the rosary for him here, if you like.' The chaplain pulled out of his pocket a small brown purse on which was tooled the word 'Lourdes' and unsnapped the clasp.

'No thank you,' I said. 'Perhaps later. I would like to go as soon as possible to see my son.'

The chaplain glanced towards the three boys as though asking for approval, but Eddie was looking at the ground while Con and Frank were gazing at me. The chaplain stood up. 'I'll leave ye for a minute, so, I'll make a telephone call,' he said.

As he left the room, closing the door quietly behind him, I wondered how often he had had to go through these conversations with grieving relatives. Did they become formulaic? Mundane? Even if the loved ones had died in the same manner as CJ?

The window of the consultants' room faced on to the blank wall of another building only feet away, and although it was almost full summer and still only afternoon, the strip-lighting over our heads was necessary to lighten the gloom. The construction jack-hammers outside were muted by the double glazing.

'Ma, you don't have to do this.' It was Con. Con is the tallest of my sons, constitutionally the strongest, I would say. He says very little, which is just as well because Amanda would talk for the Olympics. 'There's no need for you to put yourself through it, we can take care of the – ' he stumbled a little but recovered ' – the identification.' He looked at the other two, who both nodded assent.

'I know I don't have to do this,' I said calmly. 'I want to do this.'

'It might be too—' Eddie got up and stood against the wall. 'Con's right. Why don't you stay here with Father Blaise? We'll go with them and do whatever is necessary. It would be very upsetting for you.'

Frank, a gentle, unmaterialistic soul who, I suspect, will never be able to hold his own in any workplace rat-race, spoke up unexpectedly. 'Let her do it,' he said quietly to the other two. 'If she wants to do it, let her do it. He's her son. She knows what's best for her.'

Eddie and Con turned to stare at him, then exchanged glances. Eddie sat down again. Frank's intervention in any discussion in our house is rare. Perhaps that is why the others do not argue with him.

We sat quietly, waiting for the summons. The boys, who were, no doubt, suffering every bit as much as I was, stared at the dull brown floor. Continuing to feel in control, I picked a spot on the mauve-painted wall and stared at it.

Within five minutes or so, two women and a man came into the room, followed a second or so later by the chaplain. Thinking this was it, I stood up but the man walked straight over to me, shook my hand and introduced himself. (His is one name I cannot remember.)

Before I had realized it, he had taken both my hands in his cool ones. 'Mrs Lanigan,' he said, in the professionally deep tone of the authoritative male physician, 'I wish to offer the most sincere sympathy of myself and my colleagues here in the hospital to you and your family on your sad loss.'

'Thank you,' I said. I waited. My hands felt like dead fish in his. He hesitated a little. 'I understand you wish to see your son.'

I nodded.

'Trust me, Mrs Lanigan,' he said, squeezing a little,

'that would not be a good idea at this point. He has been . . .' As he searched for the right words, he now discovered difficulty in meeting my gaze and looked instead through the window at the dead wall outside. 'He was a fine young man, but he has been somewhat – mutilated. Death would have been quick,' he added swiftly, in a manner that left me in no doubt that this was far from his opinion. 'We all feel,' he continued, 'that it would be better for you and your family to remember him as he was.'

I gazed steadily at him, then looked at his two female colleagues, whose eyes were wide with sympathy but also fascination, as if they were watching a young animal being prepared for slaughter. Behind me, I heard movement amongst my sons.

I took my hands away from the medic's. I felt as though a bar of steel had laid itself across the width of my shoulder-blades. I owed my son a share in his final agony. At least that. 'I want to see him,' I said quietly.

A beat, then the doctor nodded. He turned, and I followed him and his two colleagues out of the room. The chaplain, Father Blaise and the three boys followed on. Zig and the Ban Ghárda followed them. We made quite a procession.

Clem Junior was lying on a hard flat bed in a bare room. He was covered from head to toe with a white sheet.

In fairness to Beaumont Hospital, the atmosphere in the room was peaceful, even reverent. Lit white candles had been placed on both sides of him and someone had put a vase of white carnations and a crucifix on a little table beside his head. 'All his troubles are over,' Father Blaise whispered into my ear. 'Just keep telling yourself that, May. He's with God now.'

I was not thinking of God just then. I was thinking of myself and my darling son who never knew what he had meant to me. Stretched like this on his bier, CJ looked longer than I would have thought he was. I had always pegged him at five feet nine inches but now I would swear he was taller. A lot taller. All mothers faithfully record the statistics of their firstborn children. Here was my firstborn and I did not even know how tall he had been.

I reached out to uncover his face but both Father Blaise and the chaplain, who was standing at my other elbow, simultaneously clutched at my arms. 'Don't, Mrs Lanigan,' said the chaplain. 'Let one of the boys – later—'

I shook off both of them and lifted the sheet.

From behind me, I heard all three boys react at what was revealed. Whoever had laid him out had done his or her best to conceal the full horror of what had happened but despite the dressing stretching from his hairline to his chin, it was obvious that CJ had no face left. The thick white pad was flat, as though adhering to the surface of a table. (I learned subsequently that the acid had dissolved not only all of his features and skin but some of his teeth and had taken the enamel off what was left.) I pulled the sheet down further. Under swollen, intertwined fingers with antiseptically clean nails, CJ's torso was muscular and well shaped, showing all too poignantly the beneficial effects of his health and workout regime in prison. It was also black, with striations of blue and yellow. I had not seen my son's naked breast since he was a child.

'His fingers look peculiar,' I said, staring, as though concentrating on them might remove the implications of the pad above and everything that went with it.

Eddie came forward and took the sheet out of my hands. Gently he covered his brother again while the chaplain started his decade of the rosary. I was aware that Eddie was whispering something to Zig and the Ban Ghárda. Formal identification, I supposed, and instead of saying the rosary, I concentrated on picturing their serious, grave faces. As I stood, hands balled in front of me to keep me steady so as not to attract more unwanted concern and attention, I doubted that I could ever pray again. Maybe my father had had the right idea.

Today, two weeks later, I still bear the stigmata of eight fingernails in my palms.

Zig and the Ban Ghárda must have left before we did without my noticing because they were waiting for us in the foyer of the hospital when we got back there. We had been escorted through a maze of corridors and walkways by one of the medic's female colleagues, the woman who had brought us to CJ's room. She shook hands with us, all of us, formally one by one, and before she left us I heard Eddie tell her that we would be in touch about arrangements.

Arrangements. Such a gay word for such a meaning. So unfit for its purpose.

Dirge, bury, burn, cremate, shovel, clay, dust, maggot, grave, worms, ash, coffin, hearse. These are much better words. Much less euphonious, much more suitable. Much more honest.

Zig and the Ban Ghárda came forward. 'Are you ready to go home, Mrs Lanigan?' he asked. 'We have the car right outside.' The palms of my hands had been stinging fiercely since I had unballed them. 'What are you going to do about the death of my son?' I asked him.

'We will treat this murder as we would treat any murder, Mrs Lanigan. Just the same. We will work just as hard to catch the perpetrators as we would if—'

'If he wasn't a pariah?' I asked. But then I looked into his eyes and saw kindness. 'I'm sorry,' I said.

'I know how you feel.' He glanced around at us all. 'And I do promise we will find out who did this. What's more, I promise we will keep you informed.'

At this stage, I might as well tell you what 'this' was.

When he was found, all of my son's fingers and thumbs were broken, as were his ankles, knees, pelvis, collarbone and seven of his ribs. His smashed hands had been tied behind his back and trussed with another rope to the one tying his shattered legs together – tightly at the broken knees to cause maximum pain. A plastic bag had been placed over his head and his acid-covered face. This plastic bag, a strong green one from Marks and Spencer, had been tied around his neck so the acid could efficiently do its work before most of the front of the bag that covered the face itself dissolved. It had not been so tightly tied, however, that CJ had smothered too quickly.

Because, of course, it is in general circulation that my son was a snitch, it is the opinion of the authorities that, given the method, this murder was specifically designed to act as a warning to others.

'This' I found out in dribs and drabs. I learned some of it from Eddie, whom I badgered and badgered until one evening after the funeral he broke down and told me everything he knew. I learned more from newspapers that proclaimed the details of the killing to be too shocking to print and then nevertheless went on graphically to print them. I found a pile of papers in Martin's room and could not stop myself reading them.

I learned more again from Zig, who is being true to his word and is keeping me informed of progress in the investigation. There will be an inquest but that will not happen for months, maybe even a year. The investigation so far has not turned up much. I do not find this surprising, despite Zig's assurances that they are 'pulling out all the stops'.

That first day, 3 May, I declined the offer of the lift home from Beaumont in the squad car, although I was not rude about it and thanked both Zig and the Ban Ghárda for their consideration and attention. So Eddie drove the five of us, including Father Blaise, in the Humber.

The reporter waiting for us on the doorstep was so young that I almost felt sorry for him. It might even have been his first assignment of this nature because he stumbled and stuttered and fell over what was obviously a prepared speech, requesting a recent photograph of CJ and a few words of reaction from myself.

Sympathetic as I was to him personally, however, I found his presence outrageously distasteful so I walked into the house with Father Blaise without saying a word to him in reply, leaving the three boys to deal with him as they saw fit.

Eddie's note to Martin lay untouched on the kitchen table. That brought Johnny to mind. Who was going to break the news to Johnny and how would he react?

Since this was only Wednesday, we had a few days to consider the problem. The removal to the church would obviously take place on the following night with the funeral on the Friday morning. That would be the norm. CJ would be safely disposed of before Saturday and Johnny's next visit home. With scant discussion, we all accepted that to expose him to the funeral would be unthinkable.

'Arrangements' are a great distraction. Eddie got busy on the telephone – to the undertaker, to Glasnevin cemetery – and proved what I have always suspected, that Ireland is a great country in which to die. The condolences to the bereft, even from undertakers and those officially set to profit from death – even where the deceased has been vilified by being publicly placed in a 'Dublin Gang' – do seem sincere.

A few of the old-timers amongst the neighbours had begun to call at the door. CJ's death, while in no way eradicating the opprobrium of his life, was nevertheless deemed worthy of the common courtesies, although at arm's length. None of these neighbours would come across the threshold for the traditional drink. Their sympathizing, however, appeared to be heartfelt.

The long-distance telephone operators at the Irish

exchange could not have been more compassionately helpful either, and within twenty minutes of first enquiry, Clem was at the other end of the line from somewhere within his Barcelona gaol.

'Will you speak to him, Ma?' Eddie held the receiver out to me.

I shook my head.

Abruptly I could not bear to be in the room while Clem was given the news. I left to go down to my bedroom, where I lay on the four-poster and closed my eyes. Instantly I saw that thick white pad, flat as a plank. I opened them again to stare at the underside of the drapes above the bed. Quickly, panicked, I employed the blue and yellow technique. Blue/yellow/blue/yellow, flashing on and off like neon and over-powering everything else.

'He wants to talk to you.' Eddie was at the door.

'Tell him I don't want to talk to him.' I continued to stare upwards.

'Ma—' I looked towards the door. There was no mistaking the desperation and misery in Eddie's eyes and I was left with no choice. 'All right.' I rolled over and picked up the extension on the bedside table. I noticed on the clock beside the telephone that it was now ten minutes to six.

Clem was weeping. Openly. Great mucus-filled sobs rolling across the telephone wires or satellites or whatever carries voices from Spain.

I tested myself. No. No answering emotions. At present I could not even scrabble for residual anger. I waited until he gained a semblance of control. 'I'm here, Clem,' I said.

That started him off again. I waited. Eventually he calmed down enough to ask about the arrangements. 'The removal is tomorrow evening,' I told him calmly. 'The funeral is on Friday morning.'

'You'll have to hold it. I want to be there.'

'That's up to you, Clem,' I said. 'We can't wait. It's up to you to get here in time. It's your problem.'

The hint of a fight restored Clem's spunk. He began to mouth a stream of obscenities and invective. I was not only an informer – because how else had he been caught – but I was every self-centred, selfish and foul female epithet you have ever heard. Call myself a mother? What kind of a bitch mother would deprive a son of his father at a funeral? Call myself a woman? A lump of lard, no, hog suet, had more sex appeal in it than I had – no wonder Clem had fallen in love with someone else, the soles of whose feet I was not fit to lick. Clem thanked God he had managed to find someone who treated him properly and with whom he could have fun. 'F-U-N, you pig bitch – nothing you'd know anything about . . .'

And more.

I waited until he drew breath and said, 'I'll see you if I see you,' and cut the connection. I tested. Nothing. No hurt. No rage. Nothing.

Nor did I react as I heard the police come to search through CJ's possessions.

The police had left when a distraught Martin, clutching a copy of the *Evening Herald*, tumbled through the door about four hours after we got home from Beaumont. Father Blaise had gone back to his friary across the road, having begun making whatever 'arrangements' were necessary with Eddie, Con and Frank. They had tried to glean my wishes but it was a matter of unconcern to me and I refused to participate. My ruined son could not be restored to me by all the arrangements known to man and no undertaker, no matter how skilled, could again make whole even his corpse.

Meanwhile the two wives had arrived to be with Con and Frank, so the kitchen was full when Martin burst in. He was unable to speak and crumbled as soon as he saw us all. I stood up from where I had been sitting at the kitchen table and put my arms around him, held him as I used to hold him when he was small and had skinned a knee or was reporting some dreadful injustice suffered in the street. He shook and trembled in my arms but no responding tears would come for me. My heart had withered so it banged against my ribs with the hardness of a very old conker.

Looking back on that whole day now, I think I must have been a little deranged. I know that on the surface I appeared to be behaving rationally, to be categorizing tasks in order of priority as though I were simply making a shopping list. In reality, my brain was travelling along a loop. Since lifting that sheet, all I could see now was that thick white pad. All that inhabited my imagination was what lay underneath. Yet my mouth responded to queries, my feet placed themselves one in front of the other if I wanted to walk from A to B. I had held my cool with Clem. It was all most strange. And the tears I had shed earlier appeared to have emptied the reservoir.

I could hold Martin and soothe him without becom-

ing overtly upset; over his heaving shoulders, I could
even survey the devastation in my kitchen as my other
three sons and my two daughters-in-law all exhibited
varying degrees of distress. There was Esmé, as straight
as ever, but unusually having claimed possession of one
of the fireside chairs. There sounded the telephone,
taken off the hook because of the media calls, moaning
to itself at the end of its curly flex. Over there were
the twin hearts of the kitchen – the table wiped too
clean and the sink too tidy because everyone wanted
everything to proceed as normal, the bottles of whiskey
and brandy standing on the draining-board ready for
visitors, of whom there had been none who had so far
dared to step inside our tainted door.

Discounting Clem, these, then, were my son's
mourners, this small group in this kitchen, to be
augmented possibly by a few of the wives' relatives.
Maybe Tracey, if she could stomach it and if Eddie did
not want to protect her from the excesses of this
family, maybe some of the more charitable neighbours,
who would pay their respects for my sake. Perhaps
also one or two of the priests from the church across
the road, who would undoubtedly have posited to
one another in discussion over their evening meal that
to attend a murdered criminal's funeral had to be an
integral part of a vocation.

I tried to imagine how Johnny would react. I saw
the image of his two Beanie Babies, one clutched in
each of his too-large, uncoordinated hands, and hoped
they could be of comfort to him now.

Where was Ambrose now with his jokes, his philos-
ophizing discourses and his *bons mots*?

Silently but with great dedication, I held my sobbing son and cursed Ambrose and his ilk. I cursed the God that had fooled me into His fold. But, most of all, I cursed myself for failing my son.

→ Seventeen ←

I had another of those dreams that night, similar to the one I had on the sleeper train to Barcelona. It was all there, blue sky, white clouds, the field of daisies, the feeling of airiness, light and freedom, the premonitory scent of Ambrose and then the approach of Ambrose himself. His words to me were the same as before: *This is happiness, May, this is how you should feel all the time* . . .

The bedside clock said ten minutes past six when I woke. Reluctant to let go, basking in the warm, ethereal territory midway between sleep and life, I continued deliberately to savour the fronds of the dream. Gradually, I realized that some of it, at least, had not been a dream. Ambrose's scent was all over the room. I sat up. He was nowhere to be seen.

Indolence and relaxation were snuffed out to be replaced by fury. I remembered Clem Junior, lying alone and destroyed on his hospital pallet. I remembered the prospects for the day ahead. I remembered that Ambrose was cursed and put from me.

He could not get away with this. I shot out of bed and stood firmly in the centre of the room. 'Where

are you?' I spat at the empty air. 'Where were you
yesterday? How could you let me go through all of this
by myself? And how could you let this happen in the
first place? Where were you when they prepared hell
for my son? When they gathered the ropes and ham-
mers and acid?'

I waited, but although the scent remained strong, he
did not materialize and I felt not only angry but foolish
to boot. I debated for a moment or two whether to go
back to bed but knew I wouldn't sleep. I threw on my
dressing-gown and went down to the kitchen.

Martin was sitting miserably at the bare table, his
burly frame slumped. It would have been fatuous to
ask him what was wrong so instead I offered to make
tea.

'You know I'm not in on this, Ma?' We were both
sitting at the table a few minutes later. I had made
toast as well as the tea but the plate lay untouched
between us. Martin had not got undressed and his chin
was stubbled. He might not have been to bed at all.

My thoughts had been miles away and he saw my
incomprehension. 'All right,' he said, by way of expla-
nation. 'I do know a few people, you can't avoid that
in the club business, but that's all. I just know them.
The only illegal thing I ever did in my life was to
organize that passport for you.'

'Why are you telling me this? I didn't for a moment
think—'

'I just don't want you to think that we're all like
him.' To my distress, he burst into tears as he had the
day before.

There was little I could do or say to comfort him

and, instinctively, I felt it would not be apt to put my arms around him this time. So, to let him know I was there, I merely rested a hand on his arm and let him cry.

I was the one who should have been storming the world with tears. His served to prove not only his desolation but my shame – that again I had taken my eye off the ball in relation to my sons. Or, to put a more kindly construction on it, that I had taken too literally the wisdom that mothers should let go of their children.

To take a small example: when Eddie asked me if he should set up some music for the funeral Mass, I could not answer. I had no idea what Clem Junior might have liked. (It was scant comfort to know that I was not alone in this: none of us knew what CJ's musical tastes had run to, and since his CDs had all been taken away by the police, we could not even check those.)

As for Martin, weeping salt tears at my kitchen table, if you had asked me the day before yesterday to describe him, I would have told you that he was probably the happiest of us all, a carefree, somewhat superficial sort who never let the world get him down and who thoroughly enjoyed his job and gadding with night-town companions in Temple Bar. 'Martin?' I would have snorted cheerily. 'What makes you think I know anything about Martin? I know he's supposed to be living here, but sure we never see Martin – Martin's too busy gallivanting and having a good time.'

Yet while all the others seemed to be coping well enough, he was the one sobbing like a two-year-old about the death of a brother who had bullied him. I squeezed his arm then got up from the table and fetched a wad of kitchen roll. 'Here,' I said, 'use this when you're ready.'

'Thanks,' he said, and taking the paper, blew his nose. 'Sorry,' he said then, 'I just can't seem to stop.'

He calmed down and we drank our tea.

He took a piece of toast. 'You do believe me? That I have nothing to do with – with—' he gestured towards the *Evening Herald*, folded neatly on top of the wooden box I use to store kitchen odds and bobs.

'Of course I do,' I said. Then something occurred to me: 'But you did know how to get that passport for me, Marty.'

He threw the half-eaten piece of toast back on the plate. 'Do you want to know how I got it?'

Instantly I decided it would be better if I did not know. What was done was done. He watched me. Then: 'All right. You hear things, Ma, late at night in those clubs. People get to know you and trust you so you'd always know when and how to drop the right word if it was necessary. But that's not like – like being in a gang, or being a scumbag myself.' The tears threatened again and it was perhaps only then I truly discovered what a heavy burden Clem – and I with my ignorance and collusion, whether deliberate or unwitting makes no difference – had placed upon our boys' shoulders. 'I'm truly sorry, Martin,' I said.

'What are you sorry for?' He was astonished.

'I'm sorry for the life you have had to live with us. I'm sorry I didn't mind you properly, not only you but all of you. I'm sorry that I didn't protect you from the way your da chose to live his life. I'm sorry I was so blind. And I'm also sorry about all the secrecy between us in this house. Maybe if we'd talked more openly to one another from the very beginning we wouldn't be in this situation now.'

'Did you really not know?' Incredulity had dried his tears.

I shook my head. 'I've been examining my conscience about that. I can't understand why I didn't know. Maybe I just didn't want to know.'

'I thought – I really thought – that's why I never said anything about it.'

'You were aware of what was going on?'

'I told you, you get to hear things in my line of work. I was sure you were just being loyal.'

'That too, maybe.' I thought hard in order to be truthful. 'Although not really, Marty, because, hand on my heart, I genuinely did not know about Clem. If I had known the extent of what was going on, don't you think I would have intervened earlier? Look what's happened to poor CJ. CJ has paid for us all.' The enormity of that thought, the (misplaced) biblical echoes, silenced us both. I could not bear to go down that route. Contemplation of Clem Junior in his present state needed to be performed alone.

'Will you believe one thing, Marty?' I said to him, after I rose from the table to go back to my room. 'Will you believe me when I say that I did my very best?'

I knew it was craven and he reacted with appropriate embarrassment – none of us is noted for talking openly about our feelings – but he overcame his discomfort. 'I won't let you say that, Ma. You did more than your best. None of us think that you . . .' He frowned. Then, in a rush: 'We all think you're a topper. Especially the way you've handled – well – I mean . . .'

He stopped, averted his gaze towards the sodden paper towels in his hands and then went on bravely but in a low voice: 'We all know what's been going on in Spain.'

I goggled at him.

'I'd like to kill him, I really would.' He said it quietly, almost as though he was considering a career option.

'No, no, please, you wouldn't, don't say that,' I begged. 'Whatever you think, whatever you've heard, he's still your father, Marty.'

'Yeah.'

I went back to stand in front of him but he would no longer meet my eyes. 'Marty, look at me.' He raised his face. 'You're a good lad – I don't know how some things happened, how I let things get away from me so badly, but you're a good lad. Please stay that way.' His tears came again and I had to get out of the kitchen immediately before I became as bad as he.

If I had it to do all over again, would I have been on Clem's case? I doubt it. On one occasion, only one and very early on in our marriage, I went down to the docks to see the place he and Tony Malone had rented to store the goods they imported, but once was enough. The cavernous warehouse was a bleak, leaking place where the wind whistled through gaps in the roof and where furtive flutterings and scrabblings among the

stacked pallets and boxes made me jump. I couldn't
wait to get back to my bright, warm, comfortable
domain and ever after, as I've said, was happy that our
responsibilities were allocated as they were. None so
blind as those who do not want to see.

The day was filled with comings and goings, mostly
by the boys. If we had been under any illusions about
our position in society, we were left in no doubt now.
Normally, when a death occurs in an Irish family, the
house bulges with people, the tables groan with food
and drink brought in by friends and neighbours. Ours
echoed to our own quiet footsteps and the only food
on our table was supplied by ourselves.

By the time we got back up to Beaumont for the
removal, I was so strung out and tired that the dash-
board of the funeral car seemed to waver, like the
screen of a cheap television, as I stared at it over
the shoulder of the uniformed driver. None of us spoke
and I was struggling hard to acknowledge the reality of
where we were going and why. It was raining hard and
my battle to stay grounded was not helped by the
hypnotic to and fro of the car's wipers. Pathetic fallacy.
Pathetic, all right.

There is a huge sense of unreality about removals in
any case. The deceased, wearing Sunday best and
beautifully knotted tie, lies still and waxy in a hugely
incongruous frill of white satin while, all around,
groups of people stare at him and remark on how very
lifelike and peaceful he seems.

How much more unreal would this removal be?
Where would we find the words to compliment Clem

Junior and the work of those who did him his last service?

Yet in many ways I had no one but myself to blame that I had to face CJ's ravaged body again. I could have specified a closed coffin and, as it happened, I would have got it automatically, if it had not been for Martin.

Despite my warning him not to, Martin had gone up to the hospital shortly after lunch-time. He had insisted on seeing his brother for himself and was just in time to prevent the undertakers, who had already coffined CJ, from screwing down the cover. Correctly Martin knew that I would not want to go up there merely to touch a coffin lid as if what was inside was not flesh of my flesh. CJ's agony had been my agony. I had to see it through and Martin, sensitive enough to know this, intervened and stopped the process.

But where on his face would I kiss this faceless son goodbye? My throat strangled itself with grim antici-pation as we pulled into the car park beside the mortuary chapel, our puny, two-car cortège lost in the space allotted for the friends and family of those deceased whose passing was cause for more popular mourning. Seeing the acre of rain-lashed concrete, I regretted not ordering two funeral limousines instead of the one, in which we were so tightly packed that I could smell lavender from Esmé's black toque. She secretes scented soap as well as sachets of pot-pourri in her wardrobe and all her drawers.

Our second car was small and eight years old, a Ford Escort, driven by Con's Amanda, with her parents and Sharon as passengers. Sharon's mother is dead and her father had announced he would have nothing to do with her scumbag brother-in-law's funeral. Another one down.

I have been struck before by the pecking order of death. Across the road, in Church Street, you can have a funeral that will cause traffic chaos after ten o'clock Mass, but then at half past eleven some indigent or elderly bachelor might be hurried up the road towards Glasnevin, attended by only a battered Micra driven by a social worker who is giving the presiding monk a lift.

The rain continued to bounce off the car park and to beat at the bonnet and windscreen as the driver stopped his vehicle as close as he could to the dreadful glass doors. I wanted to scream at him, 'Not yet! Not yet!' but he sprang to open the door for me and unfurled an enormous black umbrella in the gap between the door and the car. He was getting soaked so I had no option but to step outside the warm cocoon. For myself I could not have cared less whether or not I got wet but, oddly, I was suddenly grateful for the gesture, for CJ's sake. For his sake I would arrive tidy and dry. For this one last occasion, I wanted my son to be proud of me.

Father Blaise and the hospital chaplain were waiting to greet us inside the dimly lit chapel of rest where, like a reproach, trebled rows of empty chairs made a horseshoe around three of the four walls. Yet as I shook Father Blaise's hand, all I could look at was that thick, sightless visor, whiter than the cheap, encircling satin – so luminously white in the semi-dark that it seemed to rise and hover like an ascending moon.

Marooned in this glowering sea of vacancy, Clem

Junior, docile at last, lay groomed and waiting to say goodbye to me.

The power of the mind is extraordinary, because when I went to stand beside the coffin, I discovered I had not seen any pad. The undertakers had pulled the satin lining closed over CJ's body and head so none of him was visible.

No one stopped me as I gently parted the frills and exposed him again.

I was aware of Father Blaise and the chaplain whispering urgently behind my back and then of the pressure of Eddie's hand on my arm. 'They want to know if we should go ahead, Ma.' I did not take my eyes off my son. 'He's dressed in a suit,' I said to Eddie. 'Did CJ have a suit?'

'We bought it today, Ma.' Eddie's voice was low. 'We all clubbed together.'

'How did you know his size?'

Eddie did not answer. The question was irrelevant anyway. What did it matter if the suit fitted or not? It had been bought merely to quicken the flames, which tomorrow would consume CJ's sturdy body. I touched the navy lapels. The cloth was smooth and substantial. A good suit. The tie was dark blue. Probably chosen to go with CJ's eyes. Ex-eyes. Former eyes. Missing eyes. Absent eyes. Blanched eyes. Under the lapels the flesh was solid. You never know the feeling of warm, living skin until you have touched what has died. You can feel the block-like inertia, even through two layers of suit and shirt.

I kept my hand on CJ. I wanted a miracle, one more chance. Just one more chance. The phrase screamed

like a cyclone around my heart. Just one chance to say,
I love you, CJ. Words I had never uttered since he was
old enough to understand them.

Behind me I heard Father Blaise start the recita-
tion of the rosary. I stroked what was left of CJ's hair
above his suffocating visor as my sons, Amanda, her
parents and Sharon joined in. The Glorious Mysteries,
of course, the customary choice to 'celebrate' death,
for reasons I have always felt were inappropriate.
Smelling destruction, imagining the leaking already
taking place into that flimsy white satin, I was not
ready for resurrections, ascensions, assumptions or
heavenly crownings. I looked at my dead, ravaged,
decaying son, leaned nearer and talked to him from my
heart. Like I had told Martin much earlier that day, I
told him again how sorry I was for losing him.

'You're so religious, Ma,' one of my sons had said
to me recently, I have forgotten who. To address CJ, I
had now to dig very deeply into the dregs of belief that
there might be some element of him left that might
somehow hear me.

And forgive me.

'Help me, CJ,' I begged, 'help me.' I repeated it
many times until, behind me, the official prayers
finished and I heard the rustle of sleeves as the tiny
congregation made the collective Sign of the Cross.

Then descended that awful hiatus when none of the
mourners want to make the first move while everyone
knows that a move has to be made and the undertakers
want to get on to the next business. Stubbornly I kept
my eyes fixed on CJ's suit, my hand on his poll, which
was the only part of his head accessible to me. I was

still not ready for the end. Under my fingers, the combed hair was soft. CJ had always been proud of his thick, glossy hair and wore it unfashionably long. By contrast, a few matted tufts of half-inch stubble had escaped from where the visor covered the hairline.

Father Blaise came alongside me. 'God bless him, May,' he said quietly. 'God be good to you all.'

'Thank you, Father,' I said. I knew by the pressure of his hand that he was trying to move me. It was time.

One by one our small group came to touch CJ to say goodbye while Father Blaise held me tightly against his aromatic habit. When it was finally my turn, I said to them that I wanted to be on my own for a moment. Eddie was reluctant to leave me but I insisted.

When we were finally alone, I bent to kiss the top of CJ's head and wound my hands around his broken ones. Then, tenderly, I drew the satin close around him and tucked him in as I used to do when he was a little boy. 'Don't forget me, CJ,' I whispered to him. 'I won't forget you.'

Then the numbness lifted and the tears came, huge, flooding, engulfing tears. Eddie and Martin, who had been watching me through the glass doors, came quickly in and took me outside so the undertakers could do their business.

The ceremony at the church was mercifully brief, largely because the only augmentations to our original group were two additional priests from the friary and – surprisingly – Zig and the Ban Ghárda.

That night, I could not sleep. How could I when he was over there, cold, waiting in the wings of a side

altar for his obligatory centre stage appearance at the
Mass the following morning? How could I close my
eyes when they would never see him again?

Panicking, I changed my mind about cremation. I
wanted to have a grave on which to plant daffodils,
somewhere to visit, to talk to him – but it was four
o'clock in the morning by then and I could not in all
conscience go around waking people.

By breakfast time, I had sunk again into torpor, too
exhausted to make any fuss about anything.

The boys had consulted me about readings. I would
have nothing to do with choosing. As words of comfort
or inspiration they were immaterial to CJ and therefore
immaterial to me.

I did rouse myself to try to look nice. Sharon and
Amanda came early to the house. Sharon blow-dried
my hair for me and Amanda lent me a lovely black
jacket, which fitted me perfectly and went well with a
white blouse and black skirt I already owned. She had
also brought me a new pair of dark tights, had polished
my good shoes and sorted through my jewellery box
to select a pair of earrings and a brooch. When the
two of them were finished with me, they stood me in
front of the full-length mirror in the bedroom. Amanda
came to stand behind me with her hands on my
shoulders. 'You look really well, Ma,' she said softly,
as though I was a bride. Then Sharon, God love her,
gave me an amethyst to put into my handbag. 'It's for
healing, Ma, it'll help you get through the day.'

I gazed at our group in the mirror, two lovely young
women, full of life and vigour behind some faded,
exhausted woman I did not know, some suffering,

ageing lady who was trying to put a brave face on her situation. But they had done their best for me and I thanked them for it as I turned away.

So what about the outrageous, glaring fact that CJ was a criminal who had lost his life in the course of a huge robbery and who had spent most of his last years trying to defraud and steal from upright and innocent citizens? An eye for an eye, eh? He who lives by the sword?

If that is what you think, I will not bother to explain myself further. It is a very simple equation. I am his mother. He is my son.

When I entered the cool church a little before ten o'clock that morning, I saw that our crowd had swelled, by nine people to be precise, including two nuns. There were even four Mass cards on the surface of the coffin – from Joan and Tony, from the hospital, from my workshop group and, most surprisingly of all, from two people called Finn O'Loughlin and Jacqueline Sinnott. I wondered for a moment as I read it if this card had been placed on the wrong coffin but then I saw Zig and the Ban Ghárda gazing up at me from a position in the second pew between Joe Rooney and Emily on one side and Tony and Joan on the other. For a moment my suspicious mind went into overdrive but then I saw that the Ban Ghárda was not in uniform and that Zig was wearing a dark suit and black tie. They seemed to be here genuinely to pay their respects.

Giving them names had also humanized them – although Zig looked far from a 'Finn' to me. His mother had been a little optimistic in calling him after the giant warrior-hero of Irish folklore. I smiled an acknowledgement at them and whereas 'Finn' dropped his eyes, the Ban Ghárda smiled tentatively in response.

Before going to join my sons and Esmé in my place of honour – or notoriety – in the front pew on the right-hand side of the aisle, I went and shook hands with all of them, including the two nuns who sat alone and a little apart, and who, whispering their condolences to me, confirmed they had come from Beaumont. And I was glad, for Eddie's sake, to see that Tracey was there. I was instantly conscious that this would have been her first introduction to our family at large and I hoped she would not judge us as outsiders did.

So that was us all. Not a great turn-out to pay respect to a young man's life, I think you will agree. My disappointment caught me unawares. I see now that I had been hoping at a very deep level that people – for instance, some of Clem's brothers – allowing that even Jesus Christ might not have died as painfully as our son, might have overcome their prejudices for this one day. That shows how naïve I can be. In fairness, most of Clem's brothers have scattered away from Ireland but as far as I can gather, those who stayed, all law-abiding citizens, have disowned him since the trial.

Even before it, those nine boys had very little contact with each other. We used to see one or two of them at funerals and, given the lack of relatives in the senior range, there hasn't been a funeral in this family on either side since Da died.

Until now.

I tried to pay attention to the homily. Poor Father Blaise did his best but he was really struggling. The bit about Jesus preparing a place in paradise for CJ got stuck in his throat, I thought, but maybe I was just being ultra-sensitive.

Exploding my theory about pathetic fallacy, we found when we came out after the Mass that the day of CJ's funeral had turned into a pet, lifting the gloom and settling over Dublin like a warming, flowery blouse. In the sooty trees, birds sang as though obliged to cram every note as quickly as possible into this one day. The fruit market stevedores, whistling, wore only T-shirts as they buzzed about on their forklifts unloading pallets from the huge containers. 'It's going to be a scorcher, I hear it's going to last,' they called to one another, expressing the annual, age-old hope of every Irish person at the beginning of every summer.

I concentrated on detail, even trivial detail: the Tayto crisp bag under the wheel of the hearse, the horse dung flattened on the road by the passage of many tyres, the sparkle of a piece of broken glass in the gutter — anything but the big picture of what we were doing and where we were bound. This is a feature of funerals, I think, this crystallization of memory. For years after the huge funeral for my da, I had remembered every face in the crowd.

As we pulled away from the kerb outside the church, I saw that we were back to our original two-car group of last night. After shaking our hands and being suitably nice, eight of our nine augmentees had gone home to resume their own unruffled lives. Joan had tears in her eyes as she approached me. Probably for Melanie, I thought, even as I accepted her sympathy and thanked her for her Mass card.

I do not mean to sound bitter. Least of all against those who actually overcame what were undoubtedly their own misgivings to come in the first place.

I had to feel something, anything to stave off the issues raised by this journey, to play for a little time.

I achieved no delay, however. As a matter of fact, the hearse driver proceeded with barely concealed haste, even going through an amber light and leaving us in the following funeral car stranded at the red. He had let slip that he had two more funerals after ours.

We caught up with CJ at Phibsboro shopping centre where people were shopping, returning videos, taking money from the ATM machine, even laughing over the Tesco shopping trolleys. And, of course, the lights at Connaught Street were with us. So were the lights at Whitworth Road.

Even the roadway along the empty bus lane at Glasnevin cemetery, clogged with a nose-to-tail snake of cars and articulated trucks, refused to offer respite to our inexorable advance and the line willingly – too willingly – breached itself, allowing our pathetic May procession to turn without pause through the iron gates, as dreadful to me at this moment as those of Auschwitz must have seemed to the Jews and gypsies alighting from their cattle cars.

Then a hitch. A mix-up in slots. Two hearses wrangling for pole position at the door of the crematorium chapel. Two groups of puzzled mourners – ours vastly outnumbered – two negotiating priests, two hearse drivers pulling out mobile phones and punching buttons. Two helpers opening the two hearse tailgates and wheeling out two gurneys to the start line so that whoever won this race was facilitated with speedy delivery to the funeral flames. Then a third group, chatting and laughing in the temporary release after the completion of their ceremony, came round the side of the chapel and got caught up in the mêlée.

I became aware of a commotion at the iron gates behind us. Of voices raised. I shaded my eyes against the sun. A suitcase on the ground. A duty-free plastic bag. Clem was arguing with two large men. I could hear him yelling at them to remove his fucking handcuffs.

✦ Eighteen ✦

We won.

Now that it is more than two weeks later, believe it or not I can see the funny side of that scene. Up to and including the time when Clem puffed up the short aisle of the little chapel, a chimpanzee between two gorilla minders, it was slapstick. It was not funny then, of course, it was simply what was going on around me.

I would have accepted anything that happened. That was me standing there in the sunshine. That was me holding my hand to my forehead, looking at the gate and at my furious, gesticulating husband. Those were my muscles propping up my upright skeleton, but I could have been as dead as CJ.

Without my noticing, the coffin started to move and I found myself being ushered after it by one of the obsequious officials: he might have been a cleric, he might have been one of the undertakers, I have no idea which dark-clad person was bowing in my direction with one arm outstretched towards the gurney and the shadows in the crematorium chapel door. Eddie took my arm but as we moved in out of the sunshine, this feeling of objective dislocation persisted. I remember thinking how frustrated the funeral-goers on the losing side must feel and that maybe what swung it for us was the fact that our group was so much smaller and therefore able to file in and out of the chapel quicker than they could. Efficiency. Throughput. I envied them. I wanted to be on the losing side.

Without remembering how I got there, I found myself at the top of the short aisle. My hand was on the end of CJ's moving coffin. It stopped, I stopped. I was aware of gentle pressure as Eddie tried to usher me into the pew. But I didn't want to take my hand away from that wood. My last physical contact. It felt warm, very smooth under my fingers.

Ma, Eddie's whisper was urgent. Stubbornly, I would not remove my hand. Ma, please . . .

Now I'm on the inside of the top right-hand pew of the little chapel, staring at the coffin's brass handles which, I subsequently discovered, are not true brass at all but a sort of plastic. So they would melt, I suppose. Coffins for combustion are specialized – did you know that? Made of inferior materials. This is why they are cheaper.

And, of course, you know that death is actually what life is all about. Life is a preparation for it. It might sound trite but when you work out these things for yourself, through your own experience, they do not feel like clichés.

It's a small, businesslike place, this chapel: no one can be in any doubt as to why we're here. No trimmings. No messing. In the small pew, Eddie is on one side of me, Martin on the other; Con and Frank are outside them, so there is no room for Clem and his two gorillas. They are across the aisle and for that I am grateful.

That is the only thought I give to Clem. He matters less to me than the small brown moth that flutters in the sunlight above Father Blaise's head.

Because, as yet another set of prayers wafts over my own head, I am not listening to the murmurs: for the first time, I am discovering and acknowledging the hatred that stirs towards the people who did this to my son. It is a different hatred from the clean, clear hatred I had felt towards Melanie. This is muddy, murky, swirling stuff, full of sickness and ambivalent feelings.

Had they known that CJ was only twenty-five years old? Did they know about his beautiful, muscled body, which up to three days ago was not marred by even an appendectomy scar?

Do I want them to die the way they had forced CJ to die? Maybe I do. Would I be glad to attend their hangings – to watch them dangling at the ends of ropes on a public gallows while I jeer? Probably not.

So what do I want? Lethal injections, quick and relatively painless? No – but what does 'no' mean in this context? Not painless? Or no injections?

While I am thus locked in debate, Clem Junior slides away from me. Only a quake of the small red curtains at the end of the coffin runners marks the fact that my son has gone for ever. How did he go so silently?

Instantly, I care nothing about his murderers. My sights lower. I no longer beg for the miracle of Lazarus. All I want now is a return of the feeling of his coffin wood under my fingertips. All I need is one minute. No – one second will do. One more touch. Please.

He had died without a priest. Was he bound for hell?

I hear my father's voice. There's no such thing as hell. Hell is mumbo-jumbo – it's all mumbo-jumbo to keep the working class in their proper place. I am too panicked to follow the line to the end. Instead, I beseech God, I ask my mother to intercede: Please, Mammy, please, if you love me at all, I'll ask only this one thing, just this one thing, please, I'll never ask for anything else, I want CJ back, just for a minute, there's something I have to say to him.

I must have made some sound because my arm is grabbed tightly by Eddie. I turn to him and see the tears sliding down his cheeks. Selfishly, I have forgotten that I am not the only one bereaved. Shocked, I turn back to Father Blaise, but he has already taken off his stole, he is kissing it, folding it. Behind me, through the main entrance, some of the next group, the losers, are filing in. Clem's gorillas are making movements.

I hear the song of a blackbird. Our undertaker has ceremoniously thrown open the chapel's side doors, leaving us in no doubt but that we must leave. This time through the tradesmen's entrance. CJ is yesterday's business.

Here is another cliché for you, but newly minted for me. Grief is intensified when the relationship with the deceased has been less than perfect. The best way I can describe it for you is to ask you to imagine grief as a ploughed field. Normal grief rests quietly in the furrows. My kind of grief is bared on the stony ridges, each shameful imperfection shown in high relief by the blinding, unforgiving sun.

As he is led out, Clem throws us a glance over his shoulder and smiles a wan smile, not aimed at me, I would say, but at his sons. I cannot begin to imagine what he is or was feeling. We had not spoken a word to one another but I can see he is shattered, a parody of the jaunty Euro-man I had seen on that promenade in Sitges. Even the dyed, closely cropped hair, which I had quite liked on first sight, has become in the intervening weeks a skewbald travesty.

My sons, of course, probably feel for him. So I try for my sons' sake to find some residual spark of kindness but every generous impulse seems to have been leached away. At the risk of again showing myself up as a bitch, I have to say that I see him not as a sad, sorrowing father but as a zoo exhibit.

So quickly. I am ashamed of this coldness. Clem Lanigan was my husband for twenty-seven years after all. But now, within a period of just six weeks or so, I have to pinch myself to remember the good.

Perhaps this is just an interim situation.

Just outside the crematorium chapel is a stone dais where the flowers are laid. The crowds before us had had popular corpses, who attracted heaps of tributes, including a very large one in red and white roses spelling the word 'Grandad'.

No such honour for CJ. What would his have spelled? 'Scumbag'?

I had been vaguely aware of a debate about flowers amongst the boys but they must have decided against them because my single rose is CJ's only memorial. I am taking it home with me because it lay on his coffin. Something of him might have risen through that cheap roof of wood to cling to the petals. The last connection.

The wooden doors clunk behind us. We are history. The next service is already under way.

Sensing Ambrose, I turn my head a little: like a statue deliberately placed there, he is framed by the stonework around these doors. He is emanating a powerful aura of love. I don't know how I know this, I just do. I feel bathed in it just as I did in my dreams. And briefly comforted. Something to hold on to as Eddie once again takes my arm and gently guides me back to the mourning car.

As I climb into this car I see something really strange, or I think I do. Our weird poet from the workshop, the one with the long hair, is standing by one of the memorial crosses in the graveyard, staring across at us.

At least, I think it is he – which is very odd because I didn't seen him at the church with Emily and Joe. Maybe he was here at another funeral – but before I can make sure, I have almost tripped on the car door and Eddie has caught me just in time. When I look back towards the memorial, the chap has gone.

I glance towards the crematorium chapel as we leave the cemetery while the next funeral waits across the road to come in. Is CJ already in the flames? Or do they pile them up and do them in batches?

When Zig and Zag called to the house on the following Monday to rummage through CJ's room once again, I demanded that I be taken to see the place where he was found, the site of his murder. It was very strong, this impulse to associate him with some physical place, and since we were going to have to wait a while for his ashes to be delivered to us this was the only way I had of physically commemorating him. The policemen put up objections, naturally. In my own interest, they said – but I brushed them off.

It was Zig who called for me on the Tuesday afternoon at about three o'clock. I went alone with him, although all of them, even the girls, had offered to come with me. This was something I had to do alone. I was behaving out of character, I see that now, but there was a very primitive instinct in play. All I knew at the time was that it had something to do with the bond between me and my child and there was a cycle I needed to complete.

I carried fresh red roses, fifty of them, tightly budded and hand-tied in a nest of gypsophila – I had used some of the cash that Esmé had given me to buy them from a retail florist at £1.50 each. CJ deserved proper flowers to mark his passing and he was going to get them from me now. At full price for once, no deals, no haggling, no poor mouth, no favours from friends in the markets. And although I could not be certain that CJ liked roses, I did, and he was blood of my blood.

The murder site was still cordoned off with Gárda tape and I was absurdly glad to see that there was still a Gárda standing there. It meant that Zig's assurances had not been pious and that they were probably taking the murder seriously. On a nod from him, this attending Gárda, who was very young, raised a portion of the tape so I could duck under. I avoided his curious eyes.

The place itself was risible as a location for such high drama. Windswept, strewn with rubbish and builders' rubble, it was zoned for commercial development near a large shopping centre. It was also open to the gaze of any casual passer-by and, in fact, the body had been found by cleaners who were on their way to their early-morning jobs in the centre and who saw it through the windows of their minibus. It was clear that CJ's murderers cared little about concealing their crime and that the police had been correct in their judgement that this death was a warning to others.

'Where exactly was he found?' I asked Zig. 'The exact spot.'

He walked to a small mound of broken concrete blocks and indicated them. 'Just here, Mrs Lanigan, beside these.'

I stared at them. 'Were they used to break his bones?'

He shook his head. 'The state pathologist tells us he was killed elsewhere and left here.' Yes, studying those blocks I could see this was plausible. A few weeds poked scrawny tendrils through the broken cement: these blocks had not been moved for some time.

When you see sites of murder or accident on television, the flowers are threaded through fences or placed together in riotous but orderly mounds. This single bunch of roses, large though it was, was going to expose how few people regretted my son's death. Abruptly, standing there in the cold wind and clutching it, knowing that the drivers of passing cars were craning their necks to look at me, I felt naked, absurd. Where was I supposed to put it?

Then I heard Ambrose's voice, as clearly as though he was with me. 'Not long now,' he said.

Hardly aware of what I was doing, I undid the fancy ribbon holding the bouquet together, tore off the Sellotape and rubber bands and then, carefully, distributed the roses one by one around my son's resting-place. I do not know why I did it or what symbolism I was honouring – perhaps it was as simple as my aping some image from film or TV that had lodged in my subconscious. I said no prayers as I went about the task, I communicated nothing internal to CJ, I simply concentrated, counting as I went. One, two, three, four, placing each bloom precisely, aligning it at an angle to those around it, as though I was constructing a trellis. I was aware of Zig, tactfully out of my range of vision, but did not glance in his direction.

Twenty-nine, thirty, thirty-one, thirty-two . . . I have not told you about Johnny's visit home, have I? It was tough for us, as you can imagine. But, thank God for family, they all rallied around and we were able to present the Saturday as an unexpected party. We had decided that we would keep the dreadful news from him. In any event, since CJ had been gaoled for some time before he reappeared so unexpectedly, Johnny had become used to his absence from the house. We were all exhausted after the events of the previous few days. I certainly had not slept well and, to judge by their haggard faces, I suspect that the boys had not slept either.

Eddie went to collect Johnny from St Anthony's while Sharon, Amanda and I cut sandwiches and made two enormous pots of Bird's custard, which is Johnny's favourite treat. Tracey was working that day, which was maybe just as well. Getting used to us was one thing, but Johnny being added to the mix might have been a little overwhelming.

Full of beans, he roared into the house like a cyclone that Saturday, yelling repeatedly for 'Mel'. He was clutching a Beanie Baby in each hand and obviously remembering the last time he came home. You can imagine the impact that had on us all, but we managed to distract him straight away with the custard. Because of his damaged heart, he is limited in what he is allowed to eat and both whole milk and eggs are on the forbidden list, not to speak of sugar. These, however, were extraordinary times, and as I watched him float into seventh heaven as he slurped away at his industrial-sized bowl of the stuff, I forgave myself for indulging him.

From then on he was just our normal, noisy Johnny and, considering the circumstances, the weekend passed off well. For Johnny anyhow.

Forty-eight. Forty-nine, fifty.

I step back to assess my scrupulous latticework of roses on the killing field at Blanchardstown. It looks silly. A puny, silly grid. Seventy-five pounds wasted. Who will see it? Who will care? Ten seconds of wind and rain will destroy it. And CJ will never know I did this. What had I been trying to do? My grandiose instincts about completing cycles now seem pretentious. These flowers are superfluous. There is no spirit here. No remnants or relics of my son's soul, just the physical reality of broken stones, hard-packed clay and a flock of torn plastic bags chasing each other and snagging on the broken bottles and crushed cans that litter the dusty ground.

'What date is it?' I call across to Zig.

Consulting his watch, he moves towards me. 'It's the ninth of May, Mrs Lanigan.'

I almost laugh. I am doing this, and discovering God's absence, on the anniversary of my first Holy Communion. 'Let's go,' I say. 'I'm finished here.' I feel bad that he has been witness to my silliness so I walk quickly ahead of him, duck again under the tape and lead him towards the unmarked squad car. Through my back, I can detect his puzzlement.

Even now, as I write this, I can remember exactly the general timbre of every feeling I have described but I am not sure how precise I have been because, as I walked away from there, my despair and shock had given way to a type of reckless anger, against no one in particular. Against existence.

Zig respected what he probably believed to be my mourning and distress by staying silent in the car as he drove me home, although I could feel a tension from him, probably a desire to offload this crazy woman as quickly as possible. We had passed through the toll booth on the M50 and were within sight of the Ballymun towers when I was struck by severe panic. I could not face my empty house. Quickly, the words tumbling, I asked Zig if he would like to stop some-where to have a cup of coffee.

He's good, I have to give him that. He managed to

mask whatever horror he felt at the idea of being marooned with me in a coffee shop and suggested immediately that we go to the Skylon hotel in Drumcondra. I agreed. Right then I would have stopped for coffee in an opium den — anywhere to put off going back to the ghosts in Alder Cottages.

✦ Nineteen ✦

We settled into two wing-backed chairs in the lobby of the hotel and ordered coffee and sandwiches. Zig drummed his fingers on the table in front of us, and continually craned his neck to see if our order was coming. He was so uncomfortable I was almost sorry for him. But then I remembered that he belonged to the force that had let CJ out of custody to be murdered and I let him stew. (I had already asked about that, but had got nowhere. There would be an inquest in due course and all aspects of CJ's case would be covered then. That was all we were offered.)

The hotel was busy. Lethargic tourists lounged about the lobby, waiting for the next thing to happen; by contrast, a large, exuberant group of young men and women, all wearing red tracksuits and white trainers, was checking in at the desk. They were a visiting athletics team from Poland, Zig told me, then lapsed again into uneasy silence.

The coffee came and – thank God for Esmé's cash – I insisted on paying. This largesse rendered Zig doubly uncomfortable. 'You're not a new man, then?' I asked him.

'Sorry?' He actually blushed.

'Never mind.' I let him off the hook and poured our coffee. As soon as I bit into my first sandwich, I discovered I was starving; I had not eaten anything except a few biscuits since Johnny's departure on Sunday. Zig was more circumspect, taking dainty little nibbles, like an old lady with loose teeth, carefully placing the sandwich back on the plate between mouthfuls. I would have found his unease comical if I had not been so upset myself. 'Who are the scumbags who did this to CJ?' I asked him suddenly – but if I had hoped to catch him off guard I was wasting that hope. Yet he immediately brightened – this was more normal territory for him. 'That's what we're trying to find out, Mrs Lanigan.' Then, seeing my expression: 'Genuinely.'

'Well, where are the scumbags who were arrested with him?'

'They're in Portlaoise.' He watched me as I helped myself to another sandwich.

'Were they moved there deliberately after my husband arrived in Mountjoy?'

Again he shook his head. 'Accommodation problems in Mountjoy. And anyway they're dangerous fuckers—' He pulled himself up and smiled apologetically. 'Sorry for the language, Mrs Lanigan, I don't mean to offend.'

As he was beginning to seem quite human, there seemed little point in maintaining antagonism towards him. He was a policeman who was doing his job, and as a matter of fact he was probably doing more than his job by driving me today to Blanchardstown. He was certainly doing more than his job by sitting here with me. He should, no doubt, have been somewhere else thwarting some crime. 'I won't keep you long,' I said quickly. 'I'll just finish this and we can be off.'

He smiled again. 'Take your time. I'm on a day off today. Not that you're ever on a day off in my line of work, I suppose.'

Well, I thought to myself, staring at him briefly, I could feel guilty about this, but I'm not going to add to my burdens. He had volunteered to drive me today.

Tentatively, I began to ask him about himself. He was reluctant at first, but when he saw I was not trying to trap him in any way, revealed he had been widowed at the age of forty-four and had no children. 'It was a late marriage,' he said, looking at the toecaps of his black shoes. 'We had only three and a half years together. We were going to have kids but . . .' He shrugged. 'Sure that's the way of the world.'

'Do you live on your own now?' He shook his head. 'I moved back to the home place after Agnetha died. My father is still alive.'

'Agnetha?'

'She was Swedish.'

I had to struggle to come to terms with that. In a million years I would not have placed Zig with a Swedish wife. Not that I had ever given it much thought. If I had, however, I would not even have placed him in a marriage. To me he had been purely Policeman Zig, who lived on the far side of the moat between ordinary folk and authoritarianism. Now I had to struggle to readjust. To see him wearing a comfy old jumper and snuggling up to his wife's neck as they watched TV together, or ate companionably side by side. 'What happened to her?'

Again he shrugged. 'Nothing dramatic,' he said, 'the big C—' Disconcertingly, his eyes filled with tears. 'Sorry,' he mumbled, lowering his head and reaching into his pocket for a handkerchief, 'it happens some-times.' He blew his nose.

I had no idea how to handle this. Strangled in my own afflictions, I had forgotten the everyday, demo-cratic nature of death and that everyone else suffered from bereavement as badly as I did. Not wishing to embarrass him further, I waited, got busy by pouring us both a refill from the coffee pot. 'Sorry about that,' I said, when I guessed he was in control again. 'I didn't mean to—'

'No worries,' he interrupted me, putting his hand-kerchief away. 'It just gets me occasionally and very unexpectedly, you know? I should be over it by now — it's been nearly six years.'

Casting around for a change of subject, I asked him how he got Finn for a name: 'I know it's not unheard-of but it's uncommon in Dublin.'

'Oh,' he said, sipping his coffee, 'my mother had notions of upperosity, God be good to her, and we were all given these ancient monikers. All eight of us.' He counted off on his fingers: 'Oisín, Aoife, Nessa, Alil, Sorcha, Gráinne, me and Emer, the whole shoot-ing match.' He laughed. 'Hardly appropriate for Bride Street where everyone was called Nedser or Joxer or Redser or Decko. It meant we had to fight our corners. Toughened us up.'

'Eight?'

'Yeah,' he nodded, 'only three of us, though, and five of them.' He grinned. 'And I was the second youngest. It's tough living with so many women. Fighting on the street isn't the only way I learned to survive.' I grinned back, and it occurred to me that this was the first light-hearted conversation, however tentative, I had had for weeks.

In fact, it was the first one-to-one conversation I had had with a man, other than one of my sons or Clem, for more years than I could count. And with Zig of all people. Given the context, I found it bizarre that I was even able to note this. 'Are they all still alive?'

He did a double-take, as though the question was weird. Which, given the probable ages of his siblings, I suppose it was.

'You don't have a Dublin accent?' I asked him then – I would have placed his origins somewhere between Cork and Limerick. Culchie, anyway. 'No,' he agreed. 'It's mostly, I think, because of Mother and Dadeó being from the Aran Islands.'

Curiouser and curiouser. The vision of two Aran islanders cooped up in inner-city Dublin with eight children under their feet was a tough one to sustain. He saw my astonishment and mistook the reason, explaining that his parents customarily spoke Irish. Then he averted his eyes, suddenly bashful. 'The accent could also be because I also sing a bit, I'm in the Gárda choir – and I think when you're musical, you pick up whatever accent you've heard last. A lot of the lads are from the country.'

Yet another revelation. Zig singing? It was taking me some time to digest this. 'Tenor or baritone?'

'Bass.'

He seemed to relax a little then. We sipped our coffee.

'Do you like your job?' This was something I had often wondered about policemen.

He darted a glance at me and then, for some reason, decided he could trust me. He shook his head. 'Not any longer, it's a young man's job. And the lowlifes in this city have got worse even since I joined the force. They're getting younger and younger. There's a new violent breed out there I can't figure out at all.'

He then realized who he was talking to. 'I'm really sorry, Mrs Lanigan, I didn't think – I shouldn't be making things worse for you.'

'You couldn't.' It was true. And in many ways it was somewhat of a relief to be so direct with someone. This man had seen rock bottom with me.

'Have you read the newspapers?' he asked, watching me.

'I have and I haven't.' I was cautious. 'I've been selective.'

'I might as well warn you,' he said, 'there's a debate going on, letters from the public even, about our crime policy. They're using your son's murder as leverage to open up the notion that the Government isn't tough enough on crime. They mean us, I suppose, and judges. But,' to himself now, 'I don't know what more we can do.'

'What they write is of no interest to me,' I said to him, and, to my surprise, meant it. They could report or theorize about what they liked from now on and it would not bother me one whit.

He carried on, however, as though he had not heard me: 'I'm more than half thinking of early retirement.' He was continuing to talk to himself as he began thoughtfully to swirl the remainder of his coffee in his cup: 'I have a place in the south of Spain — the low-rent district, I hasten to add.' Then he grinned. 'Actually it's not that low-rent, it's a little place called Frigiliana.'

I had heard of Frigiliana, although I'd never been there: it was not all that far from Nerja, and he was right, it had the reputation of being quite posh. Yet another one for the books.

He became serious again. 'We bought it with a legacy Agnetha received shortly after we got married. I haven't been there for three years but I can tell you it's getting more and more attractive to me by the day.'

It occurred to me that, as would normally happen in an interchange like this, he was not asking me anything about myself. Then, stupid me, I thought, this man no doubt knew chapter and verse about me and my family. Including the fact that we were distant neighbours of his in southern Spain.

Of more interest, however, was something more current: 'There's something I've been wondering about — do you get training in Templemore about how to break bad news?'

He shifted in his chair and continued to look into the depths of his cup. 'We do, but there's no formula, Mrs Lanigan. It's just as bad the hundredth time as it is the first. No amount of training or rehearsal makes it any easier. I hate it.' He said this with such fervour that he slopped the coffee over his tie. He sighed as he took his handkerchief out again on cleaning duty, then smiled at me, ruefully this time. 'I definitely need a wife.' But then, as though horrified at this admission, he quickly lowered his head and scrubbed at the tie far beyond what was necessary and for far longer.

His chagrin was contagious. So much so that the ease that had developed between us had evaporated and I wanted to get out of there as quickly as possible now. I did not care to analyse why.

I had learned more about my own blinkered self in this short encounter than I had learned about him. I had judged this man to be a weed, a dull, uninteresting bobby plod who probably got a kick out of tormenting families like ours. Yet of all the surprising revelations – music, Gaeltacht parents, Swedish wife – the most jolting to me was that he wept tears as ready and bitter as my own. It was time I revised my habit of making instant suppositions about people.

I was tidying the kitchen preparatory to going to bed that Tuesday evening when Esmé came in. 'Oh,' she said, 'I didn't see you, it's quite dark in here.' She switched on the light and peered at me. 'You look peaked. Would you like a cup of coffee?'

This was a privilege offered very rarely. Esmé would drink pig swill rather than instant coffee and carries her own supply of beans, bought weekly on pension day, for grinding in her handmill. We are all under instruction not to throw out any of our used eggshells, which she crushes and hoards for use in the brewing.

I was not feeling sociable, but because of the

accumulation of events, my legs hurt, my eyes hurt —
even my teeth hurt — and I decided it would be lovely
to be served for once. I sat at the table. 'Thank you.'

Watching Esmé's unhurried coffee ceremony was
like meditating. For one year, my desk partner in
primary school had been a girl called Póilín, who could
not sit still for a moment and who fiddled incessantly.
Whether from self-protection or pragmatism, I got into
the habit of falling into a trance-like state while watching her fingers worry busily at her eraser, her pen, her
inkwell, her ringlets, the collar of her uniform, the
buttons of her cardigan. It became progressively easier
to fall into this peaceful, tranquil feeling until by the
end of our joint tenancy of that particular desk all she
had to do was reach out to pick up any object and I
was away. Nowadays this would be called meditation
but we called it daydreaming back then and it was
usually terminated by a thump on the back of the neck
from the teacher.

I fell into one of these trances while watching Esmé
as, moving deftly and economically, she measured the
beans into the mill, turned the handle with slow
rhythm, spooned the grounds into her percolator,
opened her cocoa tin and poured crushed eggshells
from it, while she added a precise measure of water
before carefully putting the battered tin jug on the gas
ring. I didn't care whether the coffee perked or not,
whether it tasted like ambrosia or slurry, I was away
with the fairies, floating, as though I had been transformed into a waterlily riding the still surface of a
pond.

Eventually, of course, the spell was broken and she

poured the aromatic brew into two of our good cups and brought it over to the table. You would not dare to sully Esmé's coffee with milk or sugar. Anyhow, you did not need to. Those eggshells really did seem to remove the bitterness.

Esmé is one of the few old people I've known who does not need to wear glasses and as we sat together in the brightly lit kitchen, whatever way the light fell on her face, I saw that her eyes were clear, her skin was barely lined. Her hands, too, although threaded with an intricate map of bluish veins, were translucent, more youthful than my own, work-roughened mitts. She saw me looking at them: 'Your nails leave a lot to be desired, May. Would you like me to buff them for you?'

I almost dropped my coffee cup. In all the years she had lived here, Esmé had never once offered to do anything at all for me, not housework, nothing. Much less a service so personal as manicuring my nails. 'Yes, please,' I said.

As if this was a common occurrence, Esmé put down her cup, opened the alligator-skin handbag that hung from her arm everywhere and at all times, took out a manicure set, a small tub of lanolin and two cotton buds. She placed them carefully on the table. 'Give me your hand,' she said, and set to work.

As she massaged in the lanolin, I gazed at her immaculate white poll and marvelled. Was this the old biddy with whom I had wrestled for possession of shopping trolleys at Broadstone so many times? The sardonic old witch I had cursed under my breath? 'I never thanked you properly for the money,' I said

softly, coasting on the warm soothing feelings gener-
ated by the long strokes of her fingers. 'It was a
godsend.'

Only a tiny shrug of her shoulders indicated that she
had heard me. She capped the lanolin and then started
gently to push back my cuticles with cotton buds:
'Drink your coffee, it's getting cold.'

For almost two years after Da's death, I found that
grief after bereavement comes in waves, throwing you
off your footing at the most unexpected moments. It
probably has to be that way because to be permanently
in a state of emotional pain without respite would
mean you had already entered insanity. Now, as Esmé
worked on the torn and tousled skin around the base
of my nails, I was assaulted by one of those waves,
seeing not this cultivated old lady but CJ's cold and
mutilated body, surrounded by its frill of cheap white
satin. The pain was physical, spreading from my
stomach to my throat and I weathered it only by
closing my eyes tightly and forcing my mind to turn
away from the vision and to concentrate on the sensations at my fingertips.

When the wave receded a little and I opened my
eyes, she was looking at me. I challenged: 'Why are
you being nice to me all of a sudden, Esmé?'

She put the used cotton bud aside, took an emery
board from the manicure set and began rasping. 'Why
not?'

I knew from experience that it would be a waste of
time to push her so I let it be. It was balm to have
someone working on me, treating me as someone
other than the live-in skivvy of Alder Cottages. How

shrunken I had let my world become in the period between Clem's arrest and CJ's death. As Esmé filed and shaped, I saw, leaving the odyssey to Spain aside, how I had paced on an endless treadmill confined to a circuit between my own bedroom, sitting room and kitchen with occasional side forays to the new Spar and the church, both less than a hundred yards from my front door.

When last had I been to the pictures or even to bingo? When had I had my hair done outside this house? All right, Sharon was a hairdresser and a good one, but she always did my hair in my bedroom. I could barely remember the feeling of being pampered in a salon. Being treated like a person who might have a life – even if it was referred to by rote, as in: Are You Going Out Tonight? Or: Any Plans For The Holidays This Year? At least that allowed for some sense of being a person in the real world. And as for manicures, no wonder my hands were in such a state. I had never bothered with hand cream, even the cheap supermarket stuff. Hand cream was for women who valued themselves as women.

Esmé finished filing the nails on my right hand and took up the left. 'I could have been an ally, you know,' she said, beginning on my thumbnail.

I wasn't quite ready for all this sweetness and light: 'So why weren't you?'

'You never made the choice.'

I stared at her. What response would be appropriate to this? All I could do was say I was sorry. She shrugged again. 'Please do not apologize.'

'All right I won't – but why did you feel you had

to tell me about Clem? You could have kept it to yourself.'

'I was outraged at his behaviour.' She stopped work briefly. 'But that is not all. It was time to tell you. You are a good woman.'

Yeah, I thought, surrendering again to the gentle proddings and buffings. Not a woman. A good woman. Martha, forever pot-walloping in the service of the Lord, never getting to sit, like Mary, at His feet and having the better part and scandalizing elders – and everyone else – into giving out about her. Still, it was nice of Esmé to say it. 'Thank you,' I said.

'You're welcome.' She pushed hard at a cuticle.

As I watched her mesmerizing fingers, the temptation to drift away again was strong, but on this occasion I felt I should take advantage of the unprecedented truce between us to find out what had bothered me for years. 'Look,' I said, blinking hard to disperse imminent trancedom, 'what's all that with the trolleys?'

'Some people climb trees,' she said calmly, 'or shoot people in McDonald's. I do not do this to inconvenience you.' A few minutes went by as she progressed through the manicure. Then, as if something had suddenly occurred to her, she looked up. 'I cannot guarantee that I will not take a trolley again.'

As I gazed into those clear, wise eyes, fourteen years' worth of minor conflicts and silly resentments lifted away. 'That's all right, Esmé,' I said.

She was doing the final polish, using a little device that resembled a miniature blotter, when I plucked up the courage to ask her about my mother. 'Please will you talk to me about her, Esmé? You're the only one alive who knew her, even if ever so slightly. I'd be interested to hear anything about her at all.'

She relinquished my hands. 'Finished.'

'Esmé?'

She started to pack away her little implements 'Perhaps,' she said, 'some other day.' I could not see her expression but her voice sounded peculiar. She stood up, making it quite clear that our session, rapprochement, whatever, was over. I stood up too and although I knew she would probably hate it, I put my arms around her. I could feel the fragile bones of her back and shoulders through the linen of her blouse. I was afraid to hug too tightly. 'Thank you.'

She disengaged herself. 'All you have to do is to ask.'

Something else occurred to me. 'The other day when they came to tell us about CJ, you were already on your way to the pawn shop. How did you know, Esmé?'

She was very still. Her face was in shadow. 'Perhaps it was a coincidence. Perhaps what I knew was that you had need of money. All families need money, is this not true?'

✦ Twenty ✦

Following advice from Emily, I have a scrapbook in which, now and then, I stick photographs, write ideas that might pop into my mind, or even proverbs that might inspire a story some day. One saying, torn off a calendar last year, is stuck right inside the cover, on the flyleaf. I think it might well be the inspiration even for a novel. Some day. 'The happiest social systems are manufactured from non-standard parts.'

Whether or not we are happy, this family is certainly non-standard and that saying, which has no attribution, sure strikes a chord with me. So much so that I mention it to Ambrose one afternoon in the context of my never ceasing to marvel at how Clem and I could have produced six sons who could not be more unlike each other in character and personality. It's bucketing outside, the fire is lit, Clem is safely in Spain – or so I think – and as yet none of the current traumas have reared across my horizons. So I am relatively relaxed.

As soon as I bring up the subject, Ambrose, naturally, cannot resist the opportunity to steer the discussion towards one of his hobby horses: I cannot emphasize enough – he grows a little in his chair – that the so-called dysfunctional family or dysfunctional group is one of those spurious categorizations beloved of humans.

He leans forward, eyes glistening: The phrase you have brought to my attention, May, could not be more apposite and I am delighted to hear you endorse it. Every family, every human group, is a collection of individuals each of whom is born to tread a unique path. Whether that path lies along a communal or societally approved route is irrelevant to the outcome of the individual's life. All that matters is that he follows it.

For once I agree wholeheartedly. Take Frank, for instance. Technically he's a failure because he can't seem to hold down a job for any length of time. But whose right is it to say that this is failure? We stream people from birth, these days. All right, we sing about all God's creatures having a place in the choir, but what we really mean is that if you step out of line, if you are not slotting into your chosen field – and you'd better damn well choose – if you are not achieving success to some degree, shove over and get out of the way.

Before I stopped listening to radio, I heard an extraordinary interview with a homeless person. The guy was in his mid-thirties and had a Ph.D. in chemical engineering, would you believe? But he hadn't been able to hack the rat-race, couldn't perform in job interviews, and had become more and more depressed until nothing mattered to him any more and he was paralysed into inaction. He could quote Plato, and did, but he couldn't organize himself to collect his dole.

Saddest of all was that he said he still found the world so beautiful it hurt his throat. Was that chap a failure?

I had started to worry about Frank when, in his teens, he slacked off in school, began to mitch and all the rest of it. I used to fight with him about it but he simply didn't hear me. His mind was elsewhere. Anyway, I knew in my heart he'd do what he wanted to do regardless – which for a while, a long while, was absolutely nothing at all. He didn't go out, didn't play his stereo or his Gameboy, just lay on his bed. I was so concerned at one stage that I confided in Father Blaise, whose advice was just to let him alone and that he'd grow out of it. As long as he's not doing drugs, May, he said, you're winning.

Needless to remark, we were all gobsmacked when Frank came home at the age of nineteen and said he was going to marry Sharon. Secretly, of course, I was delighted – although all of my protective armies rushed in and I couldn't shake off my fear that she might change her mind and thereby devastate him.

You see, although it might sound disloyal, I couldn't help wondering why she would bother with him. She was out of training and a fully qualified stylist, he had sporadically been earning peanuts behind the counter in Burger King at the Ilac Centre and was already making noises about being bored despite having stuck it for only six weeks.

On the other hand, I had always known that, despite his lethargy, Frank's mind crackled like a Geiger counter and that he was by far the most intelligent of the family.

But even I was surprised, after he moved out of the house, to find a set of drawings stuffed behind his wardrobe. Pictures of birds, tigers, sketches of this house, of the church opposite, of Johnny. And a lovely, calm watercolour of the pond in Stephen's Green. I was astonished at how vivid these were. Not only that but how accomplished. I had not known that he was interested in art. And I certainly had no idea he was this good. He had signed on for art classes in the first year of secondary school but he quit after the first term. I challenged him but he said the teacher was no good. I let it be. I thought it was just the usual teenage bolshie crap and, anyway, I was too busy to argue.

Something stops me bringing up the subject with him even now. I feel that if he had wanted me or anyone else to see these works, he wouldn't have hidden them behind his wardrobe. So back in the days when money wasn't the problem it is today I went into Eason's and bought an artist's portfolio to hold them and they're safely in the bottom of my own wardrobe now. Some day maybe he'll want them.

Frank came to see me on that Tuesday night of the site visit and the manicure. He came without Sharon, which was nice for me because the interaction between us is very different when she's here. (That being said, I have to admit that the atmosphere is far cheerier and more pleasant when either or both of the wives are with us – we all try harder to be sociable. In present circumstances, though, I welcome the times when I don't have to put on a brave face.)

I knew when he came through the door that he had something serious to say. I offered him a cup of tea and clicked on the kettle but he said he'd prefer a brandy. I joined him and we sat at the table, warming the glasses between our hands while outside the kitchen the light faded from the sky and the kettle started to sing. I let my heart settle and waited.

Throughout the few days immediately preceding this, when this house resembled Grand Central Station with all the comings and goings, Frank had kept his own counsel. We were used to that and I wasn't going to rush him this evening either. Anyway, the afternoon's adventures in Blanchardstown had drained all the false energy I had built up around the funeral and I felt, if not altogether peaceful, at least calm. He had always had that effect on me, when I allowed it and wasn't hassling him.

Who's going to pay for the funeral? he asked quietly.

I was taken aback. This wasn't something I had expected him to have on his mind. I suppose I am, I said slowly. I'll just have to apply to the courts. But sure it's not urgent, is it — we've plenty of time yet.

His eyes flickered sideways as though he could not bear to look straight at me: I don't think you should do that, Ma. I don't think you should have to humiliate yourself. We'll all chip in. I'll get another job, don't worry, jobs are ten a penny now, all I'll have to do is to walk into some place, there's such a shortage of people they're not even asking for CVs any more. He glanced back at me and hesitated. Then: What about Da? he asked, his voice very low.

I was startled and began to say that Clem had no more money than the rest of us — but he cut me off.

No, he said, I mean you and him. What's going to happen with you and him?

I stared at him. What do you mean?

You know what I mean. Are you separated now? Are you going to go for a divorce?

The kettle boiled, and although up to then I had had no intention of having tea, I got up to make some to give me a little time. Despite the knee-jerk fury since finding out about Melanie, separation or divorce wasn't something that had seriously crossed my mind as an option. Until now. Now that Frank had introduced the subject, I could see that indeed it was something I should consider. Would it bother you? I asked with my back to him.

Are you? His voice was thin with tension.

I turned to face him: I haven't seriously thought about it. And anyway, as you probably know, under Irish law I can't be divorced until we've been separated for at least four years—

That's not the point, he interrupted me fiercely. You know what the point is.

I was probably too stressed to take this on and yet I knew that whatever I said now would be crucial. I forced my voice to stay neutral: You're asking me is our marriage over? He nodded.

I abandoned the tea and came to sit at the table again. His grip on his Waterford brandy balloon was so tight it was in danger of shattering. Gently, I prised it from him: Before I answer that, what's your attitude to this, Frank? And don't say to me that it's none of your business. It is your business. You're our son.

He hung his head: It's all a mess.

Yes it is, I said softly, it's a dreadful mess. But nothing is going to happen in the near future. We all have a lot of grieving to do and I'm not such a monster as to do something like that to your da when he's just been put in prison and, I'm sure, is in an awful state about CJ.

You haven't been in to see him in Mountjoy.

I blinked at the suddenness of this: No, I haven't — but that sounded like an accusation.

That brought him up. He was horrified: Of course it isn't, Ma. But I don't know what to think any more or how to behave. He is my father. He hasn't actually done anything awful to me.

Everything clicked. You've been in to see him?

Again he nodded: Today. And yes, he did tell me about the other thing – well— He stopped. Then, bunching his hands again around the brandy glass, he stared into its depth: He couldn't avoid telling me. I met her. She was there.

He brought his head up and locked eyes with me. They wouldn't let her in, he said quietly. They gave me priority. She kicked up a big fuss. It was awful.

My stomach fried with rage. How dare that woman go into the gaol? What a fucking nerve – as though she was the wife.

Then a little voice kicked in. You didn't go yourself, May, it said. Why shouldn't she go? He's a human being, you wouldn't deprive him of having at least someone in his corner, surely?

I looked at the spiderweb of distress encasing Frank's face as he waited for me to respond, and I knew there was no point in fudging; there never is with him. Now that you've brought it up, I said to him, the absolute truth is that I have no idea what I'm going to do about that situation. You're right, I haven't gone in to see him. I don't want a confrontation.

Do you not love him any more? That's easy to know.

I shook my head. No, it's not. It's easy to know whether I'm in love with him or not, and I'm sad to say that that side of things is definitely dead. Whether I love him – that's a much more complicated question. Anyhow – I don't think he loves me any longer.

Frank's jaws tightened and, reflexively, he began to massage a point just under it – it's been a habit of his since childhood. You could fight for him, he said.

I could, I said steadily. Believe it or not, I did make an attempt to fight for him in Spain. I was defeated.

Suddenly, he stood up: Look, I'm sorry. I don't want to know the nitty-gritty of your relationship with Da. That is none of my business, whatever you say. But I had to talk to you about it so you know that I can't take sides in this. I just can't. The other three are livid with him, but I'm not. I'm sorry.

Of course that was not what I wanted to hear. I wanted everyone, all of them, the girls, the world, to be on my side, to hate her.

Do you understand? Frank's eyes pleaded with me.

I made a supreme effort. Of course I do, honey, I said. And I did. Intellectually.

But you have to understand something too, I went on. This past year has been the most difficult of my life, that goes without saying, it's been shock after shock – and I don't know what it's going to be like this time next year or who's going to be in my life or not in it. Anyway, I might be hit by a bus tomorrow so there's no point in laying down plans, I've certainly learned that much. It could be on the cards that your da and I will split. In fact it's likely. I'm sorry, Frank.

He was rubbing at the spot under his jaw again. Look, I said, there are certain things that don't change, and one of them is my love for all of you. I've been very fortunate.

Even CJ?

Especially CJ.

Slowly Frank sat on the edge of the table. What are we going to do, Ma? It's all falling apart.

No, it's not, I said quietly. Your life is not falling apart. And, although I'm amazed to hear myself saying it, mine isn't either. As a matter of fact, I'm a much stronger person now than I was this time last year before any of this happened. I haven't caved in, as you may have noticed. And you're not going to either. You and Sharon have a long life ahead of you outside of me and this family. You'll probably have children eventually and you will be amazed how that will change your priorities. All of this will recede until it's just a series of images and memories.

I tried to laugh: I'll be the nuisance knitting in a corner of somebody's kitchen and you'll all be having family conferences about me.

The corners of his mouth curved a little. Although it shows itself only rarely, Frank has a very sweet smile. What's to be done about Ma?

Exactly.

We smiled understanding at one another. He came

across and hugged me tightly. You're great, Ma, do you know that?

Will you stop? Sure, you're great too. We're a mutual admiration society.

After he had gone, I sat down in front of the two untouched brandies. I had not been exaggerating when I told him I was feeling stronger, as though the bones of me were coming to the surface of my skin. And it took Frank to show me. It's ironic, isn't it? In this dysfunctional family, it turns out I was worrying about the wrong one.

In a wider context, though, what was I at? First Eddie, then Marty and now Frank. All of a sudden opening all these floodgates, telling them upfront that I loved them.

It was as though Clem's infidelity and CJ's death had been deliberately coupled to force me into seeing what was truly important in my life. More than that, if I had told anyone about this, they would have suspected I was tying up loose strings. Was I? Or was I untying them deliberately to set everyone clearly on their own paths without being bound to me?

Frank did have a point about my not visiting Clem, I thought, as I poured the brandy back into the bottle. I had been chicken.

I decided to face up to it. I would go to Mountjoy. And if Melanie turned up, I was going to face her down – and in a strange way, as soon as the decision was made, I even began to look forward to the skirmish.

Twenty-One

In my own defence, I should say that I fought the desire for battle with Melanie as I walked towards the prison entrance on Wednesday afternoon. It was very strong, however, one of those clean, unambiguous drives uncontaminated by intellect or even liberalism where the other person's view is a factor. I was so up for it that I was almost disappointed when she wasn't among the small crowd of us, women and children mostly, who waited for admission.

I knew the drill, of course, from visiting CJ – and, in fact, a couple of the prison officers sympathized with me as I went through the entrance procedures. I think the condolences were genuine.

I think.

As I waited for Clem, memories of CJ flooded in. On the very last occasion I had been here to visit him, CJ and I had had a row – not a serious one, just our normal spat. I had been preaching at him, or trying to, about going straight when he came out, and he, as usual, was telling me to mind my own business. It was a ritual we went through every time. I guess I had been hoping that if I made the point, or pleaded with him often enough, maybe I could wear him down.

There is no point in going on about if-onlys, but if I had known that CJ was destined to die within weeks of my last visit here, would I have wasted any precious second of it in arguing with him? All those words, that energy and that time wasted, when I should have simply enjoyed being with him.

Not that 'enjoy' is the operative verb in Mountjoy prison's visiting area. Given that they're always worried about visitors bringing in drugs, they've done their best to be as humane as possible, I suppose. The barrier between you and your inmate is low enough to be tolerable and there are privacy screens between your area and the other visitors, but the whole atmosphere is artificial, somewhere between a hothouse and a menagerie, complete with keepers. It is very difficult to have a serious or an intimate conversation, for instance, unless you can take advantage of a baby crying nearby or some other temporary rise in the background noise.

Clem didn't know how to react when he saw me. He hesitated at first, before adopting a look of bravado as he sat down: Fancy seeing you here.

Yeah — fancy. I pushed a plastic supermarket bag across to him. Here, I brought you these. He looked inside, raised his eyebrows: Four oranges and a small box of Cadbury's Roses — with the price still on them. I hope you didn't go to too much trouble . . .

I stared at him. His cocky, sarcastic expression, no matter how assumed it was, ripped out every stitch that seamed my anger: You're welcome. We have a few things to discuss – like have you any preference as to what we do with CJ's ashes?

It was a low blow but it hit the target. His face crumpled. He looked right and left at the other inmates and their visitors as though seeking help. I'm sorry, I said. But you have to be civil to me, Clem. Depending on what goes on here today, this might be the last time I'll visit.

He gazed in astonishment at this May he did not know, and I could see him trying to decide how to play this. Should he get up and walk out? Should he bluster and reassert his authority? I let the silence between us drag on. In the space beside us a baby cried its heart out but on this occasion I let it cry without using the opportunity.

Where are the ashes now? Clem asked eventually.

Still in Glasnevin, as far as I know, I said, but Eddie tells me that the undertaker will want to know fairly soon. Do we want to put him in the garden of remembrance, do we want to take him for ourselves, or do we want him sealed into the columbarium?

What's that? He frowned.

I think it's that big wall inside the gate. We can put a plaque there.

Why can't you just call it the wall, then?

We argued to and fro about this – who did I think I was, being the big educated autobiography writer trying to make him feel ignorant with my posh words? Me insisting this was not the case. All the time, of course, the real fight was about the bodacious Melanie Malone who, like that cartoon girl in *Who Framed Roger Rabbit*, had draped herself in glowing technicolour across the table between us.

I got tired of pretending. All right, Clem, I said. Let's call a spade a spade. We shouldn't be fighting like this about our dead son, who isn't even finally at rest yet. And we wouldn't be, if you hadn't been unfaithful. That's what's really going on. That's why I haven't been up to see you until now. That's why this marriage is in the balance.

That really did shake him. He went pale, and for the first time, I noticed the dark circles under his eyes and so fell reflexively into caring-wife mode: You look very tired, are you sleeping?

He shook his head. Not really, I've a shithead for a cellmate. He snores like a pig.

He said this with feeling and I had to work hard not to respond with genuine sympathy. He had been very close to CJ after all. But I knew I must not yield ground. I dropped my eyes to the table to protect my armour: Back to the matter in hand – am I to assume you are going to continue with her?

When I looked back up his face had taken on that puppy-dog expression, which usually got to me. I don't know what to do, he said quietly. And I'm in bits about CJ. We both are, you're right, we shouldn't be fighting like this. Help me, Maisie.

For once I knew he was not merely trying to wriggle out of something. The appeal was truthful, and for a few moments I was tempted. It would be quite easy. I could adopt my usual, forgiving, supportive-counsellor role, we would talk it through, I could even organize marriage guidance – it wouldn't be the first time a prisoner had been through this – and I knew instinctively that right now he would have grasped at any straw in order to stave off further chaos.

I stalled. In any event, there was one question I genuinely needed answered: Why, how – no, why did you make love to me in Spain?

The unexpectedness of the question shocked him. So much so that he giggled nervously: Because you were there, like Mount Everest?

I stared at him, my expression stony. He hung his head. Sorry, that was uncalled for – sorry. No, Maisie, I love you, you know I love you, don't you? You're my wife, for God's sake.

I was certain the words were an appeal for the status quo, no more than that. However, I needed to be sure. What about Melanie? I asked.

He went immediately on the attack. For God's sake, I'm in gaol. Will you give me a break? How could I have seen her? He saw my expression: All right, she came in here to visit me. Once. Is that a hanging crime? You weren't coming up, for Christ's sake, what am to do in here – rot?

I let him peter out. You know damned well what I'm asking, Clem. Even as I spoke, quite clearly on the table between us, I saw his hands on Melanie's curvaceous, squirming little bottom and knew with certainty that no matter what he said or promised now, it was too late.

I didn't like the person who was going to dump this man when he was in such trouble. But even less would I have liked the pussyfooting, weak-livered creature who would take him back. I stood up: I'm sorry about this, Clem, given the circumstances. But I'm leaving you. We won't be able to divorce for a while, as you know, but I'll talk to the solicitor and he can draw up a separation. Don't worry, I'm not going to fleece you.

He shot to his feet. His whole body started to tremble. Maisie – please—

I'm sorry, Clem. I won't come to visit you again, but I will write to you and of course I will consult you about anything to do with the ashes – and with the boys.

Maisie – He was now reaching towards me, leaning over the barrier. The prison officer at the door was beginning to go on high alert. I stepped backwards, out of the booth altogether. My voice remained strong. I wish you and Melanie well. Genuinely.

And the surprising thing was that I did. On reflection, this may have had less to do with generosity than with this stupid little hill of beans problem being so pathetic in comparison with the enormity of CJ's murder. But I turned and walked quickly away before the profound, enveloping sadness threw me back towards him.

When I got home, I went straight to the kitchen and what we call the caboosh. This is an ancient cloth bag nailed to the wall at right angles to the sink. Its mouth gapes open to receive odds and ends too important to throw away – bus refund slips, milk bills, receipts, the odd photograph that no one, i.e. me, has put into an album.

I knew that the last snaps taken of Clem and me as a couple are saved there. On one of those photo-booth strips, they were taken during Christmas 1998, when we were out shopping for a turkey. Choosing the Christmas turkey was the only domestic chore we performed jointly – no pun intended, I think tiredness is making me high.

Anyway, as we were walking past the booth, I saw two giggling teenagers coming out so, full of Christmas spirit, I dragged Clem in there.

In the first two pictures, Clem is mugging, crossing his eyes, while I'm half out of the frame, obviously remonstrating with him. In the third, I'm back in frame – he's looking at me and laughing. The fourth is a perfect picture of two happy people. He's posing with his cheek affectionately jammed against mine and I'm smiling directly into the lens. I had planned to have that one blown up and framed but had never got round to it. I held the strip now, staring hard at the tiny images while waiting for regret to sweep me back up to Mountjoy to tell Clem that I hadn't meant it. We would start again. I would take him back no matter what he had done.

Nothing happened except an upsurge of sadness for those two people lost to each other. No urge to rush back, not even to explain my decision. Which I now knew beyond a shadow of a doubt was the right one.

The strangest thing of all is that I can detect an underpinning of relief. That is unexpected – maybe it's because at last I've decided something, done something, taken some lead instead of waiting for the world to throw more crap at me then trying to clean it up. The biggest hurdle now will be to tell the boys.

I found myself staring at my wedding ring. What

should I do with it? I'd be too superstitious to sell it or to give it away, and I wouldn't want to shove it into the back of a cupboard somewhere, where it might haunt me. Anyway, although I'm no longer married in my own mind, I was married for a long time and some of it was good. This ring is a memorial or, more accurately, a monument. I eased it off and put it on the finger of my right hand.

Our solicitor – no longer my solicitor – knocked at the door as I was still standing in the kitchen, looking at it.

I've never liked the guy and I think he knows it. Not that he's bad at his job – in fact, he is a tower of efficiency in keeping our bills paid and so forth, and he did give me a sympathy card for CJ, signed by himself and his colleagues. I didn't mean to be ungrateful, but where was he during the funeral? We could have done with a few more in the ranks.

As usual, he had papers for me to sign in connection with what I have now come to think of as our court dole, but then he introduced the subject of Clem, talking soothingly to me about early court dates and such. I cut this off by giving him the news.

If I surprised him, he concealed it. And before I got too far with detail, he explained to me that since he is Clem's solicitor, he cannot discuss the situation with me directly. Now that I am invoking family law, I have to find an advocate of my own. I will definitely be entitled to free legal aid, but he warned me that there was a long waiting list.

Pain is temporarily at bay. Could it be because the decision about Clem has been made? I'm sad, naturally, but that's a background noise, tempered with that relief I felt earlier. There is certainly a flutter of freedom. The ring looks strange on my right hand. New.

You might be surprised to hear me say that super-stition, far from being subversive, can lay down bedrock for faith – any faith and any religion. The early Irish Christians had the right idea when they fed superstition, myths and druidic practices into the new religion they preached and thereby gained interest and, ultimately, acceptance.

For instance, holy water wells, originally vener-ated by the ancients as conduits to the underworld, were quickly appropriated by the early saints and are venerated to this day as healing places of pilgrimage.

For myself, I am not enamoured of water. Never having immersed myself in it, of course.

It's Friday now, and guess who came to see me this morning? Joe Rooney. And Zig. One after the other in close formation, like a pair of ducks.

Joe was first – he came at about half past eleven while Martin was still in bed and Esmé was out collecting her pension from the local post office. I had slept hardly at all during the night and when I did manage to drop off from time to time, only fifteen or twenty minutes would pass until I woke again as alert as a pinprick.

So I had had to force myself to get out of the bed, and later in the morning, as I trudged around the house trying to do a bit of housework, dusters scoured my fingers as though they were made of pumice and the vacuum cleaner dragged as heavily as a pillar made of solid concrete. When the door-knocker rattled, I didn't even bother to pull off my apron. Expecting the milkman, I extracted the envelope containing his money from the apron pocket and opened the door to find Joe Rooney, his uniform as neat as a nun's parcel. Joe! How lovely.

Yeah, it's me. Then he took a step backwards: I was just passing, I thought I'd drop in to see if there was anything I could do for you. Are you coming to the workshop tonight? Of course, we'd all understand if you didn't, it might be too soon, but it might do you a bit of good.

This came out all in a rush, as though he had rehearsed it.

Come on in, I drew the door wider, adding immediately that I had never thanked him properly for the flowers.

He stepped across the threshold, his shoes squeaking as he wiped them thoroughly on the doormat: Sorry about that, that was a bit of a *faux pas*.

Of course it wasn't, I said, as I led him towards the kitchen, I was delighted. But I'm glad you reminded me about tonight. I didn't even realize it was Friday again. I don't know whether I'll go or not, actually. I haven't much inclination for anything at the moment. Are you just going on duty?

Coming off, he said – don't ask. We have the most peculiar rosters.

We ran out of conversation. We were in the kitchen

by this time so I emptied the kettle, taking a long time
to do it, filled it again and clicked it on while frantically
trying to think of something to say. Sorry for the state
of me, I said. If I knew you were coming I'da baked a
cake.

The effort clunked. Was he embarrassed or was I?
We spoke simultaneously:

Have you written any new pieces for tonight?

I suppose you haven't done any more work on your
short story?

That broke the tension and we smiled at one other.
It can be lonely after a funeral, after all the fuss has
died down, he said quietly. I agreed – stanching the
spring of tears and forbearing to remind him that there
had not been that much fuss about this particular
funeral. I put the teapot on the table: Or would you
prefer coffee?

As a matter of fact, if it's not too much trouble . . .
he blushed apologetically. Guilty again of stereotyping
– busmen drink tea – I took down the Nescafé.

Obviously making conversation, he brought up the
subject of Emily. What was my opinion of her as a
moderator?

I have no opinion one way or the other about Emily,
and I told him so. Then I asked him to tell me a little
about himself. This he did over the coffee. He and his
younger sister lived in a ground-floor flat on the North
Circular Road. The two of them had moved to Dublin
with their severely arthritic mother when Joe was not
quite eighteen years old. His father had just died and
jobs were scarce in his home village of Rathdowney.
Then, when his mother had died four years ago, his

sister developed serious depression and he now had to
care for her.

I told him about Johnny.

That's shocking, he said, genuinely upset. You've
had more than your share of hardship, May. It doesn't
seem fair, somehow.

I thought about this. Had I? What was a person's fair
share? And what was fair about this life and this world
anyway? Look at those poor people in Mozambique, in
Sierra Leone, in Ethiopia. I looked directly at him: I
never think about it that way, honestly. You don't.
You just live it. While it's happening you just get on
with it. You must know that – with your sister.

He shrugged. Maybe.

You never married?

He laughed at that: One near miss just after I got
the job at the depot, I wasn't exactly a prize catch,
with two women hanging around my neck— He caught
himself. Sorry. I didn't mean that to come out the way
it sounded. I was glad to help.

Your sister?

She's never worked a day in her life. He clammed
up. The vehemence had surprised him. He backtracked:
She had to look after Mother, d'you see?

I didn't get a chance to bring the conversation any
further because, just then, Esmé appeared in the doorway of the kitchen – I hadn't heard her come in. I let
him in, she announced, he was just about to knock.
She left. Revealing Zig.

Zig reacted on seeing I wasn't alone: Oh – your aunt
didn't say you had company. I'll come back.

It's all right. I stood up: Come on in, join us, have a

cup of coffee. I glanced at Joe and then back at him: Unless there's something in particular?

No – no— He did not seem comfortable, shifting awkwardly in the space between the doorway and the kitchen table: I just thought I'd call by to see if there was anything I could do for you, Mrs Lanigan, or if there was anything you needed.

Virtually word for word the same as Joe's opening speech. I surveyed the two of them. What was going on here? Ordinary human kindness?

Probably.

Maybe?

Zig moved back a little: Well, if there's nothing, I'd better get a move on, I suppose . . . He seemed to address this not to me but to Joe.

Joe rose from the table: No, no! I'll leave. You sit down. But then he too seemed to be hesitating. Was it my imagination or were these two men sizing one another up?

I don't want to be presumptuous but you know how it is when you are very tired and can't keep track of facts or rational events but instinct comes into play? I had one of those flashes right then: both of these men were interested in me, not as a suitable case for sympathy but as a woman.

Even though it had been so many decades since something like this had even crossed my mind, despite my own belief that I wouldn't have recognized a flirtatious intent if it came up and bit me, I saw that these two were jockeying for position with me. I almost laughed. I was getting giddy, probably from fatigue.

I didn't know whether to be insulted – did they think that now my husband was locked up I was fair game? – or delighted. There was no mistake. For a few seconds in my kitchen, this busman and this cop silently engaged one another like two stags in the rutting season. Was it possible that even though I wasn't doing it deliberately, I was emanating some form of subtle come-on?

I sobered up. They were both nice men – even Zig – and it would be good to have them as friends, but as to the other thing, I wasn't remotely interested. No more men in my life, thank you.

Sorry, how rude of me, I said briskly. I haven't introduced you. Joe, this is Zi – er, Finn O'Loughlin, Finn, this is Joe Rooney. Out of devilment, I didn't give either the context in which I knew the other. They shook hands.

Well, if you're sure there's nothing? Zig was the one to yield, which made sense since Joe had prior possession of the territory. Or perhaps I had watched too many programmes on the National Geographic Channel.

I shook my head. Thank you. But if there is, I'll certainly call on you.

I'll be in touch, so – nice to meet you, Joe. Zig turned and, reluctantly, I felt, left the kitchen. As I saw him out, he paused on the front doorstep: Still no developments, but I'm keeping on top of it. I didn't want to say anything in front of your friend.

I relented: He's a colleague from my writing group.

Oh, right. He picked at the paint blister on the door frame. That's nice. It's good you have an interest, that'll help you a lot. It can be lonely after a funeral.

Silence, while I tried not to laugh at how true the cliché was about great minds thinking alike. He fished in his breast pocket: Look, he said, here's my card. If there's anything you can think of that might help us — or just if you want to talk . . .

I nodded as I took the card, smiled and closed the door.

Joe left soon afterwards. He had little choice: I was dropping on my feet and couldn't stop yawning so he took the hint. In the interim I had agreed to go to the workshop.

I went to bed straight after I closed the front door after him, leaving the vacuum cleaner, the dusters and the Pledge to fend for themselves.

The hot weather of the past few days had continued and my bedroom was stuffy. I opened the window before climbing, fully dressed between the sheets. I fell asleep immediately.

Some time later I woke up, or thought I did. My arms and legs felt large, heavy and unable to move except in very slow motion and the air was thick and viscous in my nose and mouth. This, I thought drowsily, must be like being drugged. Slowly I became conscious of a high, sweet, flute-like singing with no discernible words and, turning my head on the pillow, I saw Ambrose standing in the afternoon light at the end of the bed, his head angled towards the window, his robe shot through with gleaming strands of white gold. His song penetrated every pore, spreading warmth and lightness throughout my body until my flesh dissolved and floated away like ribbons carried on a soft breeze, taking the pain with it and sending me back into deep, delicious sleep.

When I wake again I feel as silvery clean as a salmon. Through my eyelids I can sense that the sun is still high and that, for the present, pain has been kept at a distance, enclosed in an iridescent bubble. Waiting for it to pop, I don't open my eyes, fearing that as soon as I do, pain will rush towards me with horns and trident.

For now, birds sing, Friday rush-hour is belching along in Church Street, and directly outside my window, children squabble, race and bet on the future. Rich, sweet life.

I probe again for pain as, across the road, the six o'clock Angelus starts to toll: still no pain. Extraordinarily, I feel light. What's going on here? I feel almost guilty about it − disloyal to CJ's memory.

I open my eyes. Don't analyse it. Enjoy it. As soon as you start analysing what happiness feels like you stop being happy. Get up out of this bed. Get up!

I dive out of the bed and realize I am starving. And as soon as I get into the kitchen, guess who's there? Garment back to normal, he's standing with his back to the draining board, his hands splayed behind him. He's at ease: How are you, May? He's in one of his soft modes, eyes liquid, movements graceful and feminine.

How do you think I am?

He seems smaller, as light-boned as I feel, but poised as though he could take flight at any moment. You are doing wonderfully, he says.

Wonderfully? Riddle me that. Wonderfully? I think about it. Wonderfully? When most of the time these days, my life is cracking off my body like old plaster? Right now, though, I have to acknowledge that, for whatever reason, I have managed to hold on to the lightness.

You're a brilliant singer, Ambrose.

Thank you.

And thank you for my dreams.

They are your dreams, May, they come from you. He hesitates, inasmuch as Ambrose can hesitate, then: I have learned another great joke for you. Do you want to hear a great joke about a centipede?

No. I spoke more sharply than I had intended. I soften it: Not now, Ambrose, but thank you.

That is a pity. You would really enjoy this one—

Thank you. Some other time.

His face lengthens, becomes serious. Courage, May. Not long now.

A repeat of what I had heard in my head while out at the murder site. Before I could quiz him on it he had vanished.

Poor May. The last lap.

✦ Twenty-Two ✦

12 May 2000; 2.30 a.m.

The good feeling persisted right through the workshop that evening, and although I knew I was being granted only a temporary reprieve from the anguish – CJ was less than two weeks dead after all – I salved guilt about such heartlessness by rationalizing that even the poor people incarcerated in Dachau must have been able to escape into dreams for short periods of alleviation. I would enjoy it while I could.

Emily was in fine, bitchy form, pulling us up for not working hard enough in choosing the correct words. We were all lazy, she told us as, one after another, we read out our pieces. Why did so many of us use words like 'thing' or 'something' or 'stuff' when there were entire dictionaries of sparkling, wonderfully precise words that could instantly convey our meaning? And instead of starting every second sentence with 'It was', or 'There was', we had to work harder, think harder about how better to paint pictures.

She came to me last. I still could not face scrutiny of my short story so I took the huge risk of exposing my

account of Clem's early-morning arrest. I had considered fictionalizing it by changing all the names but
realized this would have been stupid. They all knew
anyway, so who would I have been fooling? So I just
retyped it, ironing out some of the halting dialogue I
had introduced.

When I had read it in all its naked, accurate glory, a
profound silence, starting from Emily, spread and
lengthened around the big table. Everyone was waiting
for someone else to react. I became self-conscious and
laughed nervously. 'It's that bad?'

'I think it's wonderful.' Joe Rooney leaned forward
in his chair. 'I really do.' His piece that evening had
concerned a runaway goose in a farmyard.

'Yes, I agree,' Emily's voice was brisk, 'it's quite
good. But there are one or two things. It's clearly
autobiographical, isn't that the case, May?'

'But that's always the most truthful type of writing,
you told us so yourself, Emily.' Loyally, Joe Rooney
fired up on my behalf. Unnecessarily, as she told him
tartly, since she had merely been making a comment,
not a criticism. One or two of the others joined in
then and I was able to relax and enjoy the ride as they
pulled my little offering this way and that. This was
the first piece of mine they had taken so seriously and
I found it exhilarating to hear them argue about my use
of words, whether I had been able to capture the
character of the minor characters such as 'The Weed',
as one of them referred to Zig, and the merits or
otherwise of using real events.

I actually found it restful not to have to be careful

any longer about who I am and from what family. This is me, myself, May.

I was still on somewhat of a high as I left the hall to go with them all to a nearby pub for a drink. Joe Rooney, Emily, the oddbod poet and another woman were in my immediate group, we were the last to leave as Emily had to lock up.

And as we were coming out into Church Street, I saw Con waiting for me: 'What's wrong?'

He ran his hands through his hair, embarrassed that others were listening. 'Nothing to worry about, Ma. St Anthony's rang me – Johnny's developed a bit of a chest infection and they've sent him to Beaumont just to have him checked out.' The home had a hierarchy of telephone contact numbers, starting with the house and moving on through Eddie and then Con. Eddie must have been out.

Although I was concerned, I wasn't alarmed. We were used to this: the medical facilities at St Anthony's are stripped down at weekends and from tea-time on Fridays until eight o'clock on Sunday nights there is only one registered nurse on duty. If something cropped up she felt she could not handle by herself, she routinely sent residents to Beaumont. 'You're sure it's just a chest infection?' As I spoke to Con, I was aware of Emily and the others waiting at a little distance. The oddbod, as was his wont, was standing a little apart, staring intently at me. He is so intense he gives me goose pimples sometimes.

'That's what they say.' Con glanced towards my little group. 'Look, Ma, you don't need to dash up there – I'll go. I'm sure it's nothing. And if I think you should be there, or if he asks for you, I can always ring you and you can get a taxi.'

I was tempted. After all, I had not had a social outing for a very long time and Con was probably right – there was no need for me to go. On the other hand, Johnny's last visit to Beaumont had not been all that long ago and any bad memories he had, of injections, for instance, would be fresh.

I am always aware, too, that one day, Johnny's trip to Beaumont will be his last. My airy mood was deflating fast. 'No, I'll go with you, if you don't mind driving me. Hang on a second—'

I hurried over to Emily and the others: 'I'm sorry, but something has come up, you go on.'

'Nothing serious, I hope?' For some reason Joe's solicitousness was now getting on my nerves. 'No – no.' I started to back off. 'I'll see you all next Friday.' He took a few steps towards me but I turned and walked briskly to Con. I glanced back towards the group as I went towards Con's car. Joe was still looking after me and so was the oddbod. Now what the hell was oddbod staring at? What business was it of his, for God's sake? More to the point, why did I suddenly find Joe's concern so irritating? Was I so unused to a man wanting to take care of me?

Yes, was the answer to that one. My marriage had not been a partnership but a loose alliance between a one-man band and his personal housemaid, cook and bed partner. Yet that wasn't all. I suppose, to someone used to relying so much on herself, such evident concern felt like crowding. I would need to watch that, probably, otherwise I might become an eccentric, lonely old lady.

It is strange how quickly I have taken to talking about marriage in the past tense. And that reminds me of something else I must be careful about: it was not all bad, after all. As I have outlined, the early days, in particular, were very happy.

Johnny was in a small room just off the nurse's station in one of the wards. He was on his back, deeply asleep, his mouth a little open and dribbling. A drip tube ran into his wrist, strapped to a board – but, more alarmingly, he had been hooked up to monitors. This had not happened on any previous admission.

The sister on duty saw my reaction: 'Try not to worry, Mrs Lanigan, he's fine at the moment – but with John's history we can't be too careful so we put him where we can keep an eye on him.' She opened his chart: 'We've given him a little something to relax him. He should sleep until morning – and we've started him on antibiotics and Warfarin. There's really no need for you to hang around. You can go home and we'll call you if there is any change.'

'Warfarin?'

'Because of his heart. It's just a precaution. And we've sent off a few bloods.'

'But I thought it was just a bit of a chest infection.'

'That's probably all it is, Mrs Lanigan.' The beeper hooked to the Sister's belt pinged. She looked at it, then patted my arm. 'Do go home and try to get some sleep.' She walked off quickly towards another room in the ward. I looked at Con. 'I'm staying.' He nodded. 'I'll stay with you. I'll just give Amanda a shout.'

'What about the others?'

Con's eyebrows shot up towards his hairline. 'Should we? It's not that urgent, Ma, surely?'

I glanced through the window of Johnny's room. From this short distance, I could see his thin chest rising and falling in regular rhythm. 'You go on, you've work tomorrow.' Saturday was always the busiest day at the bookie's.

'I got a bit of news about that actually, today—' He stopped, looked up and down the shadowy corridor. 'But I was hoping to tell you in better circumstances than this.'

'Not more bad news?'

I saw my mistake immediately. His expression tightened. 'Why should it always be bad news? We're not all like CJ, you know!'

Con had always been prickly. Perhaps it came of being the third and maybe overlooked a bit. I put a hand on his arm. 'Sorry.'

'Forget it. I'll tell you some other time.'

'Tell me now – please, Con.'

'Leave it, Ma!'

As Con hurried off, I went into Johnny's room, pulled up a chair beside the bed. I had no supplies. In the past, when this had happened, I had always come prepared with Mars bars, crisps, bottles of water and something to read. All I had with me this time was my little workshop briefcase with my writing materials.

Under the low-level night-lights, my darling son's face was as pale as a candle and without his helmet he seemed unsafe and much younger than he was. The hot, muggy air in the ward was already clogging up my breathing but I could detect a sour smell. I pulled down the bedclothes and found that they had put a nappy on him. This upset me, of course, but I understand that it's much easier for them. They cannot be checking him all the time; I know only too well how very short staffed the wards are and how each nurse and doctor is stretched to the limit. Under the bedclothes, I also saw that both his wrists were loosely fastened to the cot-sides – I hate this too but I am accustomed to it: Johnny's flailing can be damaging.

How far we have come, Johnny and I, I thought, as I tucked in the bedclothes around him as best I could. At one stage we had thought he would not see his tenth birthday, then we extended this to his twelfth, then his eighteenth and recently, he being not far off twenty, I had begun to believe that the doctors had all been mistaken.

Now, as I stroke his twig-like, inert forearm I begin to wonder if I should not have better heeded the warnings.

I am used to seeing him wearing bulky sweatshirts and pants, his helmet grossly oversizing his head and giving him an air of invulnerability; plus he gives an impression of huge energy as a result of the racket he makes with his spoons and pans. Deathly still like this, his limbs are too thin for his length, his chest concave and underdeveloped.

Like CJ, he seems taller in repose. What a lovely word for such sad usage.

I suppose I had been a bit blasé about my pregnancy with Johnny – probably because he was my sixth – and even when the pains began, because he was not

expected for a further two weeks, I figured there was
every chance this was a false alarm and put off going to
the hospital.

As this was the last Saturday before Christmas, all
the neighbours were in town so even if I had decided
to check myself in I would have found it hard to get a
baby-sitter at such short notice. (I would have loved to
see the faces on the admissions desk in the Rotunda if
I had turned up in a taxi with five small boys between
the ages of one and seven, asking the nurses to mind
them while I went in to have another!)

I started at about two o'clock in the afternoon, while
Clem was out getting us a Christmas tree. He had
taken Clem Junior with him. Marty and Frank were
running amok in the house as usual; even barely
walking as they were, those two were like Siamese
twins, always up to some form of mischief, and they
had caught Santa Claus fever from the older three.

I had finally managed to get them into their bedroom
and was trying to persuade them to go down for a nap,
but as soon as I put one in his cot and turned my back
to corral the other, the first would hop back out on
the floor. I would turn to get him and the second
would do likewise.

I am losing my patience and threatening all kinds of
dire retribution, to which neither of them pays any
attention whatsoever, when the first pain catches me
very low in the back, pushing all the breath out of me.
I have to sit down for a minute or two to recover. The
two lads start wrestling with one another on the floor
in front of me but I do not have the strength to
intervene and I just let them at it. The second pain,

very sharp but still very quick, comes while I am still sitting there. It passes within seconds. I wait for the third, but it does not come. At least, it does not come then.

I give up on trying to get the boys to have a nap and we all go back down into the sitting room, joining Eddie and Con on the sofa to watch a video of *Sesame Street*.

To this day, I grow cold every time I see Big Bird, even a soft toy of him. Because less than ten minutes later, poor Johnny decides to make his appearance. I have very little warning, just those two pains in the kids' bedroom earlier and now – wham! We are all sitting there, a jumble of arms and legs and laps and sucking thumbs, and I can feel the head descending.

The last thing I want to do is scare the boys. So, although the pain is now excruciating, so much so that sweat is running hard along the length of my entire body in my efforts to refrain from screaming, I tell them all to be good and to sing along with Big Bird and that I will be back in a second.

Somehow or other, I manage to extricate myself, to get off that couch and as far as the front door. I open it. Then I take the telephone into the lobby so they can't see me, slide down on to the floor with my back to the wall and dial 999.

The head is pressing harder now and I am terrified that to resist pushing might damage the baby. At the same time, all I can think of is getting to somewhere private so that the boys will not be scared of childbirth for the rest of their lives.

'Operator, which service do you require?' The calm male voice at the other end of the line is reassuring.

'Ambulance, please,' I gasp, 'quickly – I'm giving birth—'

'May we have your address, please?' The voice remains calm.

I manage to get this out, then, after I hang up, ease myself down to lie flat on my back with my knees up to try to slow things and slowly start to propel myself backwards, like I'm on a sled, towards the kitchen. All the time I am having to bite on my lips to cut off the screams. Thank God for *Sesame Street*: none of them has turned a head to see where I am.

I cannot describe that pain. Any woman who gives birth knows it, but this is different in scale from what I went through with the other five. I am impaled on a very thick, unyielding spike. The tiniest movement against it is agonizing.

Somehow I make it to the end of our hall but I am only half-way in and half-way out of the kitchen door when, with a gush, Johnny comes out.

I try to pick him up but then I see the cord is wrapped around his neck.

Experience in having children counts little in situations like this when all previous deliveries have been in a hospital. You are half dazed, while the post-birth procedures below your waist are quick and efficiently hidden, until in a trice, the baby is in your arms.

This new little baby on the threshold of our kitchen is very still, a tiny, slithery thing, much smaller than all the other babies I have had but he is not blue, so I decide to wait for the professionals and say a prayer that they will come quickly. I take off the cardigan I am wearing and, picking him up, wrap him in it, cord and all, to keep him warm. Then, trying to ignore the blood and the mess all over the floor, I hold him carefully with both hands, using my knees as a prop. I am afraid that if I try to unwind the cord by myself, I will do more harm than good and dimly remember from some long-forgotten magazine article that he will probably continue to receive oxygen and blood from me through the cord.

Unfortunately, that is not the case, as it turns out. You are probably not aware that when he is born, a baby's lungs are like two solid blocks of tissue but that at the moment of delivery, a reflex hunger for air develops so he cries and his lungs immediately react against the influx of air and convert to soft, air-filled bags. This was explained to me in detail by Johnny's paediatrician.

Too late, of course. If I had slapped him or unwound the cord, if I had done anything rather than lie there passively, Johnny might not have been the way he is today. It was never any use for doctors, nurses, midwives, even Clem to tell me that it wasn't my fault, that I could not have known. It was my fault. I should have known. It was my business to have known.

I keep my eyes fixed on the small, still face, willing health and life into it as we wait, Johnny and I, for what seemed like four hours, although I was assured later that the ambulance had arrived within five and a half minutes of the call having been received. While we wait, I hear a row start up in front of the television and pray very hard that it will sort itself out without one of them coming running for me. My prayers are answered because the row dies down as quickly as it had started.

I start to shiver – from stress, from the cold air against my upper arms.

Then, blessedly, I hear the siren and from then on, all is quiet, organized action. A huge presence, rustling in the heavy uniform: 'Hello there, what's your name, love? And who do we have here?'

Then another, 'Tsk, tsk,' bending low to the baby, 'Who's in such a hurry?' But there is nothing casual about it: these men, although gentle, take charge immediately, prioritizing the baby and working as slickly as whippets in the confined space. One sorts out the cord and the afterbirth while the other simultaneously blows into the tiny mouth to get air into the lungs.

It is only when I hear the first little whimper that I can let go and start to cry. Immediately, one of these wonderful men puts a blanket around me and holds me tight – 'Have a good cry, now, missus, you deserve it' – while the other swaddles Johnny and takes him outside to the ambulance.

So far so good with the other five, still safe in the sitting room and glued to the programme. Probably because they are quite accustomed to the sound of ambulances speeding up and down the main road outside, Big Bird is a closer and more immediate attraction.

The man holding me starts to help me to my feet: 'We'll have you in a nice bed in jig time.'

Then this person I have never met tells me not to

worry about the other five. 'Don't fret, missus, we'll find someone to watch them for you.'

Those few hours are as clear today, almost two decades later, as they were in the weeks following.

Tenderly, I push back the spikes of damp, fair hair that lie along Johnny's waxy forehead. I wipe the dribble and kiss his smooth, unlined cheek on which the overnight stubble is silky, like the hair of a baby, and thank God for these twenty years with him.

Have I mentioned that they are all dark except Johnny? It was as though he was marked out as being different from the very beginning. I am not sentimental about the so-called privilege of looking after handicapped people, which, believe me, is no picnic, but in Johnny's case, I rarely resented a moment of it because he was always so sweet, like a big, noisy circus clown.

Have I already begun to talk about him in the past tense?

Strangely, I do not feel frantic or desperate – maybe these enemies lie in wait – but even if this does turn out to be more serious than the medics are at present letting on, I feel that I can accept it.

Perhaps it is simply that I am numb from too many shocks, too much grieving. Who was it said that too much suffering can make a stone of the heart?

Twenty-Three

Con comes back from phoning Amanda. Continuing to concentrate on Johnny, I hear rather than see him: 'Everything all right, Amanda understands?'

'Yeah.' He goes towards the second chair in the room and pulls it up to sit beside me.

I glance over at him and find he is still not in a great mood. I turn back to Johnny: 'Look, there isn't any need for you to stay, really.'

'I want to, Ma. He's my brother, you know. You don't always have to be Mother Teresa—' Seeing he had hurt me, he broke off. 'I'm sorry, I didn't mean that.'

There was nothing to be done or said except to move on: 'What's your news?'

We had lowered our voices to just above a whisper so as not to disturb Johnny. 'Tell me. Please. I could do with cheering up.'

Con's news is that he has been promoted to assistant manager of his branch. He had been coming to see me to tell me when the telephone call came from St Anthony's. 'That's brilliant,' I said. 'Really, it's brilliant. I know you worked your socks off for that.'

'I worked more than my socks off,' he said, with feeling, and I thanked God it was as though the small spat between us had not occurred. But as he continued to whisper, telling me how he was told about this promotion and who in his office would be happy about it and who would not, I found my attention wandering. It was not that I did not care – I certainly cared a lot – but his remark about martyrdom had set me thinking. Did I really project such a long-suffering image? Had I become the kind of woman who, when asked how she is, settles in to relate exactly how she is in great and lurid detail?

'So when do you start the new job?' I made an effort to look cheerful.

Con smiled back. 'Monday.'

'We must celebrate.' I squeezed his arm. 'These achievements should be marked.'

'We'll go to a restaurant,' his eyes lit up, 'my treat. Just you and me, none of the others.'

'What about Amanda?'

'She'll understand.' At this stage his smile could have powered a small transmitter. He even seemed to sit taller in his chair. 'A bloke has to take his mother out occasionally.'

'Of course. I'll really look forward to that, honey.'

I glanced at Johnny, immobile as a plastic mannequin, and made a quick decision. 'Look, Con,' I said, 'there's something I have to tell you. Only between us, for the moment, right? I haven't told any of the others.'

Instantly, he became serious. 'Not even Eddie?'

I shook my head, equally grave. 'No one.'

I waited a little to let that sink in. Then: 'It's not very good news, unlike yours, I'm afraid, and on second thoughts, maybe I shouldn't tell you. I don't want to rain on your parade – I'm really happy for you, Con.'

'What is it, Ma? Tell me – you can tell me.' His chair creaked loudly in the silence as he leaned towards me, his face set in earnest, worried creases. 'I don't know how you're going to feel about this,' I said slowly, 'but I've decided I'm getting a separation from your da.'

His expression struggled with itself. I could see he was trying to take this in while at the same time feeling chuffed at being the son entrusted with the secret.

Conscious of my gaze, he stood up and walked over to the window of the room, a matter of just a few steps. 'I'm sorry,' I whispered, loud enough for him to hear, even though he had his back to me.

'I'm not surprised, actually.' His voice was muffled. Then he turned round to face me. 'You see, we all know about—'

'Frank told you,' I interrupted, before he had to say her name. He turned back to the window although there was nothing much to see except the unoccupied nurse's station. I let him be and again turned to the flickering digital displays on the monitor.

He came back and sat down again, but as he did so, the monitor emitted a baleful, squealing sound. I jumped with alarm but then saw that Con's feet had become entangled in a cable and the grip had come off Johnny's finger. Gently, I replaced it and everything returned to normal – if you could call it normal to be attending at the bedside of your unconscious nineteen-year-old, who is festooned with drips, tubes and cables and tied to a hospital bed. Belatedly, one of the nurses came rushing in but I reassured her that everything was now all right.

She checked, then: 'Would you like a cup of tea?'

Con declined but I was in for the long haul and asked if there was a possibility of coffee. She nodded and hurried from the room again.

'When is this going to happen?' Con asked quietly, when we were again on our own.

I kept my eyes on Johnny's oblivious face. 'Not for a while, I have to get a free legal aid solicitor and there's a waiting list.'

He considered this. 'Anyway, there's no rush, is there? Like, you're already separated, in a sense.'

'Unless he gets bailed.'

'Who'd bail him this time? We don't have the money. And with the way things are, I doubt if Tony Malone . . .' He trailed off, unwilling to go down that road.

We both turned to study the monitor again as if it held answers. 'It's a nightmare, Ma,' he said. 'The worst thing for me is that I actually liked Melanie. She was always a bit of a spoiled brat, but I put that down to her being an only child.'

I pretended to be searching for something I had dropped under the bed. When I had straightened up, he was looking at me again. 'In his defence, he didn't have to come home, you know. He put himself back in Mountjoy because of CJ.'

'I know that – but he would have been found sooner or later. They were tapping our phones.'

'Yes, but he could have fought extradition. He's here voluntarily.'

It was on the tip of my tongue to ask if a Barcelona gaol was preferable to Mountjoy but I bit it back. Con's ambivalent attitude to Clem didn't surprise me all that much, although I found it very sad – I think I may have mentioned that CJ and Con had been Clem's chosen sons. I was saved further debate because the nurse came in with the coffee. After she had left, I warmed my palms with the mug: 'So am I right? Was it Frank who told you about – you know – the other thing?' To date, I had not been able to use her name except to myself.

Con bowed his head. 'I don't know what's got into Frank. The rest of us are furious with Da. We haven't been to see him.' He looked up again. 'I suppose I will go to see him at some stage.'

He was virtually asking my permission. 'Of course,' I said. 'You must.'

He dropped his eyes. 'Look, Ma, there's something I should tell you. After I rang Amanda I rang Mountjoy and left a message for him about Johnny. I felt I had to.'

'That's all right. He should know.' I swallowed. 'Do I really behave like a martyr?'

'I'm sorry I said that, Ma, it was off the top of my head, I was just irritated. Of course you don't behave like a martyr – but you might let us take on a bit of responsibility sometimes instead of feeling you have to do everything and keep everything going all by yourself.'

There was no answer to that. We both turned to look at Johnny. Then Con pulled something out of his inside pocket. 'I actually had this for you the last time I was in the house but what with one thing and another . . .' He handed me a grubby, much-folded photocopy on which were written verses taken from the Bible, Proverbs apparently.

This astonished me: 'I didn't know you were religious, Con?'

He grinned. 'I'm not. I was handed it in O'Connell Street, some hippie with long hair and earrings who tried to interest me in sheets of his poetry. Fat chance! I suppose I'm no judge but even I could see it was complete rubbish – didn't understand a word of it.'

He indicated the Bible verses. 'I took this, though, because in my opinion, it describes you to a T.'

'Thanks.' I held the paper under the night-light, and as I read, I could feel the tears gathering:

Who can find a virtuous woman, for her price is far
    above rubies.
She will do her husband good and not evil, all the
    days of her life.
She seeketh wool and flax and worketh willingly with
    her hands.
She is not afraid of the snow for her household, for
    all her household are clothed in scarlet.
Strength and honour are her clothing: and she shall
    rejoice in time to come.
She openeth her mouth with wisdom, and in her
    tongue is the law of kindness.
She looketh well to the way of her household, and
    eateth not the bread of idleness.
Her children arise up and call her blessed: her
    husband also, and he praiseth her.

Many daughters have done virtuously, but she
    excelleth them all.

What could I say? I did not dare to meet Con's eyes
because I knew he would not thank me for it. Instead,
fighting hard to control myself, I pretended to read the
verses a second time. 'They're really lovely, I will keep
them always. Thank you.'

'You're welcome,' he replied gruffly, 'and I really
did mean it when I said that's what we all think about
you.'

He hesitated, then, ruefully: 'Sorry about the husband bit in it. Look, Ma, don't worry about us and
Da. We're all big and bold enough now to handle it.
Think about yourself for once. And by the way, thanks
for trusting me.'

He left at about midnight, having extracted a promise
that I would telephone him on the instant there was
the slightest development. The subtext was clear. Call
me first, not Eddie or any of the others.

Not long after he left, the ache for CJ returned.

Yet CJ had been almost as absent from me when he
was alive as he is now. Since he left school, his dealings
with me had been minimal at best, so why should I
now long so keenly for his presence? What was the
qualitative difference? When I thought about this, I
could come up only with the theory that this difference
might have something to do with time. I had probably
imagined we had all the time in the world and that
there was no need for me to be in any rush to
communicate with him.

Whereas now, I would gladly give up ten years of

my life for ten minutes in his company. It was also to
do with choice. Even if I hadn't seen CJ for the rest of
his natural life, at least while he was alive that choice
remained open to me.

Funnily enough I didn't pray this time – a change for
me – but watching Johnny, I started to consider the
way the world saw this damaged son.

Maybe I had not been lily-white in my knee-jerk
reactions to people. For instance, from time to time I
had harboured pretty unkind thoughts about those
unfortunate asylum seekers I saw wandering aimlessly
around Broadstone and Phibsboro. And had I been all
that tolerant of single mothers, gays, travellers, the
people I have so glibly characterized as social-welfare
spongers? After all, like me, all of them are doing their
best to live their lives, and who is to know what personal
tragedies or struggles they are going through in private?

So, May Lanigan, who gave you the right to sit in
judgement on their motivations or behaviour – which
is particularly rich given the way you resent instant
jumps to judgement on poor old Johnny?

What would my mother have made of him? How
would she have reacted to his disabilities?

And what would she have made of me? Would she
be pleased with my oh-so-quick discarding of my
husband? Had she been a liberal or a conservative in
that regard? As I tried mightily to picture her, the
exercise defeated me as usual and I started to wallow
again in regret about never having known her. It would
have been wonderful to do something as simple as take
her shopping in one of the new malls – what would
she have made of them, when, presumably, the height

of sophistication in her day was window-shopping at fusty old McBirney's on the Quays?

The most extraordinary things do occur to you in the dead hours of night, especially when you are alone and have had a lakeful of coffee.

They are coming in every fifteen minutes or so to check him and to look at the monitor. They keep telling me to go home, that there is no crisis here and there is nothing I can do, but I cannot leave. Sorry, Con. Once Mother Teresa, always Mother Teresa . . .

It is almost a quarter past three now and I can feel the blood jumping behind my eyes. My hands are so shaky I cannot write any more at present. I shall probably never sleep again.

At about nine o'clock that morning, I gave in and went home to have a shower and to change my clothes. The new shift of day nurses had promised me they would call me instantly if any serious problem developed, but Johnny remained peacefully asleep – as a result of his sedation, I was assured – all through the morning rituals and rounds on the ward. Although his own consultant would be available by telephone, he was not due to hold any clinics nor to come in to the hospital because it was a Saturday.

As I let myself into the house I was jiggy and disoriented after the long night and excess of caffeine.

The post had already arrived – I picked it up and thumbed through it: a mobile phone bill for Martin and three envelopes for me. One turned out to be the bill from the undertaker – already? They don't let the grass grow, do they?

The other two were letters churned out on a computer but personalized with my name, each purporting to sympathize with me on my loved one's death while drawing my attention to the enclosed brochures and samples of memorial and acknowledgement cards. I left all three of them on the lobby table.

In the kitchen, I found a hand-delivered note from Joan. Esmé or Martin must have put it there.

Guilt is a strangely common disease.

My dear May,

I've just heard the news about Johnny — Melanie told me. I'm very sorry and if there is anything I can do, you know that, May.

I'm real sorry about us. I don't know what to do about it, maybe we should meet and have a cup of coffee and a drink or something? We were both too upset that day you came to see me to be able to thrash anything out properly.

I don't mean now, of course, with you being so busy with poor Johnny, but afterwards, when things have calmed down. Poor you. And so soon after CJ!

May, you know they say your troubles come in seven-year cycles, well, it seems your seven-years is being all squashed into this short time. I feel terrible and guilty of course that I'm not helping you out.

I know I'm probably out of order, but because of our friendship, which I for one certainly don't want to lose, I beg you to understand my point of view about the whole Melanie and Clem thing. I'm so torn, May. I want to still be your friend but Melanie is my daughter and I love her so much.

Oh, it's all a complete mess. And Melanie is so upset about the whole thing, with him being in gaol.

There's no talking to her at the moment, she is in bits and I don't know what she's going to do next. But some day all this might die down and we, at least, can be pals again. Please?

Do ring me, May, or if you can't face talking to me (and I would completely understand that) at least drop me a note. We've been pals for a long time, haven't we? Old friends are best.

Joan

I stared at it. My emotions were mixed: on one level, there was no point pretending I could rush back to her – I could not be a friend to someone who was so heavily involved in the Melanie and Clem saga; friends confide truthfully in one another, and how could Joan and I have any conversation without it being totally superficial? If it's only chat I want or need, I can get that anywhere, from the milkman, from the girl in the new Spar. Or from Joe Rooney, or Emily – or even, Lord save us, from Zig.

On the other hand, her rambling note, whether inspired by guilt or not, was written in a very sincere spirit and I do accept that she has a problem fundamental to all mothers. Given my flawed pedigree on that score, who am I to dictate to her how she should deal with her daughter?

So here's what I sent back to her. Exhausted though I was, I wrote it straight away, while I could still feel I was responding in the spirit of what she had initiated. As you will see, I did want to leave a door open – after all, as I think I said before, half a friend is better than no friend – and I certainly did not want to be the means of making her feel any more guilty than she already was. I am able to include it here because, the way events panned out, it was never posted.

Dear Joan,

Thank you for your note. I mean that.

Please don't feel guilty, it is a useless and destructive emotion and, after all, as we did say to one another that day in your house, it is not we who have something to feel guilty about.

You are right when you say that all this will die down some day and then we can probably get together again. Just as you say you value my friendship, I value yours, I always did. I am sure we will survive this. We're both too long in the tooth not to know that these things happen in this world.

Just for now, though, I know you will understand if I keep myself to myself for a little while. I have a lot to work out.

I appreciate your concern about Johnny, it might be just the usual scare, but maybe this time it will be worse than that. I have no way of knowing, although the hospital doesn't seem to be worried about him.

Take care, love to you and Tony. And thank you again for the lovely Mass card for CJ, and for coming to his funeral. I haven't got around yet to sending out formal acknowledgements.

Your friend,

May

I sealed and addressed the envelope, took a stamp out of the caboosh and stuck it on, then scribbled a note to Martin, asking him to post it and telling him briefly what had happened with Johnny during the night and where I would be. I propped both against the sugar bowl on the table where he would find them.

I debated whether or not to go down to Esmé's room to tell her but decided against it and added her name to Martin's note. I had to have that shower and change my clothes, get back to the hospital.

Twenty-Four

I wasn't going back just yet.

My hair was already pinned up and I was running my bath when over the sound of the water, I heard the rattle of the knocker on the front door. I debated for a moment or two but as you must have noticed by now, I can rarely resist either telephones or door knockers. I pulled on my dressing gown.

Melanie stood there in all her glory.

Well, not quite glory. Far from the sleek, glossy babe I had last seen, she was bundled up in a windcheater, scruffy jeans and trainers. Her tanned face was puffy and without makeup.

I was no beauty queen, of course, in my old ratty dressing gown with my hair scraped back. Chagrined at her seeing me like this, my initial instinct was to slam the door in her face but I managed to control myself: Yes?

Sorry to bother you, Mrs Lanigan — her voice, too, was different, childish. She could have been knocking at a neighbour's door looking for her ball back.

Oh, you're not bothering me, Melanie, I said.

She didn't react to the sarcasm, cleared her throat:

Clement needs a few things, and I was wondering . . . ?

If I hadn't been so tired I might have reacted more
heatedly, not only to her presence but at the notion of
Clem's having the gall to send his doxy as emissary to
me. But fatigue, like a hangover, sometimes clarifies
situations and, looking at this sad little girl hugging
herself across her anorak, I flashed very clearly on the
track she had laid down for herself with my husband –
ex-husband – and on which she now embarked.
Melanie is going through her own private hell, at an
age when what she should be doing is scooting along
the flowerpaths of the world. As I stared at Melanie, I
knew I could no longer be her enemy. She wasn't
worthy of such a serious expenditure of my time and
emotion, it is true, but that wasn't it.

What happened was far more profound. Hatred and
resentment lifted off my shoulders on great black wings
and beat away, allowing empathy and forgiveness to
put down tiny roots. Come in, Melanie, I said, not
kindly – I wasn't yet capable of going that far – but
calmly. What do you need?

She hesitated as though I were setting a trap: Are
you sure?

I walked away from the door: I have to turn off the
bath. Close the door after you.

Alone in the steamy bathroom, I turned off the water
then paused a moment, testing again, waiting for hatred
to rush back into the vacuum. Instead, all I felt was
lightness.

As though to make sure, I rubbed a circle clear in
the mirror above the washbasin with my sleeve and

searched my face for outward signs of this release. My hair, corralled in its headband, left my face naked so there was no dissembling. I looked the same as before. What had I expected? Transfiguration?

Melanie was still hovering just inside the front door, obviously unsure how to interpret what was going on. She dropped her hands to her sides as I approached, as if I was a headmistress and she a schoolgirl warned repeatedly to stand up straight. She gave me a nervous little smile.

What exactly do you want to take? My tone was brisk.

Clem's needs proved easy to fulfil. Because he had been apprehended in a Sitges bar and taken straight into custody and had subsequently come so quickly back to Ireland, Melanie had had time to deliver very little. He had arrived barehanded in Mountjoy and what he wanted was basic: his old electric razor, his Discman, a few pairs of Calvin Kleins, a red scarf, and other odds and ends to replace the small creature comforts he was allowed and that she had not thought to take with her when she followed him home in such a rush.

I asked her to wait in the sitting room and, while I packed everything into a Tesco bag, thought how lucky my husband was to be married to a natural born hoarder like me.

There you go. Back inside the front door, I held out the plastic bag to her. The scarf was on top and I could see her looking at it.

Clem's superstitious about that scarf, I explained evenly. It was his mother's – he uses it any time he has a sore throat. Of such well-worn knowledge is a long marriage made, I thought, suppressing the desire to mock Melanie with it.

She was fazed by what must have seemed an extraordinary U-turn in my attitude and frowned in bewilderment as she took the bag from me: I – I – look, Mrs Lanigan—

Don't say a word, I cut across her. It's all water under the bridge now. Tell Clem that I'll contact Mountjoy with news of Johnny. I'm going back there now, after my bath.

How is he? She was clutching the plastic bag, like a lifebuoy, to her chest.

He's unconscious, I told her, turning away and walking towards the door so she had to follow. The hospital doesn't seem to be worried about him, not yet anyhow. I'll know more later on. I opened the door: As you probably know, Johnny is – or used to be – in and out of hospital a great deal. They know what they're doing.

I stood holding the door wide open so she would leave. I wanted her to leave now. I had forgiven her, genuinely so, but I did not care to be in her company any longer.

She hesitated again: Mrs Lanigan?

No, I said firmly. Go on now, Melanie, and the best of luck, whatever happens.

For a moment, I thought she was going either to cry or hug me, or perhaps both. Neither of which I could have borne. Goodbye now, take care – I gave her a small, gentle push and closed the door behind her.

I stood for a moment with my back to it. Perhaps I should have given her the opportunity to speak?

Really? Am I suddenly St Maria Goretti?

I was dressed and drying my hair when Ambrose appeared in the bedroom. Don't ask me how I am, Ambrose, just don't, I said, unplugging the dryer. And don't even dream of suggesting a joke to cheer me up.

I know how you are, he said. As I have told you, you are wonderful.

I can tell that he's not going to stay long this time – he seems insubstantial, almost transparent – and I'm recounting this, not to be blowing my own trumpet but because I want to give an accurate view of what it is like to live with an angel. These constant affirmations can be very comforting, to the extent that you start believing that you might indeed be wonderful. They can even balance out the constant discombobulation of knowing that this creature sees and knows every tittle-tattle of your innermost thoughts, what you have done, what you are about to do. Even this mind-reading, unnerving though it is, can prove to be rather relaxing when you stop trying to circumvent it. No fronts to keep up. This angel knows me inside out, you think, all the bad bits, as well as the good bits and yet he is still here.

Are you coming with me to the hospital? I ask him.

He smiles gently: I will be there. You may not see me, but I will be there. Then, as he starts to fade: There is something you need to remember, May. Be careful what you wish for.

Yeah, yeah, I think, not even watching his vanishing act.

I put on my coat and, rushing now, throw a few snacks and a bottle of water into a fresh plastic bag.

I have the front door open when I remember to check the telephone. We have one of those Eircom call-answering systems on our phone where you have to dial in – the phone itself doesn't show you whether or not you have any messages. It can be tiresome but at least it's free.

We have two messages, one from Joan, telling me superfluously she had written me the note. The second one is from Eddie. His voice sounds high, excited. Ring me, Ma, first thing in the morning? Well, actually, cancel that – not too early, Ma, all right? I'm not on until two o'clock tomorrow and I'm going to have a bit of a lie-in. Ring me at about noon – OK?

As it doesn't sound like bad news, I waste little time pondering what it can mean and go out to face whatever lies in store for me.

The weather had broken during the night and, outside, a stiff wind from the river whined up Church Street, making carousels from the litter on the kerbs and gutters in front of the bus stop. It wasn't yet raining but the sky threatened strongly. Our stop is unprotected by a shelter and, overtired as I was, when the minutes dragged on into a quarter of an hour, I began to shiver. I could have kicked myself, I should have blown some more of Esmé's money on ordering a taxi. Oh, to be somewhere warm, I thought. What I wouldn't give for the benediction of hot sunshine on my bare back.

I was standing half-way out into the street, watching for a taxi, when a car drew up on the far side of the road and mounted the footpath. Zig stepped out of it. Leaving the engine running, he dodged through the traffic and came right up to me: Mrs Lanigan, can I offer you a lift somewhere?

But you're going in the opposite direction – I'm going to get a taxi.

You're wasting your time trying to get a taxi at this hour on a Saturday morning. And buses are as scarce as hens' teeth. Where did you want to go?

I was too tired and too cold to look this gift horse in the mouth. Beaumont, I said quickly. My youngest son has been admitted.

Zig reacted but, thank God, didn't start into the third degree there and then. Let me take this – he lifted my bag of supplies with one hand, and with the other, guided me by the elbow across to the car. Right, he said when we were inside, put your seatbelt on, please, and without waiting to see whether I did or not, he checked his mirrors and revved the car loudly through a wide U-turn to face north. Then, as he accelerated through an amber traffic light, he saw the expression on my face: Don't worry, I'm a good driver. He was wearing glasses, the light, gold-rimmed sort. I'd never seen them on him before.

To his credit Zig seems to know the value of silence. He turned off the car radio, which had been broadcasting a news bulletin, not before noticing I was still shivering. Would you like the heater on?

Thank you. Then, as he fiddled with the controls, I pulled my lightweight coat more tightly around me, thanked him for the lift and said I hoped I wasn't taking him too far out of his way.

As a matter of fact it was a bit of a coincidence to see you like that, he said quietly. I was actually coming to see you.

What about?

Oh, it'll wait – are you all right? he stalled. You look beat.

While he drove as quickly as he could through the surprisingly heavy traffic, I told him about being up all night with Johnny.

It's tough having a boy like that, he said, then: I admire you for sticking with it the way you have. I don't think I could handle it.

I didn't waste my breath asking how he knew about Johnny. It's not only Ambrose who knows this family inside out, every cop in Dublin probably knows what every member of my family has for breakfast. I had to admit, though, that Zig's direct attitude was refreshing. Usually, where Johnny is concerned, people get tongue-tied. These days, for instance, they are not sure if it's acceptable to mention his disabilities at all in case they are breaking some unwritten code of political correctness.

I wanted to ask Zig if there had been a development in CJ's case, if that had been the reason he had been coming to see me, but whether it was because of the heat in the car or fatigue, I began to feel light-headed and nauseous and had to concentrate on not being sick. By the time we were turning into Drumcondra Road from Griffith Avenue, however, I was seriously afraid I was about to vomit. In urgent need of air, I lowered the car window and inclined my head to catch the cold draught.

You've gone very pale, Mrs Lanigan – he sounded seriously concerned.

I closed my eyes and willed my gorge not to rise: Could you pass me the bag from the back seat? My voice sounded like a kitten's mew.

I sensed him reaching back and then the plastic rustled into my lap. Without opening my eyes, I searched by touch and extracted the bottle of water. I hoped control of my stomach would last until I got the bottle open and as far as my mouth.

Have you eaten, Mrs Lanigan? Zig's voice came from very far away.

I shook my head again, but only very slightly. The world behind my eyelids was strobing and I was seriously light-headed – Please, God, I prayed, please don't let me faint in this policeman's car. It would be the ultimate humiliation. Vaguely, I sensed that the trajectory of the car had changed, it seemed to be swinging to the right. But still I did not dare to open my eyes and, after a quick gulp of the water, had now inclined my head to the extent that it projected almost fully through the open window.

The car stopped and the engine cut out. The tension of my seatbelt slackened. He had unbuckled it although I had not felt the pressure of his hands. Take your time, Mrs Lanigan. The breakfasts will still be on in here, it's only just after ten.

I felt a breeze and managed to open my eyes. We had parked outside Rook's restaurant at the Regency Hotel. Zig was getting out of the car, coming round to

my side, opening the door. I can't, I said faintly, I have
to get to the hospital.

He pulled the door open as far as it would go: Come
on, you're still on schedule. You would still be standing
at that bus stop if I hadn't come along.

It was a fair point. Gingerly I got out and, with a
hand firmly under my elbow, he helped me to mount
the steps towards the restaurant. There was little I
could do about this diversion because I was totally in
Zig's hands, not only metaphorically but literally,
because with every step my rubbery knees threatened
to give way.

As we made our way past the cash desk into the
empty restaurant towards one of the booths, he
grabbed a handful of mints from a little bowl beside
the register and thrust them at me: Here – eat these,
the sugar will help.

Ten minutes later, I'm sitting in front of a plateful
of rashers, eggs, sausages, black and white pudding,
mushrooms and tomato with brown bread on the side.
He's having only coffee. You're hungry all right, he
says, as he observes my indiscriminate wolfing. Did
you know research has shown that faced with a mixed
grill, an overwhelming percentage of people will eat
the sausage first? Did you know that?

Mmm – research is irrelevant to me as I lash butter
on my bread. It's been months since I've seen real
butter.

I'm feeling sharp and clear again. Looking at Zig
properly for the first time this morning, I realize there
is something different about him and it's not only the
glasses. He's not wearing a tie, or a jacket, just a

jumper over a denim shirt. Without the suit, he looks younger. I ask if he's on another day off.

He hesitates: In a manner of speaking. Look, Mrs Lanigan, I was coming to tell you that I won't be continuing with the investigation into your son's murder.

I stop chewing. It's all right, he says quickly, tracing the outline of a pattern in the wood of the table with one index finger, you needn't worry. There are a lot more than me involved and Jackie's one of the good ones. Looking up, he sees my incomprehension: Jacqueline Sinnott? My colleague?

She's not as senior as you – she's only—

No, but she will be. And this is one of the cases that will bring her up.

Because no one else wants it?

He stiffens. I promised you that we would do all we could. And we are working hard, Mrs Lanigan. This is a serious murder investigation at chief superintendent level. The Commissioner is taking a daily interest. There's an epidemic of this kind of thing going on and we are serious about stopping it.

So why are you going off this case?

Then he tells me he is leaving the force altogether, pulling up sticks and going to Frigiliana to live in his villa. I am conscious of a vague sense of disappointment, but rather than test it, concentrate, for Zig's sake, on seeing Zig in his new abode: Zig eating tapas? Zig propping up some bar while regaling English ex-pats with his exploits? It was hard to envisage. But what'll you do all day after – after all this? Won't you be bored?

Hardly. He grins: Don't underestimate how much of the day a person can put in on a beach counting the waves. Slowly, he stirs the coffee he has ordered but has not yet touched: Seriously, whatever about other problems, boredom will not be one of them. I'll have no difficulty passing my days. I play a little golf – not too well, but you get membership of a course along with ownership of the villa. I got to know a few of the other owners over the years and, anyway, more and more Irish people are going to live in Spain now. It's easy to get to, these days, and quite cheap so I'll be able to fly home from time to time if I get lonely. He inspects the contents of his cup.

I suppose I shouldn't be as surprised as I am. After all, he had hinted at this in the Skylon – I probably had not been listening properly. And my disappointment can be put down to the fact that Zig had been my nearest point of contact to the investigation and I had learned to trust him. Well, a little. Also, of course, he had known CJ personally and was therefore a way to hold on a little longer.

I've finished eating and place my knife and fork tidily together on the plate: But why now?

I've been thinking about it, as I believe I told you. I hate Dublin, hate the kind of people I'm having to deal with, hate all this new competitiveness in the force. It's a young man's game now. He hesitates, then having signalled for the bill, again finds something fascinating in the surface grain of the table. He scratches at it: I went for promotion recently, for the third time. I found out yesterday afternoon that a thirty-three-year-old female from Cork got it. I'll be fifty at the end of this year and this was definitely my last chance. I handed in my notice last night.

Never having worked outside the home, as they say these days, I can only imagine the humiliation of such a rebuff. I can see, too, that he is not suffering from pique but is resigned to this assessment of him. Out of the ring at fifty. Perhaps never a serious contender in the first place.

What'll you live on? Will you have a good pension?

I'll try to negotiate an exit package but I'm lucky in that I don't need to. I've been a policeman for thirty-one years so I'll be entitled to most of my pension and some kind of a lump sum. There was an insurance policy on Agnetha and she left me all of her estate too – remember I told you about the legacy? I was able to pay off the mortgage on our house, I sold it at a good profit, I haven't lived high, and the mortgage insurance paid off the holiday home which was in her name.

So – he spreads his hands wide – no dependants, no mortgages, no debts of any kind, money in the bank. Why in the name of God would I flog myself working all hours? For what? Let Mizz Carol O'Riordan from County Cork get shot at, pranged in the car, spat at outside the courtrooms of this bloody country. I've done it. I'm through.

He no longer sounds resigned. Sorry, he says ruefully, I've nothing against her. That came out badly.

What about your father? Aren't you living with him? For some reason I seem to be putting up objections to his plan.

He laughs outright. Máirtín, is it? Told me last

Christmas that I was cramping his style. He takes off his glasses and wipes his eyes. No, I've no worries about Máirtín. Not yet anyway.

I've a Martin, I tell him.

I know. He replaces his glasses.

I change the subject. So if you don't need money, why did you stay in the Guards in the first place?

He looks me straight in the eye: I thought I was in the kind of job that might make a difference. Stupid or what! I no longer believe it. We're losing. His gaze slides again towards the surface of the table.

Look, why are you telling me all this, I ask him, me of all people? I'm in the other camp.

No, you're not, he says quietly. You're another of the good ones. I've known that since the first day I saw you in that courtroom at your husband's trial.

We stare at one another. He breaks off, signalling again towards the waitress. The memory of Zig chasing my husband – and of the look he cast at me as ran past my seat – rises vividly. I'm beginning to feel strangely off balance.

He is still looking in the direction of the cash desk: Something I'd like to know, if it's not too cheeky of me?

Is it significant that you've moved your wedding ring?

Involuntarily I glance down at my hands. I should tell him it's none of his business. Yes, I say.

The waitress comes with our bill. He hands it back to her with his credit card, and she leaves. I stand up and he follows suit.

On the steps outside the doors, we see that the rain

has started with a vengeance, driven by the wind in long, arcing sweeps through the car park. Wait there, he orders. I'll bring the jalopy up to the steps. He pulls the neckband of his jumper up around his ears – as though that will give the slightest protection – and sprints through the downpour.

I get to the car with the minimum damage and slam the door. Thanks.

He removes his glasses and wipes the rain off them with his handkerchief. Bloody specs. I wore contacts for the job – you'd never know when you'd be called on to do something athletic! He flashes me a knowing grin – Zig would not strike even a doting mother as the athletic type. But I see no reason any longer to go through the hassle.

He replaces the specs: That's better. These'll do me fine from now on and I'll enjoy spending the money on more interesting things. He puts the car in gear but, before releasing the clutch, squares his shoulders. His face has gone tight. Look, tell me I'm out of order, Mrs Lanigan. But are you and your husband getting separated?

I feel there's no point in prevaricating on the issue. In due course, I say. He nods, lips pursed: And what about this Joe guy?

For a moment I'm mystified: What Joe guy? Then I remember. Oh – Joe Rooney? What about him?

Would I be trespassing if I asked you if we could have a cup of coffee or a drink or something before I leave?

A date? I couldn't believe my ears.

There's no Joe guy, I say, looking straight ahead.

He doesn't answer, just nods again then shoves the car into gear and performs another of his Fangio manoeuvres through the car park. Put on your seatbelt, please, Mrs Lanigan, he says primly, as he accelerates out of the wide entrance on to the main road and, tyres screeching, turns across the highway. I continue to gaze through the streaming windscreen. What am I at?

But I do like the glasses. Very William Hurt. And you know, now that I'm noticing these things, he's not all that small, about five ten, I'd say. He looked small only in comparison to the other one, Zag, that's probably what it was. Thinnish all right, maybe that's why I used to think of him as a weed. But actually, now that I think about it, there's something very solid about Zig.

I flood with guilt. I had not worried about Johnny for at least twenty minutes.

I remember Eddie's phone message. What time is it? My watch has stopped. It's one my da gave me for my sixteenth birthday and I keep forgetting to wind it. Zig glances at his own wrist: It's twenty-five to eleven, he says. I search through my handbag for my mobile phone and realize I've left it at home. I ask him if I may use his.

Sure. He unclips it from his belt and hands it to me.

Eddie's voice is sleepy, then fires up when he hears it's me. The most amazing thing has happened. Tracey has been offered a joint fellowship from some European business foundation together with a multinational corporation to further her studies at a business school in

Paris. It was something she had applied for and almost forgotten about at the beginning of last September.

And guess what, Ma? Eddie is almost shouting. There'll be enough money for me to go too. To Paris, Ma. Two years in Paris. I'll get some kind of a job there, Tracey says it's just like here, they're crying out for people who'll do work, like, in shops and stuff— Abruptly his tone becomes serious: Is that all right? You'll be all right?

Of course I'll be all right, I say. My reaction to this is not even mixed. I will miss Eddie, but he deserves this so much. I'm really delighted for you and Tracey, I say. I couldn't be more delighted.

Where are you? He sounds anxious now. Are you in a car?

I tell him where I am and where I'm going.

Oh, shit – I can almost see his feet hitting the ground as he jumps out of the bed, I'll meet you there.

You'll do no such thing, I say firmly, this isn't an emergency. I'll call you at work if there is any need to. We'd only be getting in one another's way. He protests but I continue to insist and we sign off.

Good news? Zig asks.

Yes, thank God, I say, as I hand him back the telephone.

Zig had the good sense to drop me off at the front entrance to the hospital and not to hang around. I'll telephone you, Mrs Lanigan, he said.

When are you leaving, exactly? I was holding the passenger door of the car open and leaning in to talk to him.

The third of June, three weeks from today, if I can get a flight for that day. It's a Saturday, he added, with pointless clarification.

I hesitated: If we are to have a cup of coffee – whatever – maybe you should stop calling me Mrs Lanigan?

He grinned but blushed brick red: So what do I call you?

You know damned well, I said, and slammed the door. I was smiling too as I hurried into the foyer of the hospital. Maybe if Johnny wasn't too bad I could slip out of the hospital some time during the afternoon to get my hair done. A colour would be nice.

I needn't have hurried, as it turns out. I've been sitting here for hours, staving off sleep and boredom while waiting for something to happen. We're still waiting for the consultant.

Until he comes, apart from amusing myself some-how, there is little I can do except to watch the monitor blinking its mysterious hieroglyphics, to over-dose on cups of tea and coffee, and to fight semi-hypnotism by the slow drip-drip of liquid through the transparent tube.

I've had plenty of time to examine the prospect of life without Eddie. I will miss him dreadfully, there is no doubt about it, but my overriding feeling is one of gladness, for him and for Tracey. They are now seriously on their way. And, anyway, as I know from personal experience, Paris is now just a cheap hop away by Ryanair.

Johnny came to, briefly, just as the midday Angelus

was ringing across the rooftops of Whitehall and Beaumont. He seemed very relaxed as he gazed around the ward, a puzzled expression on his face. Then he saw me and his face was transfigured with one of his goofy, open-mouthed smiles.

Reassured, grateful he was evidently not in pain, I immediately took his hand: You know where you are, lovey? I'm here. Going to make Johnny all better.

Continuing to smile, he squeezed my hand and kept his eyes on mine. Within seconds, though, the eyelids started to droop and the smile faded. His grip on my hand loosened — he had slipped away again.

One of the staff nurses was with us at the time. I asked her if he had been given more sedation.

She checked the chart hanging on the end of the bed then shook her head. He's sleeping all by himself. She leaned in, her face very close to his, Aren't you, John? John? John? flicking him gently on the cheek.

Johnny's response was nil. She straightened up: He's not with us. We'll see what the consultant says.

It's almost three o'clock now and the consultant is due at any minute. Maybe if he doesn't take too long with Johnny, I'll still be in time to get my hair done.

Twenty-Five

Death of Second Lanigan Son

The funeral has taken place of John Lanigan, youngest son of Mr Clem Lanigan who is in Mountjoy gaol awaiting the resumption of his trial on tax evasion and smuggling charges. The younger Mr Lanigan died early on Monday morning in Beaumont Hospital, Dublin. A spokesperson for the hospital said he had died of natural causes. Clem Lanigan escaped dramatically from a courtroom and absconded to Spain following the sudden collapse and death of Mr Justice Harvey Yelland during the course of his original trial in September, 1999. Last month, Mr Lanigan's eldest son, Clem Junior, known as CJ, was murdered and an investigation into his death continues. John Lanigan, who was 19, is survived by his parents and four brothers.

Irish Times, Wednesday, 17 May 2000

→ Twenty-Six ←

1 June 2000

I feel I live in two places at once: here is the May who is living her life, such as it is. Over there is the May who is watching this first May go through the motions. This split feeling has persisted right from the time I heard the worst was about to happen. The detached May watches the first, bereaved May with interest. I see her out there, walking, talking, dealing with medics and administrators, cleaning obsessively, and I feel enormous sympathy for her plight. I can see grief, like barbed wire, enclose her, I can even empathize with it. I know she is me but at the same time she is only of technical interest to me. I hope I am not going mad.

Loath as I am to admit it, there is even a sneaking element of relief that the inevitability of Johnny's death can no longer threaten me. Twenty years is a long wait and I think I had done a lot of my grieving in the months after he was born; each time he was admitted to hospital, I grieved again – in anticipation, and also for the life he should have had.

When you add in the fact that the mourning wound

for CJ is still open and festering, where poor Johnny is concerned, if it does not sound too heartless or barbaric, I am all grieved out.

As you know, I had always worried about dying before him – what would happen to him? who would give him the commitment and care? – but although I had never admitted it to myself, deep down I knew that, barring accidents or virulent cancer, I would survive this son.

All of this does not mean I do not miss him – I do, terribly – but if grief after CJ's death could be likened to a crushing, angry torrent sweeping all other life before it, my mourning for Johnny is like a wide, slow running river. I certainly do not seem to have the same need to pick it over in the kind of detail I gave CJ.

Late last night in our kitchen, I think I went through a catharsis, of sorts, prompted as ever by Ambrose who, I have to say, has been most attentive in the last couple of weeks.

While racing around, filling rubbish bags with what I had now decided was unwanted kitchen clutter, I was rerunning the cinema reel of this year for him. Upright and serious in one of the fireside chairs, he listened intently as I raked through the catastrophes, making comparisons, trying to decide which had been the worst time during the past year: Clem's arrest? The discovery of the affair? The deaths? And of the deaths, which would have the most traumatic effect in the long term?

As I ran out of steam at last, he readjusted his robe a little: Which horror was most horrific? Do you really find this helpful, May?'

I scrutinize him, unable to decide whether or not he is being critical, but even if he was, I knew I could not summon up energy for a counter-attack. 'Why didn't you warn me, Ambrose?' I ask him quietly. 'You knew all along, chapter and verse, what was in store for me.'

For the first time since he came to me, he engaged fully, without being enigmatic: 'Would you have thanked me for causing you to live the nightmare before it happened, May? Were there not moments of happiness when you were able to live in the present? Should I have deprived you of those moments?'

The memory reel flipped over: I saw Joe Rooney's flowers, my delight in Johnny's happiness alongside CJ as they played with the Beanie Babies on the floor of the sitting room, the sun on my face during that brief yielding to relaxation on the Sitges promenade before I saw Clem. The absorption of our lovemaking in the hotel. Would I have enjoyed that if I had known where he was going after he left our bed?

I searched Ambrose's face: 'But I could have stopped CJ – at least I could have done that.'

He gazed at me, his eyes wide and full of genuine sympathy and I finally accepted that nothing I could have done would have prevented what was to happen in CJ's life, in Johnny's life, in Clem's or Melanie's or any other human being's. That they had their own choices to make. And that this was what I had needed to learn.

Johnny never regained consciousness after that one brilliant smile and our consultant physician, having examined him, called in cardiology, pulmonary and urology colleagues throughout that afternoon. They all examined the poor sad body while the hours ticked by and I spent a lot of time in the exile of the corridor outside.

At about five o'clock that Saturday afternoon, his breathing became laboured and he was put on full oxygen. It was no longer only his heart. His lungs were full of fluid and his kidneys had started to fail. He was taken down to theatre for an emergency tracheotomy.

Four hours passed in the intensive care ward but he was still no better. Further surgery was offered, but with so many provisos that I hesitated greatly at the thought of putting him through it. Our own consultant came again at about ten thirty and I asked him, who knew Johnny best, what my son's chances would be if we did consent to an operation. He replied that no one could be sure of the outcome, and tried to inject confidence by telling me that people in this condition have survived before. I saw, however, by the gravity of his tone and the sympathy in his eyes that Johnny would probably not be so fortunate. And now I knew without doubt that even if he did survive the surgery, it would not be for long. By eleven that night, Johnny was on a life-support machine.

He lingered, sustained by the technology, for thirty-four more hours and we were all there when he died just as dawn lightened the outside sky on the Monday morning. About half an hour previously, Eddie had been warned by a sympathetic staff nurse that the end was near. I refused the chaplain's offer of bedside prayers, I knew Johnny had no need of them, and where we were concerned, I could not see any advantage or comfort to be gained by any of us. Anyhow, he had already received the Sacrament of the Sick.

Funny, the names they put on these rituals nowadays. It is as though ceasing to call it Extreme Unction will somehow make the prayers a little less final.

The crucial moment passed without my recognizing it. I do not even know how the medics saw it and I have not asked. The bellows of the ventilator continued to sigh and thump, sounds to which we had become accustomed, and I could see no difference between life existing and life ebbed in Johnny's prone body or pale face. I have read stories and articles about the bereaved becoming aware of the soul's exit. But when one of the nurses told us he was gone, even though Johnny's thin chest continued rhythmically to rise and fall, I believed it because she said so.

I walked immediately to the window and pushed it open to allow his soul to fly free. These traditions, customs, *piseógs*, ceremonies, whatever you want to call them, are very deeply embedded. I may have heard about this one at school.

When a ventilator is disconnected, the body lurches and twitches a little, gasping for one more breath. Did you know that? No blame to anyone but we had not been warned about this and all of us reacted. 'He's alive!' The cry came from Frank.

It was comforting to have a living son to comfort.

There was room in Da's grave and I decided to lay Johnny there. Believe it or not, about eighty people walked after his coffin as the hearse drove slowly along the old paths in Mount Jerome. The human heart is strange: although I appreciated the size of the turn-out for Johnny's sake, at some level I resented it for CJ's.

A few early moths and butterflies fluttered about on this hot, still day. Competing scents streamed through the sunshine from the recently cut grass, from the warming, weathered limestone and lichen-covered granite of the headstones, from the exhaust fumes of the elderly hearse and, of course, from pungent, wilting flowers and wreaths. The city's rumbling was muted beyond the old walls, and as we walked slowly along, the only sounds were the low purr of the hearse's engine, the shuffle of feet, and the rhythmic squeak from the wheel of one of the wheelchairs being pushed by the staff from St Anthony's.

I made a decision. Soon I would travel to England to visit my mother's grave. She wasn't here with Da – he had been buried with his own mother and father. She had died in London while undergoing treatment for her cancer, and although Da had never told me exactly where she was, it should be an easy matter to find out.

It was just before noon when we arrived at the spot where we had to leave the little roadway to cross towards the open grave. As we stood packed up in the sunlight while the coffin was taken out to be placed on the shoulders of Johnny's brothers for the last few seconds he would spend above ground, I realized that no one was talking or even whispering. For some reason, this disturbed me. The racketing Johnny Lanigan, wedded to the noise-making of his pots and pans and wooden spoons, would not understand such solemnity. So I turned around and smiled at the group directly behind me – Emily, Joe Rooney, two of the other women from the writing group and the oddbod poet. I think the others might have been disconcerted – too calm, she's too calm, but Oddbod smiled back; like recognizing like, perhaps, mad smiling at mad.

I hate the last sounds. The rasping of the canvas slings against the wood of the coffin, the heavy breaths from the gravediggers as they try not to grunt under the weight of their burden. But even at that moment I knew we had been right not to have Johnny cremated. I could not have faced that, not after the experience with CJ.

The Angelus rang out from the bell-tower of Mount Argus nearby as the men lowered Johnny into his grave. Although I continued to feel as though I were muffled up in an opaque grey blanket, the sight of the coffin's clumsy descent threatened to break through and I could not continue to watch it. Deliberately, I let my attention wander, looking around at the crowd. I saw that even Clem's solicitor, whom I had seen earlier outside the church, had come all the way out here. That was good of him, I thought.

Zig, without the Ban Ghárda this time, was not far away and near him, Tony, Joan and Melanie stood together near the back of the crowd. The sight of her provoked no response in me whatsoever. I continued to have the sense of floating, all feelings suspended, and with no sense of impending emotion of any sort. Clem himself, now that I took the time to examine him, was very well turned out. Head bowed and hands joined, wearing a dark suit, pristine white shirt and black tie, he might have been any businessman. Except for his closely shaved head and the two burly minders – who had found the discretion and compassion to wear civilian clothes – standing close behind him.

He had been wearing a suit when I met him at my first disco, in 1973, when I was only fifteen. It was hard to miss him: he had the bluest eyes and the longest, blackest lashes I've ever seen on any boy. Ever. He was twenty. When I managed to catch his eye, I tossed my head because I knew my hair was all bouncy from being set on heated rollers I had borrowed.

The deejay that night was poxy but Clem Lanigan and I did not care because all we heard was the beat and all we saw was one another's faces, and by the time Da came to collect me that night, I was hooked.

I looked away from Clem and into poor old Da's open grave. What would he think of me and Clem now?

Father Blaise started in on the decade of the Rosary and Eddie took my arm: 'Nearly over, Ma, are you all right?'

I turned back and smiled up at him: 'I'm fine. Grand.'

When the time came to throw my rose in on top of the coffin, I did so carefully and tenderly, making sure that it landed correctly on the blond wood. The brass plate, *John Jude Lanigan, 1981–2000*, glinted as if it were made of gold. The sun was directly overhead. The wood would be warm. Wood holds heat. At least he would be comfortable for a while, I thought, as I stepped back.

The boys threw their own roses, the green, wreath-

covered pallet was pulled over the open grave and
Johnny was Da's to mind.

The thought tickled me, made me smile again:
Would Da be up to it? His tolerance of Johnny in life
had not been great. Well, he had no choice now.
Maybe it was God's revenge.

Still grinning, I looked around and caught Esmé's
considering glance. All through the previous days, she
had moved quietly through the house, organizing meals,
quietly directing traffic and accommodating visitors.
While I walked into and out of rooms, forgetting the
reasons for my journeys, she, it seems, had effortlessly
taken control.

We were not having any reception. I could not have
faced it – even if we could have afforded such an
extravagance. So one by one, two by two, the crowd
came forward with their final condolences.

There are only so many ways to express sympathy
and only so many ways to respond, and within minutes
I was finding it difficult to keep the flow going without
sounding insincere in my gratitude. Furthermore, I was
also beginning to feel defensive. Insulated though I was,
I could see the question grow larger in people's eyes:
Why isn't she more upset? When is the crash going to
happen? Or could it be that she's been heartless all
along?

So when I saw Clem coming towards me, although I
could feel the four boys go on alert around me I seized
on his approach as something tangible to hold on to.
Clem, who had his own troubles, would not be
watching me for imminent signs of collapse. I had not
spoken to him since my visit to the prison – he had

not been allowed out to attend Johnny's removal the previous night. And even though we had parted on such acrimonious terms, looking now at his woebegone face, I could not find the iron with which to harden my heart. He stopped a couple of feet away from me and gazed at the ground: 'I'm sorry, May.'

'I'm sorry too, Clem. Are you all right?' I asked him. Then, after a pause, 'It's not too bad for you in there, I hope?'

Surprised, he looked up at me, his expression uncertain, almost shy. 'To tell you the truth, the walls are closing in on me a bit – but I'm all right.' He made a small gesture as though to touch my arm but both of us knew that this was a step too far and he dropped his hand. 'You'll miss him, Maisie,' he said.

I nodded. 'You will too – we both will.' Tears threatened the other May, that second, hazy May who hovered inches in front of my own body. They still didn't threaten me.

Clem looked towards the grave. 'I wish––' He stopped.

'Yes?' I prompted him.

'Everything all right, Ma––?' It was Eddie, stiff and proper, taking my arm, and I was never to know what Clem wished.

'Hello, Da.' Eddie nodded formally towards Clem. 'You're looking well, I have to say, considering.' Then, turning again to me: 'We should get going.'

Mutely, Clem stepped back a little. And as I gazed at this husband who was no longer my husband, I continued to feel neutral, even slightly sympathetic, and thereby made a discovery. I had forgiven Clem, not from any inherent nobility but because, as with Melanie, I had been released from caring. It was as easy to forgive him as it was to hold a grudge. And this forgiveness was not only from the detached May, it was from both of us. 'Sure, Eddie,' I said, 'we should be going.' Then, to Clem: 'Take care of yourself. We'll all be in touch, I'm sure.'

He might have said something else but his minders came alongside and the encounter was over. As the boys and I walked away from the graveside, I looked back. Clem was being escorted by his minders towards the cemetery gate along a different pathway than that taken by the rest of us. Tony, Joan and Melanie were still standing together. Joan and Tony were staring into space, away from one another. Melanie was staring after Clem. It was a sad little tableau.

I think now that although I had not realized it, Clem and I had been leading separate lives for a very long time and I had adhered only to the concept of loving, loyal and faithful wifehood rather than to the actuality. Melanie may even have unwittingly done me a favour because, although I would have preferred the process to have been a little less painful and abrupt, she had forced me into facing this.

The days following Johnny's funeral were busy enough: there were some formalities to be concluded at St Anthony's and I occupied myself with writing letters in response to those I had received. As usual, I was seized with a compulsion to spring-clean the house and went through it from top to bottom. We were undoubtedly a mourning household, but in many respects not an altogether changed one since both Johnny and CJ had been missing from the day-to-day routine for quite a while, and when you add in the fact that Clem had also been absent during almost a full year, life seemed to proceed almost as normal.

Still I have not wept.

✧ Twenty-Seven ✧

Zig has been attentive, but not claustrophobically so. He let a week pass after the funeral and didn't call on me again until 23 May, catching me in filth and glory, hair plastered to my head under a scarf, hands black from tarnish and wadding. I had been cleaning the surround of the fireplace in the sitting room, never a pleasant task but, what with one thing and another recently, I had let the brasswork in the house go to pot.

Instinctively, I rip off the turban as soon as I open the door and see who it is but of course it's too late: I know, I know – before you say anything, I know I look like one of those landlady characters from a comic seaside postcard. Come on in – I pull the door wide.

If I'm not intruding?

Not at all. I lead him into the kitchen. The sitting room is in no fit state to receive visitors.

Over coffee, he tells me he is now a free man. He's had some leave accruing to him and also time in lieu due for days worked outside his normal shift pattern. I could have worked right up to the time I went but it's like getting engaged, Mrs Lanigan, there's no point in postponing the wedding once you've made the decision. You might as well get on with the nuptials and be done with it.

Mrs Lanigan?

He clears his throat. All right then. May.

We chat easily, about nothing much, which, after all the sympathizing and watchfulness of everyone else around me, I find to be quite a relief. And by the time he's leaving, I have relaxed sufficiently to invite him to come again before he leaves for Spain: I wouldn't want you to slip off now without saying goodbye.

He shoots me a sceptical policeman's look.

I mean it. I'm not being sarcastic – honestly.

In fact, I'm surprised to find how easy I now feel with Zig. Even more surprising is the discovery that I will miss talking to him. Rare though our conversations had been, it appears that in the absence of Joan, he is now the only human being from the outside world to whom I can talk comfortably. I know the workshop people will continue to treat me with kid gloves, and although the boys are dropping in and out regularly – so regularly that I have begun to believe they've constructed a roster – conversation between us is necessarily constrained. They have their own mourning to do and consequently, with only Esmé's largely silent presence, days in this house pass slowly. All right, I have Ambrose. But really, given the choice, which would you prefer to talk to? A real live flesh-and-blood human being or an angel who is liable to vanish without even a pop? And at least with Zig I have – had – some semblance of control over what he can read of my thoughts or plans.

All of this flashes through me in an instant as we

stand at the doorstep. I realize he is watching me carefully. I mean it, I repeat firmly, I'd like to see you.

I'm not being a nuisance?

Of course you're not being a nuisance.

He smiles, his little moustache lifting: All right, so.

How long have you had the moustache? It's out before I could stop it.

You don't like it.

I didn't say that, did I? I'm abashed.

You didn't have to. He grins, enjoying my chagrin: And there was I thinking it makes me look like Errol Flynn. Ah, well, next time you see me . . . He makes a guillotine motion with an index finger across his upper lip.

I didn't mean—

Yes, you did! He relents: I'm tired of it. No big deal. I have to shave the rest of my face every morning anyway. He throws his arms wide: I'm sprung from the force, new life, new man, new face, eh?

We say goodbye, and as I close the door behind him, it occurs to me how weird it is that this policeman and I, who have nothing in common except the macabre murder of my son, have become personally so friendly so quickly.

So what? I think then. You take friends where you find them and I'm lucky that at my age I'm still finding them. In the workshop – and now Zig as well.

Yes, it's definitely a pity he is going to Spain.

He came again a few days later, shyly aware of his clean upper lip. Don't say a word. If you say a word about it, I'll put you under caution.

Don't do that. It's nice. I like it.

If the truth be told, the naked-faced Zig took a bit of getting used to. His features seemed entirely more open, his eyes larger. But it was difficult not to stare at the arc of skin, red and glistening as though denuded only very recently.

The significance of the action was only now dawning on me. I had not seriously thought he would do it. To please me? The knowledge was embarrassing yet somehow intriguing.

This time I automatically led him to the kitchen and began to make coffee without even asking if he wanted some. And this time, without waiting for an invitation, he took 'his' chair, the one he seemed to favour. So quickly adopting comfortable habits?

I rang a few people about the case – not much progress at this stage, he said, as I busied myself, but then I wouldn't expect any. It's too soon, these things take time. They're grinding through it, pulling in and questioning every lowlife and scumbag in the city. What we – what they'll need is a bit of luck, but even if that doesn't happen, you can be sure that someone somewhere is going to let something slip. We're very experienced in this kind of stuff these days – unfortunately.

I asked the million dollar question. With Zig out of the picture, was I ever going to find out why CJ had been released from custody that time and the other two weren't?

He looked at me for a considering few seconds. You will, he said, if there is anything to find out. I'm not sure there is. Not everything is a conspiracy, May. He grinned: And contrary to what you obviously think, I'm not vanishing off the face of the earth, you know. They do have a postal service in Spain. He hesitated, then, diffidently: I'm planning to keep in touch with Jackie and a few of the others. I'll keep in touch with you too, if you like. And in a rush: With whatever I hear.

Thank you.

You're welcome.

There was an awkward pause during which both of us resorted to sipping decorously at our cups. Then, to my astonishment, his demeanour changed completely, and he was off and running, chatting about the job, about Miss Dimples, as he calls the Cork woman who got the job he thinks he deserved, about anything and everything.

This garrulous Zig was a revelation. It was as though his release from the shackles of The Force, as he calls it, had freed his tongue too and that he had a lifetime of conversation to cram into whatever time remained to him on this earth. It didn't matter to me, it was refreshing actually, and I coasted along on this tide of talk, not altogether paying attention, just enjoying its novelty value and the company.

I'm boring you. I'm talking too much, he said, after a few minutes, startling me.

Was this mind-reading habit of Ambrose's contagious?

Not at all, I protested, far from it. I love listening to you, but I have to admit that up to now I had you cast as the strong, silent type.

I'm happy, he said simply. Then: I'm sorry you can't

358 DEIRDRE PURCELL

be happy. I'm sorry for myself, too, in that although it's understandable in the circumstances, we won't be going out before I leave. He stood up. I'll let you get back to it, May, I only meant to drop in for a minute.

But why not? Why can't we go out?

He was taken aback: I beg your pardon?

I had spoken impulsively but now thought about it seriously. We're not going to a night-club or a bordello, are we? It's only a cup of coffee.

Yes, but— He hesitated. Isn't it too soon?

Too soon for whom?

Who was I going to scandalize by going out for an innocent cup of coffee? And did I care anyhow? Yet seeing how taken aback Zig was by my reaction, I examined my conscience. It came up clean. Hand on my heart I couldn't see how window-polishing and floor-scrubbing was going to be of the slightest help to Johnny or CJ. To anybody at all. Even to me.

I made up my mind. I had loved both my sons and I had done my best for them; purdah would achieve nothing. I really don't see whose business it is, I said quietly. If anyone makes it his business, tough. When do you want to go?

Now if you like. He had still not got over his surprise.

Give me ten minutes to get cleaned up.

This date, if such it was, began shakily. We went to Chief O'Neill's but found it jam-packed with two enormous groups of tourists – Americans and Japanese by the looks of them – whose combined din reminded me of childhood trips to the zoo to watch feeding time.

Zig and I looked at one another and, without even discussing it, beat a retreat.

Back in his car, however, neither of us could think of any other comfortable place nearby. Tentatively I suggested the markets but he demurred. That was not stylish enough. And each of us had personal reasons for avoiding the coffee shops, pubs and hotels along the Quays. Adjacent to the Four Courts and the Bridewell, they were frequented by too many legal types and cops.

In addition, I was flustered by the sudden appearance of Ambrose, leaning nonchalantly against one of the forty-foot lanterns newly placed along the cobbled square in Smithfield. He was as tall as I'd ever seen him, and even from this distance, I could see his expression was smug. Perish the thought, but was Ambrose taking credit for this outing? I glanced back at Zig but, seemingly lost in thought, he was staring straight ahead through the windscreen of the car.

This was turning into a farce and I was about to say we should abandon the whole outing and he could simply come back to the house, when he turned to me: Let's throw caution to the winds and travel to the south side. I laughed. Whether by osmosis or detective instincts Zig had sussed my northside parochialism. I glanced towards Ambrose but he had vanished.

Zig started the car. I still could not think of him as 'Finn' but as we moved off, mentally practised tagging the name to sentences: *Yes, please, Finn, I'd love another cup. Would you excuse me for a moment, Finn? I have to go to the ladies'. Hey, Finn — look at this.*

He drove us to the Conrad Hotel on Earlsfort Terrace and, miraculously, found a parking space out-side the National Concert Hall opposite. Comfortably, he took my elbow as we crossed the road and did not relinquish it until we were inside the glass doors.

We climbed a wide marble staircase from the very large, very grand lobby, and were lucky – again – to find a table on the mezzanine above where a pianist drifted through a medley of show tunes; we had apparently arrived at a time when they were serving formal afternoon tea. Under the tinkling music, the buzz of conversation was subdued, everything was orderly, everything shone: the satiny black wood of the grand piano, the china tea and coffee services, the brass balustrades of the staircase, the polished floors. I felt privileged and cosseted as I sat in my chair.

Be right back – Zig went to the little bar to order while I conducted this brief visual survey of how the other half lives. Our companions were middle-aged women with elderly mothers, businessmen poring over spreadsheets, gaggles of young women with polished hair and briefcases, and one group of women, all wearing chic hats. Besides ourselves, I did not see a single couple.

That stopped me in my tracks. What a hoot – me and Zig classed as a couple. I nearly laughed out loud. What's the joke? He was back.

Nothing – I'm just enjoying myself.

He asked if I would like a drink along with my coffee. I thought a little, then: Yeah, why not? After all, I was a grown-up woman: A brandy and ginger, please.

Good, I'll join you.

When he brought the drinks to the table, I saw that mine was a large one. He noticed my expression and laughed: Don't worry, I'm not trying to get you drunk or anything like that, but since this might be the only time you'll ever let me buy you a drink I have to make the most of it. Me, I'm driving.

The pianist started to glide through a version of 'Some Enchanted Evening', and as he sat in his chair, Zig inclined his head, a faraway expression in his eyes: I've always loved *South Pacific* – I played Bloody Mary in school, would you believe? My voice hadn't broken yet. He grinned: My 'Bali Hai' is legendary. To this day, they speak of little else in CBS Synge Street.

I sat back in my chair, feeling almost giddy at the unexpectedness of this treat, and took a large mouthful of the brandy and ginger. We both turned round to face the pianist and I hummed along, continuing to sip.

By the time the pianist swung seamlessly into 'On The Street Where You Live', the brandy was really hitting the spot. I heard Zig laugh and swung back to face him: What's so funny? He's not that bad.

No, he's grand, very good actually, as these guys go. I was just thinking back to that *South Pacific* – and he proceeded to deliver, blow by blow, a comical account of his school production, including wicked mimicry of the unfortunate father of one of the pupils who had been drafted in to play Emil. This guy had apparently been very tall and had dwarfed everyone else on the stage. Good baritone voice, though, he added, but I was laughing so hard I missed my mouth with my glass and slopped brandy over my blouse: Oops! Sorry.

Real life was already another country. What was that Ambrose had said about living in the present? I aimed the glass again at my mouth and, with a jolt, discovered it was empty. I gazed into its depths as if by looking I could miraculously fill it again.

Zig hesitated: Will you have another?

A bird never flew on one wing! I thought this hilarious – no more hilarious, of course, than the dubious expression on Zig's face.

He watched and waited. Listen, May, he said slowly, when I had regained some of my composure, forgive me for being so forward, but are you sure you should have another drink?

I giggled at his anxious expression. Poor Zig. Do you not think I'm all right, Zig? He reacted to the name, of course – but to me his puzzlement at the private joke was so terrific it cracked me up completely. I had to clutch my stomach. People were beginning to look at me; I was short only of kicking my heels in the air.

Mercifully, the waitress came with the coffee and I managed somehow to sit up straight while she did her thing. I won't say another word, I whispered, when she had left us, ss-ssh! – sealing my lips theatrically with a finger – not a single word.

You might think it odd that I remember all of this in such detail, but I do. Every benighted, disgraceful moment of my performance.

You need water. Zig went off, fetched a carafe and a glass, poured it, watched while I drank the full of it without pausing, then poured me a second glassful: What was that you called me?

Hmm? I started to drink the second glassful, but this one seemed very cold, colder than the first. It hit my stomach hard and I felt suddenly very queasy: Listen, I have to go to the ladies' — where is it?

I made it to the bathroom in time, but only just. Thank God I was the only person in there because I did not even manage to get the door of the stall closed before the brandy, ginger ale and water all came out together in one brackish gush. Instantly I felt relieved, but so weak I had to steady myself against the walls for a minute or two. I was absolutely sober again, the alcohol had not had enough time to get proper hold of my bloodstream.

The accoutrements supplied in the Conrad's ladies' powder room are excellent and I made full use of all of them so that by the time I was ready to go back, I felt half-way like myself. And mortified that I had made such a show of myself.

Everything all right? Zig stood up as I got to the table.

Yes, fine. Look, you're right, I am not used to this. I'm sorry. I glanced furtively around the room, expecting a horseshoe of disapproving glances.

No one watching at all. It didn't help.

I've made an eejit of myself — and of you. I could make excuses. I'm very tired, for instance — and the last few weeks . . .

Please stop apologizing, May, no apology necessary. You're in your granny's when you're with me. You just drank it too fast, that's all — and that bloody ginger ale makes it taste like lemonade.

We sat down again. Look, he said then, I'm going

to get you a decent sandwich with meat. I'll bet you've been up to your old tricks and haven't eaten properly. Without waiting for me to agree, he caught the eye of our waitress and ordered a fresh pot of coffee with two ham, cheese and salad triple-deckers.

I was actually very hungry now, probably because I had voided my stomach, but also because he had guessed correctly: I had had no breakfast, lunch had consisted of a banana and a slice of toast. I could feel a headache beginning to form behind my eyes and my inexperienced heart was racing because of its drenching with brandy. Food would be good.

He would brook no more apologies or talk about my behaviour. Instead, he began to tell me about his home in Frigiliana. Temporarily, of course – and strangely contrary to the way I felt about poor old Joe Rooney's concern – I basked in having someone take charge of me like this. Maybe being an authority figure teaches you such ease and command, I thought, listening to his glowing descriptions of his villa which was apparently all that a person could want or need, three bedrooms, a little patio, garage, swimming-pool, satellite TV, and a view of the distant sea.

Three bedrooms? Obviously this villa was at the high end of the market.

Yeah, he scratched at the surface of the table, a gesture I was coming to know: We bought one of the bigger ones because we had hoped . . . You know . . . Kids. One of my brothers goes there every summer with his family, he added briskly, so at least it's being used a bit.

The food came, and as we started to eat it, I told

him how much I envied him: I love the sunshine, I love
the south of Spain, I love getting up in the morning
when the only decision I have to make is which T-shirt
to wear. I described our place in Nerja. It's not as posh
as yours, but it did us, it was perfectly adequate.
We're almost neighbours. Or we were, I added sadly.

There's no reason why we couldn't be again, he
said.

What? My mouth was full. He waited until I could
speak: What do you mean?

What's to stop you going out to Spain tomorrow?
All right, your apartment is seized but all that means is
you can't dispose of it until a decision is made about
it, which might not be for years yet. As far as I know
you can use it in the meantime. I'm not a hundred per
cent up with the play where the powers of the CAB
are concerned, but I don't see what's to stop you.

Stone cold sober, I examined this proposition from
every angle. Why had no one pointed this out to me
before? We had the use of Alder Cottages after all and
that had been frozen as an asset. And as for my being
free to go there, no one depended on me now: all of
my surviving kids were on their own path. Even Eddie,
to whom I had been closest, was off to Paris. Clem
and I were no longer Clem and I. There was Esmé, of
course, but she was hale and hearty and well able to
look after herself in the house. She already cooked for
herself and it had been a very long time since I had
even been in her room, which in reality was an
independent fiefdom.

Zig was watching me as I batted all this around in
my head. There is, of course, the question of your

passport, he said drily. That old one you travelled on?
You've dumped that, isn't that what you told us? So
you can't even get by with, what was that you told us,
that Bagman's wave? His naked upper lip trembled
with something suspiciously resembling amusement.

I fought hard against the blush I felt starting somewhere in the region of my breastbone, but as he
continued to watch me, the penny dropped.
Astounded, I stared at him: You?

Well, he had to get those photographs signed by
some Gárda or other.

Why are you telling me now? Won't you get into
trouble?

Are you going to rush off to the Commissioner?

I was stupified when I thought of the third degree he
and his partner had put me through in my own sitting
room, indignation bubbled up like lava but it proved
to be spurious and subsided as quickly as it had arisen.
What else could Zig have done or said on that occasion
without exposing his role in the acquisition of a false
passport? Thank you, I said faintly, I'm staggered. But
why? That was quite a risk you took.

I thought you deserved a break. I also owed your
son a favour – he helped me out once or twice. He's
in the kind of job where he can be useful and since he
has taken the odd risk for us I was just paying a debt.
A very small debt. In the scheme of things it was an
insignificant indiscretion. And it did lead us to your
husband, didn't it?

I honestly did not know how I felt about this. My
Martin a snitch? After what had happened to CJ?

He saw my confusion: Don't worry, it's all very

low-level stuff, he's not a grass or anything like that — far from it. He's a decent, law-abiding man.

Although he had not finished his sandwich, he placed his knife and fork together on his plate, but as he wiped his mouth fastidiously with his napkin, I saw he had confirmed that my indiscretions with the mobile had led to Clem's arrest. That would make me a sort of snitch too.

His mouth was still hidden behind his napkin and what he said next was muffled: I also wanted to do it for you.

This was too much to add to the confusion and I did not want to deal with it so I pretended I had not heard. Not difficult, because I had just then remembered an insurmountable difficulty with regard to Nerja. What had I been thinking of? The alcohol had clearly caused momentary amnesia. Trenchantly, I dismissed the idea: I can't afford it.

To scattered applause, the pianist finished his gig with a flourish of notes from 'People Will Say We're In Love'.

Oklahoma — one of my favourites. Zig turned round to clap as people around us on the mezzanine started to gather coats and handbags. Then, rather than turning back to me, he watched the progress of a middle-aged daughter as she crossed the room to fetch her mother's walking frame where it had been parked in a corner. He watched her as though his life depended on the accuracy of his observation. Let me give you the money, he said.

He faced me. Before you say no, he said quickly, please consider it. I am comfortably off, as I think I told you. My father is well taken care of and I have no one to spend my money on. It would give me the greatest of pleasure to have you as a near neighbour in Spain. He stared frankly at me. Or, better still, as a guest in my place. An honoured guest. No pressure of any kind. I'm reliable – even you would have to admit that. And, believe it or not, I can throw a few ingredients together in a pan. Agnetha was a brilliant cook and some of it rubbed off on me.

The word gobsmacked is too temperate to describe my reaction. You've thought about this, I said when the words could form themselves in my mouth. This isn't the first time this has occurred to you.

I started to think about it during your younger son's funeral. The more I thought about it, the more feasible it seemed to be. I repeat, no pressure. You'd be in safe hands – I'd make sure you wouldn't drink double brandies like they were babies' bottles.

What about your brother and his kids?

He shrugged: What about them? He already knows I want the villa this summer.

He had utterly transformed the rules of the game we had been playing up to now. I stared at him: You know I can't—

Look, he interrupted, would you accept this invitation if I was a woman?

What? I was addled now. What's that got to do with it? Then I realized how stupid this was. I don't know, I said honestly. Then: Maybe. Probably.

Pretend I'm a woman, then, why don't you? A girlfriend. A fellow writer. I'm Jane Austen inviting her dear cousin to come to stay with her in her vicarage. He grinned: We'll drink only tea, and eat watercress and cucumber sandwiches.

You can't be serious.

I'm deadly serious. He moved to the edge of his seat. How can I convince you? I'll say it again. As a guest, May, just as a guest.

Are you sure that's all? Just as a guest?

Were they my words? What was wrong with me? Was I considering this outrageous proposition? To take this man's money, to stay with him in his house? A man whom I had met through such inauspicious circumstances. A man who, up to a few weeks ago when I had invited him in for coffee, was officially opposed to me and my criminal family? Was I now completely deranged?

Of course, just as a guest – but who knows what the future holds? He threw his arms wide as though reaching for a song's high C: I'm sane, I'm sober, I'm solvent, what more can a woman ask? I could even be suave.

He saw he was frightening me: May – May, he leaned over the table, reached for my hands, I'm sorry, I didn't mean to come on so strong. I was just trying to lighten things up. I know I've a weird sense of humour – don't be scared. Bring a girlfriend with you, bring one of your sons if you don't trust me.

I made up my mind, moved my hands out of his reach. I can't possibly. No. I'm sorry. It's out of the question.

✦ Twenty-Eight ✦

But why exactly was it out of the question? Two weeks later, on Friday, 9 June, Emily, Joe and I, plus three of the women stalwarts who never missed a session, were sitting at a table in Chief O'Neill's after our workshop. The rest of our group had spread itself around nearby. We had a full house that evening because we were entertaining a visitor, an American poet who was touring Europe and reading for groups like ours along the way. She was apparently a friend of Oddbod.

Emily sipped daintily at her Noilly Prat: Seriously, May, what was to stop you?

I shifted uncomfortably, disliking the spotlight. What on earth had caused my guard to slip sufficiently that I had confided in these people? And this time I couldn't blame alcohol. Although I had been persuaded to have a drink instead of my usual coffee, mindful of my last adventure in that regard I was sipping slowly at a small glass of beer.

I had been a little late for the workshop that evening and, on the instant I walked in, recognized that my colleagues were uncertain as to how to handle me.

Being writers, they had all probably imagined how they themselves would have reacted to the accumulation of disasters I had gone through.

For whatever reason, all conversation stops as I take my customary seat beside Joe and I can read their thinking: Is she still mad? Do we refer to any of it? If we do, is she going to bleed all over the tabletop?

Emily introduces me immediately to the American – who holds her pages poised and ready – but all around me I continue to feel the smudge of awkwardness in the air so I decide to be up front. I ask permission to address the group in general before the reading starts.

Emily frowns a little but the poet puts down her pages. I take a deep breath: First of all, I'd like to thank you all for the Mass cards and for coming to the funeral. I smile at Emily and Joe: Or funerals plural. It's true what they say, I'll never forget any one of you for it. And I know you are all concerned about all that's happened to me in the last couple of months. Thank you very much, it means a lot. But please stop worrying about me now. I know it's a cliché that life must continue, but that doesn't make it any less true. I'm here tonight because I've been going stir-crazy over in that house with nothing to think about except the past, my troubles and polishing my kitchen worktops. Really, if you don't mind, I want to be treated now just like anyone else. And I certainly don't want to ruin this workshop for every-one else by casting a pall of gloom or embarrassment over it. I'll have to stop coming if I think my presence here is inhibiting – that you all think you have to look after me all the time.

They galvanize, rushing to speak over one another:
Oh, no, May—

Don't think that—

You have to keep coming—

The murmured chorus seems gratifyingly sincere but I blush as red as a ripe tomato in the full blue glare of the American's intrigued eyes.

Of course you have to keep coming, May. Emily's brisk voice cuts through as the others continue to offer reassurance. Now, please, can we all sit back and listen to our guest?

Read in a monotone with elongated vowel sounds, the America's poetry involves a lot of blood and wombs but is ambiguously genderless and I have difficulty following the meaning. So, although the others seem seriously impressed – Oddbod actually looks animated for the first time ever – the net effect on me is soporific, and after the first ten minutes or so, I find my mind wandering. Towards Zig, now departed.

He arrived the day after the Conrad experience to apologize if he had caused any offence: I was out of line, May, after all you hardly know me. Forget it ever happened.

No problem, come in for a while?

Just for a minute. He stepped in but both of us immediately felt awkward – I could tell by the way he was trying to keep from touching me in the confines of the little lobby.

Over coffee, we made efforts to behave as though the whole episode did not matter or had not happened. But of course it did and it had, so I decided to confront the issue: Look, you weren't out of line, but you did take me completely off guard. As you've said, we hardly know one another – can you see this from my point of view?

I know all I need to know about you, May.

He began the scratching trick and I could see he was gearing up to say something big. Suddenly I didn't want to hear it: I'm sorry – I don't want to rake things over, forget I brought up the subject. Just put it all down to me being a dyed-in-the-wool coward. It was a lovely invitation, I'm probably mad not to jump at it – any other woman . . .

He sat motionless until I ran out of words. Then, still without raising his head, as though I had not spoken: I'm sorry you won't give me the chance to show you who I am, or who I can be when I'm off duty. You know me only as a cop. Of course you're leery.

He met my eyes then and there ensued one of those little pauses where anything could have happened. But whatever he saw in me gave him little comfort and, abruptly, he stood up. I'd best be going. I'll come to say goodbye before I leave.

I was curiously unsettled. Maybe I should have said something after all, a holding phrase maybe, but the moment had passed and we both knew it. I stood up too: Really, there's no need – stay for another little while.

He shook his head. By the way, he said then, shoe-horning levity into his tone: If I'm Zig, who's Zag?

The guy misses nothing. Forgets nothing either. Shamefaced, I had no option to explain. He had the grace to laugh.

He came to see me again, for the last time, on 2 June, a week prior to this workshop. On that occasion he telephoned in advance so I had the table already laid and had made scones.

He made appreciative noises when he saw the little spread but our mutual ease in one another's company had evaporated and his rejected invitation still dictated the agenda. Rendering both of us virtually speechless, it lay like an enormous wet sack on my best tablecloth. Not least because this was probably the last time we would ever meet – I could visualize no scenarios where we bumped accidentally into one another in the future.

Another scone? Accentuating the awkwardness, my voice sounded artificially cheery as I broke yet another silence.

Thank you very much. As delicately as a nun, he took the scone off the plate and busied himself buttering it.

So what time is your flight tomorrow?

Ten past one. Well – he made a passable attempt at a smile – that's what it says on the ticket. But you know what it's like these days . . .

I do indeed.

I was about to add something about how it would be worth it when he got into the warmth and sunshine but bit off the words just in time. In the circumstances the remark would have been anything but anodyne. Instead, I too took another scone: Do you think you'll come home for Christmas – to see your father?

Perhaps. But it might be nice for him to come out to me. I haven't managed to budge him yet, but you'd never know . . .

It was my turn to attempt a smile: That'd be great.

Somehow the conversation stumbled on, petering out to nothing and then being kick-started again by one or the other of us until, after about a quarter of an hour, he pushed back his chair. I'll be off so. Last minute packing, all that . . .

I stood up immediately. I couldn't sort out what I was feeling. Uppermost was the desire to get out of this awful conversational swamp and to be left to think things through. Don't be a stranger now, I said brightly as I opened the front door for him.

Oh – I nearly forgot.

He reached into his breast pocket and extracted his policeman's notebook – old habits die hard – then tore out a page and handed it to me. Glancing at it, I saw it had been pre-inscribed with his address in Frigiliana. He looked out towards the street as though searching for something: There you go. And if you ever do manage to get out to Nerja . . . He turned back to me and held out his hand, quite formally: And of course I will be in touch if I hear anything of interest in your son's case. Take care of yourself, May. One quick squeeze of my hand, and he was gone. Very fast.

I was relieved as I closed the door. Thank God. I said it aloud. Thank God.

I bustled down to the kitchen and began to clear the table, but as I emptied the dregs of his coffee down the sink, the cup in my hand seeped warmth and I began to miss him. I sat down, holding the cup. I had wanted him to go. I had found the conversation between us excruciating. What the hell was the matter with me?

I already missed him.

Don't be ridiculous, May Lanigan. What age are you? Don't be ridiculous. Don't-be-ridiculous-don't-be-ridiculous—

Mantra-like, I was to repeat this phrase many times over the next few days, kicking Zig out of my way as I Hoovered, burying him deeply under the rubbish as I put out the bins, pushing him out and closing the door after him as I went to bed. Eventually, I sat down and faced it. Logically.

1. I miss him.

2. It's probably more the thought of him than his physical self. What I am probably missing is the chat. Therefore I just have to get out more. Be more sociable. Make more of an effort at the workshop, for instance.

3. To accept such an invitation would have been wholly inappropriate; quite obviously, those few mad seconds when I had considered it had been alcohol-induced.

4. I had made my decision, which was the only sensible one in the circumstances.

5. Once having made the decision I had to stick to it. What kind of respect would he have for me any-way if, having been so dogmatic, I changed my mind? I'd be beholden to him then.

6. That's settled. Now get on with your life, May Lanigan.

I counted off this abacus many times, even with Ambrose, who sat down with me in the sitting room that evening. He was back to being enigmatic again: that bloody well-worn free-will routine. To be per-fectly honest, I wish occasionally for a bit of dictatorship in my life – I could do with someone to tell me directly what to do, when and how to do it. Free will is all very well but it takes too much bloody work.

Eventually I snapped and attacked him. All right, Ambrose, if you don't want me to be with that man, what were you doing in Smithfield that day watching us in the car?

It is of little relevance what I want, May. What do you want?

I groaned, covering my face with my hands. Then I rushed out of the room and down to the kitchen where I slammed around amongst the kettle and the tea things. Something occurred to me. This was the first time I had left Ambrose and not the other way around. Was I growing out of Ambrose?

I snap back into the present, conscious of thin applause. The American's reading is over. I clap along with the rest, hoping like crazy that I won't be expected to contribute to any discussion.

I needn't have worried. Emily asks the questions for all of us – when she can get a word in edgeways. This poet can talk for the Olympics.

In Chief O'Neill's, the question of Spain arises through Emily's customary, after-session query of me as to how I am getting on with the memoir when, for some reason, I blurt out the story of the invitation, something I hadn't broached even with my family.

Emily and the other four at my table begin to discuss the issue as though it is a plot problem, almost as though I am not present. Now, May, Emily puts down her cocktail glass, I can't see what you're worried about. I think you're mad. What's so dreadful about going on a holiday? It's not as though you're emigrating or deserting your family in their time of need. It is a return ticket, isn't it? And – I hope I'm not going to say something upsetting to you here – but the idea of black, deep mourning went out with the Victorians. Go – you deserve it.

Yes, one of the other women chimes in, hoisting me with my own petard: You were dead right back there in your little speech about having to get on with your life now.

I don't quite know how to react to this as I stare around at the group.

Happiness is a choice. Choose it, offers another of our regulars, a large, dreamy woman whose rambling stories are full of *bons mots* of this nature.

The first woman, as forceful as she is vague, rounds on her: Hey, steady on, that's not original. I saw that on a Hallmark card.

So what? the dreamy one argues. That doesn't make it wrong. She beams at me: It is good, though, isn't it?

Joe Rooney has gone very quiet. What do you think, Joe? Emily, ever the moderator, shepherds him into the discussion.

He smiles tentatively at me: Is this a man who invited you on this holiday?

It's – it's just a friend. And they all see that treacherous blush . . .

The American, holding court at the table next to us, butts in: I couldn't help overhearing your conversation, May, she drawls, your friends here have been filling

me in. But what I see now are all these doors opening
for you and you won't walk through.

To what I assume is their displeasure, she abandons
Oddbod and the others at their table and scoots over
on her chair so that she is now part of our group, and
before I know it has made me the recipient of a full-
wattage onslaught about life, love, the pursuit of
happiness, and what her therapist advises when energy
channels are blocked. I don't want to sound bitchy,
but you know what I mean.

Fatally, Emily tells the American about my memoir.
She turns to me, suddenly all business: When are you
publishing, May? Have you an agent?

Oh, I haven't even thought of that — that's miles
away. It's not nearly ready.

Feebly I continue to protest while she reaches behind
her, takes her briefcase from under her chair: I'm sure
it's fine but it'll never be ready, no memoir ever is,
they're all works in progress. She is now rooting
through the briefcase: Dammit, where is it? She
pounces on something: Great.

She hands me an ornate business card: You give
Pearl a call, you tell her you're a friend of mine and
that I've recommended you.

This is getting out of control. Dazed, I look at the
card, which gives the name and address of a New York
literary agent. I gaze around at the circle of expectant,
encouraging eyes: But I told you, it's not even nearly
ready.

How much have you written? The American is not
to be put off.

Not a lot – I begin, to be interrupted by Emily: Most of it is on tape – isn't that right, May? Those pages you've actually worked on – have you got them with you?

I shake my head so hard I almost dislocate my neck, knowing full well that the pages in question are nestling together like a pair of ducklings inside the ring binder at my feet.

How many tapes? The American leans forward and fixes me with her kohl-rimmed gaze.

I don't know, I waver, a couple of dozen?

She sits back triumphantly. What you writin' here, honey? *War and Peace*? She waves a dismissive hand: It's ready – what do you think editors are for?

But I haven't even listened back to those tapes – I don't know whether I even want to.

We'll listen for you – this, amazingly, is Oddbod. Without my noticing it, he has moved his chair so that he is now with us. The American shifts to accommodate him further but he just smiles at her and stays where he is.

Silence now as they all look from one to the other. Even the American is quiet.

That's a great idea. Emily, getting excited again, is the one to break it. Let us be the judges as to whether it's ready or not, I promise you if it's no good we'll let you know sharpish, May – won't we, group?

Nods all around.

It'll be great, says Joe Rooney. A real group project. Do let us do it, May, please? Joe's expression is resolute. Whatever he had originally thought about my trip to Spain with a male has been resolved, or covered over.

It seems this is decided.

All of this left me with a feeling of unrest as I went back home. On one level I felt the whole thing was ruined. It wasn't my private memoir any more, my personal, private friend. It was now, if not exactly public, at least group property.

On the other hand, I could not ignore the bubble of excitement at the pit of my stomach. I had the name of a real agent. I had a recommendation from a published writer.

The excitement rapidly deflated as soon as I opened the door of Alder Cottages. Perhaps it was the contrast after the brightness and chat at Chief O'Neill's, but the house seemed as dim and quiet as an empty church at midnight.

I listened hard but could hear no stir of life, not even the sound of Esmé's TV. The weekends, I suppose, are when I am going to miss my Johnny most. And not only him: the others always made a special effort to be around while he was here. It won't be long before their visits tail off as they all get involved again in their own lives. Ma plus Johnny was one thing but Ma on her own, while worthy, is, after all, capable of looking after herself and sorrow must ease some-time. I must get a cat, I thought dismally. A cat might care whether I came home or not.

May Lanigan, newly wrought spinster of this parish, poured herself a cup of warm milk and went to bed, the big four-poster now permanently to remain half empty with no Clem ever again. No Johnny, no CJ to visit. For ever, I thought, the tide of self-pity rising and crashing all over me, virtually drowning me.

Canute-like, I made one last effort to turn back this wall of bathos: Snap out of it, May, stop being such a wuss! I finished the milk and reached decisively for the TV zapper to tune in to *The Late Late Show*.

Pat Kenny was interviewing a group of people involved in bringing children from Chernobyl to Ireland to give them medical treatment and holidays. Two of these children were then brought on and introduced. One had no hair. The face of the other, a boy of about nine years of age, was mutilated, yet that is too weak a word to describe what filled the TV screen. The left half of his face had been eaten away by rodent cancer.

The cameras refrained from close-ups but I had close-up lenses in my own eyes. Pat Kenny's soft, sympathetic words while he talked to these children swirled away from me and became meaningless as I fixed on that terrible wound, those exposed teeth, that patch of white bone above the hole where there should have been an ear. It brought it all back, the vision of CJ's face burning and liquefying, not slowly over time like this poor child's yet not fast enough to bring blessed oblivion. CJ's body twisting as the acid bit, each movement torturing some broken bone, some bruise—

The self-pity curled up again but this time mutated into grief. Every lump hammer of grief for all that had happened in the past few months coalesced and ambushed my body, hurling itself at me willy-nilly, so painfully that I screamed aloud.

Not caring who heard, I howled then, as an abandoned dog would howl, for CJ, for Johnny, for my own loneliness. Shockingly, I heard words, half formed but distinct, piling into my mouth from the base of my racked stomach. I heard myself crying out loud for my mother, for my father—

Twenty-Nine

I became conscious of someone standing over me. Wearing a nightgown under a shawl, Esmé was beside my bed. I struggled for control but I was too far gone.

Faintly, over the sounds I was making, I heard her say something although I couldn't make out the words. And then she was no longer there.

When she came back, she was carrying a small tray on which was a glass, half filled with whiskey or brandy — I couldn't tell which as I gulped it down between sobs. Whatever it was, it scalded like hot metal, cutting through the mire of emotion and shocking me into a semblance of composure.

Take this. She handed me one of her own handkerchiefs.

I blew my nose several times. I now had the hiccups: I'm — I'm sorry you had to see me like this.

I told you, I had been expecting it. You have been too calm. She picked up the remote control and switched off the television: I cannot understand why you continue to subject yourself to watching such dreadful things, as if there was not enough pain in your life.

Don't go, Esmé, sit down for a little while.

She sighed and, moving aside the clothes I had piled untidily on the bedside chair, sat. She folded her hands in her lap and waited. From beside her, the lamplight shimmered on her shawl and nightgown, pale grey silk over white lawn; through my blurred, teary vision, she might have been a wraith or a mirage.

Sorry. I hiccuped again.

Sorry for what? Don't be a goose.

She let the silence descend again. I'll say one thing for Esmé, she has always been good at silence.

I lay back on the pillows and stared at a money spider making an acrobatic descent from the light fixture in the ceiling. I don't know how much more of this I can take, Esmé – I need a break.

Then, perhaps because of the drink, perhaps just to keep her there or to fill the silence, I found myself telling her about Zig's invitation. She showed no surprise. So what is preventing you?

I pull myself up on one elbow: You think I should have gone?

Why can you not go even now? Esmé yawned: Why not?

But what about everything here? I scrabbled around defensively: For instance, what about you, Esmé?

She raised her eyebrows: What about me? For heaven's sake be sensible. You do not have to be responsible for me – let alone the world. She sighed as though talking to a classful of recalcitrant students. I assume you will allow me to continue living here as long as possible? From what I have gathered, even if the worst comes to the worst, this house will not be sold for at least another seven or eight years.

I think so.

Well, then. I will be well under the grave by then, at least I certainly hope so. I have no plans to linger on into helpless senility. I trust you have some years of your life left still to live. Spain is not so good as France but it is relatively civilized, these days. So, I repeat, what is stopping you? She raised a cynical eyebrow: Whose life do you now have to run?

My eyes had cleared by this stage and I gawped at her: You've got hold of the wrong end of the stick, Esmé. I wasn't talking about going for good, just for a holiday.

What would be the problem if you did go for good? It sounds like a sensible option to me. Do not always be silly. Go. Every graveyard in the world is populated by people who believed themselves indispensable. Everyone deserves time in the sun, I took full advantage of mine.

It struck me that she should be the one writing the memoir: You never talk about anything, Esmé – about France, about your husbands.

Esmé stood up. If you are feeling better now, I shall go back to my room. She turned to go but I called after her: One more thing, Esmé, please.

Yes? Impatiently she turned back to face me.

Why won't you talk to me about my mother?

She stared. Slowly, she pulled the shawl around her. Then she seemed to be distracted, as though listening to something very far away. I rose on the pillows, straining, but could hear nothing unusual: Esmé?

She remained very still. Then, her eyes milky, her voice low and breathy: Maybe it is time after all. One moment, please, May.

She glided out of the room again and within a minute – a tense eternity – returned with the brandy bottle and an additional glass. Then, as though she were mentally rehearsing, seemed to make heavy weather of pouring the two small drinks.

My chest hurt from holding my breath and my head, muzzy from all the crying, was beginning to ache. I tried to fracture the tension by being flip: My God – I'm going to need brandy?

Instead of responding, she sat again in the bedside chair: I am not sure it is wise to tell you right now as you are so upset but perhaps it is better that you should know. I am tired of keeping this secret.

Know what? What secret?

She sipped her brandy then patted her lips carefully with another of the sharply folded handkerchiefs of which she seems to have an endless supply, but I had had enough of the drama. I wanted to reach out and close my hands around her aristocratic throat: Don't keep me in suspense like this, Esmé. What secret?

Your mother might not be dead.

The sentence had no impact, sounded absurd. What do you mean?

I mean what I say. Your mother might not be dead.

Esmé watched me as I concentrated, trying to put the words into a sequence that would make some sort of sense. My mother might not be dead? I had visions of her scrabbling around inside her coffin. A person has to be dead or not dead, there is no ambiguity, no 'might'.

She is dead – of course she is dead. She is buried in a cemetery in London. I had made tentative plans to put flowers on her grave.

Feeling stupid, I look at Esmé's composed face. Please tell me I'm dreaming this – that this is some sort of black joke. She died of lung cancer because she smoked too much – what about the lung cancer?

Your mother did not have cancer. Your mother did not even smoke.

But Da—

I never approved that he should tell you your mother had cancer and that she died.

Whoa, whoa – start again, Esmé. I was half-way out of the bed by now – the only way I knew this is that one of my toes had become entangled in a fibre of the carpet on the floor. I ripped the toe clear, ignoring the tiny stab of pain under the nail: Are you telling me Da lied to me? That he deliberately told me my mother had died when she hadn't? He wouldn't do that – not Da.

Esmé allowed me to talk myself to an abrupt stand-still. Her expression was as calm as usual but the eyes were compassionate: I am sorry. But it was not my place to tell you until now.

I pulled my foot back into the bed. The handkerchief Esmé had given me earlier was still balled wetly in my left hand. As though it was an heirloom, I placed it gently on the bedside table, then moved it a little so it wouldn't obscure the face of the tiny clock. There would be time later to consider the lying of my father.

Meanwhile, the bigger question remained: Where is she, Esmé? And how do you know all this?

With her free hand, Esmé reached up to tidy away a tendril of hair that had wandered on to her neck from the diamanté slide she used to confine it at the nape: I do not know where she is. As I told you I do not even know for sure that she is still alive. The last time I heard, which was just before your father died, your mother was living in Leeds. He asked me not to tell you this secret. It troubled him and he wished to unburden himself of it to you personally. Of course, he never did.

But he spoke to you about it.

Twice. Once when I came here to live with you. I think he feared I might refer to her.

And the second time?

As I told you, just before he died. I believe it was upsetting his wellbeing, his conscience. However, he continued to insist that I did not say anything to you. He had no need to demand this, of course. It was not my place.

Why is it your place now?

It is the correct time now.

There was little point in arguing this with her because I knew I would never get a straight answer. Through the swirling in my head, I managed to make a swift calculation. My mother would be seventy-nine by now. Seventy-nine was not all that old for a woman in today's world. There was an excellent chance she was alive. The more I thought about it, the more confusing I found it.

Reflexively, I turned on the messenger: I can't

believe you didn't tell me, Esmé. I had a right to know. Even after he died, why didn't you tell me? My voice had risen sharply but Esmé seemed unfazed, which, of course, spurred me to further heights of outrage: Who else was in on this little secret – did Clem know?

She pursed her lips: Clem did not know – at least I believe so. Unless your father spoke to him.

I rejected this. Clem, for all his shortcomings, would not have kept something this momentous from me.

All right, but if she's not dead, why did he tell me she was? What happened? They just split up and she went to England? Why did she leave? When? Was it with somebody else? The questions wrestled and rolled in my mouth and tumbled out on top of one another in a heap.

Esmé leaned forward and placed her brandy, largely untouched, in a clear space on the table: I believe he was hurting very much. Not only his heart, but his pride. Your father was a proud person. Your mother departed on a Monday morning while he was at work, and when he came home for his evening meal, he found only a note. I think he did not recover from this and could not bear to reveal it to you as it would diminish him in your eyes to know that your mother had felt she could no longer live with him.

Although I was hearing it third-hand, it wasn't difficult to visualize the story – after all, it was common enough. Yet as Esmé filled in the details in her quiet, slightly quaint English, I listened with mounting disbelief and horror.

I knew, of course, that my mother had graduated

from an orphanage to the factory floor at Player Wills; I knew how she and my father had met – on separate walking holidays in Co. Kerry – and, of course, I knew about the nine-year age gap.

What I had not known about was the enormous difference in temperament. Esmé's remorseless portrait of the marriage, albeit from my father's perspective, was of a serious mismatch between a flibbertigibbet and an intellectual. According to this account, my mother married my father because he wooed her persistently, because she admired his educated, fine words – but mainly because he offered her a stable home, a pensionable future and the chance to give up work on the factory floor. He married her because, at forty years of age, he felt marriage might pass him by if he did not grasp this opportunity.

I couldn't let that last bit go without protest: That can't be true. I don't believe that was the only reason on his side – he always said she was a lovely person.

Perhaps I am being a little unfair. Perhaps he also saw an opportunity to mould her.

That's not fair either. He loved her. He did, I know he did. I was frantic.

I had to salvage something but Esmé looked away from me towards the window: Your father was not a soft man at the time of his marriage, she said thoughtfully. When he came into our office at the union, although he had no authority over us we sat a little straighter. He had a particular stare . . .

That I had to concede. I remembered that withering, narrow-eyed gaze all too well. But whether from deteriorating eyesight or a mellowing temperament,

Da had all but ceased to hurl it by the time he was visiting us and his grandchildren in Alder Cottages. Or perhaps it was I who had changed and perhaps he could no longer intimidate me.

Nevertheless, I jumped to his defence: I can't believe half of this. He never intimidated me, Esmé, never.

As you wish. Esmé folded her hands in her lap.

The bedclothes weighed heavily on my sweating body and I kicked them off. Then I was immediately too cold and pulled them back over me. I looked at the clock – it was only twenty past eleven. *The Late Late Show* still rumbled on somewhere in the bowels of the dark TV. I couldn't believe my world had shifted yet again in so short a time, but this was no ordinary shift, it was seismic. It had made a nonsense of a lot of my life: all the penny candles, all the prayers, all the invocations to my dead mother to help me in my hours of need . . .

I glanced across at Esmé, sitting patiently waiting in her chair as though she were a psychiatrist dealing with a particularly strange patient. If she was to be believed, every foundation built under my childhood was crumbling away from under it, and without the solidity of my childhood, what was I now?

She met my glance: Shall I continue? It is getting late?

Yes, please do.

She got up and began to walk around the room. You must accept that some things I will say I have heard from your father and some things I have observed for myself, but because your mother, I am sure, would have a differing view of matters, my information is incomplete.

She stopped as though she had already said too much. Shall I continue?

Go on, Esmé, please.

I listened then, trying to concentrate, as her soft, measured voice laid vivid images along the span of my parents' short marriage and the first years of my life.

Probably because the orphanage had offered an abundance of community but minimal creature comforts, my mother, according to Esmé, while remaining sociable, showed an unseemly fondness for what her husband increasingly saw as irrelevant fripperies: flowers, the cinema, dancing and pretty clothes in delicate, pastel shades. She spent his money on getting her hair curled – and for someone who loved books so much, her stubborn, continuing choice of women's and fashion magazines as preferred reading material was anathema.

Poignantly – my description, Esmé would never use such a word – my mother did try to please her new husband at the beginning by taking at least one evening course in English literature. She pretended to enjoy the books he insisted on giving her to read, and tried valiantly to discuss them with him as later he tried to discuss his books with me. In truth, however, she floundered, and before long, his encouragement that she better herself became demands and finally turned to ridicule as he began to deride her lack of intellectual abilities. Ahead of her, she saw nothing but a life of scorn.

So, one Monday morning, she got up as usual, prepared my father's breakfast and saw him off to work. She washed the dishes, cleaned and tidied the kitchen and reset the table. She made him a salad for his tea, covered it with a muslin cloth and set it at his usual place. Then she wrote a short note of apology and placed it beside his fork.

She dressed me – carefully, in my best blue dress with coloured smocking – and carried me across the low railings that divided our front garden from the next-door neighbours'. She asked the woman there to mind me while she went into town to get a few messages. I was taken in.

Then my mother went briefly back into the house. Taking with her only a piece of embroidery presented to her by the nuns on leaving the orphanage, her missal and a parcel containing a few of her clothes, she walked out again and closed the front door behind her. In her handbag was £77.80, money my father had been saving towards buying a car, always a dream of his. The story of my life had changed for ever.

Esmé was standing with her back to the window. The smell of the brandy in the glass beside me was pungent and sickening and I was suddenly very, very tired. I didn't know which aspect of the revelation to think about – the fact that my mother might be still alive, or that my father had lied to me through all those years. If she had rejected me, so had he. He perhaps more so in depriving me of an opportunity to know her.

I ground both fists into my eyes, tender from the

previous storm. My voice sounded old and tired: How did he know she wouldn't contact me? How would he have dealt with that?

We will never know. Esmé's voice usually so smooth, quavered a little – she was tired too.

There was nothing more to be said and both of us knew it. I uncovered my eyes: Thank you, Esmé, and I'm sorry if I was abrupt with you earlier. It's just such a complete shock to me.

She shrugged and, with one hand, pulled the shawl close around her as she walked over to the bedside table and picked up her brandy. Please do not apologize. It is understandable that you will feel upset. She paused by the bed and looked down at me. I do not like to have harboured this bad news for so long. I could see you did not have an easy life and I did not want to make it worse.

I gazed up at this surprising woman, the woman I had dismissed so often as a biddy or a harpy. The level of her frustration could only be guessed at. How would I feel, coming from the liveried luxury of a peaceful French château to live here, in this tumultuous family, with only one tiny space to call my own? No wonder she went out into the streets to make a protest. I pushed myself up: Esmé, I am genuinely sorry about being impatient and irritable with you all these years. I'll try to be kinder.

She shuddered and backed off, raising cynical eyebrows: Please. Do not be absurd. We are both grown women. She left then, the fabric of her night garments whispering around her.

Now, four and a half hours later, I think I have just heard her padding down towards the kitchen. I hear her moving about frequently in the night.

Through the gap in the curtains, I can see the first chinks of light. The neighbourhood blackbird has started his tentative warm-up. Although I feel burned out, weary in a way I doubt I have ever felt before, I will not sleep again.

Shall I go to Leeds? Would I find her there? What does she look like? Do I have sisters? Yet she knew where I was all these years . . .

I can hear, distantly from the kitchen, that Esmé is running the tap over the sink. She is probably making coffee.

Two women, alone at opposite ends of a house.

I plump up the pillows and lie against them, eyes turned towards the promise of the day's slowly increasing light.

→ Thirty ←

Certain puzzling aspects of my life with Da now made sense. The dearth of family photographs, for instance, and his refusal to talk about my mother, which I had seen as a reluctance to revisit old mourning. And up to this moment, I had thought Da had given me a happy childhood. He gave me books. He tried to teach me about the world outside the narrow canals of school and church, at least until he accepted that my main interest lay in dancing with Clem Lanigan.

Although he was a man who despised time-wasting and recreation, he took me to Portmarnock in summertime and read under his cap in a deck-chair while I sat cradled in the soft dunes, sprinkling Star crisps with salt from twists of blue paper and staring out at the fidgety grey sea, wondering where my destiny lay. A nurse in a big London hospital, maybe? Receptionist in a posh hotel? Maybe I might marry a rich man and travel the world – or better still, become a missionary nun and see this beautiful world under my own steam. In this latter case I would pull out all the stops. No Liverpool slum for me but a posting far away to an

exotic place that wore its name like a brilliant necklace:
the Ivory Coast, the Solomon Islands, Rio de Janeiro,
Tierra del Fuego. Those were places Da knew about in
detail. He encouraged me to dream. You're a special
girl, May, he said, over and over again.

And of course I was. As a half-orphan, my school
pals were nice to me, their mothers sometimes packed
treats for me in their own daughters' lunch-boxes.

Now it had all turned into a sham.

Warm memories were tainted: Da was not naturally
gifted in dealing with small children, yet he had come
to Clem's and my house almost every day and done
little jobs for us around the place, put up a few shelves,
that kind of thing.

Guilty conscience?

In the clear dawn, despite trying to hold on, I drifted
off into one of those half-waking dreams of such
intensity that the lines between conscious and subconscious are breached. Like a Valkyrie, this dream
swoops and catches me in its talons, carries me to the
highest point of the world then lets me tumble downwards. Falling, I see CJ, lodged in a cleft on a
mountain. He is crying and reaching out to me, begging
me to save him; his face a white sheet of paper. Small
red flames curl along the edges of his paper-flat face
and make little runs towards his beseeching eyes, which
sit in the middle like two black lumps of coal.

Then CJ's face is no longer his but my father's, CJ's
reaching hands not his but Da's. Da is now reaching
out to me, struggling to free himself from the clutching
rock while his lips, which burn and curl away from his
teeth, try to tell me something – something about my

mother. I try to divert my fall, to direct myself towards him by wheeling my arms but cannot – and then I see he has become the Viking mummy from the St Michan's vault across the road, his face wrapped in thick white bandages, his extended hand bony and skeletal. I scream, but now I have fallen past him and when I look back there is no CJ, no Da, just bare rock and sprays of small white flowers spewing like mushroom clouds from the fissures.

I fall further, and pass above a high valley between two peaks. This valley is green and fertile, sectioned like a chessboard by a grid of hedges into identical and mathematically perfect squares; each square contains a squadron of little black and white cows. They stand on their hind legs and hold each other's forelegs like Irish dancers and perform 'The Walls of Limerick', parading gravely in orderly lines between the hedges, to and fro, to and fro. In the centre of one field is a small, perfect cottage with a crimson roof. Outside it, the American poet hangs row after row of white handkerchiefs along a clothes-line that stretches to infinity. She is singing. 'Oh, the Farmer and the Cowman Should Be Friends.'

I know as she sings the second line – *Oh, the farmer and the cowman should be friends* – that this is my mother. I call out to her as loudly as I can – Mammy, Mammy – but she is singing too loudly to hear me.

One man likes to push a plough –

I scream louder. Mam-meeeeee –

– the other likes to chase a cow –

I scream and scream at her, I paddle my arms and legs in a frantic attempt to stem my descent but it is no use.

– but that's no reason why they can't be friends –

She pegs those handkerchiefs, bobbing in strict rhythm as though she is an automaton or a wind-up doll – bending to the washbasket, straightening to the line, bending to the washbasket, straightening to the line – and I can do nothing but surrender to my descent past the valley and away from any possibility that she might notice me.

Now I am falling faster and below me is a field of jagged rocks – they are rushing up to meet me and I know I am going to be cut to ribbons, I close my eyes in terror—

Impact.

Panting, my heart thumping, I find myself sitting upright in the four poster. My face is wet with tears. It is four minutes past six in the morning by the dial of the alarm clock. Less than ten minutes since last I checked.

Breathless and dizzy, I flop back on to the pillows and pull the bedclothes up around my chin. Trying to calm down, I close my eyes but the nightmare is there instantly, in full, glowing colour, and I open them again.

Hello, May. Ambrose is standing at the end of the bed between the two uprights. My heart leaps with hope then anger: he would know definitively if my mother is alive or dead. And if he is not prepared to tell me, he can go to hell.

He smiles. You truly believe in hell, yes? A place of fire and torture?

The shreds and twiglets of the dream cling to me as I rise off the pillows to confront him, my voice shaking with passion: I have a few things to ask you, Ambrose. Please answer me straight for once. I am not interested in a debate about hell. But since you brought up the subject, all I want to know about heaven and hell is where CJ is right now, and Johnny, and Da. I want to know if they're happy or going through torture or what's happened to them. However, that can wait. What I really want from you right now concerns my mother. Is she still alive, Ambrose? And if so, where?

He gets off the bed and is instantly in Clem's chair, doing that trick of his, getting there without moving. His expression is grave.

Passion drains away: Please, Ambrose, no messing this time. I'll never ask you another question again as long as I live, please.

He gazes at me for a long time, his eyes enlarging and shining like beacons, and I am reminded of that time he quoted scripture at me. On this occasion, however, there is no organ burst. You will rest now, May, he says eventually. Instead of the organ, his voice rests on the notes of a flute: You are free. He comes a little closer, his expression inscrutable: Are you the same person you were when we met?

The absurdity of this conversation hits me as I hear a car engine revving in the street outside, then the first police siren of the new day. Anger gives me energy: Of course I'm not – how could I be? Two of my sons have died, my marriage has ended, I've just found out my father was living a lie – why wouldn't I be the same person, Ambrose? I leap off the bed and lean forward so my face is very close to his: What about my mother? Are you going to answer me or not?

He sighs. As you will . . .

Slowly, he bestows on me a smile as incandescent as I have ever seen. I am reminded of that last smile of Johnny's and, for an instant, think I might weep but instead an extraordinary feeling of calm comes over me as he starts to grow and to metamorphose.

We are almost done.

I have decided I will answer May's question but she touched on the existence of a physical heaven and hell. I have wished to address this and I cannot let the opportunity pass.

Consider the following: human beings and animals are composed of matter; so are birds, rodents, insects, dinosaurs, whales, trees, rocks, vegetables. Matter, as I am sure you know, does not decay but mutates. It is therefore immortal.

Consider this also: if heaven is a place and love the key to its gates, do not domestic pets that have loved until their hearts burst not deserve to be admitted also?

Beasts of burden that have served so faithfully their backs have broken under the burden?

Species and matter in universes unknown to man?

Do you yet believe heaven and hell are specific physical places – infinitely elastic?

Finally consider this: the span of human life is preparation for contented – and thereby perfect – solitude; bliss is not permanent togetherness but permanent, happy and eternal self-sufficiency.

*

I've seen Ambrose's transformations before, of course, but this is something special, even for him. His robe lengthens and spreads, its iridescence shooting wide, dazzling rainbows. The walls of the room fall away as these palettes of colour begin slowly to rotate like a kaleidoscope – except that this is no children's toy but a slide show: a field of small trees, blooming white; a sky of cobalt blue over a yellow, blowing prairie; a panorama of rocks and stones, whorled with fossils; an emerald wave curling over an island of coral; stags and salmon in a brown, rushing stream, an Arab stallion racing across a desert, a hovering dragonfly, a pair of colourful parrots . . .

People. Black, white, yellow, ochre, Aborigines with painted faces, Africans with necks extended by multitudes of metal rings. A babel of voices, drums, music. Babies with young mothers, doctors wearing surgical masks, crowds in St Peter's Square, Joseph Stalin, Balinese dancers, a cross-gartered actor on a medieval stage, a traveller woman begging on O'Connell Bridge.

I finally understand. Ambrose is showing me the beauty and diversity of the world, unmediated by experience or prior conceptions. He has returned me to non-judgemental childhood. And as I watch, I recognize what has changed in me. A child sees patterns in a rock, not a weapon to crush a skull. She sees a human being, not a dole sponger or a person who has no right to a share in your spoils. She sees a man who may be good or bad, but whether he is a policeman, a reporter or a homeless drunk will not affect her immediate reaction to him.

It's all too much. I begin to suffer from vertigo:

Stop, stop – please stop. Immediately the kaleidoscope slows, resolves itself, becomes static.

In a candlelit bedroom covered with sprigged wallpaper and furnished with neat, pastel-painted cabinets, a white-haired woman lies in a clean bed, pink coverlet tucked in hospital-style at the ends. Beside her, an elderly man kneels on the floor, his head beside hers on the pillow. I notice his hands, hanging loose by his side, palms to the back. They are calloused and thick, a workman's hands. The woman is dead and, although the lined face bears little resemblance to my mother's wedding photograph and is not familiar to me, I know it is she.

May's mother was not heartless – she thought often of her only daughter – but believing herself to be deficient in mothering skills, she felt, generously, that May was better served by her absence.

The illusion fades slowly, the colours leaching first and then the figures, like ghosts in a film. I am spent.

Just tell me one thing, I say quietly to Ambrose, did she have a happy life? Who is he?

He is almost dreamy. His name was Tom Crabbe. They lived together in Leeds as man and wife. He was a carpenter from the town of York and they were very happy.

Was?

He died shortly after her, he suffered from no illness, he simply died because he no longer wanted to live without her.

How did they meet?

I have overreached, Ambrose's eyes becomes opaque.

It doesn't really matter, now, I say, meaning it. Esmé had opened a Pandora's box, but Ambrose had closed it again, saving me the further pain of dashed hope. At least I know now and I would go some day to Leeds in search of details and information. And I would find her grave and put flowers on it. But not for a while. I needed to readjust my memories.

And as for anger at my da — what was the point now that everyone was dead? I had loved my da, still loved him, respected his memory, that was unchanged. To rage at him would be inappropriate because he had done the best he could. Like I did. Like almost everyone does.

Now, May — Ambrose seems to come even closer, although I have no impression he has physically moved — are you going to walk through those doors?

The room is so quiet I can hear the beating of my own heart. Outside, the milkman whistles. I stare at him. You?

And not only me, he says gently. We are all around you, May.

Some image starts to scratch at my overburdened brain. I play for time: What do you mean?

I mean what I say. We are all around you. As we choose. When and where we choose.

The scratching at my brain is more insistent. Abruptly, I remember Oddbod's amazing intervention. I am so astonished I almost gag, and my voice is not a voice but a whisper: Oddbod?

Ambrose smiles. The door remains open, May. You

will be aware from now on, will you not? I did warn
you to be careful about what you wished for.

He is making no sense now. I am still caught in the
notion of Oddbod being another Ambrose – whose
eyes, I see, have fixed themselves on something far
away. At the bus stop? he prompts, sounding impatient
now: You wished you were in Spain?

Zig? You sent Zig that day to give me a life?

You mean lift, do you not? Despite his impatience,
his lips twitch with amusement. Of course I did not
send Zig – he put quotes around the verb – Zig has
free will . . . He is openly grinning now.

I swallow hard to find my real voice again: Not
the free-will lecture – please, Ambrose, I couldn't
stand it.

He yields gracefully. This time I will not be travelling
with you to Spain. The underlying finality is unmistakable.

And perhaps it is my imagination, but as the city
quickens outside, he seems less substantial, his robe
less bright: You mean you won't be travelling with me
at all, that's what you mean, isn't it?

You will not need me any more. Then: As for me, I
have said what I need to say.

Not me. I had unfinished business: Ambrose, please,
once and for all, why me? And don't, for God's sake,
turn it around and say why not me.

You were ready for me, May, you were willing to
entertain my presence.

Too late, I realized I had not properly appreciated
the privilege of his presence. In the months he had
been with me he had become so much part of my life

I had never envisaged him leaving it. I was frequently furious with him for the capriciousness of his comings and goings – mostly for not being around when I wanted him – but looking back on it, I could see what had been going on. He had set me up, let me go through whatever it was I had to go through, then stepped in to show me the pattern.

Of course, frequently one doesn't want to hear the truth, even from angels.

So is this it? I ask him, as though I'm starring in one of those films that went straight to video. This is goodbye?

Ambrose cocks his head to one side: You will not miss me, I promise you. But you will always love me. His grin is wicked: You know, May, love comes in many disguises.

I laugh outright, surprised that I can: Since when did you start talking like Jonathan Livingston Seagull?

Probably since I met you, May. Then Ambrose makes a peculiar, strangled sound. If I didn't know better, I would think he was trying to laugh.

You're wrong, I said ruefully, I will miss you.

He shakes his head, sober again: You will be surprised. I will trickle away as quickly as the *son et lumière* I showed you until you will think you have imagined me, or that adversity has been playing tricks with your mind. But you will remember what you have learned – that nothing is as it seems. He has started to fade. Please be kind to yourself, he says gently. And then I can no longer see him.

Unbelievably, despite all that has happened during that night and morning, I feel peaceful. And then, like a stream in flood, I feel energy return. I should be exhausted but I am as fresh as though I am fifteen years old again and waking up on the morning of my first grown-up ball.

I test: What about the revelations? How do I feel?

Regretful, nostalgic, forgiving of Da. Although I would have liked to have known her, although I already missed the idea of her, I have lived my life with an image of her that cannot be superseded. That white-haired lady was someone other than my mother, moulded by the life she chose to lead. My mother lives in my imagination and my heart.

Yes, she abandoned me and I have always felt that loss, but I no longer feel like an orphan or a motherless child. Whether she left me by death or deception is relatively immaterial because she left. She obviously loved me. She had me taken care of. She dressed me in a blue smocked dress.

I had a happy childhood.

Now – Ambrose. How do I feel about Ambrose being gone from my life? Sad? Resentful? Amazingly, all I feel is fondness and gratitude. Although I can remember vividly the texture of his robe, I am having difficulty in picturing his face.

I suppose the realization that he will no longer pop in and out will hit me in a few days' time. I do know he is correct about one prediction: for me, no one will ever again be as he or she seems on the surface.

And I have made two decisions.

I am going to go to Spain – if Zig will still have me.

Second, I am going to pack up all of this, the tapes, the foolscap and, with it, my life over the past few months. I am not going to waste time going over it, reliving all the grief, trauma and self-questioning. I will take up the offer of the workshop group and will give them this memoir, in its raw, naked glory, to fend for itself. If it sinks, so be it, if it swims, that will be terrific.

With it, I might even earn my own money, for the very first time in my life.

In the meantime, I will take Zig's money. Humility, it would appear, has not been my strongest virtue, although six months ago I would probably have challenged anyone who suggested this.

A quick sting: am I not an unnatural mother to feel this good, however temporarily, so soon after my sons' deaths?

I will not give it house room. Enjoy this, May, it mightn't last.

Like a girl, I jump out of bed, throw on my dressing gown and kill the self-analysis by humming loudly as I go into the kitchen to face the day.

The main thing now is to arrange the family meeting.

→ Thirty-One ←

First things first, I thought then — no use getting everyone in the family all het up for nothing, I had to contact Zig to make sure he had really been serious about the invitation.

And therein lay the first problem. I couldn't find either of the notebook pages he had given me, either the one with his mobile number or his address in Frigiliana. The pages weren't in my bedroom, in my ring-binder, in my handbag — they had vanished. I tried the caboosh, even cleared it out thoroughly — and wasted half the morning browsing through the years of rubbish that had collected there. I discarded all but what we really needed to store, including the Mass cards — which offered me the solution to the problem. Jacqueline Sinnott.

I gussied myself up and walked down to the Bridewell. I was recognized, of course, as I went into the front office, but this new blithe me didn't give a sugar. I asked for the Ban Ghárda and lucked out. She was on duty and in the office.

Hello, Mrs Lanigan, she was immediately friendly, what can I do for you? She looked different without her hat and jacket. Far less starchy.

There was nothing for it, I asked her straight out if she had Zig's address. I called him Finn, of course, and it was only when the name struck oddly against my tongue that I remembered this was the first time I had said it out loud. The Ban Ghárda smiled: Good, she said.

I frowned. Good? Then I realized he must have told her. A blush threatened but she was already opening her notebook. I'll tell you what, she said, copying out the address on to a piece of paper for me, why don't I give you his mobile number? He's still using the Irish one until he gets fixed up with one locally.

Good luck. She smiled again as she said goodbye to me.

It was only after I got back to the house that I began to have doubts. Maybe I had been a little hasty.

My euphoria deflating rapidly, I sat on the settee in the sitting room for at least an hour, staring at some race meeting on the television while trying to decide whether to make the call or to abandon the whole stupid idea. Esmé was keeping herself to herself and, it being a Saturday afternoon with no Johnny to focus on, the rest of the house was very quiet around me.

I became aware that, on the TV, a horse called Mandy's Shoes was leading the current race, just ahead of another one called Mobile Nellie. I decided that this was an omen and not only because of the mobile: Little Nellie had been the imaginary best friend of my childhood, a feisty, fairy-sized creature with spectacles, a tight perm and the behaviour patterns of a human adult.

If Mobile Nellie won this horse race, I would pick up the phone immediately.

With half a furlong to go, I was on my feet, inches from the screen, my hands bunched into fists at my side. A third horse, Skeheenarinky, had joined the other two at the head of the posse and the three of them were battling it out as they approached the finishing post. I found myself muttering aloud, willing Mobile Nellie on, come on, come on, straining into the TV as though I could physically pull and push her over the line.

Unfortunately, Skeheenarinky won, with Mandy's Shoes second and Mobile Nellie, as the commentator said, a disappointing third.

I stared at the TV. I decided that third was good enough and rushed out to the hall to pick up the telephone.

Zig's voice was as close in my ear as though he were in the next room, but I could hear a lot of noise in the background and he was finding it difficult to hear me. I told him I would call him back.

No. He almost yelled it. Don't do that, please, May, don't go away – hold on.

I waited, my heart beginning to speed up, while I heard the noise decrease and then a different atmosphere. He was back on: Is that better? I was in the supermarket, I'm outside now.

Much better. But what about your groceries?

Feck the groceries, he said. Then he took all the hard work out of the situation. You've changed your mind? You're coming out?

Of course, I should have guessed: Jackie Sinnott had telephoned him in the interim.

He became businesslike, gave me very specific instructions. I was to go to Budget Travel in Finglas for my ticket – my return ticket, he emphasized – and they would bill his credit card for it. Then I was to go to the Bank of Ireland branch in Glasnevin to collect a bank draft, which they would cash for me, giving me half in pesetas. When all these arrangements had been made I was to call him again to tell him when I would be arriving. He would be at the airport to meet me. I wasn't to worry, I was to take my time, I didn't have to ring him until everything was in place. All he needed was a few hours' notice to give him time to get to the airport – he'd make sure the mobile was always on.

He was cordial but not gushing, said he was genuinely delighted I was coming and he hoped it could be soon. I couldn't have faulted him in any respect. And yet I was vaguely dissatisfied as I hung up the receiver at my end.

Had I been expecting him to fall over with excitement?

Of course I hadn't – so why was I left with this feeling of anti-climax? He had given me the reassurances I had sought. This was a holiday. I was a guest. While out there, we could each come and go as we pleased as adults. That was what I wanted, wasn't it? And I had even accepted his money. How gracious of me.

I shook off the feelings. The decision was made, the arrangements in train, I was going to go through with this. If he had indeed regretted asking me, that would become apparent within days and I could come straight home.

On the following Sunday, I looked around at my assembly in the sitting room, meeting all the curious, expectant eyes. Only Esmé wasn't staring at me, she was working at a small wooden frame, stitching one of the intricate pieces of embroidery with which she sometimes passes the time.

Within a few short years, how the balance in this family had changed, I thought. Discounting Esmé, we used to be a household of seven males and me. Now, here we were, four boys, me, two wives and a fiancée, four and four.

This discovery underpinned the decision I'd made. I had been given no choice in any of the changes: each of my lads was now making decisions with no reference to me.

Was I to sit growing old with Esmé, waiting for titbits of information and the occasional visit, when there was a world full of people, beauty – and, yes, even angels – available to me if I stirred myself to go out and meet it?

I launched in and told them what I proposed to do.

The reaction was somewhat similar to that when I had announced I was going to visit Clem in Sitges. In other words, everyone seemed distinctly underwhelmed. They started to discuss it amongst themselves, referring to me in the third person. I noticed, however, that Frank was very quiet. What about you, Frank? I asked. What do you think?

What about Da? he said quietly. He's in prison, with

a big trial coming up and you're just going to abandon him and go off with another man?

That's outrageous, Eddie rounded on him. You know very well what Da's been up to.

Easy, Eddie.

I walked over to where Frank was sitting: I'm sorry about your da. I did my best, but there's no way to make this easy on you, if that's the way you feel.

He stood up, his eyes flaming: Well, I think you're being a total bitch.

Mayhem. You can imagine. The two wives just raised their eyes to heaven, but Tracey, whose first experience of a Lanigan family barney this was, didn't know where to look as the other three jumped on Frank to defend me. I wasn't all that bothered, really, I've been called worse things, so I sat on the settee beside the two wives, waiting for the row to blow itself out. Frank's reaction had not been unexpected. I had thought this through carefully, and I had reckoned that if there were to be objections, they would most likely come from him.

Stop this! Esmé's voice pierced through the babble.

Stunned, all four boys stared in her direction. Esmé always – but always – stayed above rows or arguments, even when they were all small, and this public intervention was therefore all the more effective. She stood up and walked towards Frank, every inch as tall as he. Do not be disgraceful. Your mother is a grown woman. She does not need permission from anyone to go anywhere and my nephew has forfeited his right to have any views on the friends she chooses. You should be ashamed of yourself, Francis. I think you owe your mother an apology.

Then, quietly, she picked up her embroidery frame and glided out of the room.

All eyes were on Frank, with whom I now felt huge sympathy. His neck was like a turkey cock's as his fury abated and was replaced by embarrassment. Sorry, Ma, he said sullenly, I was out of line. I shouldn't have said what I said. Then he fired up again: But that doesn't mean—

Shut up and sit down, you jerk – who do you think you are? This was Martin, shooting to his feet and confronting his brother, nose to nose.

Frank continued to look upset but nevertheless backed away from Martin and sat down. Martin searched all the other faces, saw nothing to bother him and resumed his own seat on the couch. After a moment or two, Con spoke up: Well, that's settled that, then. When are you off, Ma?

First things first – Eddie nudged Tracey and looked past her at the two wives: Any chance of a bit of grub, girls?

The wives and I exchanged looks. It was over, thank God.

The first thing I did after that family meeting was write a note to Clem. I had toyed with the idea of going to talk to him in person, but had decided against this for two reasons, the first and most powerful was that I didn't want to, and the second was that it might seem to him as though I was rubbing his nose in it.

I did my best with the text, wished him the very

best of luck in his trial. I mentioned the good times we had had together, saying that those memories were still valid, but that now it was time for both of us to move on.

Then, after some hesitation because I didn't want him to think I was being sarcastic, I chose my words very carefully and wished him and Melanie the very best of luck.

I genuinely meant it.

Dropping that note into a pillarbox felt to me as though I had reached a staging post in a journey. On the way home, it occurred to me that it hadn't been the only one. In a way I had said a mammy's goodbye – but not May's goodbye – to all of the boys individually before that family meeting. The two dead ones, of course, with awful finality, but the others too: Marty on that morning he had broken down in the kitchen, Con at the hospital, Frank on the evening he had come without Amanda to see me in the house, and Eddie during the course of his breaking the news to me of his engagement.

So that was Sunday. Next day, Monday, I telephoned Joe Rooney at the Broadstone bus depot. If he was serious about listening to and transcribing the memoir, could I call in and see him as I would not be at the session on the following Friday? He seemed to be delighted.

On the way up to McGowan's pub to meet him, I debated whether or not to warn him about the angel stuff but I decided against it. Let them discover it, I thought, enjoying the vision of how they would react. Would Oddbod be there during the process? I doubted it.

The big pub was quiet, populated by a few middle-aged men poring over the tabloid racing pages. Over coffee, I asked Joe to be kind to my work. Of course we'll be kind, May – he was wide-eyed with responsibility and gravitas. He was also going pink.

I scrabbled for something else neutral but encouraging to say. I trust you completely to do the best for me, I said quickly. Then, when he blushed even pinker: Look, Joe – you're a really lovely person.

Don't. He stood up. Don't say anything, please, May. I'll be happy to look after your memoir for you, we all will. Now I'd better get back to work.

As I followed him out of the pub, I felt sorry that I couldn't have offered him more. Joe is charming, delightful, courteous in an old-fashioned way. He's a decent man.

Over the next few days, the boys – all except Frank – continued to drop in and out but I was away from the house more than I was in it. I went to the early summer sales and bought myself a pair of colourful flip flops, a new beach towel and, feeling quite strange about this, a peachy-coloured nightdress. When I got home, I stuffed this into my luggage, complete in its plastic bag from the shop, without looking at it again – as though this would take the harm out of it. Yet every time I passed the half-packed holdall from then on, I seemed to hear it it rustling.

Frank, who was obviously still upset, came to visit me on the Saturday, and by then I had splashed the rest of Esmé's money on a surprise for him. I had dithered a bit, unable to make up my mind whether I could be seen to be offering a bribe or a consolation prize, but decided I'd go ahead and do it anyway. If it was indeed a bribe, or even a conscience or reparation gift, so what? I was through apologizing.

They aren't the most ritzy frames in the world, I said, as I showed him what I had had done with two of his paintings, but I think they really point up what a good artist you are. Then I handed him the portfolio, which contained the rest. He hugged me, hard.

There were tears in his eyes as he stood away from me. Then after a moment: Thank you, I really appreciate this but I have to be honest. I can't help it, Ma, I'm still unhappy about this. I'm sorry, but that's how I feel.

I touched his face: I'm sorry you're unhappy, love, but Esmé is right. I don't have to ask anyone's permission any more and I won't.

I understand. He hugged me again. I love you, Ma. We all love you very much. I hope you know that.

So here it is, my last night. The tickets and money are safely in my handbag and I'm all packed, including a supply of rashers and cheese and onion Tayto crisps because that's what Irish people always miss when they're abroad.

I'm nervous, fearful I'm making a fool of myself at my age, yes, but these fears are in a different league from the terror I went through before my last trip to Spain, not least because I'm leaving my worries in the hands of fate, or God, or Ambrose, or whoever wants to handle them for me. It could be his legacy, but for the first time in my life, I'm trusting myself to the world.

The difference is that this apprehension is even a

little thrilling: it's akin to standing looking up at a huge roller-coaster just before you step on board. I'm excited at the prospect of starting out on an adventure. I have no idea what lies ahead but then, on this night and at this time approximately three months ago, I had no idea what lay ahead of me either. It's just as well you never know, isn't it?

I'm taping this last bit while ensconced in the four-poster. The padded Jiffy-bag is on the floor, the whole shebang is already in it — tapes, foolscap, the New York agent's card, stamped addressed envelope — everything except this last tape. I have the strongest intuition that I'm shedding my old life by getting rid of it all and letting someone else take care of it. This is how a snake must feel every time it sheds a skin.

I should be making an effort, I suppose, with my last paragraph, as Emily has taught us. But I can't concentrate, I'm too wound up. Sorry, Emily. Think of this ending as a dying fall. Write your own last sentence. And thanks.

In the meantime, this is May Lanigan, signing off for now.

And this is Ambrose, as May has so charmingly named me. Before she does pack away her tape, at the risk of repetition or cliché, I need to underscore the following in the unlikely event you have not already discerned it: my personal mission has been to open your mind. Received wisdom may long ago have wandered off the path, learned tomes can miss the point, authority can obfuscate the truth.

Neither rationality nor evidence is the last word.

Look for us. As I told May, we are all around you and although we are not what you may have imagined, we will be happy to join you in making the most of this wonderful planet earth — you do not need to ask, just listen and look, touch and taste. This is your fore and after time.

And now that I have the floor, I am determined to leave you with this:

A man goes into a pet shop and asks for a useful pet. The pet-shop owner thinks hard. What about a centipede? They are very useful as pets. They can do anything.

The man is sceptical but buys the centipede and takes it home with him. As soon as they arrive in the house, he says to the centipede: Clean the kitchen. Ten minutes later, the kitchen is gleaming, worktops spotless, dishwasher humming.

Right, says the man, tidy up the garage, please.

Ten minutes later, he goes into the garage. All the rubbish is neatly in the bins, the tools are racked, the floor is spotless.

This is marvellous, thinks the man. All right, he says to the centipede, last one for tonight, will you run down to the shop and get me the evening newspaper, please? He goes into his living room to relax and await the centipede's return.

Ten minutes pass, twenty minutes pass, but there is no sign of the centipede returning with the newspaper. The man, seriously worried, goes to the front door and opens it. From the doorstep, the centipede looks up at him: Sorry about the delay, I'm lacing up my shoes.

I am putting this one on the Internet. I might design my own website. What a good idea. See you on the web.

I have enjoyed speaking to you as I hope you have enjoyed listening. You have been a great audience.

Sorry, Joe, Emily and group, this is a postscript. I forgot one thing, two things actually. The first is a message for Ambrose because even though he's no longer in my life, I suspect he'll remain aware of what's on these tapes and since he figures so prominently in them I don't believe he will be able to resist a shufti through this last lot. I never thanked you, Ambrose. I mean it. Thank you.

The other thing is, I forgot to record the latest phone call to Zig.

As instructed, I ring him to tell him when I am coming – and to thank him for making such meticulous arrangements. This time, I catch him in the kitchen of his villa. I can hear *West Side Story* blasting out in the background.

Hold on – I can hear his shoes clicking on tiles as he rushes to turn down the volume. When he gets back, I tell him I'll be arriving in two days' time and give him the flight number and times. This is followed by a long silence. In the background, very faintly, I can hear Officer Krupke getting a going-over from the Jets.

Zi – Finn? Finn? I call out anxiously. Are you there?

I'm here all right, he says, but his voice sounds funny.

Is there something the matter?

No, nothing. When I didn't hear from you, I thought you weren't coming.

But you said you only needed a few hours' notice.

I know what I said.

I'm puzzled by the way he has articulated this. He has almost shouted it. Finn?

May?

We have spoken simultaneously. You first, he says then.

No, you.

Look, he blurts, all in a rush, I'm really sorry about saying this, and please, I don't want to scare you into changing your mind, but I have to say it or I'll burst. You've made me very, very happy.

I can't think of how to answer that. I mumble something about having to go now and that I'll see him in two days. But my pulse rate soars off the scale as I replace the receiver.

Something has dawned on me: regardless of what I have said, implied or even believed about this trip being merely a holiday, I can no longer avoid admitting that it is much more than that, not least because I recognize a very strong desire I have never before acknowledged. I want to come first in someone's life.

Maybe, just maybe, I am now being offered a chance for that to happen.

I am not abandoning motherhood, I am easing up on the centrality of the role. Nor am I leaving the pain behind, but pain and loss can be a companion to my life from now on rather than a component of it.

What was it Da used to say? *Per ardua ad astra.* Onwards and upwards. Face to the stars, May Lanigan.

Today, as Scarlett O'Hara might have said if she'd met Ambrose, is another day.